C90 1879648

LIBRA[illegible]
WITHDRAWN

D0296837

JOAKIM ZANDER

THE BROTHER

Translated from the Swedish

by Elizabeth Clark Wessel

First published as *Orten* in Sweden in 2015 by Wahlström & Widstrand.

First published in the UK in 2016 by Head of Zeus Ltd. Published by agreement with the Ahlander Agency.

Copyright © Joakim Zander, 2015
Translation copyright © Elizabeth Clark Wessel, 2016

The moral right of Joakim Zander to be identified as the author of this work has been asserted in accordance with the Copyright, Designs and Patents Act of 1988.

All rights reserved. No part of this publication may be reproduced, stored in a retrieval system, or transmitted in any form or by any means, electronic, mechanical, photocopying, recording, or otherwise, without the prior permission of both the copyright owner and the above publisher of this book.

This is a work of fiction. All characters, organizations, and events portrayed in this novel are either products of the author's imagination or are used fictitiously.

9 7 5 3 1 2 4 6 8

A catalogue record for this book is available from the British Library.

ISBN (HB) 9781781859216
ISBN (XTPB) 9781781859223
ISBN (E) 9781781859209

Typeset by Adrian McLaughlin

Printed and bound in Great Britain by
CPI Group (UK) Ltd, Croydon CRO 4YY

Head of Zeus Ltd
Clerkenwell House
45-47 Clerkenwell Green
London EC1R 0HT

WWW.HEADOFZEUS.COM

For my parents

'I paid for my betrayal
but then I didn't know
you were gone forever
and that it would be
dark'

—Zbigniew Herbert, translated by Alissa Valles

Chapter 1

Bergort—Winter 2011

We're moving low to the ground through Bergort at night, our momentum perfectly calibrated, our formation solid and compact. We're silent, our eyes pinpricks or dashes. We're the X-Men, Band of Brothers, the elite.

A car is burning on Drivvedsvägen, and we hear the windshield exploding from heat, see the glass shatter across the snow like ice, translucent shards of frustration and pleasure. This is just like every other night this winter, except the kids don't even bother to run up onto the pedestrian bridge over the train tracks anymore. They stand so close the flames are reflected in their wide eyes, and their skin ends up singed. They know exactly how long it takes for the sirens to go off. They're in no rush, have no deadlines to meet, don't even have anything to run from anymore.

But we don't stop, we have a greater goal, we're not just kids setting cars on fire anymore. We're eagles and falcons, predators with razor-sharp claws, pointed teeth, and big appetites. Lois, Räven, Mehdi, and Bounty. I turn my head and see my brothers—shadows in the glow of the fire—and something in my heart expands. I have stopped chasing you. You started to leave all this a long time ago. And even though your shadow still falls across the gray walls of our room every night as I lie in my bed, it's my friends—my brothers—who are like me. Lost and clueless. Empty and tired.

"*Ey*, Fadi?"

Bounty's voice is high and hollow, as if he's not getting enough air in his lungs.

"Shut up, faggot," Räven hisses.

He gives him a nudge on the shoulder, pushing Bounty into the deeper snow.

"Stop it," I say. "This is serious now, got it?"

"But..." Bounty says.

"No fucking buts, *sharmuta*."

Räven hisses again and raises his hand.

"So you're sure about the door code?"

Bounty continues while taking a step backward to elude the blow.

"You're sure they didn't change it?"

The concrete looms over us, enclosing us, holding us fast. The air is cold and smells like burning gas. I shrug, feel my lungs tighten. Feel what I always do: I don't know anything, am never sure of anything.

"Yes, damn it," I say. "So shut up."

We wait in the shadows on the other side of Pirate Square even though it's empty, even though it's one-thirty in the morning. We wait until we hear the sirens cut across the highway, wait until we see the sky above the playground illuminated by blue lights. Wait until we see Mehdi trudging across the icy flagstones outside Sami's kebab shop, his steps muffled thuds in the winter darkness. The sirens are gone now, the only sound kids screaming on their way across the footbridge in the opposite direction.

"All clear," Mehdi pants, his lungs whistling with asthma.

He leans forward, groaning.

"Only the fire department, they don't even send the police anymore."

We all nod in silence, as solemn as a funeral. This is serious now. The key burns in my pocket, the code in my memory. I bend backward and let my eyes drift toward the other side of the square and then up—to the windows covered with the sticky handprints of children, the cracked façade, the tangled blinds, the bedsheet curtains, the satellite dishes, the Somalian flags, and then up to the roof and beyond. The sky is black and cold, and not even the stars are out tonight, not even a sad sliver of a moon, just empty, black clouds, and nothing. Still, I let my eyes rest there, as frozen as my fingers and the night. This is the real choice. You or my brothers.

I force my eyes away from the sky, like pulling a tongue from a frozen flagpole, and say: "What are you waiting for? *Jalla!*"

We rush in formation across the square, as stealthy as fucking drones. We're a unit, we're gangsters, we're elite. We make no sound, only smoke comes from our mouths, just breath and blood rushing in our ears, just us and our mission.

It's easy. Punch in the front-door code, don't even look over my shoulder. Everybody in, and then I do what I've seen you do—head straight for the white keypad, my heart beating, punch in the code and see FROM on the display, only a thousandth of a second wait for the long beep that means it's worked, and we're inside. Fast high fives, silence, flashlights on, and down the hall into the studio.

Two MacBooks on the table in the mixing room. *Swoosh!* Ours now. Two Samsungs charging. *Swoosh!* Ours now. Three small tablets. *Swoosh!* Mics and guitars. We look at each other. Fuck it. Too heavy. I bend down over the mixing table, squatting, groping in the darkness until I find it. Slowly I pull out the Nike shoe box. Open it, bend my face in closer, and let the sweet smell of weed wash over me.

"*Ey!*"

I hold up a joint for the brothers, whose eyes widen as they give me the thumbs-up. But there's more. I saw it when I was here with you, saw Blackeye take two thousand and give it to some fucking hanger-on to buy liquor. That's when this first occurred to me, when the idea was born.

I sneak into the other room, the office. Pull on the top drawer, but it's locked. Jackpot.

"Räven!" I whisper into the studio. "Screwdriver."

Räven is the king of the screwdriver, chisel, and crowbar. There's no window, no door he can't open—so this is easy. He braces himself against the desktop and bends over and the drawer jumps up and out. The cash box is green and heavy, and I stop Räven from prying it open.

"Fuck it," I say. "We'll do that later."

And then it's over. We run out the door like water, our hands full of loot, down toward the playground, where we divide it roughly. I'll take the cash box and a MacBook.

"Lie low. See you Thursday."

And then it's over. The night is cold and empty and quiet. Not even the cars are burning anymore and exhaustion washes over me like an ocean, like snow, like darkness, and I stagger home, quiet and empty, not at all like I expected.

In my room the grayish-yellow light of the streetlamp outside my window won't let go of me. It finds its way under my eyelids and into my pupils, even when I close my eyes and burrow my head into my lumpy pillow. No matter what I do, it won't let me sleep. Finally, I give up, open my eyes, and sit up in bed, but I don't turn on the lamp. Time slows down and changes shape until it finally stops completely, and I hear the door to my room creak, the floor squeak. I don't turn, just keep my eyes on the wall.

You bring the winter into my room with you and sit at the bottom of my bed. The air stands still.

"Remember when we were little?" you begin. "You must have been around ten or so? Remember when I started to say I had to get away from here?"

I know what you're going to tell me, it's one of our stories, part of our mythology, but I say nothing. Just sit there, empty, with my back straight.

"I'd had another fight with them. Don't remember what it was about. Someone *khara*, some bullshit, who knows? And I ran out, didn't come home until late. And you were too big to play with your dirty old thrift-store LEGOs? But when I came home, you'd put all your blue pieces on one of those green plates, some white here and there, and placed it on my bed before you went to bed. Do you remember?"

I nod weakly. I remember. I remember everything.

"Do you remember what you'd made?"

I don't say anything. It was too long ago. Too much has happened since then.

"You said it was an ocean. That you'd built us an ocean to sail away on. And you were going to build a boat for us to sail away on."

I feel it burning behind my eyelids and in my chest. I feel it all crashing down, drowning in the past, drowning in the future. You don't need water to drown.

"But you never built that boat, Fadi, just the ocean."

I want to say something, try to explain, beg you to forgive

me, forgive me, forgive me. But I know that all I can do is whimper, all I do is cause chaos and stress. We sit in silence.

Then, finally: "Maybe you've finally made that boat, Fadi," you say. "But it's only big enough for one."

I finally turn and look at you. You are tired and thin, your skin pale in the dim light. I knew you were on your way somewhere else since I was little. But I've never seen you like this.

"What do you mean?" I say.

You look so sad when you look at me. Not disappointed, not angry. Just sad.

"What did you think? They wouldn't figure out whose code was used? Everybody has their own code to the studio. So you always know who's been there and when. That's the first thing Jorge will check tomorrow, and he'll see my code was used, won't he?"

What should I do? Shame burns inside me. Betrayal. My fucking stupidity. I'm a *khain*—a traitor. Then comes the terror.

"Jorge and Blackeye," I say. "They're gonna kill me."

"Not them," you say. "But Biz or Mahmud or the Russian probably will."

Now I feel the tears running down my cheeks. The tears are shameful, of course, but the fear paralyzes me.

"Fadi, *habibi*," you say. "How could you be so fucking stupid? You know they're not gonna be content to just get their stuff back. Anybody who does something like this to the Pirate Tapes... Damnit, Fadi, it's the only thing we have to be proud of. Whoever does something like this is a traitor. To Bergort. No one will lift a finger to stop them."

Through my tears, I see you stand up from the bed and go to your closet. You're almost never here, just a few nights of the week, but I know you keep your sketchbooks here. Now you reach up for the top shelf, rummage around through notepads and books and drop them into a Pirate Tapes tote bag along with your Swedish dictionary.

It feels so far away now, how we thought it would be enough to learn all those words. You stop, remove the dictionary, put it on the bed.

"It's better if you take this," you say. "I don't need it anymore."

I hide my face with my hands, can't see you anymore.

"How did you know?" I say quietly. "How did you know about Pirate Tapes?"

I glimpse through my hands how you shrug, how you shake your head.

"I saw you up on the bridge this afternoon, chain-smoking. You were obviously up to something. You're not exactly smooth, Fadi. Then I heard about the burglary. I put it together. I'm not stupid."

"What are you going to do?" I say. "Where are you going?"

"It doesn't matter. It's better that you don't know right now. I'll contact you later."

You crouch down in front of me, force my hands away from my face, force me to look at you.

"Here," you say, and your voice is so severe it causes the air to tremble around us. "As far as they know I'm the one who was at the studio last night. It's my code. If I disappear into the night without a word, there's no reason to suspect anyone else."

You hold my wrists, stare straight into my eyes, through my tears and shame, through the mirrors and smoke of my illusion, straight into who I am, straight to the bottom.

I don't know what to say. I open my mouth and close it, trying to turn away, but you won't let me.

"But I don't understand," I try.

"It's simple, *habibi*," you say. "In the end, you did build me a boat."

You stroke my hair.

"Forgive me," I say. "Forgive me, forgive me."

I close my eyes and feel your dry lips against my cheek. When I open my eyes again, you're gone.

Chapter 2

Brooklyn, New York—Thursday, August 13, 2015

The feel of concrete through the thin mattress on the floor; the rattle of a truck on the street so loud it makes the dirty windowpane tremble; sporadic voices and clattering heels on the asphalt; sirens on Atlantic Avenue; heat pressing down; your pulse echoing between the brick walls; the key in the door.

Yasmine sits up. She is immediately wide awake, eyes open, ready for anything, or almost anything. All those sounds, and the light from the streetlight falling over the floor. Darkness, reflections, and signals that she can't identify immediately. Just a key in the door. She looks around, pulls yesterday's black tank top over her head, steps into a pair of jeans, runs her hands through her thick dark hair, and stands up quietly. The rough floor is surprisingly cool against the soles of her feet.

The lock jams and *chickchackchackchick*. The key is forced in and turned. The sound echoes through the empty apartment. Blue light from the street flickers in through the windows and over the half-finished canvases leaning against the walls.

It's the middle of the night. How long has she been sleeping? Has she even slept at all? The jet lag crackles inside her. It is as if all her senses were being filtered through a weak radio frequency, making her slow and sluggish. She shakes her head again, trying to clear the noise, before she starts moving softly toward the sound at the door. Outside the sirens fade away down the cracked asphalt, leaving something that resembles calm in their wake. Now only the sound of the key in the lock.

She moves closer to the door, so close that her lips touch the metal, and she whispers in Swedish: "David? Is that you?"

She still has remnants of airplane air in her lungs and her voice is dry and hoarse. The key stops scratching in the lock.

"Yasmine?" he says from the other side.

The way he says her name. The flustered intonation and the aggressive, impatient tone. Everything they've built is destroyed in an instant. She turns the bolt and the door crashes open.

David looks almost normal, almost like he did a week ago. The same gently curved lips, the same deep furrow in his brow. Same collarbone and the dimple on his left cheek, the shaved head, the same gray T-shirt with the same spots of spray paint and ink; the same jeans in thick, old denim that she bought him in Shibuya on her first trip to Tokyo. But there's also the stubble and the dirty nails, the shifty gaze and the grinding jaw.

"Yasmine, baby!"

He throws his arms wide, steps over the threshold, his teeth bright yellow in the glow from the street. She backs up a step and turns away from his attempt to embrace her.

"Baby, I didn't realize… What time is it?" he says in English.

He touches his wrist in search of a watch that isn't there, pats his pockets, looking for a cell phone, finally finds it, takes it out, and pushes its buttons frantically, but gets no reaction.

"What the fuck? I'm outta juice! What time is it, baby?"

He drops the phone, which bounces on the floor. He moves toward her again, now with his hands cupped in front of him, as if to grab hold of her face. She backs up until she's standing in the middle of the room or the loft as David calls it, though it's no bigger than a dorm room, even if the ceiling is high and sometimes fills with light early in the morning.

"Why are you speaking English?" she says.

He stops and looks at her as if he hadn't actually registered that she was there until now.

"How'd you get in?" he says in Swedish, in an accusatory tone buzzing with paranoia and aggression.

"David," she says, her head cocked to the side now, like a child. "What happened?"

She stands in the middle of the floor with her arms crossed over her chest. She feels anger penetrate the pain and confusion inside, feels it expand. There is a hole inside her, inside them, inside this room. Every time she thinks she's grabbed onto the porous edge of this pit, she feels it expand, feels her fingers start to slide into the gravel. No matter how hard she fights, kicks, and bleeds, she fumbles, then falls forever downward.

"Happened?" he says. "What do you mean happened?"

He opens the refrigerator and pulls plastic containers in and out, rearranging leftovers on the shelves. A tub of butter falls on the floor, but he doesn't seem to notice.

"Timmy and Aisha had a party," he says. "Then we went out with Rasheed and some other people."

He turns to her, surprised: "What are you doing here? You were supposed to come back on Thursday."

"It is Thursday," she says, pressing her fingers against her temples. "Or maybe Friday now."

The noise wasn't going away.

"Timmy and Aisha had a party last Tuesday," she says. "So you haven't been home since then, I guess?"

He shrugs, as if trying to think.

"Thursday?" he says. "Rasheed and I got stuck in some beats he found. Then we went to a party in Bushwick. Lauren was there."

He looks as if he expects some type of credit for mentioning the name of a gallerist who they both know will never exhibit any of his paintings.

"She seemed really interested in my new project, you know, the birds and the churches. Have I told you about it?"

Yasmine sinks down to her knees.

"A million times, David. But you haven't painted shit, right? Not one fucking brushstroke!"

She stands up again and goes over to the double mattress in the corner and picks up two sheets of paper. She puts them on the counter in front of David without saying a word.

He leans forward and squints at them.

"Oh," he says. "Fuck it. It'll take them forever to take us to court. We're artists, baby! Evictions are just part of the story."

"We're going to court in ten days, David. Then we'll be on the street, OK? I've fucking been giving you money every week to pay the rent. What did you do with it? Drugs? Partying in Bushwick?"

Deeper and deeper into the pit. She doesn't even have the energy to fight it.

"I need a drink," he says, and opens the freezer door.

He roots around inside the icy space until he grabs hold of a foggy bottle that he holds up in the gray night haze.

He shakes it and turns it upside down before throwing it full force against the gray brick wall. The bottle misses the window by a couple of inches and shatters.

"Why the hell did you drink the vodka?" he hisses and turns to her.

Maybe it's the eviction notice, maybe her trip, or the jet lag. Maybe it's the last month, the ever-expanding sadness and confusion inside her. Maybe it's because the pit just keeps getting wider. Maybe it's the dirt under his nails. Maybe that's what makes her see the dark and bloody bottom of the hole. Maybe it's nothing. But suddenly she knows what needs to be done.

"I haven't touched your vodka, David," she says.

And not only that. Her voice doesn't tremble, she doesn't look away or back down or leave. Instead, she puts her arms across her chest and takes a step toward him. She can feel glass cutting deep into her left foot, feel how cold the shards are, how cold her blood feels in the heat.

David looks surprised. What she's saying isn't consistent with their history, a history full of episodes where she ends up on her knees in the corner sweeping up the pieces. For a moment he looks puzzled. He grinds his jaw.

"What the fuck did you say?" He takes a step toward her as the corner of his mouth twitches, either from speed or tension or lack of sleep.

She knows she could end it now. She could back down and surrender. Grab some toilet paper and sweep up the bloody shards. She could run down to the bodega on Classon Avenue and buy him some beer. He could suck down a six-pack and scream for a while. She could turn his hatred outward, toward gallerists and agents, and all the other people who are to blame for the fact that he hasn't made a decent painting since they came to Brooklyn. She might be able to borrow money from Brett to stop the eviction? Take a couple of trips to Tokyo or Berlin. Continue saving up for her own apartment to disappear to under the cover of darkness. She can do exactly what she's done a hundred times before, let herself fall slowly down into the pit again.

But she doesn't.

"I told you I was in Tokyo for ten days," she says instead. "And you know very well I didn't touch your vodka."

He takes a step toward her and for a moment seems to be weighing what she said.

"While you were here partying away the rent money for the thousandth time with your fucking loser club, I've been busting my ass for us to move forward, out of this shit," she continues.

She's gone too far now. Further than ever before. But lack of sleep makes her light and volatile. For a moment it's as if she's no longer a part of this anymore, not fully. It's as if the past month temporarily loosened its convulsive hold on her, as if what she and David had together was no longer real, just matter and myth and dream.

It's been a month now, a month since Fadi disappeared for good, a month since her phone buzzed in her pocket on the subway somewhere between West Fourth and Spring, and the world slowed down around her. It's been a month since she started running from her grief and her past faster and further than she ever thought she could. And then, just when she thought she couldn't get further away, just when she felt the terrible sorrow overtaking her, she received the second message four days ago. The blurry picture of someone who might be Fadi in Bergort. Fadi is dead. Fadi is alive. Nothing makes sense anymore. There is no pattern.

"You bastard!" she screams now and feels how sharp and raw her voice is.

"Shut up!" David roars, louder and deeper.

He holds a hand in front of her face.

"You should just shut your mouth! Who the fuck do you think you are? Huh? I don't owe you shit. You know that."

He's in her face now, and she can feel his chemical breath, smell in his clothes and skin the pungent sweat of two full days of partying. His voice is quieter now, more threatening.

"Who the hell are you to come in here with this shit? If it weren't for me you'd still be in the ghetto. If it weren't for me you'd be working in that fucking nail salon your friend's mom started, you ungrateful little cunt. Or you'd be dead like your retarded brother. You waltz in here with your fucking Tokyo trips... As if it wasn't me who arranged all that for you. Fuck you!"

She feels his saliva on her cheek, and she knows that what he's saying is true. He's said it many times before. She's thought it so many times before. That her debt to him is so great that it justifies the pit, justifies everything.

At that moment she almost lets go of the edge. Almost puts her arms around him instead. Almost puts his head on her shoulder, almost moves his arms around her waist.

But something is different tonight. It's as if there's a rope ladder hanging down into the pit, nearly within reach. Fadi's death and his resurrection. The world is spinning so fast it gives her vertigo. The journey between time zones makes everything seem easy and surreal. But she knows she can't grab hold of the ladder by herself, she still needs him, even for this. Maybe especially for this. She needs his hands to get out of this bottomless pit and wrest free from their story. She needs him in order to save what can still be saved.

So she hardens herself and pulls back, forcing that tenderness to become hatred with nothing more than her own will. She pushes him as hard as she can in the chest and yells.

He stumbles a step backward, disoriented for a moment.

"You're such a fake," she yells. "You're a fucking clown, David! You think you're an artist..."

She laughs an empty, joyless laugh.

"An artist! What a fucking joke! You haven't done shit for a year! You're a junkie, David. One step from the street. And you think you saved me? Don't you get that I'm the only thing standing between you and a park bench?"

She doesn't get any further before David's fist slams into her temple. It burns and her head buzzes—she feels weightless. The room spins around her as she falls backward onto the concrete floor. The taste of metal on her tongue. It tastes like sadness and emptiness. Like the end of the story.

It tastes like a victory.

Chapter 3

Bergort—Autumn 2000

It's called Bergort. Call it what you want, we don't care. We can't pronounce it anyway, and we're still better at this than most. We know now that the ones who brought us here, our parents, will never make themselves understood here. They'll be mute outside these walls, worse than dumb, because they'll try. They'll hem and haw and stutter and think that they're rolling their consonants and curling their vowels well enough to get along, believe it's enough to stumble your way to what you want. But it's not enough, it will never be enough. Their old-fashioned, black dress pants, shawls, and jewelry. How could that be enough? We've known this from the first day. How could it escape them? We're foreigners here. And we will never be more than the sum of our limitations. For people like us it's never enough to do our best.

So we decide right here on the scratched-up wooden floor of the living room in our new, old, shabby apartment with its toddler graffiti on the kitchen cabinets, with our stupid memories still in moving boxes next to the wall, still waiting for someone to grab hold of us. Someone to unpack us and connect us to all this newness. Here on the floor we decide we're not like the things in the box. We can't wait for anyone, and we can't rely on the people in the kitchen, the ones who brought us here and then surrendered. They are nothing more than old clothes, old thoughts, and old languages.

We sit in silence. We hear them chopping and mumbling in the kitchen, complaining about the tahini in the store on the square, about the acidic tomatoes, about the parsley, the olive oil, about how there are no vegetables worth the name. We look at each other, and you smile at me and stroke my cheek, push a lock of hair from my forehead. You've just learned a word that's so funny. *Kåldolmar.* It's something they served in the school cafeteria, something brown and gray that might contain meat. We're not supposed to eat pork, but we don't care. They serve it with potatoes—they serve everything with potatoes.

We sit on the floor and listen to them nagging and whining in the kitchen, and it feels like we're alone here, just you and me. Like there are oceans and worlds, galaxies and universes, between us and the kitchen. A cold wind streams in from the warped balcony door and you whisper to me: "Maybe we should eat *kåldolmar* instead."

And we laugh until we can't breathe. This is where it begins. This is where we decide—it's just us.

In the beginning, we never leave home except to go to school. I wait for you outside the barracks and hide behind bushes that lose their leaves in the fall, becoming just as bald and ugly as everything else. While counting the minutes on the big clock on the brick building on the other side of the schoolyard, I pick white berries from those bushes and feel them explode and drain through my fingers.

It's always gray, and it's always raining—until it starts to snow. I can't believe it at first, those flakes seem to come from nowhere, as easy as thoughts, as dreams, as wind. I'm freezing and jumping and shaking and waiting and waiting and waiting.

And I wonder who goes to that big brick school, and why we have to go to these barracks, and I count the seconds that feel like minutes, like hours and days, until you finally come out the door, always first, always alone, always peering down toward the bushes until you catch sight of me. And then it's not cold anymore, not hopeless, then the seconds don't feel like hours, the afternoon is no longer empty and endless, completely beyond clocks and time.

This is autumn, this is winter—we exchange their *Wayed Wayed* for our "Razor Tongue" and "7 Days" and Britney. This fall, this winter we walk over the asphalt, between the sparse hedges and frozen grass, through a world that gets darker and darker until I doubt I'll ever see the sun again, that it's disappeared and left me alone. Just like everything else left me. Everything except you, my sister.

And we walk slowly back to them across the frozen asphalt, dragging our feet through fresh snow between the buildings, creating ditches and furrows, a trail to follow back. As if we're Hansel and Gretel and don't need to find a way home, but a way out.

It gets cold so fast, and my feet are freezing in my old tennis shoes—the snow finds a way in under the tongue, through the hole in the sole, or up under my too short pants.

"You grow too fast, little brother," you say. "Soon we're not gonna be able to afford those legs anymore."

The cold finds its way through my polyester jacket and my mustard-yellow thrift store sweater, through T-shirts and skin, and pierces bone and marrow.

"We're almost home, *habibi*," you say. "Then we'll run you a hot bath."

And we laugh because we have no bathtub, just a shower with a thin, weak stream of lukewarm water, but laughing warms me up.

You say: *"Cord, board, lord, afford."*

New words you have learned. They sound like bird calls in your mouth, completely alien, inhuman. But we know that they are the key, they mean everything. We're here now, we have no choice, can't change our short pants, our crappy shoes, our cramped, depressing home. But we can practice this melody until we sing it more beautifully than anyone else. And when spring finally sheds its pale light over the yellow grass I chirp: *"Row, hoe, mow, cow."*

"That doesn't rhyme," you say.

And we laugh again, helplessly, breathlessly, until we collapse into the melting snowdrifts—two scrawny, lonely kids in an alien world.

Sometimes when we get home the apartment is dark and empty, and we regret not hurrying more, running through the winter so we could have had more time alone in the almost warm darkness.

Those afternoons by ourselves we put pillows on the floor so close to the TV we are almost inside it, and it is as close to happiness as I get in those early days. We learn the word *flip*, and we *flip* past the Arabic channels and straight to Ricki Lake or Oprah or reruns of *Beverly Hills 90210.* We dip dry bread in hummus or baba ghanoush or whatever we find pushed into the back of the refrigerator, behind the acidic tomatoes and tasteless, rotting peppers. Then we just lie there, still cold but drowsy, eyes half-open, and you read the subtitles aloud to me in a voice so heavy and tired and warm that I dream I can wrap it around me like the thickest, softest blanket, and sleep until the cold rolls away, and the sun streams in through the gaps in the broken blinds and gives us back our world again.

But usually one of them is home from their classes or their temporary jobs, with their sighs and groans, their tired eyes, their paltry quarrels, their halfhearted questions about homework and angry tirades and a raised, open palm when we say we don't have any. How will we ever learn anything? This society is too weak, too easy. They will make up their own math quizzes and Arabic homework because they hear us drifting away from it, drifting away from them, whispering and creeping.

"Eat, sleet, meat, feet, beet, sweet."

"Threat, wet, net, let, set, bet."

They can hear us croaking, almost singing. They can see our wings are growing.

Chapter 4

Manhattan, New York—Saturday, August 15, 2015

The sun is rising into a gray summer haze as the train rattles across the Manhattan Bridge. It's already hot, and Yasmine's left eye is throbbing. But if she's worried about anything it's her foot, which she dug glass out of yesterday morning before pushing it into her black canvas shoe. Just removed, not washed or bandaged until much later in the afternoon in the bathroom of a diner in Prospect Heights. She can feel the wound now bleeding onto the rubber sole, the blood staining its awkward bandage. Of course, it didn't help that she'd wandered the streets of Brooklyn for hours last night—like an insomniac or a zombie—before finally checking into a hotel she couldn't afford on Dean Street for another sleepless night.

Now she stares out over the river and the city's compact, gray skyline, and it feels like her life is ending again, like she's reached the limit of whatever her life is or has been—again. It surprises her that despite everything else that's happened the feeling is connected to David. She'd always imagined the moment when she finally left him as very different from this. Cleaner and clearer, somehow monumental, not as part of something bigger and more important.

Now everything she owns is lying next to her on the seat. A U.S. Navy duffel bag she'd bought before her first trip to Ljubljana six months ago. Inside is her sketchbook, computer, some underwear, T-shirts, a few pairs of socks, a dark-blue, knee-length skirt by an English designer that was so expensive it made her dizzy when she ordered it from eBay a few months ago, and an M51 parka in the smallest size, but still too big, which came from the same army surplus store as her duffel. Plus a phone and a maxed-out American Express card in her pocket. That was all she'd brought with her. Everything else belongs to the past. To another one of her pasts.

She takes her phone out of her pocket again, feels the vibrations of the bridge reproduced in the tremors in her hand, feels the phone shake and jump. It feels warm, just as it did a month ago when she sat on another subway heading uptown to a customer near Grand Central. She doesn't remember anymore to whom or what, just that the phone buzzed in her hand, and she felt a slight rush that was equal parts shame and joy when she saw who the sender was. An email from Parisa. Shame because it reminded her of all the other emails she never answered. Shame because it dragged her thoughts back to Bergort, to her old life, to everyone she'd abandoned, to Ignacio, to Fadi.

But also joy that Parisa persevered and still wrote to her occasionally, maybe once a year, even though Yasmine never responded, even though Parisa couldn't know if Yasmine was reading them. Even Fadi stopped writing to her at some point. In the beginning she'd intended to at least answer his emails. She'd formulated letters in her head as she lay on the mattress on the floor in Crown Heights. Long and detailed letters full of explanations and promises to come back.

She still did that, even now, even though it had been three years since Fadi's last email. But she never wrote them. Not because she didn't want to, but because she didn't know where to begin. Her break with Bergort had been so sudden and so complete. It had also been the only way:

she'd left Fadi and gone directly to the airport with David. And Ignacio? Had he known what was going on? That she was going away? That that was why she'd left him even before she met David? Ignacio's emails finally stopped too.

She and David were drunk when he bought the tickets with his scholarship money, and she closed down her Facebook and Instagram. Erased everything that held her captive in Bergort's net. Everything except an email address, one tiny lifeline. Everything except her shame.

How could she have left everything behind so quickly? Bergort, which shaped her. Ignacio, her first love. But most of all Fadi. How could she? Her brother, her own blood, who she protected and watched over as long as she could remember. But there was no other way, it was as if Bergort was threatening to pull her down into something deep and dark, something she always had known was there, and had somehow always expected to become a part of.

But when she met David, it was as if a completely different path appeared. Another direction, another life. And she chose it, almost without thinking. Sometimes in order to move forward, it's better not to think through all the consequences.

> Hi Yazz,
> Is this even your email address anymore? Anyway, I don't know how to tell you this, but your brother is dead. I don't know what you know, but he went to Syria. Now they posted on Facebook that he died in battle. Mehdi talked to your parents. I'm sorry, sister.

She remembers pulling into West Fourth just as she read that last short sentence, standing up, and pushing her way out of the train, then running up the escalator toward Washington Square Park.

Then nothing else until late in that night when David found her huddled beneath the window facing the street in their messy studio in Crown Heights. It was as if the rest of that day had been erased, as if it never existed.

"You have to call your parents," he whispered and crept up behind her, for once not impatient or speedy, but quiet and warm.

But she'd wriggled out of his embrace and just shook her head and stared at the wall.

The following morning she woke up with a new feeling in her chest. A desolation she didn't know was possible. David had disappeared, and the room was empty and cool. A glowing ray of sunshine had found its way through the dirty window, splashed like a spilled glass of orange juice all across the concrete floor.

She didn't leave that room for several days, not until Brett finally tracked her down after she missed a meeting with him and forced her to go to a café where she choked down half a bagel. They'd never spent time together outside of their work relationship, and Brett wasn't exactly the comforting type, nor was she the type to be comforted. So they mostly sat in excruciating silence until she met his uncomfortable gaze.

"Get me an assignment," she said. "Anything. Just as long as it's far away."

Anything to avoid thinking about Fadi, to avoid having to talk about it with David. Anything to avoid having to call her parents or to go back to Bergort. Anything to escape herself and her own betrayal.

Brett nodded and paid for her breakfast. Three days later she was on a plane to Detroit then Baltimore and finally

Tokyo. She hardly had time to wash her clothes in between. She ran from hotel to airport, between meetings with artists and advertising agencies, uninterested in content or the world around them. The only thing that kept her upright was her direction and speed.

It was on a Tuesday in Tokyo, in Shibuya somewhere, in a dull, modern hotel full of right angles and blond wood, sometime in the middle of the night, when she got the second message. It was the first time she saw her mother's email address, and for a moment she considered deleting the email unread. But she was too exhausted to resist and opened it. The text was brief, just a few sentences:

> It says on Facebook that Fadi died last month, but he was in Bergort just a few days ago. I don't understand, Yasmine. Please come home.

She had sat up in bed and turned on the lamp. Four images were attached to the message. She clicked on the first one, and the phone's screen filled with the image of a young man in front of a concrete wall, side toward the camera. He seemed to hold a spray can in his hand, with which he was writing or painting something on the wall.

Under the light of the streetlamp, the man's profile was surprisingly clear. Yasmine had dragged her trembling fingers across the screen and enlarged the photo as much as she could until only a grainy, pixelated face appeared on the screen. He was thin and haggard, thinner than ever, thinner than when he was a child, almost someone else. But Yasmine would have recognized her brother anywhere, in any image. It was Fadi, without a doubt.

*

Yasmine limps off the train at Bleecker and up the stairs toward Houston. Brett is in the parking lot of the gas station, leaning against a black SUV monstrous enough for an oligarch. "ARE YOU SAFE ENOUGH?" asks some company called Stirling Security in meter-high letters on the billboard above him. Yasmine steels herself and tries to will away the pain in her foot. There's no room for that now.

David has spent all the money she'd tried to save up. Only Brett's contacts and her own street smarts can get her on a plane to Stockholm. She sent Brett the three other pictures her mother attached in the email. Three images that show something is up in Bergort. It's enough to make it worth the trip, a chance to make things right again.

Chapter 5

Bergort—Spring 2007

It's spring, a miracle, impossible to believe, and the jackets we shoplifted from a sports store in the inner city in November melt off of us, revealing our pale, gaunt arms, our eyes still reflecting a winter spent playing Halo and FIFA. We have no references beyond TV screens. With weak sun on our faces we sit on the broken, graffiti-covered benches of the playground and start to remember, start to invent another life.

"We could grill, *len*! Get some good sausages!"

"When can we swim again? In May, I guess?"

"*Ey*, just sucking down a cold one in the sun is enough for me, man."

But it's not summer yet. We're shivering, even if we refuse to put on our jackets. We bounce the ball between us down to Camp Nou, our joints stiff, our breath still smoke streaming out of our mouths.

When we get to the coarse, artificial grass of the field, there's shitty, hard-packed snow still lying in its corners. We shoo away the kids kicking around a plastic ball, and then divide into teams of three. We stretch ourselves and kick the ball so hard that the rattling of the chain-link fence around the field vibrates like thunder through the concrete. It's Lois, Fox, and me against Mehdi, Bounty, and Farsad, and it's unfair of course—Bounty is two hundred pounds and Mehdi's asthma whistles in his breath—but I don't care, I just want to win, just want to feel the wind on my back, feel spring on my face, summer so close you can touch it. And today I can run forever. I can do a fucking back heel and scissor kick. I'm Thierry and Eto'o. I'm Zlatan. And when I put the ball into the top corner from midfield, I can feel the whole world inside my chest, and when I stretch out my arms and run in a circle on that stupid-ass artificial grass, I hear the crowd roar all around me, feel my arms grow, my wings unfurl, my body getting lighter until I take off and soar over the artificial grass, high above Mehdi's asthma, high above the concrete.

These early spring days never end, even after the sun sets, even after the temperature drops, even when it's almost winter again. Not even then do they end, but when the shadows return, we pull on our jackets. It's a retreat, not a surrender. We sit on the benches in the playground and smoke and drink Cokes and dream new, vast, meandering dreams, with the sweat from the game drying off our skin.

"Daaaamn, Ana Maria, you know her? Jorge's little sister? Great tits? *Wallah*, I swear man, she's hotter than Rihanna."

"We should figure out how to get some cash and go to Barcelona, *yao*. Go see a match. Doesn't Jorge have an uncle there?"

"I wanna go to Australia, *len*. That shit is cool, kangaroos and all that?"

"Australia? Jesus, what a fucking *bati* you are, Bounty. Kangaroos? Ha ha ha ha ha!"

"Kangaroos!"

We laugh at Bounty until we're lying on the hard, still-frozen sand, until we can hardly breathe, until Mehdi's lungs almost give up with asthma, until Bounty almost cries and finally gives up and walks away.

We stay there until the laughter drifts away over the rooftops and leaves us silent and restless, while the light around us turns from a clear, pale gray to the deepest blue. The evening isn't spring, it's freezing, the stars are still winter stars, clear and distinct against the blue, and I turn away, close my eyes. Perhaps it's the strange light or a spring that comes and goes in just one day, but suddenly anxiety rushes through me like a wave, and I gasp, barely able to get any air. My heart is pounding so hard that I lie flat on the ground in the sandbox.

It's not something you talk to your brothers about, unless you want to end up like Bounty. I pant and take in gulp after gulp of ice-cold air, feel the frozen sand against my lips, forcing myself to calm down, forcing my heart to stop pounding.

"*Ey*, Fadi? What the fuck are you up to?"

I force my eyes closed, force that feeling down into my stomach, force myself onto my feet.

"Nothing, faggot," I say. "Let's go."

So we go. Up toward the footbridge that crosses the tracks, freezing with just T-shirts on under our winter coats, but with spring still crackling on our skin. We hang out on the bridge above the subway tracks with our backs to the fence. We spit and smoke and watch trains roar by beneath us—white light and single-minded direction.

We high five Adde, who arrives from the row houses wearing his Canada Goose and carrying a jingling bag.

"Damn, it's cold?" he says. "Thought it was spring."

We nod. I think of you when I see him. I haven't seen you in a week, not even your shadow. I want to ask him if he saw you at the studio, but I choke. I pull on the fur collar of his enormous coat instead.

"Niiiice," I say. "You're like Diddy in that coat."

He shrugs, his bag clinking.

"You got booze?" Mehdi croaks. "Give us some!"

"Knock it off," he says. "There's a party at Red's. Wait a few years and you might get invited too, brats."

He laughs and disappears across the bridge.

"You're fucking cheap!" Mehdi shouts after him.

Adde doesn't even turn around, just flips us off and continues walking toward the concrete.

So we walk up and down the cracked asphalt, across frozen, yellow grass, under the broken streetlights. We tag buildings and electrical boxes with our worthless signs. *Boing*. But the *o* is a star. It doesn't mean anything, we don't even know where it comes from, but we tattoo all of Bergort with our trashy pointlessness. I keep my eyes on the black asphalt or the dark gray buildings, because if I slip up, look up at the dark blue emptiness above, I don't know what will happen.

Something has to happen. This can't be it—so endless and quiet and empty and poor. So I leave the others in the playground with their smokes and stupid jokes. I unbutton my coat and pull my jeans even farther down on my hips.

"I'm just gonna check something," I say.

"What's that, *bre*?" they ask.

"Nothing, I'll be back soon."

I cross the square, pass by the kebab shop where the Finns are drinking themselves to death, pass the Syrian's store and the yellow light from the subway, pass the high-rises, and head for the low-rises, whose façades are barely visible behind the satellite dishes that cover them like ivy, nostalgic wormholes to another time, another context, another reality as false and static as a fairy tale.

It doesn't matter that I've forgotten where exactly Red lives because I hear Ghostface and Trife through an open balcony door on the ground floor, hear the whole party rapping along to the chorus of "Be Easy." And I see you at the railing wearing a green plaid flannel shirt, tight tank top underneath, jeans not tight like the other chicks, but loose and sagging like a guy. Your hair is straight, your skin lit softly by a lighter you're using to light a joint. I carefully slip up to the balcony railing, don't want the whole party to see me, clear my throat.

"*Shoo*, Yazz," I say quietly.

But you can't hear me. You're talking to Blackeye, Igge, and Ignacio, and you take a deep drag on your spliff and let the smoke flow out of you, away from the balcony and out toward the streetlamp. I'm standing just below your elbow in the shadows. "Be Easy" ebbs away, and I hear your laughter for a moment before the beat starts again. I open my mouth again, extend my hand to touch you, to tell you I'm here. But you withdraw your arm, take another drag from your spliff, and hand it to Igge, before you rush off the balcony and back into the apartment and the party and what is very much your own life.

I stand still for a second, unsure of what to do, or why I'm here at all. Behind me I hear the door open and Adde stumbles out, pupils almost floating in his eyes, his face contorted and green. He bends into the bare bushes and pukes up the whole bag of beers he had with him just a couple of hours ago. When he's done, he turns around, a half smile on his lips. He wipes off his mouth with the back of his hand, slurring slightly and swaying.

"What the hell you doing here, *len*?"

I shrug.

"Nothing."

"Get outta here then, *abri*. Nothing here for you, right?"

Len? *Abri*? He's not even from here. He's from the row houses, a *suedi*. Fuck him. But I don't say anything, just stare at him, button up my jacket, and leave.

They're still in the park when I get back, looking at something on Mehdi's phone.

"Damn, look who's here!"

Jorge stands up.

"Come on, let's go over to Bounty's and play some FIFA. It's freezing."

I shake my head and feel the emptiness growing inside me.

"Räv?" I say. "Do you have a tube, you know, for gas?"

Räven nods and smiles.

"I got everything, *bre*. You know that."

"Good, go get it. And a crowbar."

It takes Räven less than five minutes to go home and dig up what we need. Not even five minutes for him to get back, his face is red, his eyes narrow and ready for anything.

"What're we doing, brother?"

"How much do you hate the Syrian?" I say. "How much do you hate his sorry style and his cheap fucking store?"

They nod. We've all been caught stealing by him, all had his farmer hands on our ears, all had a talk with the police.

"It's goddamn time we teach him a lesson, *ey*? Time to school him."

They look at me with something else in their eyes now—FIFA is forgotten, the cold is forgotten. This is something else.

"Have you seen him in his new Audi?" I say. "New? Ha, it's a hundred years old, but new to him. Have you seen him in it? Proud as a fucking beard, like he thinks he's somebody, that fucking faggot. "

"A-ight," says Mehdi. "About fucking time, I swear."

So we gather together, put the hose and crowbar under our coats, put our hoods up over our heads, feel the blood pumping healthy and strong through us for the first time since Camp Nou. It takes a few laps around the parking lot to find the Audi. A station wagon that's probably ten years old, green, dirty, a piece of shit. At first we walk past it, pretend not to see it. Take a couple of rounds to make sure the parking lot is empty. We don't talk, we just glide quietly over the asphalt, Shaolin, Wu-Tang, like fucking gangsters.

Then, in the shadows: "So how long will it take, Räv?"

He shrugs.

"Ten seconds for the cap, a couple of minutes for the doors. No more."

"And then?"

"Oh, easy, just a few minutes. Chill, *bre*. I got this."

So we look at each other, unable to hide our smiles or how much we've been waiting for this, for the spring, for the gangster life. So we glide through the yellow light of the parking lot, floating soundlessly toward the Audi, our eyes on nothing but revenge and chaos.

And Räven is a genius, he just braces his feet and pries off the gas cap, which pops off with a bang, then we suck the gasoline into a couple of Coke bottles. One liter should do it. We nod at each other, and Räven swings the crowbar against the glass. One time. *Boom*. Nothing. His eyes narrow, but Mehdi takes the crowbar from him without a word.

He puts all of his two hundred pounds behind a swing

that is destined to become legendary, which will live with us all summer, and the windshield explodes into thousands of tiny crystals that cover the asphalt, and before they've all even landed, Räven is inside the car emptying bottles onto the backseat and opening the doors to increase the draft. Then he crawls out again and looks at us. Holds a matchbox toward me.

"It was your idea, brother. It's only right that you'd get to light this shit on fire."

I take the matches, look him in the eye, look into Mehdi's eyes, into Jorge's eyes. They nod, red in the face, excited. And I do it. I light three matches at once and hold them in front of me for a second. Then I drop them inside the car door, watch fumes turn to blue and red flames above the seat, and we all turn around, and fly away over the parking lot with the fire still building behind us. We're already at the square when the gas tank explodes.

Chapter 6

Manhattan, New York—Saturday, August 15, 2015

"You look tired," Brett says as Yasmine sinks into the soft, blond leather seat beside him.

He'd just woken up when Yasmine called a half hour ago, but you'd never know it now as he sits there in his tailored suit, white shirt unbuttoned an extra button, Italian shoes, his dark hair wavy and sculpted.

Yasmine folds down the sun visor in front of her and throws a quick glance at its small mirror. Her left temple is swollen and has turned a pale reddish-purple. She runs her fingers over the swelling and feels it throbbing slightly.

"I've had a few long days," she says.

She flips the leather sun visor shut, leans back, and closes her eyes.

Until she ran across Brett at one of David's friend's openings in Williamsburg a year ago, she'd never met anyone like him. Sure, she'd seen pictures of people like him, seen them in Sweden too, bent over plates of seafood and rosé basking in the sun at open-air cafés in Stockholm. They were there when she used to go by Stureplan on her way to McDonald's with her teenage friends. There they sat in their expensive suits, with their elegant nineteenth-century apartments, a race who lived isolated lives in the expensive neighborhoods of

Stockholm's inner city. They had their housing prices and their educations to keep them safe, walled off from the kind of chaos she experienced in her daily life.

Brett is all that and more. He's the American dream, more than the American dream. He's Harvard and sockless feet in boat shoes and a house in the Hamptons. He is eighty-hour weeks at the office and Christmases in the Caribbean. But at the same time, there is a dissonance about him, something rebellious and ironic that cuts against his perfectly polished surface. It slips out in an unexpected joke or a dejected expression in a meeting with some hopeless client.

Now he struggles to back the SUV out between the gas pumps and throws a quick glance sideways at Yasmine.

"Looks like more than long days," he says.

Yasmine pretends not to hear him, just keeps her eyes closed. Brett is an agent in the advertising industry. He finds what he calls *talent*—creative young people with some special skill—which he sells to various advertising agencies and other clients who need those skills for their projects. Before she met Brett, Yasmine never knew there was such a job. She didn't know anything about the advertising industry. It had amused her when, after a few glasses of Chardonnay at that little gallery on Roebling Street last spring, Brett started bragging about his job and his contacts. She'd assumed that he was hitting on her, and she had to work hard to keep his clumsy performance under the radar as David stared at them from the other side of the gallery.

When Brett really did get in contact with her a few days later and offered to set her up with what he called the "street intelligence unit" at a huge energy drink company, it surprised her. And she was even more surprised when they wanted to meet her that same week in something they called their "clubhouse" in a neighborhood of the Bronx balanced on the edge of gentrification. No wine bars or organic stores yet, but a few of the early markers—the logo for Stumptown Coffee in the window of a café and bearded men in faux working-class clothes sitting on the other side of the dusty window. She'd asked Brett if he was coming to the meeting, but he'd had an uncomfortable look in his eyes and had nervously ran a hand through his hair.

"It's in the Bronx," was his only explanation, before offering to drive her to the closest subway station.

The "clubhouse" was housed in an old commercial space with large windows that faced a gritty sidewalk right next to an old diner that was ironically called Energy. The intelligence unit consisted of five kids in their twenties who seemed to represent an array of ethnic groups and subcultures.

After they talked about Banksy and Shepard Fairey and their "street capital," Yasmine briefly presented a few street artists she thought were interesting at the time. She got the job after ten minutes. The next week she was on a plane to Tokyo for the first time. She had a paid hotel room, various brand-new digital cameras that she had no idea how to use, and just one mission: find "the next Banksy."

So she'd walked like a shadow over the streets she didn't know, in a country that felt like another planet, with its impenetrable language and alphabet. All she had were her cameras and a couple of phone numbers for advertising people the energy drink gang were apparently friends with. The Japanese ad guys had been kind, took her out to bars and parties, showed her the best noodle shops and malls that were like luminous, autonomous worlds. But it seemed like the ad guys were as clueless about how she should fulfill her mission as she was. They showed her the graffiti and manga murals in neighborhoods like Shimokitazawa and Koenji, which looked like glittering, densely populated versions of Hornstull or Williamsburg. And she photographed everything dutifully, but it all seemed flat and empty, expressionless and mass-produced global art for bearded art directors, nothing you couldn't find in any city. Nothing that was worth going halfway around the world to discover.

She'd given up, determined to say the hell with her assignment, figured at least she got a trip to Tokyo out of it, could get away from everything for a while, that was something.

But on the last night at a party in what seemed to be a student dormitory, she ended up next to a tiny girl named Misaki who looked about twenty years old. Yasmine was actually on her way to the airport but had a few hours to kill, and the ad guys, in their desire to show her everything, had insisted.

Misaki was quiet and serious and there was something about her that spoke to Yasmine. It was nice to just stand quietly next to each other, to hide from the rest of the night. But after a while Misaki turned toward Yasmine and in apologetic, tentative English said she had heard that Yasmine was a curator and asked if she could show Yasmine her *architectural art*. Yasmine had laughed, she hardly knew what the word *curator* meant, but she happily agreed to look at her art. Misaki produced a computer as if from thin air, and soon they were sitting side by side on a brown couch in what seemed to be an enclosed balcony looking out over a dark alley.

On the computer Misaki showed her scans of hand-drawn, architectural sketches of identical cuboids attached to one another to create various angular robotic figures, figures that seemed to be doing different kinds of exercises. Some crouched with arms outstretched, like a kind of gymnastics or yoga; others sat on their knees with arms thrown wide in a kind of plea or prayer. A few more stood on one leg. Probably a dozen characters in total.

Yasmine didn't know what to say. They were extremely well made, well thought out, and good-looking. But at the same time simple, like the drawings of a talented, mildly autistic child. She smiled, hopefully encouragingly, and nodded. Misaki pointed and leaned toward her.

"Architect," she said. "They are durable. Containers."

And through Misaki's faltering English the image of what she had created slowly emerged: drawings and strength calculations of how the figures could be put together from freight containers. Monumental sculptures hundreds of feet high. It was the first time during the trip that Yasmine felt like she had found something really interesting, and before hurrying to the airport she asked Misaki to email her the sketches.

Back in New York the energy drink gang loved Misaki's sketches.

"That is exactly what we're looking for!" a bearded guy, maybe Rainbow, exclaimed and hugged Yasmine. "So *fresh*!"

Brett had called her a *Rebel Curator*—even printed it on business cards that Yasmine, embarrassed by the corniness of the title, consistently refused to hand out. And after Tokyo Yasmine became part of Brett's stable of trend-conscious young people from all over the world who came to New York for a thousand different reasons. Brett paired her with other companies, other kids in camouflage who wanted something *fresh*, or men in suits in Midtown who wanted to understand the *street*. And thanks to Brett, she'd be sent all over the world. Ljubljana, Detroit, back to Tokyo. Always for different companies, always the same obscure mission.

Sometimes she found something really interesting, like Misaki, and sometimes nothing at all. But over the past six months it started to dawn on her that she had a nose for scouting new, unexpected projects. And the missions just kept showing up, and the money continued to roll in—which David always went through quickly. But the missions gave her the opportunity to stay in New York, in exile, and then disappear when David's partying escalated. They gave her the opportunity to both be in exile and escape from exile.

And now, here in this grotesque car with Brett, she's hoping her reputation is enough to give her one more chance. One more opportunity to escape. Or maybe the opportunity to run from who she's become back to who she was.

When she opens her eyes she sees Brett glancing at the swelling near her eye again.

"It's nothing," she says, anticipating him. "Nothing I want to talk about."

She pulls out her phone, scrolls through nonexistent messages. From the corner of her eye, she sees him nod, maybe relieved not to have to ask anything else about her eye. He keeps his focus on the traffic on Lafayette.

"Is your pitch ready then?" he says at last. "No offense, but you're looking a bit rough?"

"Pitch?" she says. "I don't even know who we're going to meet?"

"You're the one who wanted a paid trip home?" he says, lifting an eyebrow. "We're meeting Shrewd and Daughter, one of the world's most prestigious PR agencies. I mean, this was your idea, right? You called me and asked me to find a customer for a project you have? What do you think? Agencies want to throw money at you because you found some Japanese container artist six months ago?"

He glances sideways at Yasmine, clearly annoyed.

"You're not the only one in this business, and seriously, your reputation isn't that solid? Sure, everybody's heard about the container lady, and that'll get you in the room, that's the only reason they'll meet with you. But when you're there you better fucking deliver. Please tell me you've prepared something? I didn't just throw my Saturday morning away on nothing?"

She feels the pressure welling up inside, the pain in her injured eye, the throbbing in her foot. That *was* what she'd thought. That it would suffice for her to say that she had something going on in Stockholm, pictures of something interesting, and Brett would find somebody to pay for her trip. She hadn't thought she'd have to show anything at all, just those three pictures from her mom's email. All she can think about is Fadi. All she can think about is that he was dead, and he might not be anymore. All she can think about is a chance to make things right.

Now a kind of desperation takes hold of her, and she has to fight the impulse to open the car door and throw herself out onto Lafayette Street, fight the urge to run as fast as she can, as far as she can. Because she knows that won't help, nothing helps, what you can escape from is always crushed by the weight of what you can't.

Instead she closes her eyes again, breathes calmly, looks at the buildings of SoHo and wipes away something that might be a tear as discreetly as she can.

"You saw the pictures I sent?" she says, doing everything she can to sound neutral and confident. "There's something there. Why do this if you don't think so yourself?"

Brett sinks into his seat with a sigh.

"That's a good question."

Chapter 7

Bergort—Winter 2011

Eventually I wake up, so I must have slept. The room is grayer now, whiter, no darkness or yellow from the streetlights outside, so it must be morning. The sheets are all tangled up, and for a moment I think that yesterday might not have happened yet, maybe it's still just a plan, unrealized and far away. But when I lift up my thin mattress the metal box of petty cash from the studio is lying in the hollow space under the box spring. On the other side of the room, the closet door where you grabbed your sketches is still ajar. Everything happened. Everything.

I stretch out my hand and pick up the phone, try to call you, but don't have enough money left on my prepaid phone. I text: WHERE ARE YOU? and push "send" but it doesn't go through. Not even enough money for that. I drop the phone on the floor and lean back against the wall, remorse and anxiety tearing me apart. I beat my fists against my forehead, halfheartedly at first, then harder and harder until I'm afraid I'll split my eyebrows, so I stop, collapse into a ball on the bed, whisper: "No, no, no!"

I sneak out of the apartment sometime after ten. It's quiet and empty, they're at one of their jobs, earning money we'll never see, sent home to family, or squirreled away, always for the past or the future and never for the here and now. I open the old laptop and try again:

Where are you? I can fix this.

I see that my brothers are online, and send them a quick message, without explanation

Camp Nou. Now. Need to talk.

Ten minutes later I'm breathing in frost and ice on the corner of the plastic field. It must have snowed again last night, because there's a fragile, fluffy layer on every chain-link of the fence around the field. A field of snow, surrounded by a net of snow. It takes them a half hour to show up, red-cheeked, laughing.

"*Shoo*, Fadi, what's happening, brother?"

"Damn *len*, you should have gone to school. The plan, bro, the plan!"

They thump each other's backs, happy and unconcerned. I look over their shoulders. I stomp, jump, spin, and worry.

"Listen," I say. "Everything's gone to shit, OK? *Wallah*, really fucked up."

I light a crooked cigarette and tell them about the code, how they'll see that it was Yazz's code we used in the burglary. But the brothers just laugh, just look at each other like I'm an idiot.

"So she gets blamed?" Bounty says. "What's the big deal, brother? She wants to go away, *yao*? So let her take the rap for this then?"

The others nod. They don't get it. I just keep smoking—exhale a jagged, gray cloud that rises above the jagged, gray concrete, up toward the jagged, gray sky.

"Fuck," I say. "It's not about her, OK?"

I'm looking at Jorge, trying to catch his eye, don't give a shit about the others now, don't give a shit about Bounty because he's a fucking retard. Don't care about Räven because he's already a criminal, always has been, he doesn't care about this, he's already turned around and started messing with his phone. I don't care about Mehdi because he's fat. I'm only looking at Jorge, because he's always the last one to join in with our bullshit, always skeptical, always half a step behind, always one thought ahead. But he only shrugs.

"What can I say, brother? What's done is done. And your sister is gonna do it, right? Just chill, *yao*. Lie low."

The cigarette's done, but I take one more drag so it burns down to the filter, before I throw it onto the snow. I look at Jorge again, but he's already laughing at something Mehdi said.

"Well, fuck it then," I say.

I don't care anyway. I don't give a shit about their stupid fucking risk analysis. That's not the point anyway. I don't give a shit if it works. All I care about is that you left for good. You've floated above me for so long, and now you've left the atmosphere. Your shadow will fall somewhere else. But that's not something you share with your brothers. That's not the kind of thing you share with anybody.

It's started snowing by the time I leave Camp Nou and head home, pass by the playground, which is empty and pointless without swings or children, its benches hidden in snowdrifts. The brothers' voices are still audible though muffled by the snow as they head in the opposite direction, past low-rises and the park and down toward the school. I can't do an afternoon there today. Can't just pass the day doing nothing.

It's completely empty between the buildings, there aren't even any bums sitting on the benches outside the liquor store, and the ads—always for the same damn seventy-nine-kronor chicken—sway and creak in the wind. It's as if I'm the only one here, as if everyone else has left, like there was an evacuation that nobody told me about.

I take a detour around the tracks because yesterday pushes me away from Pirate Square, makes it impossible for me to cross there. Repels me. Repel, compel, dispel. We got good at it in the end, Yazz. We learned the words. But we were the ones who were wrong. It wasn't enough to imitate. They wanted something more. From people like us, they always want more.

By the time they're finally standing in front of me, I know it's over, everything is over.

It happens fast. I'm on my back in the snow, the taste of steel in my mouth, the back of my head pounding and my ears ringing from the fall, snow pushing in under the collar of my coat, snowflakes on my face. I don't even know who they are until they lean over me.

"There you are, *sharmuta*," somebody says, maybe the Russian. "There's the little whore."

They drag me up onto my feet again, my head still so heavy from the fall that it feels like it's going to roll off my shoulders. I see Mladic, the Russian, and Blackeye. Somebody is holding me from behind, but I don't know who.

"Is it him?" Mladic says and turns to Blackeye.

Blackeye just nods and looks away. The Russian punches me in the stomach, and even though my thick winter coat protects me, it knocks the wind out of me. I gasp for air. It feels like I'm going to die. Am I going to die now?

Tears run down my cheeks, the man behind me lets go, and I fall forward into snow, which fills my mouth, my nose. They kick me in the stomach, I roll to my side, but even there somebody is kicking and kicking. But they can't hit me properly, the snow is too deep, and when they realize that, somebody pulls me to my feet. Mladic pushes his pock-marked face, his shaven skull, his crazy eyes, close to mine. He spits in my face. I feel the saliva flow down the bridge of his nose and drip onto my chin.

"How fucking stupid can you be, you little cunt?" he says. "What kind of fucking *sharmuta* would be so stupid that he steals his sister's code? And breaks into Pirate Tapes?"

He pulls back and then throws a punch that hits me above the temple—a flash of light explodes in my skull and all I want to do is fall back down into the snow, but whoever is holding me won't let go. I moan, don't want to moan, don't want to beg for mercy. But that's what I do, while the piss runs down my leg, and the fear of death grows inside me.

"Please," I say. "Please, please."

"Please?" The Russian is laughing somewhere beside me. "Get it together, you little prick."

And then he pushes me forward, and I fall down in the snow again. Then they grab hold of my legs and pull me on my stomach along the path, pull me over to the train tracks, my cheek bouncing and bleeding onto the mix of snow and gravel.

"No, no, no!" I scream.

They hoist me through the rusty gap in the fence, then drag me onto the subway tracks. I feel the rails, cold and smooth against my cheek.

"What are you doing? Please, I have everything. You'll get everything—"

They kick me in the stomach, and my head thumps against the track. The Russian leans over me, his breath full of tobacco and acetone.

"You're gonna die here, faggot," he hisses in my ear. "You're gonna die now."

And I cry and scream, like a fucking pig. I feel my whole body shaking, bursting, refusing to function.

"Your little faggot friends helped you didn't they?" Mladic says. His voice close to my ear sounds reasonable, almost sympathetic.

I nod and tremble.

"Yes!" I say.

"Bounty, Räven, Mehdi, Jorge."

They look at each other and grin.

"Not only are you a little pussy, you're a fucking rat too. You're disgusting, *sharmuta*."

They spit on me, all of them, one by one.

"Everything should be back in the studio by this afternoon, faggot," the Russian says.

I hear the train rattling somewhere inside the tunnel to the station. Feel its power vibrating through the tracks.

"Sure," I whisper. "It was a mistake. Forgive me, forgive me, forgive me."

They stand up and brush the snow off. Walk away without a sound.

I can feel the vibrations increasing in the track, hear the sound of the train's acceleration. I feel piss, wet and cold in my pants. Everything is over. Truly over. I should just leave my head here. Just end it now. What a relief that would be, such freedom.

But I can't even manage to do that. I don't even have enough honor for that.

Chapter 8

Manhattan, New York—Saturday, August 15, 2015

The elevator door opens directly onto an open-office space that is unexpectedly dark, despite the bright sunlight streaming in through the windows facing Madison Square Park. It's as if the dark red carpet absorbs whatever light bounces off the deep green walls.

The room is furnished with a dozen identical aged cherrywood desks arranged in straight rows. Black office chairs match the black metal office lamps, most of which are lit to compensate for the rest of the lugubrious interior. If it weren't for young people in jeans, chambray, and mustard-colored cashmere, it could be some English government agency in the 1930s.

Yasmine glances at Brett, but his gaze is already far inside the room.

"Brett!" a sharp voice cuts through the open space from the back of the room.

Brett stretches to see over the desks.

"There you are!" says the woman, who is now moving toward them through the rows of desks. "And you must be Yasmine? I'm Geneviève."

She's in front of them now and extends her hand. She's short and thin with a thick, steel-gray mane that sweeps from a transparent forehead, back over the dainty crown of her head, and down behind her ears, from which sapphires and gold earrings dangle. She's wearing a floor-length, moss-green caftan with what appear to be plants and insects embroidered intricately onto its sleeves and chest. Around her neck hangs a carelessly tied, scarlet silk scarf. How old is she? Sixty? Seventy? It's impossible to say. She looks like she's lived an extraordinarily interesting life, which is only getting more interesting with age.

"That doesn't look good," she says, and makes a careful gesture toward Yasmine's eye. "But there's nothing we can't solve."

She turns back toward the rest of the room.

"Hermione?" she says in a transatlantic English accent that evokes clinking glasses of champagne or Sunday excursions in the Jaguar in one of those English miniseries they used to show on Swedish public television when Yasmine was small. A young blond woman in a dress shirt, gray cardigan, and large horn-rimmed glasses looks up from her small screen.

Hermione, Yasmine thinks. Not only is there a *Geneviève*, there are people named Hermione here.

"Would you be so kind as to call Gretchen? Tell her to come here. It's urgent."

The woman nods and reaches for her phone.

"It's really nothing..." Yasmine begins.

Geneviève waves a hand to stop her, as if what she has to say is irrelevant, then takes Yasmine gently by the elbow and leads her toward a large, dark cube in the far right corner of the room. The self-assured way she does it should irritate Yasmine, but right now, right here, in this strange office, after that horrible night, all she wants is for Geneviève to never let her go.

But she does once they arrive at the cube, where she

opens a hidden door in one of the otherwise perfectly identical sides.

"The office was short on conference rooms," Geneviève says with a shrug. "So we built our own here in the corner."

The cube turns out to be lined with fluffy, deep purple egg cartons, and it takes Yasmine back to Affe and Red's cave, the recording studio on Pirate Square, where she hung out when she was fifteen. She can almost smell the beer and weed. But it's an illusion. This room smells like the expensive vanilla-scented candle standing on a small pedestal in one corner. And if this is a cave, it's an infinitely more exclusive one. The furniture consists of a table in that same worn cherrywood used in the rest of the office, surrounded by eight modern, ergonomic office chairs in black leather. Geneviève gestures to Yasmine to sit.

"Welcome to Shrewd & Daughter, Yasmine," she says.

The room mutes her voice and makes it sound as if everything but the core of the words has been polished away. Yasmine follows Brett toward the long side of the table. A white girl around Yasmine's age, dressed neatly, with a ponytail and sparkling silver earrings, smiles and sits down next to Geneviève.

"We're delighted you could come," Geneviève continues. "This is Mary, my assistant."

Mary waves to Yasmine and winks.

"We've heard such good things about you," she says, smiling again.

A man of about thirty-five wearing chinos, a dark blue blazer, and horn-rimmed glasses with dark, tousled hair enters the room and closes the door behind him.

"And here's Mark," says Geneviève. "One of our trend analysts."

She turns to Brett and smiles softly, tapping the watch on her wrist.

"We better get started," she says. "It is Saturday after all, and we try to be home by lunchtime. Brett says you have something exciting for us? I assume you're familiar with what we do?"

Yasmine nods as Mark sits down, takes off his glasses, and polishes them with the back of his striped green tie. He seems friendly. Of course she's familiar with Shrewd & Daughter. It's one of the names she's heard repeatedly since she entered this industry—a legendary PR company with an almost supernatural ability to identify the latest trends and use them for their clients just moments before those trends emerge on a broader scale, while they still feel fresh. They find subcultures and ride those waves out into the crowd, and their work encompasses everything from campaigns for major footwear brands to the representing of international artists. Always with an ear toward the street. Always with campaigns targeted at young people. Yasmine wishes that this pitch would have taken place somewhere else, someplace a bit less hip. Delivered to people who wouldn't be so hard to deceive.

"This is, as you know, a summer of rebellion, which is always difficult to anticipate," Geneviève continues. "There have been demonstrations against trade agreements and the war and everything else. Both here and in Europe. We're very interested in this. It's important for our customers to know what's happening on the street, and it's important we understand where trends come from. I don't want to sound cynical, but this unrest is going to be very marketable come autumn—if you know how to use it."

Something about the lighting in the meeting room has changed. What had been warm and deep has now become clearer and colder. Yasmine looks around but can't detect the source.

"LED lights," says Geneviève, as if reading Yasmine's mind. "Underneath those wall tiles."

She gestures to the velvet-clad egg cartons covering the walls and ceilings.

"We worked with a psychologist at NYU who developed a lighting profile to maximize concentration during our meetings. Who knows if it works?"

Yasmine swallows deeply. Feels her eye throb, her foot throb. Sees how they bend toward her, how they prepare to listen, to hear what she has for them, what paths into street culture she might be able to illuminate for them. She looks at their shimmering green caftans, their cashmere and horn-rimmed glasses, their silver earrings. She thinks of those pictures and of Bergort. Suddenly she feels disgusted by these people, by their exploitative eyes, their search for something genuine, something that can be bled until it's nothing more than surface. Disgusted that she's playing along with it, that she's abandoned where she came from. She left her blood and her background. More than that. What she was supposed to protect. She left it for this. For windowless meeting rooms with the kinds of people she never met until adulthood.

Slowly Yasmine turns the screen of her computer so that everyone can see, but Mary quickly plugs a cord into the computer, and before Yasmine knows it her desktop is projected onto the only wall in the room not covered by egg cartons.

She fumbles with the images. Clicking to find what she wants to show, not really knowing what to say. Finally, she finds the first picture sent to her a couple of days ago. She double-clicks it and hears the people on the other side of the table gasp, from the corner of her eye sees Mary avert her gaze. She looks up at the projected picture and understands their reaction, but somehow she's enjoying it. This is what it looks like, she wants to scream at them. *Wallah,* this is fucking reality! Make a fucking campaign out of this, *bre*! But she says nothing. She lets the image of a pixelated black cat, hanging lifeless from an electrical cord strung up on a lamppost, speak for itself.

Chapter 9

Bergort—Spring 2014

I haven't been living here for weeks. I sleep in my old, dirty sheets, eat what I can find in our almost empty fridge, only leave the apartment to buy smokes and Red Bull. But I don't live here. I'm not Fadi anymore.

I live in San Andreas now and drive a fucking Ferrari. I'm packing heat and robbing banks, shooting up cops and civilians. I respect no one and nothing, hijack fucking boats and airplanes, go on missions and burn through car after car after car. If you mess with me, you pay for it tenfold.

Or I just say the hell with all of it and drive around. Tune the radio to *West Coast Classics* and wait for "Gangsta Gangsta." Push some *shuno* off a chopper, push a Glock up under his chin and see the fear in his animated eyes before I blow his head off and speed away down Mount Vinewood Drive. Lose the cops in the hills and glide down toward the ocean at sunset with "Gin and Juice" in my headphones.

I don't live here anymore. I live in a fictional California where the sun doesn't get lower every day, where my options aren't limited, where my solitude is self-imposed and as tough as titanium.

This is as close as I can get to leaving. This is as close as I've gotten to being somebody else since I stopped waiting for your emails. Since I stopped waiting for you to come back. In the end, I stopped waiting for you to forgive me, stopped waiting for Mehdi and Räven and Bounty to forgive me. You make your mistakes, and you live with them. You get used to solitude.

But in San Andreas, I'm only alone when I want to be. I have Psych7876 and Amirat to hang out with online, and we're blood brothers in bank robberies and car chases, back each other up until we get bored with that and jam submachine guns into each other's faces. Sometimes we don't feel like playing, just steal a car and drive to the tennis court, play a few rounds while the sky turns from blue to orange.

Like tonight, it's just me and Amirat. It's been only two weeks since we found each other online at GTA V, but we call each other brother now, we're cut from the same cloth, different coasts, but the same kind of neighborhood. Tonight, we've done a couple of races, won some, lost some, and we don't feel like chasing around, not right now. Amirat is lousy at tennis, but it's fun to make him run around like a little *sharmuta* on the baseline until he gets pissed off. But tonight I take it easy, too tired to tease him. We've been playing quite a while when an email pings on my cell.

I open the email. He sent me a YouTube link, long and blue. I click it, only half looking while I lob forehands at his backhand.

It begins with a black box, Arabic text I don't feel like reading, something about Allah and jihad. We've talked about it before. Or Amirat's talked about it. He's a few years younger than me and goes to some Muslim school in the suburbs, and he says his elder brother is a beard, a radical.

In the film someone's reciting the Qur'an in the background—it sounds like a song, like an unexpectedly beautiful

Friday prayer. Then there's a clip of a rocky hill with a few low bushes. In the middle of the picture stands a group of guys with black ski masks over their heads, wearing black uniforms. They recite a long chant in Arabic that's difficult to hear, and then they chant *Allahu Akbar* maybe ten times.

When they're done, the man sitting in the middle starts to speak in Swedish, immigrant Swedish, Bergort Swedish, my Swedish. He talks about injustice and shame, about how it's time to do something about that, about how Muslims are suffering all over the world, and we have to resist. There is no choice, jihad is not a choice, it's something we have to do.

I don't know why, but my heart starts to pound. They overwhelm me somehow, those guys in masks, in black, dusty uniforms. It's not what they say exactly, that's nothing new, it's the kind of thing you've heard people harping about in the square for a hundred years. But that's just it, the guys in this film aren't just whining, they're doing something. They speak Swedish just like I do, they're like me. Except they're sitting in the dirt in Syria, with their guns and black uniforms, maybe just came back from a battle. I'm watching this from out of the corner of my eye the whole time. The Islamic State and the war, the suffering in Syria, our brothers and sisters are suffering. We all think it when we see the images flit by. This hell, created by al-Assad and the Jews and the Americans and the Swedes and all of them. Everything they do to hold us down, to humiliate us, putting us in camps or into fucking ghettos, forcing us to be like them, and then not even that helps. Not even when we learn all the words and sing better than anyone else, not even then does the concrete release its grip on us. My heart won't stop pounding.

"*Ey*, Amirat," I say. "I'm done for the night, *yao*. Pretty fuckin' tired."

*

After we hang up, I sneak out into the living room, grab the laptop, and crawl back into bed. I play the video again. It's not the first time I've seen this kind of video, but it's the first time I've seen one in Swedish, and there's something in that *shuno*'s voice, something so earnest, so sincere, so genuine. He says he hopes to die out there in the dirt, hopes Allah will take him. He hopes he will have the chance to serve Allah well first, to help as many Muslims as he can, to build the State one battle at a time. And there's something about his eyes underneath that ski mask. They're neither angry nor accusatory, just sad, honest, and sincere. They want something, those eyes, something bigger and better. Those eyes radiate a force that cuts or burns through all this bullshit and concrete. Those eyes make my heart beat faster, and my thoughts fly in directions I didn't know they could.

I keep clicking, searching for Swedes in Syria on YouTube and Facebook. I can't believe I never have before. There are stories, you hear about it in Bergort, legends, brothers who went down there. Nobody knows how, they just packed up and left late one night. Just a message a few weeks later to their family about Allah and making sacrifices. But it's always seemed daunting, and has always been brothers on the outskirts, brothers you don't know, who kept to themselves and then—*boom*—they're gone, just tall tales and ghost stories, not real.

But now I look around the room, heart still racing. It's as if something is stuck in my head, something that pushes and squeezes itself into the solitude that has been there for months, for years, since you disappeared, since I forced you to go away, since I ratted out the brothers and became an outcast.

I look at your bed, which is still there just a few yards away, still made, as if it's waiting for you, as if you might come back at any time. But I know now. I know you're never coming back. I stare at the gray wallpaper with white squares where posters of Messi used to hang, team pictures of Barcelona, the Pirate Tapes logo. All things that have been torn down now, all things that I tore down, tore into tiny pieces. Because I have never ever been able to leave anything whole.

There's a TV in here and a PlayStation console, video games and socks and underpants covering the floor. Gray light, a sun that keeps sinking, yellow light from streetlamps outside, concrete and gray. There's nothing here.

It's as if I see my own life through that jihadist's eyes. See how poor and empty my life is, how utterly useless. Just waking up and going to sleep. Just the same thing over and over again, the same emptiness.

Everything is nothing, nothing, nothing.

And it fills me up now more than ever. An emptiness that allows me no space, no room, which encloses me from the inside and out. I sink into it like a diving bell, black and heavy and completely alone. It's as if my brain embraces the full extent of something no one should be allowed to understand: nothing matters.

I curl up on my bed and feel my chest heaving faster, feel the flash of eyes, feel the oxygen running out, feel like I'm dying now, I might die now.

It has to end, this pressure on my chest and temples.

And suddenly I see those eyes from the YouTube video in front of me. See that they're not indifferent, not alone and hopeless, but strong and warm and full of a clear sense of meaning and direction.

I curl up like a newborn on the bed, my head filled with images of black-clad brothers in a row, kneeling in the dirt, backs bent. They fall simultaneously forward in prayer. Without my noticing it, I feel my lips start to move, first slowly and hesitantly. But then faster and louder as I close my eyes and let the words rush through me.

The more words I get out of me, the more air I get in. The louder I mumble, the less pressure on my chest. I fall out of bed, get down on my knees, hands over my ears, lips mumbling words I don't recognize, words I didn't know I had in me. Louder, louder.

With each repetition the press of the clock is reduced. With every word the ocean's pressure is reduced, changes shape, color, goes from black to gray to blue to light. I fall forward on that shitty floor, put my forehead against an old towel, let my arms fall forward, like the brothers in the dirt, feeling the emptiness give way, feeling a gap open in the emptiness through which light, or something like light, falls down over me, the faintest of rays of sunlight, the most fragile grace. And I hear my own voice in the silence: *"Ashaddu an la ilaha illa-Ilah ashaddu wa anna Muhammadan rasulu-Ila."*

Chapter 10

Manhattan, New York—Saturday, August 15, 2015

Yasmine tries to gather the words to explain what they're looking at. The light from the egg cartons has changed to a duller, deeper purple.

Geneviève finally turns her eyes from the cat to Yasmine. Her expression is quizzical, those slated, accentuated eyebrows raised halfway to her gray hair. Yasmine clears her throat.

"This is a picture that was sent to me just a couple of days ago," she says. "As you can see, it's a cat hanging from a lamppost."

"Yes, that's pretty self-explanatory," Mark says and takes off his glasses, polishing them again against the back of his green-striped tie while turning toward Yasmine.

His gaze is also questioning, but not necessarily curious.

"Horrible of course, in every way. But I don't really see what this has to do with anything. It's Saturday, and I'd rather..." He makes a rolling gesture with his hand, apparently in order to explain he'd much rather be doing anything besides this.

Yasmine drags her fingers across the trackpad, centering the picture on the noose around the cat's neck, zooming in on the tiny patch that sits attached to it. She zooms until the image becomes grainy. But the image on the label is simple and clear, easy to see.

"This symbol is attached to the cat's collar," she says.

They lean in toward the screen to see it better. Mark puts his glasses on again, squinting at the wall where the picture of a red, stylized fist is silhouetted against the background of a five-pointed star. Four identical rectangles represent the fingers of the hand, with a tight thumb lying across them. It's a simple image, like something from a propaganda poster or an eight-bit video game. Almost childish in its simplicity, like an enlarged emoji. Meanwhile, the symbol is remarkably powerful. Self-explanatory in a way that makes you feel like you've seen it before but can't place it, as if it's already part of a canon of rebellious symbols, along with the anarchist's *A* and Che Guevara stencils.

The symbol on the cat's collar is what Fadi is spraying onto the wall in the fourth picture, the only picture she won't show them.

When she's sure they've got a good look she zooms out and changes the image. A high, rusty fence appears on the wall. Through the fence, concrete apartment buildings can be seen, which extend up and out of the picture. In front of the fence stands an electrical box covered with old graffiti and dirt. On top of the graffiti the same image appears—a fist sprayed in bright red. Mark turns from the picture to Yasmine.

"Where is this?" he says.

But Yasmine doesn't have time to explain before Brett gently, almost imperceptibly, puts his hand on top of her arm.

"We have reason to believe that this is in Sweden. In the suburbs of Stockholm. Exactly where we don't know yet. You might want to show them the last picture too? "

Yasmine glances at Brett, unsure why he wouldn't want her to tell them that the place is an artificial grass field in Bergort, which the kids call Camp Nou. But still she's grateful that he's trying to help. She clicks the trackpad.

The last picture shows another stencil sprayed on the side of an apartment building. The same symbol as in the previous images. Yasmine knows exactly where it is. Just around the corner from Pirate Square, near the newsstand.

"This is also in Sweden, but in a different city. In a suburb of Malmö, in the south of the country," Brett says.

Yasmine turns her head way too fast. Why is he doing this? She's about to protest, but he sends her a look that indicates that she should trust him.

"And this is all you have?" Geneviève says. "Three pictures from at least two different places? A dead cat and a stencil?"

Yasmine nods.

"Yes," she lies.

The image of Fadi is not for them.

Mark seems impatient, almost halfway out of his chair.

"Seriously," he says. "Not to be rude, but this is a waste of time. What are we supposed to do with this? It's sad about the cat and all, but it feels a little bit like you just want us to pay for your trip home to Sweden, to be perfectly honest."

A throbbing foot. A throbbing temple. Tears that threaten to finally break through. Geneviève leans over the table toward Brett. Her eyes are small and shiny like Mary's polished earrings. The light has changed again, pale blue and cold now.

"Brett," she says. "I really don't understand. This could be anything. Why should this interest us? It could just be some maladjusted children? Hardly something for us."

She seems about to rise. But Brett is still sitting quietly in his chair.

"I thought this was your specialty," he says. "Finding out what the kids are up to?"

"Sure, sure," Geneviève replies wearily, standing now, and looking straight at Brett with a reserved expression. "If it can be assumed that there's a coherent symbolism or an activity that's representative of a group or some tendency, but this..."

She points distractedly toward the crooked, badly lit photo on the wall.

"This is nothing. Just graffiti. And some disturbed sociopath kid who kills cats."

She turns toward Yasmine.

"The symbol is very nice. If it's not generic we could surely sell it to another agency who'd use it for something. But we work more broadly than that. We want to see big shifts, not just individual expressions. Not your fault, darling, but I really thought Brett had better judgment."

Yasmine turns to Brett. Why isn't he standing? Why doesn't he put an end to this torture?

Instead he bends down and takes out his computer from his calfskin briefcase. It's shiny and impossibly small. Without asking for permission, he takes the cord from Yasmine's computer and connects it to his computer. A dark green wave appears on the wall. Apparently his desktop image.

"Is this really necessary?" Mark says, already reaching for the door of the meeting cube, which is camouflaged by the velvety egg cartons and impossible to discern if you've forgotten where you entered.

But Geneviève has stopped and gestures for him to come back.

"Give them a moment," she says and turns to Brett and Yasmine. "But believe me, a moment's really all you have."

Yasmine turns toward Brett, but he does not meet her eyes, just clicks methodically through folders on his computer until he finds one called *Protest*. It contains four images. The first one shows some kind of demonstration—Yasmine sees placards and flags with words written in French.

"Very well," Brett says. "Let's begin here."

He smiles confidently and leans back with his arms crossed over his soft navy blue blazer.

"This is some antiglobalization thing in Paris a few weeks ago. Pretty large, but they have them all the time. Nothing to get too worked up about."

He sways forward on his seat, swipes his fingers over the trackpad, and zooms in on a placard far out to the left of the picture.

"But perhaps you recognize this?" he says.

Yasmine is surprised to see the same red symbol on the placard, the fist she sent to him, against the same backdrop of a five-pointed star. She turns toward Brett, who blinks calmly at her before closing the image and opening another.

"This is Williamsburg," he says. "Maybe half an hour from here?"

The picture shows a dark alley surrounded by brick walls and concrete. At the far end of the alley on the dirty wall sits a red fist inside a star. The stencil is much larger than in the image from Bergort, maybe a yard by a yard. Brett zooms in. In the middle of the star a cat is hanging in a noose, almost identical to the one Yasmine showed.

Yasmine turns from the picture to Geneviève and Mark. They've sat down again and are leaning forward, their expressions now predatory. Brett clicks on the third image.

"This one I took myself the other day," he says. "Here in Manhattan, at Bryant Park."

The picture is undeniably Bryant Park. And there is the fist again, sprayed on one of the walls that leads down to the subway.

"You just took this?" Geneviève says.

"Maybe three days ago," he says. "I was surprised at first. But you know, once you've started to look for something you see it everywhere. Pattern recognition."

"I'm pretty sure I've seen it too, now that I think about it. Sprayed somewhere near the PATH train in Jersey City," Mary says suddenly and leans back in her chair, thoughtful. "Not the cat. But the stencil. I'm pretty sure."

Geneviève turns to Mark; her impatience seems to have shifted focus.

"And you don't recognize this?" she says. "No scout reports? Nothing?"

Mark shakes his head, even he's thoughtful now.

"Not that I can recall," he says. "I'll check again, but I'm pretty sure that this is the first we've heard of this."

"Sweden, Paris, several times here in New York?" Geneviève says. "Such a simple symbol? How is that possible?"

She bends over the table, turning her tiger eyes toward Yasmine.

"And someone sent images of this to you? Who?"

"An old friend," Yasmine lies. "Someone who knows I'm interested in street art."

"And you think you can figure out what this is about?" Geneviève says. "What the symbol means? Who's behind it? Through your friend in Sweden?"

"Yes," she says. "I don't think it will take more than a week to figure out what this is about, actually."

Geneviève nods and turns to Mary.

"Book the next flight to Stockholm for Yasmine," she says. "Put her in our usual hotel there for a week."

She spins her chair and looks coolly at Mark.

"And you follow up in New York, right? We have some

contacts too, don't we? I mean, this is your job after all, isn't it?"

Mark shakes his head, suddenly confused.

"So weird," he mumbles. "We don't miss this stuff."

A subdued knock on the door interrupts Mark's introspection.

"Ah!" Geneviève says and stands up. "Gretchen."

Gretchen turns out to be a blond, middle-aged doctor in jeans and a burgundy sweatshirt with NOTRE DAME printed in thick letters across the chest, who arrives with a bag that holds enough medical supplies to equip an ambulance. Gretchen isn't at all interested in listening to Yasmine's confused assurances that she's fine, and simply applies a cooling salve around her eyes and cheeks and even manages to get her to reveal her injured foot.

When Gretchen leaves twenty minutes later, Yasmine is patched up. It's just Yasmine and Brett in the conference room now, and she feels like Malik, the beige toy dog she inherited from their Croatian neighbors when she was little, the dog that she never let out of her sight. Malik was carefully sewn together, had new button eyes and a tail that constantly fell off. Every time he split, more of his stuffing fell out until he was only plush and thread. She feels like that now, not leaking anymore, but made of only plush and wire and nothing more.

Brett conjures up a glass and places it in front of her, fills it halfway with mineral water.

"Feeling better now?" he asks.

Yasmine ignores the water.

"What the hell just happened?" she says.

"We'll talk on the way to the airport." Brett gives her a satisfied smile.

And now she sits slumped in the leather seat of Brett's monster of a car as they drive through Queens on Atlantic Avenue toward JFK. She can feel the credit card that Mary from Shrewd & Daughter gave her rubbing against her hip bone through the thick fabric of her English skirt. It's her winning ticket, and she can hardly believe it. She's on her way. Everything that happened is fading, David's bullshit, all the breakups and deceit. None of it matters. Fadi may be alive, and she's going to find him. The credit card is proof that she has the ability to do so.

"Use it responsibly and keep receipts," Mary had said, winked, then lowered her voice. "But don't be *too* careful."

Her foot feels soft and muffled, not even her temple hurts anymore. She probably has one of Gretchen's pink pills to thank for that.

"Ozone Park," Brett says and drums his fingers on the light brown leather of the steering wheel. "I've always loved that name."

Yasmine looks out the window at the dusty nail salons, at the plastic bags drifting across the vacant lots, plywood on the windows of abandoned houses, liquor stores. It seems far from Brett's world and closer to her own.

"What the hell just happened up there?" she says and turns from the exhaust and boarded-up dollar stores toward leather and wood paneling—and Brett.

"What happened at the meeting?" he asks.

"What else?"

He laughs, drumming the steering wheel again.

"Oh," he says. "Just a little bit of *Brett magic*, that's all."

"Where did you get a hold of those photos? Did you know about this before? I only sent you my photos twenty-four hours ago."

He glances at her sideways, a smile at the corner of his mouth.

"Twenty-four hours is all I need, baby. More than I need, actually. "

They stop at a red light, and he turns to her.

"You think the photos were real?" he says.

Yasmine shakes her head, trying to make this afternoon, these last few days, all of it fall into place.

"I don't understand anything," she says. "Anything at all."

He pushes quietly on the gas pedal, and they start moving slowly over the bumpy road again.

"You sent me the pictures," he says. "I knew right away it wouldn't be enough. My God, Yasmine, I asked you to prepare properly?"

He glances at her with a bit of irritation in his eyes.

"Luckily I didn't trust you to do that, and took the initiative to do it myself. Those people aren't just any old losers. They sell trends. Their clients are paying them millions to stay abreast of whatever the kids are up to. So their clients stay in a good position to tailor their products and campaigns so it feels like they've created the trend themselves. But what do Shrewd & Daughter really sell? Nothing! Just smoke and mirrors. They're hustlers. Albeit rich and successful hustlers. And you know what they say: if you're gonna hustle a hustler, you gotta take it to the next level."

Yasmine focuses her gaze on the traffic and the decaying concrete in front of them.

"So what did you do? Photoshop them?"

Brett shrugs, drumming happily on the steering wheel.

"Well, what was I supposed to do? What you sent me wasn't enough for them to start a project with you, as you may have noticed. That was clear from the start. I gave the pictures you sent to a client who does photo editing and asked him to make it a little bigger, if you know what I mean? Paste the pictures into other contexts. Nothing all that strange really. He owed me a favor, and I knew what they'd want. The same thing that everyone in this industry wants: trends, new things that pop up in different places simultaneously. Ideally, an American angle, and preferably something they can relate to directly. Like Manhattan. They want rebellion and youth. Something a little dangerous, but not too dangerous. They've been looking for a way to make money off all of those demonstrations this summer, the protests and riots, antiglobalization and all that shit. And that symbol was simple enough. The cat was a bit dirty, maybe, but it gave it a little edge. Those people love edge."

He laughs and leans back.

"*Voilà*, as you Europeans say. Now you have a week to do whatever you want. But you better send me something after all I've done."

Chapter 11

London—Sunday, August 16, 2015

From the elevated railway tracks leading in from Gatwick, London still looks like the future, the horizon filled with diamond and cobalt, skyscrapers, twisted and self-confident, sparkling in the early-evening darkness. But beneath the futuristic skyline, streets and alleys meander like stairways at Hogwarts, always in a different direction than the one you've been promised. Overcrowded, dirty, and smoggy. Pale faces under the yellow light of the bus ride home and a bag of chips for dinner. Underpaid Ukrainians and Greeks jumping out of the way for Chinese limousines. London is Dickens remixed by an oligarch.

Klara Walldéen is sitting at the window, letting the city pour over her again, streaming in through her temples, into her skull, her skeleton, until even her heartbeat changes pace.

It's a relief to be back. Three days at her grandparents' in the archipelago is all she's capable of at the moment and not a second longer. She has to make an effort to sit still, to stay seated while her grandmother carefully pours boiled coffee into thin porcelain cups and serves freshly baked cardamom buns. It's as if her body can't handle it anymore, as if her brain is too fast for Aspöja, and this morning she counted the seconds until it was time to go duck hunting with Grandpa. She felt like she needed it—the concentration and anticipation, the calm and explosion.

But as soon as she was headed out in the boat with her grandfather's basset hound, Albert, facing the wind in the bow, his small eyes full of anticipation, her discomfort began to grow—with each rock they passed, with every ripple on the calm, beautiful sea. Memories of that Christmas out among those rocks and islets a little more than a year and a half ago washed over her again. The storm that drove in over Smuggelskär, where she and Gabriella hid out in Bosse's old barn from black ops soldiers who were hunting them down and planning to murder them.

And before that. Brussels and Paris. Mahmoud calling her with a voice so unlike the one she remembered from Uppsala. How angry she'd been at him. She'd nicknamed him Moody, her first love. Maybe her only true love, who betrayed her, but came back to tell her why, and because he needed her again.

Then that snowy evening in Paris. She still remembers the smell of spilled wine in the grocery store. Soundless bullets twisting around them. Mahmoud's heavy hand in hers before she realized he was hit. The small, round hole in his forehead. The blood spreading across the cold floor. The moment she decided to run, to abandon him, to survive.

And then, just days later, the American who suddenly banged on the door of the barn in the middle of the storm out there among the islands of the Sankt Anna archipelago. Her father, a word that she found difficult to accept.

Within a few days she saw the love of her life and her previously unknown father die in front of her, in her arms. How do you get back to yourself again after something like that?

*

Grandpa had sensed it, the atmosphere around her, and when he stopped the boat at one of the small islands they'd been going to on mornings like these as long as Klara could remember, he put his arm around her, pulled her close to him.

"How are you these days, little Klara?" he said.

But she couldn't take it, couldn't stand that he was worried. Her grandparents had worried enough about her in recent years. They'd seen too much of her lying in bed in her old room the first few months after it happened, and then worried too much when she took on Mahmoud's doctoral work on war crimes and finished it. She saw their pride when the book was published with both her and Mahmoud's names on it, but what she felt most was shame—it wasn't really her work. She couldn't escape the thought she'd stolen something from Mahmoud, pulled it out of his dead hands, and presented it as her own.

And she couldn't escape the fact that everyone was coddling her. Lysander—Mahmoud's supervisor—who managed to convince her that her name should be on the book; told her she'd edited and written more than most coauthors. It was true: she'd worked twelve-hour days for almost a year to put it together. Yet still it felt like theft. And they were all coddling her, tiptoeing around her. Nobody seemed to realize she'd failed to protect the ones who died. Why were they so kind to her, why make things easier for her?

Like Charlotte Anderfeldt, who arranged for her to work on her PhD in law in London and made sure she received a scholarship to finish Mahmoud's book in London. Or Gabriella, her best friend, who pulled her out of bed and persuaded her to keep working.

She hadn't earned their help and patience.

So she shook off her grandfather's arm and gave him a shaky, hollow smile.

"It's nothing," she said. "Just a little tired, it's early. Come on, let's go find our spot."

And when she started to head toward their usual place, she could feel her grandfather's eyes on her back, feel his worry and curiosity and willingness to help. It made her angry. She wanted to turn around and scream at him, scream at them all: *Leave me alone for fuck's sake! I'm nothing. Less than nothing. I'm a traitor, a murderer! Somebody who doesn't know anything. Let me be! Don't love me!*

And when they were in place, sitting in silence, invisible among the bushes with the sea glittering in front of them in the early-morning sun, it gave her no peace. Not even this, not even here, doing what she had always loved more than anything else.

But then Albert started barking, and seconds later the reeds rustled and six woodcocks fluttered up and out of the bay. There, in that moment, only that moment, the weight of it lifted, leaving Klara empty and alone, with no history or future. She aimed her shotgun, held it still until she was sure, and pulled the trigger. Once, twice. The recoil hit her like a wave, and her head felt light and clear.

But by the time she lowered the gun that wonderful emptiness had disappeared.

Albert came back with the woodcock in his jaw, and her grandfather gave her an approving pat on the shoulder.

"You certainly can shoot, Klara."

He took the bird out of Albert's mouth and patted him as well, gave him a treat from one of the pockets of his oilskin coat.

"Coffee?" he said and smiled at Klara.

"Irish coffee?" she said and regretted it immediately.

He looked at her with new concern in his eyes.

"A little early for that, don't you think?"

Klara put the rifle over her shoulder and started walking back down toward the boat.

"We should probably get going," she said.

She gets off the train at Blackfriars and flags down a cab. She doesn't have the energy for the Tube or bus tonight.

"Shoreditch," she says. "Navarre Street."

She feels the taste of red wine in her mouth, loves that harshness, looking forward to the taste of a cigarette when she gets out of the cab.

She drank a glass at the airport and then a small bottle on the plane, which she nursed as slowly as she could to avoid the shame of having to order another one. It's Sunday, and she worked on the report all day Saturday and half the night out on Aspöja without a single glass. Tomorrow's going to be a long day, so she surely deserves another glass tonight. Just one or two, it's not even seven yet.

"By the way," she says to the driver. "Do you know that bar Library? On Leonard Street."

The Library is half full when Klara arrives, which suits her. It'll be full soon enough—Sundays are just like any other day for the bar's freelance clientele. Pete, the bartender, winks at her when he sees her, and she goes over to the bar, waits for him to finish pouring some locally produced IPA for two "creative" men with beards, striped shirts, and baggy shorts.

"How's it going, Klara?" he says and puts a glass on the counter in front of her while reaching down to grab a bottle of red wine.

"Okay, I was in Sweden over the weekend, just got back."

She nods toward her carry-on and laptop bag standing next to her on the floor. Pete fills her glass and waves her off as she fumbles in her purse for her wallet.

"It's on me. Glad you came straight from the airport."

He pauses and his expression changes.

"If you help close up later I'll offer you a drink at my place too."

Klara takes a sip of wine and looks at his tousled blond hair, his clear blue eyes, his collarbones and toned shoulders, which are clearly visible through his thin, white T-shirt. She remembers, or barely remembers, three clumsy, drunken, and unsatisfactory nights at his home in recent weeks.

She shakes her head.

"Not tonight, Pete," she says. "But thanks for the wine."

By ten, the bar is full, and Klara feels drunk. How much did she drink? Obviously more than she'd planned to, and with each sip of wine her mind feels emptier and lighter. With each glass, it's easier to relax, to let go of the past, to let go of the job and the stress and the bullshit. But tonight, she must have misjudged, because her head is spinning, and she's regretting that last glass. Like a fucking rookie.

"I think I..." she says to the dark-haired photographer she'd been flirting uninhibitedly with just three minutes earlier.

"I think I have to go."

He looks surprised, as if she's joking. What's his name—Martin? Not that it matters.

"I have to go home," she says, and is relieved she isn't slurring.

Her bags and then air.

"I can take you home," says the man who might be named Martin.

Klara shakes her head and waves her hand.

"I live around the corner," she says. "I'll be fine."

"Are you on Facebook at least?" he says against her neck as Klara winds her way among guests and out into the still warm London evening.

The air is stale, smells of exhaust and frying oil. The last few weeks have been tropical, and Klara's head starts spinning faster and faster. She tries to take a few steps and discovers she can't really focus her eyes. It feels as if the buildings are moving in her peripheral vision.

Slowly she starts to head toward home, and dread overcomes her. Damn, is she really going to be hungover tomorrow? So incredibly stupid. She cuts across one of the small streets that lead to Great Eastern Street; after just a couple of yards, she thinks she hears footsteps behind her. She stops and turns around. Nothing. It was probably the wheels of her rolling carry-on. Suddenly overcome by fatigue, she forces herself to start walking again, speeding up her steps, relieved that she lives just ten minutes away.

But as soon as she starts moving, she hears footsteps again. Now she's sure of it and glances over her shoulder without slowing down. The alley is dark and flanked by beat-up brick walls covered with graffiti. Intoxication makes it seem as if the concrete is rocking back and forth. But in the middle of the asphalt, between the walls, she sees the silhouette of a man. He stops when she sees him. She stops too.

"Martin?" she says.

The concrete spins and shakes beneath her, and she finds it difficult to focus. The man raises his arms and says nothing. Klara stumbles, takes a few steps forward, then squats down onto all fours. Her head is buzzing. The asphalt beneath her looks like the sea, the concrete like rocks in the archipelago. The waves around her move, as if breathing and swaying, as if she's still in her grandfather's boat. She turns away from everything moving and transitory, tries to focus, while her nausea grows. But it's in vain; the red wine and nuts she ate force their way out of her. After she vomits, she rolls onto her side and closes her eyes. In another universe, unfolding outside her closed eyes, she hears a whisper, feels hands pulling and pressing. Then darkness. Warm and silent and black.

Chapter 12

Stockholm—Monday, August 17, 2015

It's morning in Stockholm, Yasmine realizes as she pays her taxi outside of Story Hotel on Riddargatan. The clock on her cell phone says morning, but her body has given up and now exists outside any earthly concept of time. Thirteen hours' time difference between Tokyo and New York. Another six hours' difference with Stockholm. She feels both heavy and ephemeral, equal parts lead and helium.

For a moment she holds her breath as the taxi driver swipes the card. It's the first time she's used it since the meeting, and the last few days in New York feel like a dream, so she can't be sure it will work.

But the card reader accepts it, and she totters out into a warm late-summer morning, stumbles through the automated reception and up to her—according to the website—"bohemian" room, where she falls headfirst onto the sheets, not even bothering to take off her shoes.

When she wakes up, the light is streaming through the thin curtains at a different angle, and she turns over to check the time on her cell phone. Just after twelve; she slept for two hours. It feels like a whole night, and yet her head is full of sand and her body restless. It's strange to be back, even if this hotel room with its raw, untreated walls and minimalist decor doesn't feel like Sweden, or at least not her Sweden. She gets up and goes to the window, looks out over the mix of clean, bourgeois modernism and elegant *fin-de-siècle* architecture on Riddargatan, and down toward the Östermalmstorg subway station and Birger Jarlsgatan. Not her Sweden either. But Fadi must be somewhere out there, she thinks.

"I'm coming, *habibi*," she whispers quietly. "Don't disappear again."

She draws the curtains and goes into the bathroom. The face in the mirror makes her wince. It's not exactly a black eye, more like the right side of her eye has swollen up, and a bright purple sunset is radiating from her temple. No wonder Brett bought her a pair of cheap, huge sunglasses at JFK. At the same time, she's thankful for that eye, thankful for the vague, throbbing pain, thankful for what the swelling has done to her face, what it's done to her. It's concrete and unambiguous, an etching, an obvious and simple symbol to turn to when regret or remorse or doubt sets in. She picks up the cell phone and centers her face as close as she can to the viewfinder and snaps a picture. Never again.

Sitting on the bed, she opens the message from her mother. Looks at the dark picture of Fadi, twisting and turning it. Trying to get the pixels to line up, trying to make them add up. It's him, she thinks. It must be him.

She closes the picture, but doesn't close the message from her mother. How long ago has it been since she spoke to either of her parents? She left four years ago, but she'd hardly said a word to them for several years before that. She stayed out when they were home and made sure she only went home when they were out, when she knew only Fadi was there. All she remembers is their tired faces, their long stares, their harsh words, and hard fists. And now? She shakes her head. Tomorrow. First, there's somebody else she has to see.

Slowly she scrolls through her Swedish phone list. So many names and so many years since she's contacted them. People who were her whole world, who she grew up with. Parisa and Q, Malik and Sebbe, Bilal, Red, Soledad, Henna, Danny, Amat. Math classes and after-school programs, weeds in the playground, the mast in the woods behind Valgatan where they climbed until they almost touched the stars and fainted from the height. Day drinking at José and Mona's when their parents were in Chile and their uncle ended up in the hospital, hanging out on the square and smoking under the kitchen fan at Miriam's. And then the studio, but she can't think past that. It doesn't matter. She takes a deep breath. She has no other option, she has to confront it. She scrolls through the names in the phone until she finds what she's looking for.

He answers on the first ring, must have had his phone in hand.

"*Shoo*, this is Igge."

Yasmine swallows an impulse to hang up. She forces herself to breathe calmly and musters her courage.

"Ignacio," she says. "It's me. Yazz."

There's silence on the other end of the line.

"I know," she says. "It's been a long time. I..."

"Where are you, *len*?" he says.

His voice is exactly like she remembers it. Large and full of space, big enough to disappear inside of.

"I'm home again. In Stockholm. Where are you?"

He laughs.

"*Ey*, what do you think? I am where I always am, *bre*. I'm no international traveler, right?"

"Are you working? Same place?"

"Like I said, Yazz, same ol' shit. What about you? You're in Stockholm now?"

He sounds surprised, almost taken aback. No wonder.

"Yes, I'm in Stockholm. I got in just now, this morning."

Silence again. It's been such a long time. And quiet for a long time. She knows this is up to her.

"I'd like to see you, Ignacio," she says.

He hesitates and sighs.

"Ignacio?" he says at last. "You're the only who calls me that, sister. You know that. OK, where do you wanna meet?"

"I can take you out to dinner, it's the least I can do, right?"

"You gonna take me out? That's a first, *len*. But sure. I'm at work right now in the city. How about Flippin' Burgers at five o'clock? Before the rush. You know where that is?"

"I'm sure I'll find it," she says. "See you there."

Vasastan is quiet and strangely lethargic, the summer has been a long one, and even if vacation is over the laziness remains. The occasional thirty-something media type saunters home in shirtsleeves, and a few fathers on paternity leave wander by, pushing a stroller with one hand and holding a coffee in the other. The traffic inches forward.

Yasmine spots Ignacio's broad back at one of the tables at Flippin' Burgers outdoor seating as soon as she swings around the corner from Upplandsgatan onto Observatoriegatan. Even from behind and from a distance, Ignacio makes his surroundings seem smaller than they are, as if the proportions don't quite make sense.

Seeing him again makes her somber, and she deliberately slows to put off their reunion as long as possible. It's been four years since she disappeared without a word. And not until now, when she's actually in Stockholm again, does she realize how far away she's been. How far away she might still be.

"Ignacio!" she says with a forced cheerfulness and slides down on the bench beside him. "*Que pasa?*"

He turns so quickly, he almost tips over the picnic table. His shaved head is hidden under a blue Knicks cap, and he's let his beard grow out, dark, thick, and trimmed square. It makes him look older than his twenty-four years. He's come straight from his job, still wearing blue work pants and a T-shirt with the name of a moving company printed across the back. A wave of old love flows through Yasmine.

"Yazz!" he says and puts his huge arms around her. "Damn, it's been a minute, *len*."

"Four years," she says. "Time flies."

He doesn't say anything, just lets go of her gently but leaves his huge hands resting on her shoulders while he inspects her.

"You're skinny, Yazz. Don't you eat anymore?"

Yasmine shrugs and smiles. Ignacio shakes his head in resignation before letting go of one of her shoulders and gently lifting her large black sunglasses. His squints and his mouth narrows to a line when he sees the sunset radiating from Yasmine's temple. Before he can say anything, she shakes free of him and grabs her glasses from his hand and puts them back on again.

"We better order before all the *suedis* start rolling in," she says. "What do you want?"

*

Forty-five minutes later they've finished their burgers, and Ignacio is halfway through his second cookie dough milk shake, spiked with two shots of Jack Daniel's. Yasmine takes a sip of her Stockholm IPA ("You're home now, Yazz, gotta drink local," was how he'd dismissed her attempts to order an American beer) and leans back on the bench. Alcohol has stabilized her somehow, reduced the jet lag to vague background noise. The evening is still warm, the sky clear, bright, and endless.

They've gone through a good deal of what happened in the last four years. Who's left. Who put out a record. Who moved, died, or is serving time. For a moment, Yasmine can almost forget everything else, almost forget her eye and David and New York and Shrewd & Daughter. Almost forget Fadi and exile, because it's such a relief to just lean back, drink a beer, and listen to new versions of the same old war stories and legends. For a moment, coming home is almost like coming home.

But she knows that they're just circling around, and they can't keep on like that, and in the end they fall silent and let their eyes wander over the almost deserted street, over the cobblestones and Art Nouveau façades. After a few seconds Ignacio turns back to her, looks at her with a different expression.

"I heard about Fadi," he says calmly. "I'm really sorry, Yazz."

Yasmine just nods and looks down at her beer.

"I swear," Ignacio continues. "I didn't know it had gone so far. You never saw him around anymore. If I'd known..."

"I know," said Yasmine. "I know, Ignacio."

She puts her hand on his but can't meet his eyes.

"This is on me," she says quietly. "Nobody else. I'm the one who left."

She turns to Ignacio and takes off her sunglasses, looks him in the eye.

"It was fucked-up," she says. "To flip out and leave like that, without a word. It was really fucking wrong, Ignacio. To Fadi and to you."

Now it's Ignacio's turn to avert his eyes and let them sweep out across the dusty pavement.

"You don't owe me anything." He shrugs. "It was already over between us, wasn't it?"

"But to just take off like that? I owed you more than that. I wrote so many emails to you in my head, but I never sent them."

Ignacio turns back to her with a wry smile.

"It is what it is, sister," he says. "You do what you gotta do, right?"

Yasmine nods carefully and takes a sip of her beer.

"So *que pasa*, Yazz?" he says gently. "What are you doing here? Four years? You disappeared without a sound, baby. You didn't just come back to see me?"

"He's not dead," she says quietly.

Ignacio seems to flinch, then leans across the table.

"What? Who isn't dead? Fadi?"

Yasmine takes her phone out of her pocket and opens the picture her mother sent. She pushes it across the table to Ignacio.

"See for yourself."

He picks up the phone and drags his finger across the picture, enlarging it, and holds the phone close to his face to study it. Finally, he puts it down on the table again. There's sadness in his eyes.

"Maybe," he says. "Yazz… Don't get your hopes up. It could be him. But seriously, it's pretty dark and blurry, don't you think?"

"It's him," she says calmly.

"So you came back to try to find him?"

"Not try. I will find him."

Ignacio looks worried but nods calmly.

"Where you staying?" he says.

"Story Hotel, at Stureplan."

Ignacio whistles.

"Sweet. You've come up in the world, sister."

"I have a job," Yasmine says. "Or, I do stuff for advertising agencies. Find artists and shit. Trends. You know, big companies want to be down with the kids."

She bends her arm in an ironic hip-hop gesture.

"Anyway, right now I'm working for an agency that wants to find out what's up in Bergort."

Ignacio shakes his head and sucks on his milk shake.

"What the hell are you talking about? What do they want with Fadi?"

"They don't know anything about Fadi," she says. "But there's something else out there. Something that Fadi might have gotten mixed up with."

She shrugs again.

"I don't know what. Fuck that anyway, but it was enough to make them pay up."

"I don't get it," Ignacio says. "Some ad agency in New York wants to know what's going on in Bergort? How the hell did that happen, *len*?"

Yasmine smiles tiredly and takes a sip of beer.

"Just an old-school hustle," she says. "You're not the only one that can shake money outta the trees, brother."

Ignacio laughs, leans back.

"So you made them pay your way home? Your hotel? Shit, Yazz, I'm proud of you."

"I have to find Fadi. But David… He made off with all my money. I needed somebody to bankroll this."

She takes out her phone and opens the image of the cat hanging in the snare.

"Here," she says and pushes the phone across the table again. "I was sent three pictures, which seem to be related to Fadi."

He takes the phone back and glances at the picture but closes out the screen almost immediately before handing it back to Yasmine.

"No idea," he says defensively. "Where did you get that?"

She looks at him questioningly.

"*Ey*, Ignacio. There are more pictures. A stencil of a fist inside a star."

She picks up the phone and turns the screen on.

"I don't know nothin' about that, okay?" he says.

His voice is suddenly curt, almost aggressive, and she quickly looks up at him, but he's turned his gaze to the street, to the Art Nouveau façades that look soft and matte in the afternoon light.

"Come on, man," she says. "You haven't even looked at the pictures."

She bends over the phone again, but he takes it from her and places it on the table.

"*Wallah*," he says. "I swear. I don't know anything about that."

He looks her in the eye, his expression no longer warm and ironic now, but more like Bergort itself—all concrete and complicated loyalties. There's worry there too, and something else. Something he's not saying.

"Seriously, Yazz," he says.

He puts one of his hands on hers, so big it completely covers her own and presses, not hard, but enough to remind her of the past—of Bergort and growing up, of claustrophobia and confinement. Of helplessness.

"There are things you just gotta forget about, okay?"

"There are things you can't forget about," she says quietly. "But I hear you, brother."

They drink in silence for a little while. Until Ignacio can't hold back anymore.

"Your eye? It was him, right? That Swede you left with. The artist."

He spits out the word *artist* with the satisfaction of someone who's had a piece of food stuck between their teeth and finally got it out.

"It doesn't matter," she says. "I'm here now."

She takes a deep breath. They had to end up here eventually.

"What the hell, Yazz—"

"Fuck it," she interrupts. "I had to take off, right? After the break-in and all that. I did it for Fadi. I thought I was doing it for Fadi."

Ignacio leans forward, his eyes are soft again, familiar.

"But Yazz, *querida*. Didn't you realize everyone knew anyway? Did you really think they'd believe you pinched that stuff from the studio?"

She feels a cold wind blow through her. Of course, she knew it was an excuse, just something that pushed her over the edge. Something that gave her the strength to go.

"You do what you gotta do, *ey*?" she says. "I'm here now. What do you want me to say?"

She takes a sip of beer. Ignacio shrugs and glances at his phone.

"Gotta go," he says, and gets up. "It was good to see you, Yazz."

The shadow of his huge body blocks the sun and falls across Yasmine. She stands up too, kisses him on the cheek, but he grabs her shoulders and pushes her away a bit, looking at her seriously again.

"Don't run around flashing those pictures, OK?" he says. "Seriously. You don't wanna end up in the middle of that."

"In the middle of what, *len*? Tell me then. They're all I've got."

"There are some things you just don't talk about. Mind your own business. Bergort style, ya' know."

"But you'll check about Fadi, right? Check if anyone's heard anything?"

"Sure. But don't get your hopes up. Seriously, Yazz, it's better to lie low here. If he's alive he'll get a hold of you. Believe me."

Chapter 13

Bergort—July–October 2014

It's a hot summer. That's what the Swedes say over their thermoses and cheese sandwiches on the loading dock behind the vegetable wholesaler in Fittja where the unemployment office eventually forced me to work. It's nice in the sun, they say, and turn their pale hungover faces to the sky to make sure they burn.

"What do you think, Abdullah? Just like home in the desert, right?"

I don't sit in the sun on my break. Eat no cheese sandwiches, drink no coffee. Just nuts and tomatoes I pinch from a pallet, while I wait for them to take their plastic lunch boxes and bullshit and go out onto the dock, then I wash myself in the dressing room and go into one of the coolers, spread out the worn carpet I bought for forty bucks at the Sunday flea market under the overpass. Didn't even try to bargain, not for this, not for my new life.

Now, I don't even have to look at my Mecca app anymore—I know to turn toward the cucumbers and eggplants. Behind them, if you draw a long, straight line, lies Mecca. It's the same at home in our room, just turn toward your pillow, or what used to be your pillow, and a straight line from my forehead, through your pillow, that stops at Mecca.

Every day, at every prayer, I think I'm a bad Muslim, a bad brother, because I don't feel God inside me while I pray. I don't feel the light flowing through me, and I steal tomatoes and can't remember my *rak'at*, my Qur'an verses, so I always Google them and read them on the screen of my phone. With the Swedish transcription, because the Arabic is too difficult.

Every day I curse how hard we tried to be part of what we could never be part of. We learned the entire Swedish dictionary but forgot our Arabic. Every day I promise to get better, to learn, stop bullshitting. You can't bullshit in this new life.

When I've finished praying, I hear the Swedes coughing and snickering outside the storage-room door and I quickly whisper my *as-salamu alaykum wa Rahmatullah* twice, stand up, roll up the mat, slide it under the shelf of pears, and leave the fridge and go back to carrying boxes of bananas, lettuce, apples, and cabbage until the time to take the subway home finally arrives.

I'm the world's loneliest Muslim. I pray in solitude. Read in solitude. Believe in solitude. Sometimes I go down to the mosque on Fridays. I stand on the other side of the square and watch the old men heading down to the basement, always the same men. Mehdi's father and grandfather. Old man Jamal, who fixes shoes by the subway. See their dress pants, quilted jackets, mustaches and bent, submissive necks. How could I be a part of that *umma*? It's not for me. It's a fucking club, not serious. They just nag and whine. I need more. I'm waiting for more. Until I find it, I'm a brotherhood of one.

And while I wait, I have no congregation, no one to pray

with in a religion that is all about community, justice, and solidarity. While I wait I'm preparing. Forcing myself to read more than ten consecutive lines in the Qur'an. Forcing myself to remember my prayers.

I'm preparing myself and finding new, virtual brothers online. They aren't like the men in the square, they're serious and militant, and my faith grows stronger with every video from Syria, with every sermon they send me. My new brothers have handles, not names, and they're as angry as I am, as ready to blow this shit up as me. Just as lonely too. Brothers from whose eyes the veil has been lifted, just as it was lifted from my eyes, to reveal the world as it is: oppression, colonialism, imperialism, and injustice. It's incomprehensible that I couldn't see it. I lived it, forced myself to adapt to it, and even tried to become a part of it. It fills me with hatred and self-loathing. How could I have been so blind for so long? How could I choose the Swedish dictionary over the Arabic? But that's all over now.

Now I see it on the screen in front of me every day after work, gritty films, pixelated evidence of oppression, blood in the sand, my brothers and sisters driven from their homes, murdered, and raped in the blue twilight. Now I see the ignorance and evil in Gaza and Syria, as well as here, in Bergort, where we're imprisoned and locked out at the same time, stuck in the concrete, with no future, no history, completely at the mercy of corrupt people with no morals, people who are impossible to respect, a godless government that lacks all legitimacy.

It's so obvious now that my whole life has been wasted, but that doesn't matter, none of it matters. Everything is new now, and I kneel on the floor, on the carpet I use at home, and I bend toward your pillow, toward Mecca, and I can't help thinking what you'd say if you saw me now. Would you be relieved or horrified? And I feel that sea take hold of me again, the emptiness, the endlessness, feel it spreading like mercury through my bones and my blood, and I mumble what I remember of my prayers and fall down on the mat to keep it inside of me, to force it back into its nest at the bottom of my stomach, at the back of my chest.

And it works. I push it away with prayer. So what if I wasn't filled with God instead? So what if I can't feel his love and grace? This is one of his tests. I have to prove myself worthy before he'll allow the golden light to descend upon me.

Months pass by without me talking to anyone except the Swedes at work, which I do my best to avoid, and the anonymous brothers who I chat with online. I'm in my room or in the gym where I do what I can to prepare myself, and I feel my body growing and aching, and I know I should thank Allah for each weight I lift, but that's hard for me, seeing God in the everyday. I need something bigger, more important.

I'm a bad Muslim. I know I should respect and honor my parents, but I hide from them, at work or at the gym or in my room. I don't know what to say to them, what they'll say to me. It's easier since you disappeared. I'd like to tell you that, because I know that keeps you awake, the idea that I'm still here. But he's calmer now, maybe older. I was always better at avoiding him and rarely provoked his rage, despite all the shit I got up to.

It worries me even more that you probably don't live righteously. I pray to Allah that you'll understand and open your heart before it's too late. And when I think about it, the darkness grows inside me until I have to recite lines from the Qur'an aloud, words I don't even understand, but they help me, and I stop thinking of what I cannot change.

Sometime in October I run into Mehdi down by the bridge to the subway. He's still fat and short of breath, and he's sitting on a bench down by the gray tiles outside the Syrian's, drinking one of those Turkish liter bottles of cola that the old man sells. I consider just walking past. I don't even remember the last time I talked to my old crew. Probably not since you disappeared?

But now Mehdi looks up with his shiny cow's eyes, and he sees me and straightens up on the bench before raising the hand with the cola in it.

"*Shoo,* Fadi!" he says. "What's up, *bre*?"

So I can't just keep walking, I have to stop and go over to him.

"It's been ages, man," he says, and stands up, fist bump, and hug with one arm. "I swear, you're a hermit, brother."

I shrug.

"You know how it is. I got a job in Fittja. Go to the gym. No free time."

He takes a step back, tilts his head, laughs, bends forward, and pulls on my stubble.

"What the hell is this, *yao*? You got a beard now?"

I don't answer, my heart starts to pound, I feel exposed, my private life suddenly out in the open. Is it a sin to deny your faith? I don't remember, I don't really know anything about the Qur'an, and I just shrug again, pull back.

"It's just a beard, bitch," I say. "What about you, what's up?"

He smiles and takes a sip of his soda.

"You know Parisa?" he says. "Your sister's friend?"

I nod. We used to be in love with her, her tight tops, her bare skin and slim jeans, and I still see her outside her mother's salon. She's still hot, but thicker around the hips.

"She's my chick now, *bre*!" he says, holding up his hand for a high five I don't give him.

"*Ey*, you lying?" I say.

It's crazy that Mehdi of all those dudes would have landed Parisa. Fat fucking Mehdi with his asthma and his squeaky little voice, got the hottest girl in Bergort?

"No, no!" he says. "I swear, brother!"

He leans toward me, whispering.

"The sex, *len*... Ajajajaj! So hot, I swear!"

I pull back, this has gone too far, the Qur'an must have something to say about this.

"Seriously," I say. "I don't wanna hear about it, OK?"

"Don't be so uptight, brother," he says, laughing. "Anyway, gotta go."

He holds out his fist, and I put my own against it.

"Nice to see you, Fadi," he says. "The whole gang's gonna grill if we get some good weather. You should come. It's been a long time since we saw you."

I nod and suddenly feel overcome by a strange melancholy. We'll never grill again, I know it. We'll never talk about chicks again. Never smoke a spliff or torch a car. All of that is behind me now. It should be a relief. It is a relief. But it's also sad.

I'm almost home when I see him—squatting down and staring at the withering bushes next to my door. He looks like a

Habesha—or Somalian, maybe, with a long beard, thick and combed, a caftan and a string of prayer beads, and I break out into a cold sweat, because I know what this is about, that now my life begins. And it scares me, the thought of what that might entail, but I know fear is a part of this, part of Allah's test, something I have to endure in order to prove myself worthy. I take a deep breath and walk quietly toward the door.

The man stands up. His beard is not as thick as I thought, his cassock not as clean and freshly ironed as I thought, instead, he looks weary, and his small, skeptical eyes inspect me carefully.

"Fadi Ajam?" he says.

I nod silently.

"Speak so I can hear you," the man says. "You have nothing to be ashamed of."

I swallow.

"I am Fadi Ajam," I say. "*As-salamu alaykum.*"

I bow slightly toward him, showing my respect.

"*Wa alaykum salaam,*" he replies.

Without looking away from me, he gestures toward the parking lot with one hand while continuing to finger his prayer beads with the other.

"Come here," he says. "Otherwise we'll miss *isha'a.*"

Still I hesitate. This is what I've dreamed of. What I tried to explain to the brothers online. That I need something more, I can't handle being alone, can't deal with the day-to-day, that I have to get away, *inshallah*. And now Allah has heard me and sent this Habesha to lead me forward. Still I hesitate.

"Come," he says again, holding out his hand. "Allah, may he be glorified and exalted, needs you."

And I throw a glance up at our old windows where the blinds are always down, and I take a breath and close my eyes.

Then I open them and follow the man across the asphalt toward the parking lot.

Chapter 14

London—Monday, August 17, 2015

It's the headache that wakes her up—heavy and dull, aching, rather than intense—and she opens her eyes gently. The room around her is filled with a gray light that she finds familiar and alien at the same time. She's not home. She closes her eyes again, pressing them together tight.

Where is she? What happened? Slowly, in short intervals, yesterday tumbles back to her. The hunt with Grandpa, a glass of wine at the airport, the taxi to the Library. And then? She remembers that she got much drunker than usual. She remembers that she left the bar and that the streets were unsteady like suspension bridges, the buildings sagged and changed location. And she remembers a silhouette behind her. Then nothing.

In panic, she sits up and opens her eyes. Runs her hands over her body. She's wearing a way-too-big, white T-shirt. It's not hers. Just panties underneath. She feels her chest tighten even farther, her pulse quickens. She starts to sweat, her head is pounding. The room is familiar, but she can't place it: a bed, a desk cluttered with paper and pens, a clothing rack with a man's clothes hanging on it, a white sheet on the only window, through which gray light streams in. She puts her feet on the carpet, sees her suitcase standing in the corner with her clothes folded on top.

Her phone? It only takes a few seconds to find it in one of her jeans pockets. It's seven o'clock, no missed calls.

She stands up and realizes she needs water. Her mouth is sticky and dry. She moves hesitantly across the floor, out through the door, into what appears to be a living room that looks out onto a street. A small dining table for two stands in the middle of the floor, and there's a sofa against the wall—on which a man is sleeping. She tiptoes into the room. She's extremely thirsty now. But first she has to figure out where she is.

Halfway into the room relief pours through her. It's Pete's apartment. She's only ever seen it at night, in various states of intoxication, always left before sunrise. Pete. It could have been worse. Much worse.

She finds the kitchen and a glass. Fills it to the brim and gulps down three of the same until she feels like she might vomit from rapid rehydration. But her headache recedes slightly, and she puts the glass down and goes back into the living room. She drops down to her knees beside Pete and feels a rush of tenderness mixed with her increasing anxiety. How drunk was she?

"Pete," she says, and gently nudges his arm.

Pete snores and turns a half turn away from her, so she shakes him gently again. This time he opens his eyes and turns toward her, seemingly immediately wide awake.

"Klara?" he says. "You're awake?"

He sits up on the couch and looks at her with clear blue eyes. She shrugs and is overcome by immense shame. How could she get so drunk? How can she not remember what happened?

"I..." she begins, but doesn't know what to say and falls silent.

Pete sits up on the couch now and looks at her worriedly.

"Are you feeling better?" he says with genuine concern in his voice.

She nods gently.

"Bloody hell," he says. "You were completely wasted. Do you remember what happened?"

"Kind of," she says. "I must have lost control for a bit."

She smiles wryly and blushes. The headache makes her temples vibrate gently.

"How much did you drink before you got to the Library?" he says.

She can feel herself getting redder, and it makes her feel warm and raw. She's not sure she can handle this discussion, not with Pete, not now.

"A glass on the plane," she says at last. "But I don't know. I lost control at the Library, I guess."

Pete shakes his head, an uneasy expression in his eyes.

"You drank three glasses of red wine at the Library," he said. "I kept an eye on you. Didn't want you to get too drunk, you know. Three glasses? That usually isn't a problem for you?"

Klara isn't sure that's a compliment, so she shrugs again. What does he mean?

"Also," Pete continues, "you were completely out of it there in the alley. You vomited. Do you remember?"

She stiffens. She remembers fragments—collapsing in the alley, the world shaking. She remembers vaguely that she threw up. But she also remembers the outline of a man in the alley.

"Oh my God," she whispers. "There was somebody there, in the alley. Was it you?"

She looks straight into his eyes. "Were you there when I fell down?"

Pete frowns, and his eyes get even smaller, even bluer and more intense.

"Klara? You don't remember? I came out there because somebody from the bar found you in the alley and wondered what he should do about it. You were lying there alone."

Memories flash by and pull away. Her legs feel weak and unsteady. She remembers falling down on all fours. Remembers vomiting. A whispering voice. It gives her goose bumps now.

"My bags?" she says. "Did you bring them here?"

"Bags?" Pete says. "You only had the one? A roller bag?"

The silhouette in the alley. The memory of hands and a whispering voice.

She stands up and runs back into the bedroom, pushes her clothes off the carry-on, turns it over, opens it, roots around inside. Nothing. She turns around and shouts over her shoulder: "Did you see my backpack? My computer bag?"

Pete is standing in the doorway behind her.

"No. When I found you, that's all you had."

He points to the carry-on. Klara sits up and runs her hands through her hair. Fuck! She bends over the bag again, opens the top compartment and sees her passport and wallet. It gives her some relief.

"Do you mean you lost a bag?" Pete says.

She pretends not to hear him. Her thoughts and anxiety rush through her like water, like a waterfall. Someone took her laptop bag. Nothing else. She turns to Pete.

"Are you sure I only drank three glasses? I don't know, I lost count. Besides, I thought I left the last glass half full. All of a sudden I just felt incredibly drunk."

"Yes. One hundred percent. I mean, there weren't that many people in the bar."

"There weren't?"

In her memory, it was quite full, rowdy and noisy.

"Just a regular Sunday," said Pete. "A little more than half full."

Klara nods slightly. She remembers the shadows and hands pulling and prying, and it makes her tremble.

"So what happened?" she says. "If I only drank two and a half glasses of wine? What the hell happened?"

He shrugs and squats down beside her.

"Are you on any medication?"

She pulls back and puts her feet down on the bed next to him, irritated by his sudden intimacy. Sure, she's grateful he took care of her, but now she just wants to get out of here.

"No, I'm not on any fucking medication."

He stands up again. He's only got his underwear on, and she tries her best not to look at him. She can't handle this intimate, unaffected situation.

"Maybe you ate something bad?" he says. "And the backpack might still be at the bar? We'll check."

She nods.

"Sure," she says. "We'll check."

But she already knows it's not there.

Chapter 15

Bergort—October 2014

I follow the Habesha over the parking lot under the afternoon sun. He doesn't have a car like I expected, instead, we walk slowly toward the low-rise apartment building that Bounty lived in until his family moved to a row house. I've hardly been there since we were little. There's nothing over there, even less than where we live, and it's in the opposite direction of the main square or the subway.

The grass at the edge of the parking lot is yellow and unkempt, full of wilting cow parsley, nettles, and thistles, but the Habesha points to a narrow path that crosses the small field. It seems to lead in a half-circle around the low-rise, toward the little grove where you and I used to have adventures when we were little, where you'd tell me the story of Ronia the Robber's Daughter, which your teacher read to you in school, and I was so afraid of trolls and robbers that you had to hold my hand on the way home at dusk, even though I was far too old to hold someone by the hand. I think of all of that as I follow the Habesha through the grass and bushes and nettles. And it occurs to me that I'm scared now too, but I don't have anybody's hand to hold. Nobody but Allah, *subhanahu wa ta'ala*—may he be glorified and exalted. But he's quiet tonight, and his hands are cold. This is a test, and I keep going step by step through the growing grass.

The grove is much smaller than I remember it and the subway tracks much closer, the rocks are not like the ones from storybooks, but more like big, gray boulders with plastic bags and rusty beer cans wedged in between them. We place our feet carefully and make our way up the gentle slope toward what I vaguely remember as a clearing in the middle of the grove.

It's in this patch of woods that it begins. My new life consists of three men in beards, one is dressed in a caftan similar to the Habesha's, the other two in jeans and dress shirts that are buttoned up to their Adam's apples. They stand in a line, as if they're waiting for us, five prayer rugs spread in a row behind them, facing an opening in the trees through which you can just make out the beginning of the tunnel and behind that a high-rise building and shopping center. I'm outside of myself now, above myself, and reality seems sharp and angular, light falls from an unnatural angle and turns us gold and emerald.

The Habesha goes over to the men and kisses them one by one on the cheeks, muttering greetings in Arabic, and then turns back to me.

"This is brother Ajam," he says in Swedish.

I don't know what to say, don't know what language to speak, what gestures to use. I don't know anything, so I just hold up my hand in greeting, like a dork.

"Hi."

The man in the caftan smiles and takes a couple of steps toward me, holds out his arms in an embrace, and pulls me toward him, kisses me on both cheeks, and then pushes me away. He has red hair, a red beard, and green, inquisitive eyes. He's Swedish, not an Arab, maybe a convert.

"Welcome, brother Ajam," he says and smiles.

There's something sincere about him, something warm and deep, and I want him to hold me again, want him to pull me close, whisper to me that everything will be all right, that faith is what's most important, that God sees my heart, and it doesn't matter that I'm such a bad Muslim as long as my heart is true.

"I'm imam Dakhil," he says.

Imam Dakhil's Swedish has the rolling sounds of a Gothenburg accent. He's not from Bergort.

"And this is my congregation," he says.

One by one the men approach me, first the Habesha that led me here.

"Brother Tasheem, you've already met," imam Dakhil says.

Tasheem kisses me on both cheeks and murmurs something in Arabic, which I don't understand.

"Brother Taimur," the imam continues, and the youngest of the men in jeans comes over and kisses me on both cheeks, he doesn't look much older than me, maybe five years. Maybe your age.

"And finally brother al-Amin," the imam adds.

Brother al-Amin is in his forties, tall and large, with a large well-groomed beard, a leather jacket, and a *kufi* on his head.

"Welcome, brother Ajam," he says and embraces me.

And I feel it from him too, that warmth, which I would really like to feel from Allah, that hand to hold, and the tears well up in my eyes, and I feel myself being pulled into the warmth they radiate.

"You're not '*ajam*' anymore," says brother al-Amin. "You're not a stranger anymore, now you are a part of Allah, may he be glorified and exalted."

He puts an arm around me, and then we kneel on the mats and say the *Shahada* together. Then we say the *isha'a*, and during the prayer I finally feel something like joy that makes me soar and quiver, because these brothers have found me, because Allah, may he be glorified and exalted, allowed these brothers to find me.

"How did you find me?" I say afterward, when we're sitting on the grass together in silence, watching Bergort turn purple in the afternoon sun.

Brother al-Amin points to brother Taimur, who holds up his hand in greeting.

"We know each other from chat," Taimur says, smiling. "I'm Righteous90."

I'm surprised and bend over to see him properly. Righteous90 was one of the first people who contacted me online, the person I chatted with the most. I told him I lived in Bergort, and where in Bergort I lived. I told him my wish to leave everything behind for jihad.

"It..." I begin. "It's incredible to see you in reality."

"Praise be to Allah," brother Taimur says and bows. "I should have contacted you earlier, but I wanted to be sure that you were genuine first. There are a lot of posers who say they're interested in jihad. Not many are serious. But not you, brother Ajam, your heart is true."

When he says it, I am once again overcome by gratitude, my throat swells and tears threaten to break through. My heart is true. Maybe I can't pray, but the brothers can see that my heart is true.

I look around the grove, trying to gather myself.

"You always meet outside?" I say. "What do you do if it rains?"

They exchange looks and smile in agreement.

"We meet in different places," says imam Dakhil and points down toward Bergort. "We're... careful, you might say. We don't want to draw attention to ourselves, don't want to have any ears other than the ones we decide for ourselves. Not when we have new members like you, brother Ajam. Not when we have important things to discuss."

I feel my heart start to race, my cheeks getting hot. Imam Dakhil takes my hand in his and puts his other hand on top of it. He looks at me with his green, sincere eyes, and I feel that nothing has ever been more important in my life than this, that this is more important than me, or even you, or us.

"Brother Taimur says you are devoted?" says the Imam.

I nod enthusiastically. I have never been more eager to express my sincerity.

"That you feel strongly about the injustices that our brothers and sisters are subjected to? Brother Taimur says you've had your problems, brother Ajam, just as we have all had our problems, but that you've chosen to let Allah, may he be glorified and exalted, take over your whole heart, not just a small part?"

"Yes," I say. "My whole heart belongs to Allah, may he be exalted."

I say it with conviction, just like I say *Shahada*, just like I pray and read the Qur'an. I say it because I want it to be true. I say it even if I don't feel it, because there's nothing I want more than to feel it.

Imam Dakhil nods and holds my hand tighter.

"Brother Taimur also says that you're very eager to seek out jihad? That you want to connect with our brothers in Syria, that you're not afraid of martyrdom, that you would be happy if Allah, may he be exalted, were to allow you that?"

"Yes," I say, my heart pounding. "I don't fear death, I yearn for paradise, I long to serve Allah, may he be glorified and exalted."

They look at me calmly. Imam Dakhil presses my hand harder, then leans forward to stare deeper into my eyes.

"There are many ways to seek jihad," he says. "Jihad is not just accomplished on the battlefield and in martyrdom, if you were to be so blessed by Allah, may he be exalted. It is not the only way to reach paradise, do you understand?"

Brother al-Amin moves closer to us so that he can look me in the eyes.

"You understand that we're fighting our jihad here?" he says. "By doing what we're doing now? By finding believers like you and helping them to carry out the will of Allah? That's also jihad."

But I can't do that, I want to scream. *If Allah has a plan for me it's not here! It can't be here!*

"Yes," I say. "I understand. May Allah's will be done, may he be glorified and exalted."

It feels uncomfortable to praise Allah here, among these scrawny trees, in this long grass. It feels uncomfortable to praise him at all, when all I want is for him to fill me up, not just test me.

"It's possible that you have potential," imam Dakhil says. "We have contacts and opportunities. If your belief is strong, brother Ajam, it's possible that your dream to serve Allah, may he be glorified and exalted, on the battlefield may come true."

Now I feel that gas fill me again, that warm, hopeful, volatile gas that's thicker than blood and lighter than air or thought. Maybe it's God, I think, maybe it's Allah, may he be glorified and exalted. Perhaps he's come to fill me, to reward me for my patience and trust. But I know that's not true. I know I'm a bad Muslim who can't feel God, who longs for something greater but can't feel the greatest of all.

"Thank you," I say. "Thank you for contacting me."

"Don't thank us," says the imam Dakhil. "Thank Allah, may he be glorified and exalted."

Chapter 16

London—Tuesday, August 18, 2015

It's just after nine in the morning when Klara arrives at the four steps that lead up to 33 Surrey Street, just around the corner from the Strand and the roar of morning rush hour. The air is heavy and warm, saturated with the smell of exhaust, the river, and coffee. A small, shiny brass plate above the doorbell announces that she's outside the King's Centre for Human Rights Study.

Yesterday's dull headache has died down but still hums somewhere in the back of her head. She really didn't have time to be sick yesterday, but it had been impossible to work. Her hangover and anxiety kept her in bed most of the day. Of course, she was grateful for what Pete did for her, but she'd refused to borrow clothes from him and instead made her way home in her own disgusting clothes. She could never face him again after that, better to just forget that night as soon as possible.

Now she takes a sip of the coffee she bought from a Belarusian teenager at Starbucks and regrets it immediately when her nausea returns. Whatever happened on Sunday night led to at least a two-day hangover, and coffee obviously doesn't help.

In order to gain a little time, allow the nausea to pass, she walks past the front door to number 33, and instead takes the stairs down to the courtyard beneath a sign that says Strand Lane. She remembers reading that behind the window at the back of the small courtyard an ancient Roman bath is hidden.

On the way down the stairs, she takes out her phone to check her email and jumps when she notices that she's not alone in the yard. No more than thirty feet away, she sees the tall, slender silhouette of her American colleague Patrick Shapiro. He seems to be squatting but gets up quickly when he sees her, then runs a hand through his blond hair and adjusts his titanium frames.

"Klara," he says seriously, slightly embarrassed. "Good morning."

"Good morning," she replies and realizes that she has no other choice but to approach him.

They shake hands, which seems oddly formal, but over the year she's been at the institute they've barely spoken to each other outside of the weekly meetings their boss, Charlotte Anderfeldt, insists on having with her employees. And Patrick's not the kind you can have a chat with when you're headed back to your office with a cup of coffee in hand. On the contrary, he keeps to himself, comes in early, leaves late, always keeps his door closed. Rumor has it that he refuses to use the Internet or even a computer for some reason.

Klara notices a window behind Patrick, and she takes a few steps toward it and leans in toward the dirty glass while she puts a hand above her eyes to minimize the glare. All she can make out is something that looks like a worn, sunken sandstone bathtub. A ruin of a bathtub. She turns to Patrick, a wry smile. The headache remains ensconced at the back of her head.

"As tourist attractions go, it's not exactly Disney World, is it," she says.

He nods seriously. His smooth, elongated face looks like sandstone too, she thinks.

"Well, I like it," he says, almost offended. "I go here almost every morning. Dickens apparently used to bathe here."

Klara nods, she's also heard that somewhere.

"And Guy Fawkes and his men met here to plan the attack on Parliament," he adds, his voice slightly lower.

"Really?"

She didn't know that.

"So you come here every morning?" she continues and glances in through the window again. "Feels a bit like if you'd seen it once..."

She lets the sentence hang.

"I like the idea of it," he says. "The layers. The story within the story. It's probably not even a Roman bath, probably more recent. But just the fact that it's lying here beneath everything else, quiet, almost forgotten. First, the Romans—maybe—then the city grew for thousands of years, then Fawkes, then Dickens. Everything has grown around that old tub, and we don't even really know what it is. And finally, here we are with our 'human rights.'"

He adds air quotes around the last two words. It's the longest speech she's ever heard him make.

"What do you mean by that? 'Human rights'?" She imitates his gesture. "You don't think that's what we're working on?"

He shrugs and seems to inspect her more closely.

"I just mean it's like this bath here. Things aren't always what they seem, there are layers. And in the end we don't even know if the core is what we think it is."

She shakes her head, gently massages her temples. This is way too existential for her today.

"I think I have to go to work now. You coming?"

*

Up on the third floor, outside Charlotte's door, Klara takes a deep breath before knocking. The old wooden floor creaks as she nervously shifts her weight from one foot to the other.

"Yes?" Charlotte's voice comes from inside the room.

Klara gently pushes the door open. Charlotte is sitting in the bay window facing the street, behind an antique desk cluttered with papers and highlighters, cell phone chargers and half-empty coffee cups. In the middle of all this chaos stands a large aluminum-colored computer screen that's probably connected to a computer somewhere under all the papers and debris. The walls are covered with bookshelves full of books, binders, and more chaotic piles of paper.

"Excuse me, Charlotte," Klara says in Swedish. "But something happened."

Charlotte gets up from her desk and gestures for Klara to join her on one of the small sofas. Charlotte looks relaxed and bohemian today in a wide skirt and a loose-fitting top. Her thick, dark hair is held up in a messy ponytail.

"Sit down, honey," she says. "What happened? Have some water. Or would you like some tea? Are you feeling better at least? You were sick yesterday?"

Klara nods and can feel herself turning red.

"Yes," she says. "Much better. Must have been... food poisoning. "

Charlotte looks kindly at her with big, dark eyes and the sincerity in them makes Klara feel more deceitful than ever.

"Ugh," Charlotte says. "Glad you feel better!"

"Definitely!" Klara says and nods with excessive enthusiasm. She swallows deeply, preparing herself.

"I don't want to disturb you, it's just that I lost my computer on Sunday."

She knows she's blushing more, there's nothing she hates more than admitting failure. And she can't tell Charlotte what really happened, so she's decided to present an edited version, one without red wine or vomit or bartenders or collapsing in dark alleys. Yes, a story with no bars at all. Charlotte's eyes widen.

"What? How did that happen, Klara?"

"I must have left it at the airport or on the train," she lies. "I contacted the lost and found department, but, you know how it is, nothing yet."

She shrugs, feeling small and completely worthless.

"It's OK, Klara, we'll figure it out, of course. We'll find you a computer to work on. But you've followed the instructions regarding all your documents?"

Klara nods eagerly, relieved to finally be able to say that she's done something right.

"Yes of course," she says. "Everything related to work was saved on the server."

"And only on the server?" Charlotte says and presses her hand a little harder. "You know, so close to the Stockholm Conference, it's important that nothing leaks out."

Klara nods again.

"Only on the server."

"Are you sure about that?"

"Yes, definitely," she says.

And she is. She's followed Charlotte's instructions to the letter, been careful to save every document onto the encrypted server, especially every document related to the large EU conference in Stockholm. She knows what an honor it is for Charlotte and the rest of the center to be presenting their assessment of the opportunities and risks related to privatizing prisons and police forces at the biggest annual meeting of EU justice ministers in about a week. This particular report was the main reason Klara was hired by the center a year ago. Charlotte won the contract not because she happened to be Swedish, and the report would be presented in Stockholm, but because of solid academic experience, and she needed a right hand that could help her with organization and writing.

Charlotte's offer arrived suddenly, just as Klara was getting herself out of bed at Grandma and Grandpa's on Aspöja and had decided to try to finish Mahmoud's thesis.

"What a great opportunity. Of course, you should take it, Klara," Professor Lysander, Mahmoud's supervisor, had said. "You'll get the chance to work on the thesis, and it will be good to get away. And it's at King's College! That'll look good."

She looked up the center, and indeed it belonged to King's College London, was relatively new, and focused on researching human rights issues in the gray area between the private and public market. It was concerned with precisely the questions Mahmoud's dissertation touched upon, and she saw that some of Anderfeldt's articles appeared in Mahmoud's bibliography. She thought about it for a week and then went over to meet Charlotte.

It turned out that the institute was composed of Charlotte, Patrick, two other researchers, and later Klara. Over the past year a few graduate students had joined them together with a couple of undergraduates who did background research for various projects.

Klara had liked Charlotte's laid-back, intelligent attitude from the beginning. It was clear that she had ambitions, both for herself and for the newly established center. Klara had felt a kind of excitement awaken inside her. Maybe this would be good for her?

"But why me?" she'd asked Charlotte. "How did you know about me?"

Charlotte had only smiled at her.

"Good researchers get noticed fast," she said, and winked at her.

Klara didn't really care how Charlotte had found her, she was just happy to leave the archipelago. To get out and move on. She'd already signed a contract by the time she flew back to Stockholm later that evening.

"Typical," Charlotte says now. "To lose your computer right now, I mean. But, like I said, these sorts of things happen."

She pats Klara's hand and reaches for a mug, which she fills with green tea from a thermos bottle on the coffee table.

"And how's it going for you?" she continues. "The draft on legal constraints?"

Klara's job is to compile a background text on the legal problems of privatization as it relates to democratically sensitive agencies, such as the police or prison system. She's been as accurate and objective as she could, even if she thinks it's appalling that anyone would seriously consider it democratically defensible to privatize a police force. It's lucky that Charlotte received such a sensitive assignment, she thinks. Charlotte is objective and honest, both in her research and in her private life. At the same time, it's almost a dizzying thought that the institute's research will form a kind of basis for such an important discussion among EU countries. This is precisely the kind of job that is able to consume Klara, stop her from thinking about the past or the future.

"Good, I think," she says. "Just read through it again. I'll send you a link this afternoon."

"Fine," Charlotte says and takes a sip of tea. "Talk to Dawn about getting a computer, she knows what you'll need in order to sign for a new one from the university."

It's with relief that Klara climbs the creaking stairs to the attic floor she shares with Patrick. Charlotte and the other researchers all sit on the floor below. The rest of the building's five floors are taken up by various university administrative activities, which Klara has never really had any reason to explore. Charlotte has indicated that they'll soon get another floor and at least three more researchers. There seems to be money in any case, which is an unusual level of security in the academic world.

As Klara enters her floor, her head throbbing weakly, she grabs an ibuprofen from her purse, and swallows it without water. Just as she's about to go into her office, she notices, to her great surprise, that Patrick's door is ajar, something she can't recall ever having seen before. She stops, hesitates. She and her colleagues have joked so much about Patrick and his oddball ways that the temptation to peek into his office is overwhelming.

She glances at the door to the tiny restroom and can see that it's locked. He's probably gone in there and forgotten for once to close his office door behind him.

She glances once more toward the locked door and then tiptoes over the creaking floor to Patrick's office. Just a quick look, surely that's OK? She carefully pushes on the faintly squeaking door.

The room inside is surprisingly dark, he's pulled down the blinds of the garret window that looks onto the backyard. She's not sure what she expected—perhaps creative madness, papers pinned up with colored yarn connecting them, like the movie version of academic mental illness?—but that's not what his room looks like. It's tightly organized. Smooth piles of paper lie in straight lines on his desk, and the books are placed orderly on the shelves in the low, dark wood bookcase that covers one wall. A single paper is taped up on the wall, a letter-size page with just a few words in large font: *A Dangerous Remedy*.

She freezes. There's something about those words. *A dangerous remedy*. Something familiar, something that makes the hairs on her arms stand up, and she shudders. What does it mean? Is it the name of the book he's working on?

She continues searching the room with her eyes, but the only strange thing that she sees is a computer screen—identical to the screen in her own office, university standard—standing on the floor with its cord hanging behind it. Instead, a large whiteboard hangs above the desk, on which something that looks like a mind map has been drawn. Klara leans in inquisitively—maybe she'll get a few more details about what Patrick actually does with his days?

In the dark, it's difficult to make out what he's written in red ink on the white background, but at the center of the mind map she can make out a rectangle with "Ribbenstahl" written inside it. She takes a half step over the threshold. In one of the other rectangles she sees what looks like "Stirling Security." An arrow leads from that to Ribbenstahl. Below Stirling Security is a circle with "Russian Embassy?" written inside it.

What is he up to? she thinks.

At the same time, she hears someone flushing the toilet and throws a quick glance over her shoulder before bending forward and squinting at the board one last time. All arrows seem to lead through King's Centre for Human Rights toward a large jagged circle at the top of the board. Inside it reads

"The Stockholm Conference." And beside it: "Charlotte's report?"

Behind her she hears footsteps on the carpet and pulls back quickly, turning toward her own office.

"What are you doing?"

Patrick's just come around the corner. She jumps—caught in the act—and feels herself blush.

"Nothing," she says as calmly as she can.

He pushes past her and into his office, turns around and looks at her furiously.

"I thought you had more respect for me," he says.

"Give me a break!" she says, suddenly irritated by his dramatic behavior. "I peeked into your office, that's all. What the hell is wrong with you?"

Patrick doesn't say anything as he simply turns around and closes the door on her.

Chapter 17

Stockholm—Tuesday, August 18, 2015

The subway stations are cool and clean in the inner city, the tiles polished, the light muffled and warm. Yasmine sinks down onto a blue seat in a half-full train headed toward Bergort and tries to collect her thoughts. It's bewildering to be back in Stockholm. She was once a part of this city, part of this subway, part of the concrete and rails and tiles. But now it's as if she doesn't fit. She has no function here anymore, no system to operate within.

She should have gone out yesterday, of course. She has no time to lose. But after the meeting with Ignacio, jet lag beat her into unconsciousness, and when she woke up sometime late in the evening, her body felt full of sand and water, too heavy and cumbersome to maneuver. All she could manage was to order room service with a whispered thank you to Shrewd & Daughter for the credit card before falling back into a jerky trance-like sleep and a recurring dream, in which she hunted Fadi through snow in Bergort. His short pants flapping in the wind, his laughter bright and shrill like a child.

Now the train moves slowly southward. The sound of the doors closing, movement over the rails, hip-hop leaking out of the headphones of the short guy opposite her. It's exactly as she remembers it, but in an inverted form. She has never returned to Bergort, not even back then, when the train was moving in this direction with her on it. Even then she was moving away from there, maybe even more so. She always closed her eyes and dreamed of something else. After basement clubs in southern suburbs, she'd stumble out of the train and up the escalators at dawn completely oblivious to her surroundings, still drunk on beer and the future. She never even thought about where she was before she put the key in the door to Parisa's or Abdul's or wherever she happened to be crashing. She dreamed about the future until the future became a part of her, until she lived inside it. Until the future turned out to be something other than what she'd imagined, until suddenly she's sitting on this blue seat, riding through these tunnels, finally on her way home.

Yasmine holds her breath and closes her eyes for a moment when the train leaves the tunnel and rushes out among the pines and shrubs and the light of a late-summer afternoon. That shaking, swooshing noise the train makes as it tears itself free of the darkness of the underground used to make her happy. It was the only time you really felt the speed and direction of the train—the force of it, how it could keep moving forward forever.

Now she opens her eyes and sees Bergort emerging like a gray, cubist fortress next to the tracks, high-rise apartment buildings standing like a forest of watchtowers around the shopping center and beyond that stand the low-rise buildings. She sees the parking garage, cars in jagged lines on its roof, sees the satellite dishes stretching their beseeching arms to the sky. Home, she thinks, but all she feels is her chest constricting and her breath becoming shallower.

The train stops on the platform, and for a second, she considers just staying put, but at the last second before the doors close, she gets up and exits onto the heat of the platform. She's barely stepped out of the train car when she sees the symbol on one of the worn concrete pillars holding up the roof of the station. Simple and compact, newly sprayed, no more than a week old. A red fist inside a five-pointed star.

She walks slowly down the ramp from the station, down toward the shopping center, down to Skutvägen and the Fregatten block, toward Mistlursgången and Vasatorget. All those Swedish street names were so provocative and exclusionary that the kids tore down the signs and renamed every corner, made Bergort their own. Skutvägen became Shoot Road, Fregatten became Fuck Street, Vasatorget became Pirate Square.

She takes a deep breath, trying to find a rhythm, a way to take in all that is so familiar. The rusty railing, the tags she and Red sprayed on the electrical boxes when they were thirteen still visible under a new layer of tags. Farther and farther down the ramp, farther into the past, farther into herself. The ragged buildings, the grass between the flagstones on the square, the signs outside the grocery store, the eternal chicken, Faruk's pizzeria, which seems to have made a half-hearted attempt to change its name to Paradise, but the drunks remain. The men in the square with their prayer beads and suit pants, their broken Swedish and perpetual unemployment, the truant kids outside the Syrian's shop wearing caps and tank tops and sneaking cigarettes in the sun. All of this is her. All of this is what she created herself from, the material she used to build her wings, all of this is the air through which she flew.

Parisa sits smoking outside her mother's hair salon, long nails, long lashes, slightly wider hips, slightly bigger hair.

Otherwise, it's as if nothing has changed, as if this summer has lasted for four years and Yasmine just went into the city for an hour to buy new boots.

She watches Parisa from afar and stops, unsure how to begin, how to approach this. Yet it's so safe, so natural, how Parisa wobbles on the plastic chair, clicking her nails on her phone. Without really knowing how, Yasmine is suddenly beside her, the smoke from Parisa's cigarette sweet and full of mint.

"*Shoo, len*," Yasmine says and squats down beside her.

Parisa jumps, looks up from her phone, turns her head, her eyes wide, getting bigger and bigger.

"What?" she says and stands up, the chair falling backward down onto the concrete. "Yasmine!"

Yasmine smiles, stretches, and open her arms.

"Yazz!" Parisa shouts. "Baby!"

She turns back toward the small salon where her mother stands working on a hair treatment.

"Mama!" she screams. "Look who's here! Yazz, my *gahar,* my sister!"

Afterward, they sit on the benches in the playground. Yasmine takes one of Parisa's menthols and can feel the nicotine, sharp and unfamiliar, flow through her, leaving her light-headed and shaky. Parisa puts her arm around Yasmine, pulling her closer. Her cheek is smooth, oily with makeup and the August heat. Yasmine feels Parisa's fake lashes flutter like an insect against her temples. She turns toward Parisa, smiling.

"So are you still with Mehdi?" she says.

She got a long, cheerful, almost happy email from Parisa a year ago. It was strange. Mehdi. Little fat Mehdi. Fadi's friend. But fuck it. It made Yasmine happy, too. She'd printed out the email and saved it, but never replied. Just as she'd never responded to anything Parisa had sent over the last four years.

Parisa sighs, smiles halfheartedly, before looking away and shrugging.

"I guess," she says. "A lot has happened, sister. So much has happened. But to hell with that now."

She pushes Yasmine away, pinches her shoulder, gently strokes her collarbone.

"You've gotten skinny, sister!" she says. "And I got fat."

She slaps her thighs.

"Shut up," Yasmine says. "Everybody likes a booty. You were always Beyoncé, baby. I look like a guy, as usual."

"But a skinny *shuno* anyway," Parisa says. "Where you staying, Yazz? Out here?"

She shakes her head.

"A sweet hotel in the city, on Riddargatan. It's a long story."

Parisa whistles. "Nicely done, sister," she says seriously.

Yasmine shrugs and smiles.

"I'm not paying."

Parisa nods and runs her finger gently across the swelling near Yasmine's left eye.

"I knew he was no good," she says quietly.

Yasmine stands up, shakes herself, takes one more drag before dropping the cigarette on the sand and stomping on it.

"We all did," she says. "But he was there, right? When I needed him."

"You could have fixed it yourself, Yazz. But you were so impatient that you couldn't wait. You just wanted to get away."

She shrugs again. If only it were that simple.

"And now I'm back," she says.

Parisa nods and extinguishes her cigarette.

They look at each other in silence for a moment, the past hanging like fog between them.

"I'm sorry about Fadi," Parisa says at last. "I can't believe he went away. That he turned to air, *bre*. That's what happens to them when they get sucked in. Like air, you can't reach them anymore."

Yasmine nods and squats down in the sandbox, lets hot sand run through her fingers, squints up at the dazzling reflections of the sun from the windows of the high-rises.

"You haven't heard anything more?" Yasmine says. "Since they posted it on Facebook that he was dead?"

Parisa sits down beside her in the sandbox.

"What do you mean?" she says. "All we heard was what those jihadis posted on Facebook. You saw it for yourself? His squad down there was on some frontline, and they were bombed."

Yasmine shakes her head slightly, takes out her phone and opens the picture before handing it to Parisa.

Parisa stares at it for a while, magnifies it, then turns back toward Yasmine.

"Is that him, sister?" she says.

Yasmine just nods. "It's him."

"How do you know it wasn't taken before he left?"

"My mother sent it to me. And she said it was taken last week."

Parisa looks at the picture again, closer now. She shrugs.

"It's probably not even him," she says. "Better to just accept that he's gone, sister. Nothing we can do anyway, right?"

Yasmine looks at her in surprise. What is it Parisa doesn't understand?

She's standing here with a fucking picture of Fadi in her hand.

"You were so close when you were small," Parisa continues. "He used to wait for you after school, right? You couldn't even speak Swedish yet. But everyone noticed you two. There was something about you even then, baby."

"Stop," Yasmine says.

She can't stand to hear more, can't stand to hear about the past.

"But why did you stop talking to each other?"

Yasmine gets up again, brushing the sand off the knees on her jeans.

"Why does anything end?" she says. "I was angry at him at first. You know after the Pirate Tapes thing, which was so fucking stupid. So I didn't answer his messages. I didn't answer anybody. We left right away. The morning after all that fucking shit. David just booked tickets, and we flew to New York. It was..."

She falls silent, can tell she may not be able to hold back her tears, clears her throat.

"It was like a fairy tale. *Wallah*, I swear. Everything I dreamed about, you know? I just couldn't deal with Fadi. Couldn't deal with Bergort and my parents..."

By now tears are flowing down her cheeks, and she hates herself for it. Hates that she can't stop them, she doesn't deserve the relief of weeping. Parisa goes over to her now, puts her arms around her, pulls her close, and Yasmine lets her for a moment, before shaking herself free. Suddenly she feels it again. How the concrete leans over her, shutting her inside.

"Never mind," she says and wipes her cheeks with her palms, feels the remnants of the sandbox scratch her face. "He's not dead, Parisa."

But Parisa says nothing, just continues to stare up at the concrete and roofs, not meeting Yasmine's eyes.

"Don't talk like that," she says. "It's not good, sister. Not healthy."

Yasmine takes her phone out of her pocket again and scrolls down to the image of the cat in the snare. She hands it to Parisa, who receives it with some surprise, her eyes widen.

"Do you know what this is?" she says.

Parisa almost immediately returns the phone to Yasmine, as if she wants to get rid of it as soon as possible.

"Never seen it before," she says.

Yasmine puts a hand on her arm.

"What about this?"

She flips to the next image, the stencil, and puts the phone on Parisa's knee, but Parisa only throws a quick glance at it before turning off the phone and handing it back.

"No idea," she says curtly. "Never seen it before either."

Yasmine feels her frustration grow. First Ignacio's bullshit and now this?

"Oh for fuck's sake," she says. "They're sprayed all over the place, are you serious, you've really never seen it?"

Parisa stands up and brushes the sand from her thighs, throws a dark look sideways at Yasmine.

"I said I'd never seen it, OK?"

Back in town now, Yasmine is so tired she can barely make it the few steps from the subway to her hotel. The jet lag and the toll of seeing Bergort again have drained her completely.

After she said good-bye to Parisa outside the salon, Yasmine's legs carried her as if of their own will toward the building she grew up in. The same dirty walls. The same blinds and dirty windows.

She should go up to her parents, to her mother. She should find out what they know and check out her and Fadi's old room. But it was as if an invisible force field repelled her. As if she weren't strong enough yet. Still, she sat on a bench in the parking lot outside her old building until the sun disappeared behind the high-rises and exhaustion forced her back to the subway.

Back in the city, in the soft light of the fourth floor of Story Hotel, she takes out the note with the door code the receptionist gave her, punches it in, and opens the door to her room. Immediately she gets the feeling that something's not right. The lights are on, and she's almost positive she turned them off this morning.

Carefully, as if on tiptoe, she continues inside. One of the reading lights is on and angled up toward the wall above her bed. She follows the beam of light up to the wall and sees that someone has sprayed a fist inside a five-pointed star. On the pillow beneath lies a photograph.

She slowly lifts it up. It's a zoomed-in version of the same motif she was sent: a cat hangs in a noose from a lamppost. She turns the photo over and reads the short message on the back.

Stay away from Bergort, whore.

Chapter 18

Bergort—February 2015

Autumn turns to winter, Christmas comes and goes without me even noticing. I do my morning prayer, *fajr*, at home because I won't make it to work if I go meet my brothers at the imam's home in the low-rise building. I pray *dhuhr* and *asr* in the fridge at work, but I don't hide it anymore. To hell with those Swedish bastards, they can say whatever they want. But it's as if they can see it in me now, that I won't stand for it, that I don't need to put up with it, and they leave me in peace, no more jokes about terrorists or camels or deserts. They just keep their mouths shut and chew on their dry fucking sausages. They're so weak, even weaker than me, with their greasy lunch boxes, body odors, and forgotten Christmas decorations.

After work one of my brothers usually comes by, and we go to the shopping center and get a cup of coffee at the café, whisper to each other about Syria, leaning close. I like brother al-Amin best. He's quiet and calm, lets me talk and ask about anything that I don't yet understand, everything I'm trying to learn. About the rules and the prayers, about *shari'a* and *haram*. But mostly we talk about the struggle and our brothers who are fighting. How Allah, may he be glorified and exalted, has rewarded our brothers in Syria by giving them the possibility of martyrdom.

Brother al-Amin says he wishes he were younger, he's too

old and slow for the battlefield now, though grateful for the role he's been given. He says people like me are what they need in Syria, men like me will build the Islamic State.

And it fills me with pride and confidence when he says that. It makes my wings start to grow again. They're big now. As big and black as the Prophet's flag. Then it's easy to forget that God's hand still feels so cold. Then it's easy to avoid thinking of your eyes, of what you'd say if you saw me now.

One afternoon, sometime in mid-February, brother al-Amin is waiting for me outside my door when I come home from work. That's not unusual in and of itself, the brothers know my parents don't sympathize with the struggle, they know it's better not to provoke them, so they always wait outside.

I'm happy to see brother al-Amin standing there; he told me earlier this week about how the courts are organized in the Islamic State, and he's promised to tell me more about daily life there next time we meet. Several of his relatives have joined the fight, and he receives reports about how wonderful life is there every week via Skype.

But today, I can see already from the bike path that there's something different about him. There's something almost solemn in the way he stands, straight-backed, his eyes searching for me in the pitch-black, winter darkness, even though it's not yet four in the afternoon. When he sees me, he takes a few steps forward and waves impatiently for me to hurry up. I start jogging along the bike path with expectation rising in my chest.

"*Salaam alaykum*, brother Ajam," he says and kisses me on the cheek. "We have no time to lose, brother Dakhil is already waiting for us."

My heart skips a beat, and I feel my whole body fill with something like carbonation, something effervescent and exuberant.

"What has happened?" I say.

"Come now, you'll know soon," he says and walks ahead of me toward the parking lot, away from the house where I grew up, toward a future I haven't even dared to dream of.

Brother Dakhil is standing in the snow in the middle of the glade where I met them for the first time a few months ago. It's so dark now that we can only see him because his face is illuminated by the screen of his phone. When he notices me and brother al-Amin coming up the slope, he walks toward us with a smile on his face, arms held open for an embrace.

When we've greeted each other and praised Allah and the Prophet and he's kissed me lovingly on both cheeks several times, he holds out his hand in front of him.

"Your phone, brother Ajam," he says. "For security's sake."

I take it out of the pocket of my jacket and give it to him, surprised. He turns it off and puts it in his own pocket.

"Brother al-Amin?" he says then.

Brother al-Amin fishes a small, black box the size of a cigarette pack with three short, rubbery antennas out of his pocket. When he presses a button, a small red light illuminates on the box. He nods to brother Dakhil to continue.

Brother Dakhil turns to me with a little smile on his face. Snow flies between us, and I wonder why we have to be here, why we can't be in his apartment as usual. Despite the darkness, his thick red beard seems to shine as he gently strokes it.

"We can't be too careful," he says, pointing to the box in brother al-Amin's hand. "That's a signal jammer. It knocks out all frequencies within twenty-five meters of us. No cell phone signals, no eavesdropping."

He points to a thick blanket he's laid out on top of the snow, and we sit down. Brother Dakhil looks at me without saying anything, and I don't know what to say or what's expected of me. So I stay quiet, rest my gaze on the railway tracks, which look cool and quiet under the electric lights of the bike path. Beyond that stand some mangy birches, concrete towers, dark and menacingly frozen in the light from the shopping center.

"You're a devout Muslim, brother Ajam," Brother Dakhil says at last. "Devout and impatient."

He laughs, leans forward, and pats me on the cheek.

"It's good," he says. "You're young and passionate to serve your God, just as you should be."

He stops again and looks at me calmly. I sense something serious in his green, shallow eyes now. I still say nothing, just try to meet his eyes as calmly as possible in the dark.

"It was easier a year ago," he says. "Now we have to be more careful. That's why we meet out here. That's why brother al-Amin jams phones with his little device. We keep our congregation small for now, and we don't think we've attracted any attention. And you are also clean. A few run-ins with the police in your past life, but who hasn't had that? We think there will be no problems if we act fast."

I clear my throat.

"Excuse me," I say, my mouth dry. "What's going to happen fast?"

Brother Dakhil says nothing at first. Instead he digs something out of the nylon backpack lying beneath his caftan-clad legs. It's three letter-size pages, which he places on the rug in front of me. The snow whirls and lands as small dots on the top page. I brush off the flakes and lift the papers in order to read the text, then flip quickly through them. There are two flights with different airlines. From Stockholm Skavsta to London. Then from London to Istanbul. Departure is tomorrow morning at 7:35, and I feel my throat close up. Brother Dakhil doesn't release me from his gaze.

"Thanks to Allah, may he be glorified and exalted, your dreams have come true," he says. "You leave tomorrow and someone will meet you by car to take you to the border. Someone else will help you over. You'll be in Syria before the week is out."

I swallow and hope the world will soon go back to its true colors, that everything will stop jumping and shaking.

"You'll be placed in a Scandinavian brigade. Brother al-Amin has explained it all."

But I don't hear what he's saying anymore, I see only the tickets.

"Brother al-Amin will take you to the airport tomorrow morning," Brother Dakhil says. "It's an early flight."

He stops and regards me calmly.

"Often, it's better not to tell your family if you're not sure they support the struggle, brother," he adds.

Brother al-Amin takes me back to the parking lot, down the hill, and over the snow-covered field, where a cold wind whips ice crystals at us. His car is a surprisingly new and shiny blue Volvo V70. I want to ask about it, but I'm too stunned by what has happened, and what is going to happen that it feels like I've lost the ability to speak. He opens the trunk and removes a black rolling carry-on, the kind used on business trips.

"This is yours," he says. "Pack light, brother."

Then he falls silent and takes what looks like an old, bulky Nokia phone from his bag. There's something almost mournful in his eyes as he presses it into my hand.

"This is a satellite phone," he says. He puts his hand on my shoulder.

"You are important to us, brother Ajam," he says. "We want to be able to reach you, and we want you to keep us informed of whatever progress Allah, may he be glorified and exalted, allows you to make."

"Thank you," I say. "Thank you for doing this for me, giving me the chance to serve Allah, may he be exalted."

He looks deep into my eyes, leans toward me, and lowers his voice.

"There is one thing you should know: There are traitors in Syria," he whispers.

I'm not sure I heard him right so I take a step toward him and shake my head slightly.

"What did you say?" I say.

"There is a traitor in the unit you'll be fighting with. It consists of brothers from Sweden, Fadi. All are from the projects. But someone there is *khain*, brother. Someone is a traitor who leaks information to al-Assad's troops. Do you understand?"

I shake my spinning, whirring head and feel the weight of the phone in my hand.

"We don't know who it is," al-Amin continues. "But there have been too many coincidences, brother. Too many operations at the front where the brothers have prepared to attack, but al-Assad's troops were already there to stop them. Too many times it seemed the enemy knew what we were thinking. Do you understand?"

I nod my head, doubtfully.

"But we don't know who this rat is," he continues. "Just that he's there. And it's good for you to know about it."

Now he lets go of my shoulder and takes hold of my face with his warm, slightly damp hands. I can smell the garlic and peppermint on his breath as he pulls me closer.

"You have to keep the phone on you, brother," he says. "And you have to keep us informed if anything unusual happens. It's the only way. Do you understand?"

I nod again.

"And most important of all," al-Amin continues, "you can't tell the brothers down there."

He releases my face and kisses me on the cheek.

"I'm proud of you, brother," he says, smiling. "Allah will richly reward you."

Chapter 19

London—Wednesday, August 19, 2015

The windows of Klara's studio apartment are open, and she's awakened by the early deliveries rolling across the cracked asphalt of Navarre Street. Klara stretches out her hand for her phone and is relieved to see it's six-thirty, a totally reasonable time to get up. The night has been an uneasy one, filled with disjointed dreams in which she lay stretched out on a cold street, unable to move, while whispering voices approached her. She had repeatedly woken up in a state of terror just as she felt the breath of someone bending over her.

When she sits up, she realizes that the headache at least seems to be gone. She'd gone to bed early yesterday evening, just two glasses of Chardonnay and a few cigarettes out on the fire escape overlooking the courtyard. But it feels as if she's hardly slept at all, and when she stretches out her arm a pain shoots from her elbow. She grimaces and massages her arm gently as she walks over the wood floor of her tiny kitchen and turns on the coffeemaker.

The night in the alley still won't let her rest. How could she be so damn irresponsible? Anything could have happened in that dark alley. Something much worse than being mugged—that is, if mugging was all that happened to her.

She sits down at her small kitchen table. She's almost certain someone was with her in that alley. It's more than just a feeling. That breath and arms pulling on her.

Why would anyone want to get to her or her computer? It couldn't just be some junkie who saw her lying there and seized the opportunity to grab her backpack?

"Damn, damn, damn," she murmurs to herself. "Why the hell did I have to get so drunk?"

She shakes her head and opens the computer she borrowed from the institute.

The last site she looked at last night pops up. She'd been curious enough to look up Stirling Security, one of the names Patrick had written on the whiteboard in his office. Lots of hits, but nothing that she could connect to anything. After that, weariness overcame her.

But now that she's feeling more alert, she sees something farther down on the search screen that might be interesting and clicks on the link:

> Stirling Security is one of the world's leading security companies. We offer consulting and comprehensive security services to individuals, companies, and governments worldwide. The question you need to ask yourself: Are you safe enough?

She opens a new tab and Googles "Ribbenstahl," the second name on Patrick's whiteboard. Again she has to search through Facebook and LinkedIn profiles before finding something that might be of interest. There seems to be a private bank named Ribbenstahl & Partners in Liechtenstein.

She's never heard of Stirling Security before, but she knows there are hundreds of companies more or less like it. They perform everything from intelligence analysis to missions in war zones to personal security for companies in the Western world. Mahmoud's doctoral thesis had more or less been about companies like that. The only thing new here was an arrow that pointed to the King's Centre for Human Rights. And that arrow to the Russian Embassy. Maybe she should simply ask Patrick?

She pours a cup of coffee before turning on a Swedish morning television program to distract herself. It's a habit left over from her years in Brussels, where it was part of her job as political secretary to keep an eye on what was said on those morning sofas. Nowadays it's just a reflex, part of a routine; she doesn't even like the artificial coziness, but it's too early for the cold objectivity of the public television alternative.

She turns her back to the computer and opens the door of the empty refrigerator. Damn, she completely forgot to go shopping. All she sees is the package of chocolate bars she bought at the airport.

When she gets back to her computer, her mouth full of sweet, melting chocolate and her nausea increasing, there's a policeman, famous from a stint on *Swedish Idol*, talking about the upcoming demonstrations expected to take place during the meeting between EU ministers of justice. The whole segment is so silly—what would a singing cop know about demonstrations and the EU?—but the discussion still sets her pulse racing. This concerns a meeting she's going to be a part of. Sure, she'll be on the periphery, but it still feels huge that she'll be there.

She picks up her phone to text Gabriella. She suddenly misses her intensely, and the singing cop who's babbling on without the least bit of self-consciousness on a subject he could hardly have any expertise in, cheerfully egged on by the two tan and speedy presenters, is exactly the sort of thing she'd find hilarious.

If it hadn't been for Gabriella, Klara wouldn't be here

today, would never have climbed out of bed at her grandparents' house.

It was Gabriella who got her to go back to Stockholm, Gabriella who got her to quit the job in Brussels and finish Mahmoud's dissertation, and it was Gabriella who got her to accept the job in London when the opportunity arrived.

And what has Klara ever done for her?

Just used her. First, putting her life at risk last Christmas, and then forcing Gabriella to solve all the problems Klara had been facing. She hasn't even thanked her.

This is what I've become now, Klara thinks. That's who I've been for the past year. Someone who other people take care of, fix things for, coddle. Darkness washes over her again and takes away that moment of joy she had at the first thought of Gabriella. She closes her message app.

There's so much she wants to say to Gabriella, so much she wants to repay. But it's as if she's still too weak. She has to get stronger, and she has to do it herself, without help. Just as she's putting down the phone, it pings. It's a Facebook message from Pete. She hasn't given him her cell phone number, but on one of those blurry evenings when she went home with him, he managed to ensure they became Facebook friends.

The message is short:

> Hope you're okay. We found your computer last night. Come and pick it up at the bar when you can.

She puts the phone down and stares out at the red brick on the other side of the courtyard. From the other side of the apartment, she can hear traffic and voices coming from the street. A warm breeze blows through the apartment and a ray of sunshine has found its way from Navarre Street, across her wood floors, almost reaching the kitchen. That fleeting fragment of memory from the alley skips and flickers through her mind. She's sure she had the computer with her when she left the bar. Something isn't right. It wasn't at the bar—it was stolen.

And on the computer screen behind her, the news shows archival footage from a demonstration where young people in Guy Fawkes masks march in step through an unknown capital, flanked by helmeted riot police in an absurd theater where rebellion is just as faceless as the oppression.

Chapter 20

Stockholm—Wednesday, August 19, 2015

Yasmine has forgotten how light it is here, how it never really seems to get dark. In the gray light, she sees ships docked all along the quays that surround the new hotel. Many of them are antiquated beauties—old, dented, rusty, and badly painted. Still there's something glamorous about them. As if they denote a special class of people she's never before been aware of, a class for whom it's completely normal to keep a berth for your old hulk right in the center of Stockholm. She wonders what would happen if someone set fire to one of those ships, if they burned instead of the cars in the parking lots of Bergort.

She sits up in the Egyptian sheets of Lydmar Hotel. This was where she ended up. She couldn't have stayed one more second at Story after what happened. She'd asked her cabdriver where the hip-hop stars stayed when they were in Stockholm. He'd suggested Grand Hotel or Lydmar. The Grand felt too old, so here she was, paid for by Shrewd & Daughter's credit card, booked under an assumed name and with repeated assurances from the skinny, blond guy at reception that no one would enter her room, not even the maids.

She tosses and turns. There are a thousand things she can't let go of, a thousand things that make her unable to relax, a thousand imaginary footsteps in the corridor outside her door, a thousand thoughts like needles pricking her skin.

When her body no longer has the energy to fight, it's like falling off a cliff. As she falls swirling images of cats and stars fly past her, images of Fadi when he was small, behind the snowball trees in winter, his hand in hers, her mouth to his ear.

I will never leave you.

The room is dark when she wakes up, but she knows it's late in the day, she feels it in her bones, she slept deeply and for a long time. It's not until she pulls back the curtains and looks out over sparkling waters, shaking her head at the complete absurdity of the Royal Palace towering on the other side of the bay, that she remembers where she is. It's as if she has to scroll through Tokyo, Crown Heights, airplanes, and Story Hotel to finally end up here at this window, looking out onto this gorgeous August morning.

Turns out it's nearly twelve and breakfast has been officially over for several hours, but apparently there are advantages to staying at the Lydmar Hotel with Shrewd & Daughter's credit card. One seems to be that you can get breakfast whenever you want. She orders eggs Benedict from a menu that a serious-looking twenty-year-old with glasses and a well-groomed beard hands her, mostly because he recommended it, and she has no clue what it is.

The breakfast room is like a library in a modern, tasteful castle and the eggs are "poached" according to the earnest waiter. They're served with some sort of bread and a light, yellow sauce so creamy and smooth it takes Yasmine's breath away. Right here, for this brief moment, she feels cared for and maybe even safe. No wonder all the Swedes strive for this, she thinks. Nobody's eating eggs Benedict in Bergort.

But for her, this is nothing more than a tear in her existence, an illusion, and she's on the subway again before the waiter even has time to take away her scraped-clean plate.

She touches the thick cardboard-like paper of the photograph she found on her pillow, which lies inside her pocket now. Why did she even save it? And above all, who left it in her room?

She sees Ignacio's eyes in front of her. How they only glanced at the phone when she showed him the symbol. How his eyes changed to something else, something much harder and colder. Despite all of Bergort's alliances and ties, all the winding paths of loyalties, she thought she could trust him after everything they'd been through. If anyone, him. Her first love.

But she's been gone a long time, and loyalty is short-lived in Bergort. It's obvious someone feels threatened by her asking questions about that symbol. Why she's not sure yet, but Fadi is involved in some way. And apparently even Ignacio. But that he would threaten her, or tell someone to threaten her, she hadn't expected. She hadn't thought there was any risk in contacting him. The quiet glow she felt for Ignacio transforms into another kind of heat. He betrayed her. He should pay for that.

As the subway starts to shake into motion headed back in time, toward Bergort, she takes out the photograph of the cat. She carefully tears it into the tiniest pieces she can and throws them in the first trash can she sees at the station in Bergort.

She stood here yesterday, in this very place, hesitant, already aware that she couldn't do it, that it was too much. But sleep has given her strength, and she doesn't hesitate now.

What they fled to, what she fled from, is a high-rise apartment building with four entrances. Their entrance had been tagged back then, and it's tagged now. Different words and patterns, different kids, the same concrete houses and barren pine trees, the same words and patterns.

She walks calmly across the asphalt to the door, pulls on it, sure it won't be locked, the door code pads are broken so often that no one bothers to fix them, it's easier to just turn off the locks, allow anyone who wants to go inside.

The elevator doesn't work, same as always. The note hanging up that says it's broken could just as well be the same one that sat there four years ago, yellowed and frayed with its edges burned by a lighter.

She takes the stairs and every step is a memory. How they raced here the first few months, up and down, up and down. The time Fadi stumbled, and she thought he'd knocked out a tooth, but it was just his lip, which bled and bled, and no matter how hard she washed his T-shirt with that shitty, off-brand detergent, she couldn't get rid of those brown spots. She remembers how she hid the sweater at the bottom of the laundry basket, and how they still found it, how she crouched in the corner of the kitchen while her father pulled out the chairs to reach her. Then nothing after that. Everything always ends just when it begins.

She doesn't even hesitate when she reaches their landing, not even at the front door of the apartment. Just steps left to the door, glancing at the other names: Ahmadi, Ghazemi,

Lehtonen, and her parents: Ajam. Same as it's always been. She doesn't even hesitate to push the bell, nor when it doesn't work, doesn't even knock, just puts her hand to her neck. Grabs hold of a chain and pulls a key up over her bra, between her breasts until she's holding it in her hand, and moving it toward the door. Not even then does she hesitate, just slides it into the lock, turns the bolt, and opens the door.

The apartment is dark and smells like soap. But at the same time, it's stuffy and old, as if the windows have never been opened, as if no one really lived here. And perhaps that's true. Her parents reside here. Sleep here. Exist. But do they live?

Is there guilt in that? Shame? That Yasmine hasn't called her mother once since she left Bergort or since Fadi disappeared. If so, it's hidden behind everything else, which is deeper and easier.

Yasmine doesn't bother to turn on the light, just heads down the dark hallway into the living room. The blinds are pulled shut as they always are. Everything is cleaner now than it was. Neater. More in order. No plates on the coffee table, no bills or empty cups. She goes over to the bookcase where the photographs used to stand. The ones of her and Fadi in the old country, before they came here. Even then, on that beach with bright sunshine in his eyes, Fadi looked scared.

But that picture is gone now. There are only old pictures of relatives, of a grandmother and cousins, and her father's sister. But none of that is what she came here for, and she turns around, crosses the scuffed wood floor, and stops for a moment. Takes a calm breath before opening the door to the room she shared with Fadi and stepping over the low, worn-out threshold.

Like the rest of the apartment, the room is dark and hot.

Here too the blinds are drawn, but a ray of sunlight streaks through across the speckled gray carpet. She sees that her bed looks exactly like she left it, maybe it hasn't even been touched. Covered by a white Ikea bedspread. Other than that, the room is not at all like it used to be. The TV is pushed against the wall, the game console stowed, no clothes on the floor, no forgotten, half-drunk Red Bulls on the desk or plates next to the bed. Fadi's bed is made in the same tight, painstaking way as her own.

She walks quietly over to the window and pulls up the blinds, looks out at the paved bike path and the little grove of trees behind it. Sunlight transforms the room from a tomb to something else, to what it is, an abandoned room in an abandoned part of the world. She absently opens closet doors, pulls out drawers. Everything is empty and clean. As if they never lived here, neither she nor Fadi. Carefully—as if she were afraid to leave anything behind, not even wrinkles on the smooth bedspread—she sits down on what used to be her bed.

At first, she thinks it's the bed that squeaks, but then she hears it again, and she freezes and listens more closely. The sound is coming from the other side of the small apartment. It's the sound of a key being put into a lock, a bolt slowly turning. Somebody is on their way inside.

Chapter 21

Bergort—February 2015

I can't sleep, how are you supposed to be able to sleep when God has answered your prayers, given you exactly what you've been desiring for so long? My body trembles under the clean sheets. I've been chosen. I've shown that I have the courage and strength, and the confidence of my brothers. The passport and the satellite phone are in the rolling bag that brother al-Amin gave me, which now stands packed on the floor.

I sit on the edge of the bed. The yellow light from the streetlamp turns the lowered blinds into tired, weak shadows on the carpet. Otherwise, everything is so dark, I wouldn't even see you if you were curled up in your bed. But it's been a long time since you slept there, so long ago I can hardly remember it.

I get up and go over to your bed, lie down on it without getting under the bedspread. I think that if God can flow through my body and wipe out everything except my desire to be close to him, maybe I can be filled with you. When I close my eyes, I'm nine years old, waiting for you outside school behind the snowball trees. Later we're in front of the TV, me half asleep, you reading the subtitles aloud from the American talk show. Then we laugh and wrestle on the living-room floor to keep warm in the freezing apartment. Then you hold my hand and whisper that there are no trolls, it's just a fairy tale, nothing more. And even if there were, you'd protect me, you wouldn't let their beaks reach me, you would keep their claws from scratching me.

I open my eyes and feel tears streaming down my cheeks, down onto your pillow. You can't protect me now. No one can protect me now. Not even God can protect me now. And I sit up and dry my eyes, stand up and push my hands through my hair. The handle of the suitcase rattles and the wheels make a muffled thumping sound along the floor as I pull it out into the hall. But I don't make it through the living room before I see his silhouette detach from the darkness and stand in my way.

He's in the doorway, and it's been so long since I even saw him. He's just shadow, not real. Just an atmosphere and a bad conscience, ballast and anchor.

It occurs to me how short he is, how he's collapsed over the years, as if every adversity and loss cut him off at the ankles, one inch at a time, until now he doesn't even reach my chin.

"Go back to your room!" he says, pointing with his hand—pathetic, trembling—back toward our room.

I stop, but keep my hand on the suitcase handle.

"Lay off," I say. "Go back to bed."

But I feel my heart pound, of all the things that could have happened this was the last thing I expected.

"We'll talk about it tomorrow," he says. "Go back to your room now."

It's so absurd. He's giving orders and expects to be obeyed. I shake my head, unsure of how much strength this will take. How much violence.

"No," I say. "I'm leaving now. Just move aside. It'll be easier that way."

He takes a step toward me, waves a stubby forefinger in my face. I can see that his cheeks are red from excitement, his eyes shiny, and it fills me with unexpected tenderness.

"I know where you're headed, Fadi," he says. "I know where you think you're headed. Don't you think I understand? You think I'm an idiot? Well? I've seen your friends, Fadi! Their beards and *kufi*. Don't you think I know who they are?"

There's desperation in his voice now, resignation, and loss. It makes me sad and even more determined to get past him. I focus my eyes on him, empty them of all I feel, making them cold and violent.

"Do you think I care?" I say. "Do you think I give a shit about what you think you know? Huh? Do you think you have any power over me?"

I take a step toward him, feel his sweaty finger touch the bridge of my nose before he draws it back.

"You're nothing to me, do you understand that? Nothing! What have you given me? What did you give Yasmine? What?"

I've raised my voice now. And I hear my mother moving in their bedroom, hear the door creak, but she doesn't come out.

"Is it any wonder that she left?"

The tenderness is gone now. All I feel is hate, and I bend over the little man in front of me, and he backs up until he's pressed against the thin, cheap, stupid plasterboard wall.

"All you gave us were blows, Papa."

I spit out the word *Papa*. My saliva lands on his cheek. I see it shine faintly in the dark.

"All you taught us was fear. Do you realize that?"

I push him away from me, toward the wall. He holds up

his weak, old hands and grips my forearms. I put my hands around his neck. My fury grinds away inside me, wrestles with my self-control. My fingers close around his thick neck, his pulse rushing now, and his Adam's apple bobs as I press harder. I can feel him struggling, feel how helpless he is, how powerful I am. I don't really want to, but it's as if I have to finish this, as if I need to close this door and I push harder, as he gets weaker and heavier in my arms.

In the end, she's the one who brings me back. I hear her yelling behind me, and I turn my head and see her eyes are wide and frenzied, her mouth is open, and from it comes a desperate, animal-like scream, unlike anything I've ever heard before. It scares me, that sound, and it forces me back into the world, away from what I'm close to finishing, and I release the man I'm holding, and he falls heaving and gasping to the floor. The scream stops, and she falls down on the floor beside him, holding his head in her lap. I turn my back on them, grab hold of my bag, and leave the past behind me.

Out on the bike path a quiet winter rain is falling. I shake myself off and take a few steps. Then my black wings unfurl, lifting up through the rain and the light of the streetlamps, lifting up over the empty parking lots and satellite dishes, up above all that asphalt and concrete. Gone.

Chapter 22

Bergort—Wednesday, August 19, 2015

Her muscles constrict, and she shudders when she hears the sound of that door. She stands up carefully, leans forward to listen, and the front door opens with a sucking sound. It's the middle of the day, her parents shouldn't be coming home yet.

Slowly, tentatively, she takes a step toward the door to the living room. Whoever has entered the apartment is no more than thirty feet away from her. She thinks about the symbol on the wall at Story Hotel, the fist inside the star, and she reaches out and grabs hold of the thin door's plastic handle. Is someone following her? But nobody knows that she moved to the Lydmar. Someone must have seen her in Bergort? Ignacio? Or whomever Ignacio ratted her out to?

She closes her eyes and prays the door won't squeak as she slowly pulls it toward her. She hides behind it, leaving a small gap that offers a glimpse of the living room.

The footsteps in the hall subside and are replaced by another sound, a *clip-clop* across the living-room floor. She leans against the door crack waiting for the person to appear in her field of vision. And when that finally happens, she feels the whole apartment tremble, her past and the future are suddenly the same thing.

Slowly she pushes open the door and goes out into the living room.

Her mother stands in the middle of the room, still wearing her gray-green scrubs, her makeup faded after a double shift, maybe even triple shift, but her hair still tight in the little knot on her neck. When she hears Yasmine open the door she turns around, not overly fast, not as if she's shocked or scared, more as if she's been waiting for this moment.

Yasmine stands there, quiet, hardly breathing. She looks at the person she and Fadi stopped calling Mama a long time ago. They never talked about it, but when they switched to Swedish "mama" and "papa" disappeared—replaced by "he" or "she" or "them." As if she and Fadi had to leave certain words and constructions behind them, as if there was no longer room for them.

"Yasmine," she says in Arabic. "You came back."

Yasmine clears her throat.

"I got your email," she says.

Her mother approaches her with hesitant steps. Yasmine smells the sterile scent of hospitals and disinfectant combined with her floral perfume.

"Yasmine," her mother says in a voice that's lighter than the one Yasmine remembers, not as heavy with dashed hopes.

She allows herself to be embraced, lets her forehead fall on the starched, stiff fabric of her mother's scrubs. For a moment, she's a child again, and she feels tears welling up in her eyes. For a moment, it's so close she just stands still and lets time take its course. It's so long since she let herself be held by her mother. So long since her mother let herself be held. But it doesn't work, there's too much between them, so she pushes her away and looks into her mother's eyes.

"Did you talk to him?" she says. "After you took the picture?"

Her mother's eyes are tired and confused.

"I didn't take the picture," she says quietly. "Shirin took it. You know, my colleague? She lives around here too, on Briggvägen. She was on her way home after a late shift and saw that cat. I don't know why she photographed it. But while she did, a boy started painting on the wall."

She falls silent.

"Then she showed it to me because she thought the boy reminded her of Fadi. And she helped me to send it to you. I don't know what it is, Yasmine. I don't know what to believe."

Her mother sinks down to the floor and puts her head in her hands.

"It looks like Fadi," she whispers, shaking her head. "But Fadi is dead. They say he's dead, he died a month ago. Yasmine, I don't understand, I can't take it, I..."

She falls silent. Yasmine hesitates a second then sinks down next to her mother on the floor and wraps her arms around her. They sit like that in silence for what might be a couple of seconds or maybe an afternoon. Finally, Yasmine gets to her feet and leads her toward the bedroom. Gently, almost tenderly, she puts her on top of the bedspread and wraps a cardigan around her. She sees how heavy her mother's eyelids are, maybe she's already taken a sleeping pill on the way home, like she usually does after long shifts. But she struggles to keep them open and raise her head to Yasmine.

"Is he dead, Yasmine?" she whispers. "Is Fadi dead? Do you know? Please Yasmine, you must know."

Yasmine gently strokes her hair. All she felt for her parents. All the hate and contempt. Still there's a gap in that sticky, coal-black anger. A gap that could never be closed completely. She takes her mother's dry hands in hers.

"I don't know," she says. "But I'm going to find out."

*

Afterward Yasmine is alone in the living room. Her mother is asleep in her room, just like so many times in the past, with earplugs and sleeping pills after eighteen hours at the hospital. So many times Yasmine has found herself in this living room, listening for the front door to open, waiting for him to come home, exhausted and humiliated, ready to be set off by anything or nothing.

So many times he came across that floor full of exaggerations and gossip, rumors about her or Fadi, things he heard from his friends in the square at Radovan's crappy café. So many times she's pushed Fadi behind her, tensed up, prepared herself, and waited.

So many times she directed his rage at her instead of at Fadi. So many times that her quota was ultimately met. And in the end nothing was left. She sacrificed the one she was supposed to protect and ran away with someone like David.

She goes over to the window and looks out onto the small balcony, letting the afternoon sun flood inside, opens all the doors and windows. The afternoon smells like spruce and hot asphalt. She feels the same stress as always. He could be on his way home. He may already be on the stairs. She doesn't want to stay here any longer than she needs to.

She returns to her room, pulls up the blinds there too, opens the window and sits on the bed with phone in hand. She doesn't care about creasing the bedspread now. All the shelves and drawers are empty, even the desktop is cleaned off, and the beds made. But there's something whispering to her in here.

Something that tells her he's been here—and not that long ago. If he returned alive from Syria and is in hiding, he's been here. She can almost feel him. Like her, he would have returned to his starting point.

She gets up and goes over to his bed. Suddenly she remembers a space under the bed where he used to hide his stuff. His prized shoes and his beer.

She bends forward and pulls the mattress onto the floor. Carefully she lifts up the base of the bed and pulls it out as well, puts it on top of the mattress.

And indeed something is there: a light blue nylon bag with a zipper. She grabs hold of its strap and coaxes it upward. The bag is heavy and unwieldy, difficult to remove, but finally she gets it onto the floor. The zipper jams at first, but she works at it and manages to open it enough to lift the flap. Underneath she finds something that makes her heart stop.

Two weapons.

On top lies a scratched, black handgun. She lifts it out with trembling hand. It's cold and solid, as if molded from one piece. Carefully she puts it down on the floor beside her, leans over the bag again. The other weapon is even more surreal. Everyone's seen them in movies, in photos of wars or robberies. A weapon so deeply embedded in the culture that it's difficult to believe it's real, that it would work. That it could kill.

She widens the opening in the bag to see it better. It's a Kalashnikov. Also old and scuffed, with a worn, wooden butt and bent magazine.

Her head is spinning. What are these weapons doing here, in their room, in her room? What is Fadi up to? What has he turned into?

She sinks down onto the floor now, her head on the bed,

and she feels the tears finally come, there's no way to hold them back any longer. She cries for Fadi. For the rifle in the bed, the cat on the lamppost, for every blow dealt inside these walls. Cries because she and Fadi were never good enough, so escape was all they had. But most of all she cries because she abandoned him, because she betrayed him. Because she didn't take him with her, away from this.

She allows herself to sink into self-pity and regret, allows herself to wish the story were different, that she were different. But when she opens her eyes, the room is the same. She is the same. She can't change the story.

Gently, she gets to her feet and picks up the rifle.

This ends now, she thinks. This ends here.

The rifle feels surprisingly good on her shoulder, and she wraps her hand around the handle.

"Fadi," she whispers quietly. "No matter what you're mixed up with, no matter what happens, I will find you."

Chapter 23

London—Wednesday, August 19, 2015

Klara walks into the Library a little after seven, straight from the office. The place is buzzing and murmuring against the background of an unsteady beat from invisible speakers. Pete stands behind the bar, flirting with a girl with long, brown legs and an even longer, thick red braid. She bends her head back and laughs at something Pete says, but he excuses himself and waves to Klara instead.

"Hey, Pete," she says, leaning over the counter, both so he'll hear her, but also because it gives her some kind of superficial satisfaction to see the braid struggle to keep from glancing at her.

Pete leans over the bar, and Klara kisses him lightly on the cheek. The braid makes a point of turning away and slurps her beer.

"What was that for?" Pete says.

"Because you found the computer," Klara says. "Where was it?"

Pete holds up a bottle of red and looks questioningly at her, but she shakes her head.

"Chardonnay," she says.

Pete bends down under the bar and takes out a bottle of white wine. He fills her glass almost to the brim.

"You obviously left it hanging there on the side," Pete says and gestures toward the bar's short side.

She walks over to where he pointed, and sure enough there are hooks there for hanging jackets hidden under the protruding bar.

"I didn't hang it there," she says when she returns to Pete again.

She takes a sip of wine, and immediately things feel easier, the world opens up slightly, releasing some of its claustrophobic pressure. Pete shrugs and smiles at her.

"Maybe some customer hung it there after you left? Who knows?"

She looks at him, at his tousled blond hair, his sinewy muscles under his green tank top, his laid-back surfer attitude, and his whole fucking leisurely, positive way of being. It makes her want to throw her wine in his face, but she gets a hold of herself and takes a deep sip instead.

"Did you find it?" she says.

"Nah, a customer found it and turned it in."

She puts the glass down and bends over the counter, catches his eyes.

"A customer turned it in?" she says incredulously. "Who?"

Pete shrugs again and smiles, puts his head to the side, taking a sip of the kale smoothie he's always sipping on behind the bar.

"How should I know? Somebody. Not a regular."

She takes calming breaths and another big gulp of wine. Like a child, she thinks. He's like a fucking child, and she's filled with disgust at the thought that they actually had sex, or anything resembling sex, several times in the past month. How old is he? Twenty-two?

"What did he look like?" she says. "Do you think you could try to remember, do you think you're capable of that, Pete?"

Pete holds his hands up and takes a theatrical step backward.

"Hey, hey! Is this an interrogation? I'm not the one who drank my computer away, right?"

He sucks on his stupid smoothie again.

"What did he look like, Pete?"

Now he really seems to be thinking, glances up at the ceiling and nods quietly.

"A little nerdy. Like a heavy-metal geek, you know?" he says. "Skinny, kinda scrawny? Pale. T-shirt with a monster on it or some bollocks like that. Jeans. And wait..."

He closes his eyes and seems to really search his memory.

"He had a tattoo on his hand," he says at last. "Text, not that unusual. You know, like old typewriter text?"

"OK, OK," she says impatiently. "But what did it say?"

"Just two words. *Remember, remember* and then three dots after that, like it was supposed to continue, you know?"

She freezes and sits down on the barstool. The hair on her arms rises. The dream she had last night. The shadow, the silhouette, arms pulling at her. Those fleeting images that she tries to hold on to. That rough voice whispering in her ear while she's lying on the ground in the alley, close to losing consciousness.

Pete leans toward her again.

"Is everything all right?" he says.

She shakes her head to rid herself of a terrible feeling of helplessness that suddenly runs through her. Then she gets up, takes the computer bag from the bar, hangs it over her shoulder.

Remember, remember, the fifth of November.

Someone whispered it as they pulled the computer from her arms.

"See you later?" Pete says.

She takes the wine from the bar and swallows the last it, before turning toward the door.

"No, Pete," she says over her shoulder. "You won't."

Outside the bar she avoids the alley and presses the computer more tightly to her chest. On Shoreditch High Street, she goes into Tesco and buys a bottle of Australian Chardonnay and a new mobile phone with a prepaid card. While she pays, she quietly rattles off a phone number she never wrote down, just memorized. She'd hoped to avoid having to call Blitzie for much longer than this—they'd agreed to be in touch only in the case of an emergency. But if anyone understands cryptic messages and missing computers, it's her. And this is definitely starting to resemble an emergency.

Chapter 24

Turkey—February–March 2015

They're spraying something on the wings in the pitch darkness outside the little round window, and I guess that's what the captain or whoever was just on the intercom was talking about. The water bounces and sputters against the metal, and I silently recite verses from the Qur'an that I memorized with brother al-Amin, praying with all my heart that this is normal.

The only other time I've been on a plane is when we moved to Sweden fifteen years ago, but I don't remember that. I only remember that it was dark then too, that I felt cold in the bus on the way from the airport, and that you were sitting next to me. You took my hand and smiled. Sweden smelled like diesel and newly waxed floors, and I was so relieved that you were with me, even if it was so quiet and dark that I thought I'd died.

That memory overcomes me now. It crowds out everything else, that memory. It pushes out yesterday, my hands around his neck, her howling, my feet walking out the door. It replaces my memorized Arabic phrases and my dream of the Caliphate. It pushes out Bergort and my brothers. It drives away God.

I close my eyes as we accelerate and take off from the frozen tarmac, and I don't open them until I'm sitting in the backseat of a taxi in Istanbul next to a small, round man in a gray shirt with a long beard who calls himself Ali—and the whole world slows down, stops, and starts over. I lean back against the vinyl seat and look out through the dirty windows at all the small dusty cars. Somewhere behind the Turkish pop streaming out of the taxi's cracked speakers, I hear the muezzin. Only then do I make the switch from our past to my future. Only then do I let go of you and fall headlong into my own destiny.

How long am I in Istanbul? Long enough to stop counting days and learn where Ali's wife buys their tomatoes and eggplant. Long enough that I no longer feel wide-eyed and frightened like a child caught in traffic or among the raised voices in cafés; long enough for my Arabic to improve so that I can discern outlines of what Ali and his family talk about around the table. Every day I ask if we should go soon. Every day Ali responds in the same way.

"*Bukra, inshallah* —Tomorrow, God willing."

I help Ali with his job delivering boxes of what appear to be office supplies across this endless, winding city and pray in his mosque, where men hold my hands hard and tell me the favor Allah has granted me by giving me the opportunity to die for my beliefs.

And then one day, in the middle of a rainy spring, it's tomorrow.

A minibus picks me up one humid dawn. Ali wakes me up and holds the door open, while his wife presses into my hand a paper sack filled with hard plastic boxes of cold chicken, tabbouleh, and hummus. I'm on my way before I even have time to open my eyes.

When I finally do, I realize I'm not alone on this bus, there are five of us around the same age scattered among the seats. I look at them and see myself. We are five young men from different parts of Europe, but we all have the same studied indifference in our eyes, the same memories of police batons and empty apartments. We shoplifted the same jeans, burned the same cars, dreamed the same dreams. We're from different cities, but the same economically depressed suburb, the same Ort.

It takes two full days to drive through Turkey, and we barely speak, still unsure of our Arabic, our common language. It's late evening when one of the drivers turns to us, points through the window at the gray silhouettes of sandbags and Turkish military vehicles. I can feel my temples vibrating as he opens his mouth. For a second, I think I might throw up from the tension.

"*Al-Dawla*," he says. "The Caliphate. There, on the other side of those sandbags."

Chapter 25

London—Thursday, August 20, 2015

It's still dark outside when the ringing prepaid phone wakes her. She rolls over on her side, her mouth dry and bitter, and reaches for it. No number on the display. She grabs hold of the glass of water standing on the floor beside the bed and washes the aftertaste of wine from her mouth. Barely any headache, even though she drank two-thirds of a bottle last night. She takes a deep breath and looks at the ringing phone. Finally, she presses "answer."

"Two hundred euros," she says into the phone.

"Three hundred euros," the metallic voice answers. This was the code they'd agreed on.

Three hundred euros, the price Blitzie, a teenage hacker, had demanded in order to help her with another computer—which sometimes seems like an eternity ago and sometimes last week. The events of a year and a half ago had left Blitzie in charge of information that could topple governments and start revolutions.

Afterward, they'd agreed to stay out of touch, to become invisible from each other, in order not to attract any attention from the powerful forces they'd stirred at the time. So Blitzie created a system that consisted of two anonymous email accounts. If one of them really needed to contact the other, you could email the number of a new prepaid phone. Then the other one could call you, also from a new prepaid phone. According to Blitzie it wasn't 100 percent secure, but close enough.

Klara feels stuck after the code is completed. Where to begin?

"How... how are you?" she says at last.

"Good," Blitzie says. "But you didn't get a hold of me to ask how I was doing, I hope?"

Klara smiles at the memory of Blitzie's complete lack of social skills.

"No," she says. "Something happened. Where are you?"

"Come on."

"OK, OK." She backs down. "Sorry."

"Go ahead. We can exchange small talk some other time. What happened?"

She takes a deep breath.

"Somebody stole my computer. Then they gave it back to me."

She hears Blitzie take a deep breath on the other end. She's smoking a spliff, Klara thinks. Without a doubt.

"You smoking?" she asks.

It sounds like Blitzie giggles.

"Fuck that now. So what? Someone stole your computer?"

"The circumstances were suspicious. At first I thought I lost it."

"OK," Blitzie says on an inhalation. "Have you been installing what you were supposed to on your computers?"

Klara goes out into her darkened kitchen. It's already hot, oppressively so, as if there's a thunderstorm in the air. She sits at the kitchen table and opens her old computer.

"Of course," she says. "After what happened how could I be anything but paranoid?"

"Paranoia is good," Blitzie says. "It saves lives. Open the

program. It should be hidden in your documents folder and not with your other programs. It looks like a spreadsheet program. Quarter Q3 2013. Can you find it?"

Klara scrolls through the programs in the documents folder until she locates it. She double clicks on the program, and a spreadsheet opens on the screen, filled with incomprehensible number and letter combinations.

"Double click cell G 17," Blitzie instructs.

Klara obeys and a dialog box appears. She inputs her access code and a small program opens in another window.

"Then double click on *Threat*," Blitzie says.

A file name appears in the small search box.

"Something that seems to be an .exe file comes up. There's a date and time after that. What is that?"

"It's a fishing program and the time stamp of when it was installed. If it was during the period when the computer was gone, you can be pretty sure it was infected then. Unless you picked it up surfing porn."

Klara smiles, checks the date, August 17. She counts backward. Three days ago. That was when the computer was lost. She shudders. She wasn't just drunk. It's no longer possible to ignore the reality that someone actually stole her bag from her in order to access her computer.

"Yep," she says. "Somebody has installed something."

She takes a sip of water and finds an aspirin in a box next to the computer.

"What did you get yourself mixed up with now?" Blitzie says.

Her voice sounds thick—maybe from marijuana—but also genuinely worried.

"I really don't know," Klara says. "I have no clue. Maybe nothing. I don't know."

"How did it disappear?" Blitzie says on an inhalation. "You were mugged?"

The blurred memory fragments run through Klara's consciousness.

"Yes," she says. "Or, I think so anyway."

"You don't know if you were mugged?"

"I'd been drinking," she says quietly. "I kind of blacked out. Lost consciousness. And then the computer was gone."

Blitzie is silent for a moment.

"That doesn't sound like you," she says. "Not that I know you that well, but you seem a little too stiff to drink yourself into oblivion."

"A lot has happened since then," Klara says quietly.

"But why would anyone want your computer? Is it something you're working on?"

Klara takes a sip of water and gently massages her forehead.

"I'm writing a report for the EU. With my boss. On privatization basically. It's supposed to be a kind of foundation for the EU justice ministers to base their decisions on, but my part isn't particularly controversial. And I haven't even seen my boss's part yet and don't have any documents stored on my computer."

"You don't think..." Blitzie begins. "You don't think somebody's looking for those documents that we... You know, from last year?"

She falls silent. The same thing has occurred to Klara, but she hadn't wanted to admit it. What else could it be?

"I don't know," she says quietly. "But I don't have anything. You're the only one who has access to those documents. That was the deal. And if they want to check my computer, couldn't they have hacked it from outside?"

"Maybe they're clumsy?" Blitzie says. "Plus the program

I gave you has a pretty hefty firewall built in. They might have tried to get into your computer from outside but didn't succeed, so they had to install that shit manually instead. By the way, that program has a function you're gonna like. Click on *Location*."

She obeys and a map of northern Europe opens up. There are dots marking what appears to be London, but also the Swedish east coast.

"The program has a GPS tracker. You can enter a time, and it tells you where the computer was at that moment. It's good for theft protection. But you can also check where the computer's been while it was gone."

"Thank you," Klara says. "At least now I know something really weird is going on."

"You seem to attract trouble. Hope it resolves itself. Be careful and contact me later, OK?"

"Sure, I'll take it easy. Wait! Don't hang up. One more thing. *Remember, remember, the fifth of November*. Do you know what that means?"

"*V for Vendetta*," Blitzie says. "You know that movie about some futuristic Guy Fawkes? Patron saint of all hackers. Anonymous and some anarchists use it as a sort of motto. The Internet is full of people talking about the revolution. Why do you ask?"

"No reason," she says. "Just something I saw somewhere. I'll be in touch, Blitzie."

A hacker slogan tattooed on the robber's arm? What the hell is this all about?

After Blitzie's voice disappears, she feels completely alone. Despite the early-morning heat, she's freezing, crawls back into bed again, and pulls the covers over her. The headache slowly recedes as she clicks on *Location* in Blitzie's programs. A map opens immediately and a red pin is dropped in west London. She zooms in as close as possible.

Formosa Street, number 3. It seems like her computer spent a few days in Little Venice.

She shuts her computer and stares out at the dawn light on the street outside. Little Venice. Not exactly an area you'd think was full of anarchists and hackers. But at least it's a place to start.

"Are you coming?"

Klara jumps and looks up from the screen. It's been five hours, she's very close to finishing her part of the report now, and has been so engrossed in her work that she hadn't noticed when someone appeared in the doorway of her office.

Charlotte is standing there in one of her usual long, flowing dresses. Big earrings and her dark, curly hair pulled back in a messy bun at her neck. Klara thinks, not for the first time, that there's something encouraging about the fact that Charlotte always seems to look like she's headed for a yoga convention. But she hides a spine of steel beneath that bohemian façade.

"You didn't forget that we're having lunch today?" Charlotte says with a smile.

Klara glances at the screen. Is it already twelve-thirty?

"No," she says, guiltily. "I didn't forget, just didn't realize it was so late."

She saves the document just as the first heavy drops of rain hit her attic window. As she rises, bright lightning streaks across a dark sky.

"Dear lord," Charlotte says. "I hope you've got your umbrella."

There's something liberating about the sudden storm, and Klara has no objection to the warm rain on her bare legs as they run along Catherine Street to the little Italian restaurant where Charlotte made a reservation.

The waiters seem to know Charlotte, and they quickly relieve them of their umbrellas and find a table by a window facing the street. After they sit, Charlotte cautiously dries her face with a linen napkin and smiles.

"Is there mascara all over my face?" she says.

A thick line is actually smeared slightly at the corner of Charlotte's eye, but it doesn't look bad, quite the contrary. Combined with her big, brown eyes, high cheekbones, and messy bun, it looks rather sexy. Klara shakes her head.

"Not at all."

Charlotte bends over the table and winks at her.

"Shall we have a glass of wine?" she says. "I know you have to finish your part of the report, but one glass won't hurt will it?"

A pleasant anticipation awakes in Klara's body.

"Gladly," she says. "If you're having one, I will as well."

They order their late-summer pasta with porcini mushrooms and white truffles and sip their wine. The feeling of relief when the alcohol hits her blood makes the stress of work and the stolen computer fall away for a moment. She feels so relaxed she suddenly decides to tell everything to Charlotte, but it's too complicated now, especially after she glossed over what happened last Sunday. She'll go down to that address in Little Venice first. Maybe after that. Depending on what she finds out.

"So what do you say?" Charlotte says. "You're almost

done with your section now, right? It's just a few days left until the presentation."

Klara takes a small sip of wine, dry and mineral rich. She feels like closing her eyes and escaping into that feeling for a while; the taste for some reason reminds her of early summer mornings on Aspöja when the sky is clear and warm, the grass still damp with dew or light rain. She wants to forget about the report and the computer for a while. Instead she nods.

"Yes, of course," she says. "I'm almost done. How's it going for you? You're the one who's doing the heavy lifting."

Charlotte also takes a small sip of wine and looks out onto the street where the rain bounces on the cobblestones.

"Well, it will most likely be fine," she says, nodding thoughtfully. "But it's certainly not simple."

"A lot of people have strong opinions about this, I suppose," Klara says, searching Charlotte's face.

"Definitely," Charlotte agrees and turns her gaze from the street toward Klara, looks her straight in the eye.

"Things aren't always what they seem," she mumbles quietly and takes another small sip of wine, then breaks off a piece of white bread and dips it thoughtfully into the dish of olive oil on the table between them.

"What do you mean?" Klara says and lays down her own piece of bread on the plate in front of her.

There's something about how Charlotte said it that reminds her of her meeting with Patrick in the courtyard the other day. He used the exact same phrase. Now she sees Patrick's mind map in front of her. All the arrows and names.

But Charlotte just shakes her head, as if trying to wake up, and a renewed focus appears in her eyes when she looks at Klara.

"I don't mean anything really," she says. "Just that issues like these are... complicated."

The waiter puts two steaming plates in front of them, and their little universe by the window is filled with the wonderful scent of truffles. Charlotte spins some spaghetti on her fork, puts it in her mouth, and chews with intensity while turning toward the window and rain gushing down outside.

The days since Klara came back from Aspöja have been confusing—computer theft and Patrick's strange behavior. And now this vague talk with Charlotte—she's tired of running into question marks. She takes a deep gulp of wine and musters her courage.

"Do you know a company called Stirling Security?" she says.

Charlotte turns toward her quickly and raises a glass of water to wash down the food she has in her mouth. Something glimmers in her eyes and then rapidly disappears, replaced by a blank, puzzled expression.

"What's that?"

"Stirling Security," Klara says quietly. "I don't know, it was just a name I saw somewhere, in some context."

"In what context?"

Charlotte leans back in her chair, now with wineglass in hand, and looks calmly at Klara. There's a tone in her voice that's equal parts indifference and threat, and Klara knows instinctively that she's stepped onto thin ice, that she probably never should have brought this up.

"Nothing," she says. "Just a name I saw in some report, I think. I'd never heard of it before. But I guess you haven't heard of it either?"

Charlotte shakes her head but doesn't release Klara from her gaze. Slowly she takes a sip of her wine.

"But this naturally leads to why I wanted us to have lunch today. The report, Klara, it's time to wrap it up now," she says. "We're presenting on Sunday. I should have had your section the day before yesterday. It's time to focus on work."

Klara's cheeks get hot. It's the first time she's heard anything critical from Charlotte at all. And for no reason.

"Yes, I know, but I lost the computer and all of that. I'll give it to you this afternoon... I'm basically done."

"Yes, but you're usually a little sloppy and biased in your writing," Charlotte continues. "And this time it's especially important to have all the facts and formulations done well, so I may have to rewrite part of the text. All the more reason that you send it to me *pronto*, rather than holding on to it. Do we understand each other?"

Klara's head starts to buzz and her throat starts to close up. *Sloppy and biased?* As if objectivity weren't the foundation of her reasoning. Is there anything worse you could accuse a lawyer of?

She nods but isn't ready to surrender completely.

"I haven't seen your section either," she says quietly. "It's a little hard to finish the background if I don't know what your recommendation is going to be."

"Klara," Charlotte says, and her voice is as smooth as steel. "This is my report. You are my assistant, nothing more. If you can't deliver then maybe we need to rethink our arrangement? Can I be any clearer than that?"

Klara shakes her head and feel tears rising behind her eyes. She reaches for the wineglass.

"You'll have my section after lunch," she says quietly.

"Good," Charlotte says, smiling only with her mouth.

Chapter 26

Stockholm—Thursday, August 20, 2015

When Yasmine pulls back the heavy curtains of her window at the Lydmar and looks out at the gray morning, she sees a late-summer rain perforating the surface of the bay like tin foil pierced by thousands of tiny needles.

The news is on the TV behind her. It was a restless night in Bergort. There are images of stones being thrown and cars burning. Police officers in riot gear and teenagers in tank tops are so far away from the camera they hardly look real. Yasmine sat glued to the story the first time it was played a half hour ago, her heart pounding, her eyes searching, searching for a glimpse of Fadi, or whatever, whoever. But the feature was short and void of any real information. The police said they didn't know what was behind the riots, but they'd also "noticed signs that something had been going on for a long time."

Signs, Yasmine thinks. All of Bergort is fucking papered with signs. Stars and fists. A cat hanging from a lamppost. Symbols that no one seems to want to talk about, not Ignacio, not Parisa. Symbols that get you threatened if you ask about them.

When she turns, her gaze falls on the gun she took from the apartment, which she put on the bureau in front of the bed. It looks even more insane here, on that natural-colored bureau under a shining, polished mirror with a matte frame, in this clean, upper-class environment.

She's never felt as much like an outlaw as when she packed the guns into an old football bag, threw it over her shoulder, and walked out the front door.

But what was the alternative?

She couldn't leave the weapons in her childhood home, couldn't allow them to be used for something unimaginable. And she couldn't call the police. Not the police they hid from the whole time she was growing up. The ones who dislocated Red's shoulder, who knocked Karim's teeth out and left him in a field in Botkyrka. Police put them in the back of the police van and called them *cunts*, *sand niggers*, *camel fuckers*, *monkeys*. The police would kill Fadi if they found him. And she's already betrayed him enough. If this was going to be fixed, she was going to have to do it herself.

She almost took both weapons on the subway, but at the last second she decided to hide the Kalashnikov in a dense thicket of rose hips in the grove behind the school, where they used to hide their shit when they were kids. It seemed like walking around with one gun in her waistband was enough.

She'd left a note under Fadi's mattress. Just her phone number. Nothing else. You don't lose a machine gun. Not even in Bergort. Especially in Bergort. He'd have to call her now.

In the meantime, she's gonna find who has been talking about her and caused someone to threaten her. And then she's gonna lure the little snitch out of his hole.

Ignacio sounds completely calm and relaxed on the phone, happy to meet her after work. But fuck it. It doesn't matter how you sound on the phone. Lying is the first thing you learn in Bergort.

She can't wait to find out exactly why Ignacio didn't want

to tell her what those symbols meant. And she's even more anxious to know why he would get people to threaten her.

What the hell is going on? Could he really have turned into that big a coward?

Stay away from Bergort, whore.

On TV clips from Bergort are still rolling by, and she's sure that symbol has something to do with the riots. And she's sure Ignacio is involved. The question is how involved is Fadi.

She stands up and looks into the mirror above the gun. Everyone says she's skinnier, and maybe it's true. The swelling next to her eye is purple now. It seems to change color like the light in the conference room at Shrewd & Daughter.

She takes a deep breath and gently picks up the large, dull gun, takes it by both hands, and backs up a step toward the bed. David forced her to go to a shooting range in Flatbush last spring. They'd shot several different guns, and she'd found it unexpectedly liberating. They went back several times over a period of a few weeks when David was trying to cut down on partying and just drank in the evenings, smoked some weed, nothing more.

Slowly she raises her gun and points it at her own reflection. She sees the muzzle, large and dark, her face taut behind it. She feels the strength inside her now. A single direction. Despite all the bullshit. Despite David, her mother, and all of fucking Bergort. Despite Ignacio's betrayal. It's all about this now, she thinks. This is about Fadi. There is only one thing to think about. Only one thing to do. Find him and do what she should have done from the beginning: protect Fadi from himself.

*

When she finally leaves her room around five o'clock, she sees the quiet Swede at the reception, so orderly and clean with his little mustache and fancy, dotted bow tie that she has to stifle the impulse to tell him she has a big black gun pushed down the waistband of her jeans. Would he have raised his voice then? Would his perfect service be compromised?

Instead she asks him to order her a taxi and sits down in one of the tasteful armchairs in the lobby to wait. The gun is cold and feels surprisingly secure against her lower back.

It's still raining, or raining again, as she climbs onto the loading dock in the parking lot near Kärrtorp Centrum and squats down in the shelter of an overhang, pulling her hood down over her forehead to avoid being recognized. In the taxi, she looked up directions from Johansson's Moving Company, where Ignacio works, to the subway, and she's guessing he'll cut through this parking lot. And here, in this alley, she'll ambush him.

Johansson's Moving Company, she thinks. She'd be very surprised if anyone with that surname worked there. She leans back against the brick wall and stares out over the half-empty parking lot where rain has turned the asphalt shiny and smooth, while the feeling she woke up with continues to grow. It's neither fear nor anxiety. No, it's resignation, which makes her suspect it might be too late. Fadi might already be lost, maybe she lost him when she left him four years ago. Meanwhile, there's a kind of power in that feeling. If the only thing that matters is already lost, then she might as well sacrifice whatever's left. No one is more dangerous than someone who's lost everything.

When she turns her head back toward the alley, she sees

Ignacio's big body in a soaking wet varsity jacket and a Braves cap, baggy jeans, and black Air Maxes, coming around the corner and into the alley. She feels the gun cold and hard against her spine as she stands up. That fucking snitch. Her heart starts to pound as she moves across the loading dock. His time has come.

Chapter 27

Syria—March 2015

Finally, I'm alone in the dust and the cold. The night is quiet, only crickets and the sound of the minibus disappearing over the gravel, between abandoned, half-finished buildings. I've never felt so alone and confused, not even after you disappeared. Not even then.

Back then the feeling crept in, you'd been on your way for so long, and besides Bergort was a cage I knew well. But this? I look around and listen, sink down onto my haunches in the dirt. This is loneliness.

I bend back and see a starry sky that's so magnificent I lose my balance and fall backwards onto the road.

I don't know how long I've been there when I hear footsteps approaching through what I now think, after my eyes adjusted to the darkness, looks like a village. Maybe even a small, empty town. Quickly, I sit up and grab the bag, get up on my feet.

At the same time I hear a metallic clicking through all the crickets and darkness. A gun being cocked.

"Who are you?" someone asks in broken Arabic.

"*As-salamu alaykum*," I say, and my voice is so shrill that I have to clear my throat. "I'm Fadi Ajam from Sweden. Imam Dakhil sent me."

That's what they told me to say when I arrived. It should be enough, but it feels like grasping at straws now, here in the dark with footsteps and crickets and unsecured weapons.

"Fadi from Stockholm?" the voice says.

He speaks hood Swedish, but not from Stockholm's hoods. From the countryside, and I feel my muscles start to relax, and my heart starts beating again.

"Yes, yes!" I say. "Fadi from Bergort. Imam Dakhil sent me."

That metallic clicking again, maybe he's securing his weapon. He's closer now, close enough for me to make out his silhouette, his scarf wrapped around his head like a mujahid, his dark soldier pants tucked into his boots.

"Yes, yes," he says and laughs. "I heard you the first time."

Now he stops in front of me. I can see he's Somali, and that he has a sparse beard and long hair, his teeth gleam in the moonlight.

"Welcome, brother Ajam. Thank Allah, may he be exalted, that you arrived without any problems. I'm Abu Umar."

Abu Umar leads me down a village street, where all the windows are gaping black holes, even though it's no later than eight in the evening.

"Where is everyone?" I say. "Doesn't anyone live here?"

"This is war, brother," Abu Umar says and throws a quick, condescending glance sideways at me. "I thought that was why you were here, *ey*?"

"But," I begin. "What do you mean? Are they dead?"

Abu Umar shakes his head and looks tired.

"Dead?" he says. "We only kill enemies and traitors, brother. They fled when the fighting was at its worst. Before we liberated this village, thank Allah, may he be glorified and exalted."

"Were you part of that battle?"

I know I shouldn't ask so much, since it only exposes how fucking green I am. But I don't know anything. Everything is new. And I'm curious.

Abu Umar shrugs.

"Not in that battle, brother," he says. "But in many others. As you too will be if Allah, may he be glorified and exalted, lets you."

As we walk down a small hill to what appears to be a small, depressing square, I see a couple of houses where a faint light is burning. I get a whiff of mint and grilled eggplant.

"But a few are still here?" I say.

"There's nobody left in this part of town, brother," Abu Umar says. "No one but us. And this is where we live. You too now."

We head up a small alley and enter the door to what appears to be an ordinary apartment building with broad, new stairs. There are no lights in here, but a weak, yellow light falls across the stairs as we climb up in silence. It reminds me of the light from the streetlamps at home, and I swallow something that tastes sweet and wet, maybe tears.

Abu Umar comes to a door, and without bothering with a key, pushes down on the handle and opens the door to a modern and dark apartment. We step over the threshold, and I see a dim light inside what appears to be the living room.

Two men are sitting on the floor around the faint blue flame of a small camp stove. They stand up when we come into the room.

"*Shoo* brother!" says the larger of the two and holds out his hand.

He's tall and broad, not fat like Mehdi, but not exactly muscular either. Just a larger version of a regular person.

A thick, smooth beard covers his broad chin, and his hair is hidden under a scarf like the one Abu Umar wears. I take his hand, which is warm and dry, and a little too easy to hold on to. I let go reluctantly.

"I'm Shahid," he says. "Welcome, brother."

The smaller and slimmer man takes my hand. He doesn't have a beard, but he's unshaven and has his hair hidden under an army cap.

"Welcome," he says. "I hope Allah, may he be exalted, offers you an honorable death."

He looks at me seriously, and I feel a discomfort so intense it surprises me. Everything we talked about with brother al-Amin. Martyrdom. How we long for it, how we can't wait to enter paradise. In this dark room, in the middle of a ghost town, it doesn't feel quite as desirable anymore. Rather than clean and beautiful, it now feels dirty and far too real.

"But we won't die tonight, *brus*," Shahid says and pulls out a pillow for me to sit on. "Tonight we're going to drink tea and get to know our new brother, Fadi."

He turns to me.

"Brother Tariq is eager," he says. "He can't wait for his virgins. It's because he's not married. "

Shahid laughs at his own joke as he pours hot water over mint leaves in a dented tin mug, which he hands to me. Tariq doesn't say anything, just looks down into his own cup and drinks quietly.

Tariq wakes me up before sunrise, and we mumble prayers until the sun hangs somewhere behind the buildings. Then he disappears before I even have time to stand up.

Tariq and I share the apartment, because we're not

married. The others live with their families, the ones who have been here over a year already have children.

I don't understand who we are, how many we are, or what our task is, either. But it seems like war is the brothers' job. They go to the frontline, do their eight-hour shift, and when darkness falls, go home to their families again. Just like a regular job, like when I was working at the warehouse. The soldiers are mostly Syrians and Iraqis, and they live scattered throughout the almost deserted village in order to make it harder to bomb them. But it seems that we Swedes stick together.

There's tea in a jar, and I struggle to get the camp stove started. I find a couple of flat pieces of bread and a little leftover hummus in a plastic jar beneath them. I'm still not hungry but force myself to eat the dry bread. No sooner do I finish than I hear the door open and brother Shahid comes into the room.

"*As-salamu alaykum*, brother," he says. "Come with me, it's time to get started."

As soon as I get to my feet, he presses a gun into my hands. It's heavy and cold and makes my blood race. A Kalashnikov with a wooden butt and a curved magazine. I don't know where to point it, but Shahid has already disappeared out the door and is headed down the stairs.

We exit onto the dusty courtyard and take a gravelly path to a parking lot, where only a few burned-out cars stand. I shiver in the gray dawn, and Shahid tells me to stay put and goes over to a car that's about sixty feet away. I have a thousand questions, but I push them away, force myself to do only what I'm told.

Shahid comes back and asks for my gun, which I give him. He turns and twists it, checking it from different angles before putting it to his shoulder and firing off a salvo at some jars he's placed on the hood of the car. The sudden noise is deafening.

"Yes, yes," Shahid murmurs and eyes something through the gun sight.

He takes a couple of shots at the cans. Then the choppy sound of machine-gun fire followed by a whistling sound and an explosion come from not far away. I crouch instinctively and look around for protection, the blood rushing to my head. It starts now, this is just the way it will be.

But Shahid turns his head and grins when he sees me crouching against the wall.

"*Ey*, what are you up to?" he says. "*Wallah*, you look so freakin' funny."

He aims the gun toward the ground and turns toward me.

"Are you afraid of that?"

He points the gun in the direction from which the hacking machine-gun sound came.

"That's the frontline, brother, it doesn't go anywhere."

I stand up, legs still shaky.

"But that explosion?" I say.

"Barrel bombs that Bashar's swine release from their helicopters. Get used to, it sounds like that all day here."

He points the gun up at the gray morning sky.

"Get up now, and we'll see what you've got," he says, and hands me the Kalashnikov.

Shahid can't spend the whole day with me, in the end he has to head to the frontline. When he mentions it, I feel my excitement and anticipation start to grow again. I'm close now, so close to what I want. But Shahid just laughs at me.

"There's no frontline for you today, newcomer," he says. "You take care of maintenance, and then we'll see."

And with that he jumps into an old Fiat, lays his gun in the passenger seat, and disappears in a puff of smoke, a small, fleeing cloud of dust.

So my job is to go shopping with the wives in a village farther from the frontline, and after that, to try to get the electricity working in one of the houses along with a Syrian man with a dialect so thick I can't understand a word he says. As soon as I turn my back, I hear the women giggling at me, feel them staring and pointing. When the temperature falls, and the sun approaches the hills outside town, I drag myself back to my room and wait for the others to come back. I feel useless and superfluous. We couldn't even get the electricity running.

I'm already asleep on my mattress when a buzzing phone awakens me. It takes me a moment to realize the vibrating sound is coming from my own bag under a window that looks out onto the deserted street.

"This is Fadi," I say when I dig the satellite phone out of the bag's outer pocket.

"Brother Fadi!"

It's brother al-Amin's voice bouncing, warm and static, up above Bergort through space and all the way here into my solitude a few miles from the front.

"We don't have much time, this is expensive!" says brother al-Amin. "How are you? Have you arrived?"

I'm so happy to hear from him that my eyes fill with tears, and I sit down on the rickety windowsill and tell him everything as fast as I can. About the trip through Turkey in the minibus, the border, and how dark it is here at night. About the brothers and my useless day. And brother al-Amin lets me go on, lets me get everything out, even though it's expensive.

"It'll get better," he says finally, laughing. "You just got there yesterday? Just relax."

My cheeks get hot, and I feel ashamed. It's true, I got here yesterday, what did I think would happen? I can't even shoot. How could they send me to the frontline?

"Sure," I say. "Sorry. I'll be patient and wait for Allah to choose a role for me. "

"It's good, brother," he says. "No news otherwise, I guess? Regarding what we talked about. You remember?"

The traitor. Of course I remember.

"I haven't heard anything yet," I say as quietly as I can.

"No big plans discussed? No visitors?"

"Nothing yet."

"You know all of that may be what the traitor is looking for," brother al-Amin says. "As soon as you hear something, we'll get our chance. The most important thing is that you keep your eyes and ears open and be ready when the time comes."

I hear the door to the apartment open and what is probably Tariq's shuffling steps across the stone floor.

"And remember that you can't share this with your brothers, Fadi," he says. "Not even that you are in touch with us. The fact that you have this phone may be enough for them to be suspicious. "

Outside my door, I hear Tariq getting closer to my room, his steps getting louder.

"I have to go," I whisper, and press the red button.

I've just stuffed the phone into the pocket of my combat pants when Tariq pushes the door open with his Kalashnikov.

He's grimy and dirty from the front and has an exhausted, disgruntled expression on his face.

"Who were you talking to?" he says.

I swallow and feel the heat of the phone inside my pocket.

"No one," I say. "Allah. I... was praying."

He looks at me for a moment without saying anything. He doesn't believe me, but the lie is untouchable. He turns around without a word and leaves me alone.

I wait until I hear him go into his own room before I slump down on my mattress on the floor. Tariq's suspicious expression, his foxlike stealth and arrogance. What's his problem? Is he worried? And about what? Being exposed?

Chapter 28

London—Thursday, August 20, 2015

Klara is leaving the office early. She felt empty and tired after the wine at lunch and with the stress to finish the report, but now, after having uploaded it to Charlotte's folder, her energy has returned.

After all the turmoil surrounding the computer, it feels almost liberating to have a mission, a plan, or at least a direction. To find out what's hiding at 3 Formosa Street in Little Venice.

Which is why she doesn't jump onto her bike to head home to Navarre Street immediately like she usually does, but instead heads in the other direction, toward the river. This afternoon's sudden and heavy rains have moved on and taken the oppressive heat with them. She feels like she can think again.

She walks out onto Waterloo Bridge just far enough to see the enormous city spread out on either side of the bend.

She lights a cigarette and smokes it, leaning against the thick, damp railing, where the remaining drops of rain look inexplicable in the bright afternoon sun. The cigarette burns out, and she throws it over the railing, bends over to watch it fall down toward the brown river. When she can no longer see the butt, she closes her eyes.

*

She blushes at the thought of her lunch with Charlotte. It was a mistake to bring up Stirling Security. Charlotte's reaction was unmistakable and as close to hostile as she's ever seen her. There's definitely something amiss. And the question remains, What is Patrick doing inside his shadowy chamber? Stirling Security, Ribbenstahl, and the Russian Embassy.

She leaves the bridge and walks along Lancaster Place and Bow Street, past the tourists and their late-summer pints, around Covent Garden, their laughter and shopping bags. She pushes away the idea of stopping for a glass of wine. Once she's finished with what she needs to do. Only then, when she's earned it.

She follows the meandering shopping streets around Covent Garden, up through Seven Dials and continues on to Old Compton Street and up toward the Tube station at Oxford Street. Somewhere far away she hears drums and whistles and something that sounds like chanting. Another demonstration, a meaningless riot. This summer is full of them.

She's never been to Little Venice—except for Kensington Gardens, she's actually never been north of the Westway—and even though she knows the area is famous for its beauty, she finds the canals and greenery surprisingly picturesque. Here there are no speeches or drums. The streets are almost silent, only a taxi or an occasional BMW, no tourists, not even a stencil of a Guy Fawkes mask or an anarchist-*A*. The neighborhood seems to be a sanctuary for an upper middle class with creative jobs, flexible hours, and children in Montessori. Subcultures and the discontented need not apply. Neighborhoods like these always made her nervous. The complacency in these oaks, these canals with their small houseboats safely moored, these empty streets. But appearances can be deceptive, she thinks. Somewhere in this Potemkin village the person who stole her computer is hiding.

It doesn't take long to find 3 Formosa Street. The door is wedged between a tasteful café and a clothing shop with a selection of orange silk scarves and airy, natural-colored linen skirts tailor-made for the area's wealthy bohemians. She'd already decided when she checked the map that the pub across the street would be the perfect place to wait.

Wait for what? She's not sure. Judging by what seems to be three separate doorbells next to the door, the house seems to contain more than one apartment. She doesn't dare go and look more closely, not yet. She's decided to be careful, start by surveying the door this evening. Watching who goes in and out. What she'll do with that information, she's not exactly sure.

The Prince Alfred pub on the other side of the street fits in well with the area. Or, rather the area fits in well with Prince Alfred, as if the area itself were here to give Prince Alfred's Victorian façade a sufficiently polished surface to mirror itself in. Wherever you turn there's engraved glass, a black cast-iron pillar, and ornate woodwork. She walks through the door to the bar, hesitates a moment before she feels the words "orange juice" forming on her lips. But at the last moment, she swallows them and orders a glass of white wine. She sits by the window that looks out onto Formosa Street. Just a glass while she waits, she thinks. That's not the end of the world.

But the evening ends up long and uneventful. The pub slowly fills up with ideal representatives of the English middle class while a gorgeous blue darkness slowly falls on the street outside.

The streetlamps light up, one by one. She's on her third glass of wine, and has momentarily left the door to 3 Formosa Street unattended for a moment, when it finally happens.

The first thing she sees is a silhouette from the corner of her eye, and she turns her head in a flash. A tall and lanky figure digs into the pocket of his chinos outside the door. It takes a second for her to realize who it is. But there's no doubt. The person on the other side of the street is Patrick Shapiro.

Chapter 29

Stockholm—Thursday, August 20, 2015

Yasmine stops short and squats down while throwing a quick glance across the parking lot. The rain is good, it keeps people away from the open asphalt and inside under a roof. It makes her task easier.

She stands up quietly, her eyes on Ignacio's calm, swaying figure. He has headphones on and is quietly rapping along to some song, completely in his own world, doesn't even seem to care about the rain. She feels her fury growing again.

Of all people—him. After they shared so much. So many nights in the studio and in Red's living room down in the low-rise apartment buildings. So many days of dreaming and cutting school and not giving a shit. Maybe the only one she ever really counted on. And he subjects her to this. When all she wants is to find Fadi.

When she stands up, she can feel how the weight of the gun pushes her jeans lower on her hips.

When Ignacio is within reach, Yasmine jumps down from the loading dock and calmly walks toward him, still with her hood pulled down over her forehead. He doesn't notice her immediately, but he must be aware that someone's coming because his jaw stops moving, maybe because it's embarrassing to be seen rapping to himself.

She lets him go by before she stops, removes her hood, feeling faint rain more like a film than drops on her forehead.

Her breathing is faster, the adrenaline like mercury in her veins, and the taste of iron and rust is in her mouth. Before she even realizes it, she has the gun in her hand, heavy and still warm from her body.

Ignacio continues walking, still in his own world, and she takes three steps behind him. Speeds up for the last two and turns to her side, kicking him full force against the back of the knee, Bergort-style, always the knees, always with all your might. Ignacio screams, loses his balance, and falls down on his knees, dazed. He turns around, rips the headphones from his ears and looks up at her.

"What the fuck!" he shouts, holding up his hands. "Yasmine? *Que pasa, len?* What are you doing?"

But she doesn't answer, just surveys the area. It's empty, no one here, just them. And she grabs hold tight of the gun without hesitating, holding it with both hands, and walks slowly toward him. She sees it in his eyes—he understands that this is no joke. She's standing in front of him now, the gun just a few feet from his head.

"Who the hell did you rat me out to, *sharmuta*?" she says. "You cunt. I trusted you."

She spits on the wet asphalt, but her mouth is so dry, she has almost no saliva.

"*Ey*, Yazz!" he says. "What is this? Stop playing around."

His breathing is shallow, and his voice thin and fragile. He knows that she's not kidding.

"This isn't a fucking joke," she says. "This is serious as fuck now."

She presses the gun against his cheek, like in a movie, and she sees real fear in his eyes. And something more.

"What?" Ignacio says. "What do you mean, Yazz? What the hell?"

He looks into her eyes, not beseechingly, just genuinely confused. But she's not ready to accept that, only surrender, nothing else.

"Do you understand what you've done?" she says. "They came after me immediately, you fucking asshole. They found me right away. You knew where I lived, *bre*. You knew what I was looking for. So now it's fucking time to tell me who they are, OK? "

She presses the gun harder against his cheek, but the confusion in his eyes makes her conviction waver, makes her hands shake.

He remains on his knees, his huge hands on his sides, his gaze on her. It's not the first time someone has threatened him with a gun.

"Seriously, Yazz," he says. "*Wallah!* I swear, Yazz, I have no idea what you're talking about, OK? "

She sees it in him, but she can't accept it, it has to be this way. How else could it have happened?

She feels how Ignacio leans into the gun, how he does nothing to escape or counter her. And his eyes are so open and honest that the gun feels heavier and heavier in her hand, until it's too heavy and she drops it, and it falls down onto the ground between them with a thud.

It's as if all her energy suddenly drains out of her, this whole last day, this last week, the last four years, her whole life, suddenly washes over her, flooding her and she falls to the ground—her legs no longer legs, just twigs or grass, nothing at all. Somewhere, in another world, she feels strong arms placed around her, pulling her into a broad chest, a bearded cheek leaning against her head, a voice whispering.

"It's okay, Yazz, you're okay."

*

Afterward, they end up at a café near the subway. It's about to close, and there are only a few elderly Swedes inside with buns in their trembling hands. She can't even remember how they got here, how she got a cup of hot chocolate in front of her and a cheese sandwich. The gun is tucked in her waistband again, and Ignacio doesn't say anything, he just looks at her quietly from the other side of the table, crumbs in his beard, a cup of coffee in hand.

"It wasn't loaded," she says quietly, looking around to make sure no one is listening. "Just so you know, *len*."

Ignacio laughs.

"Good to know," he says and takes a bite of his Mazarin cake, nodding happily. "These sure are delicious little bastards."

They're silent again. Yasmine sips her hot chocolate. Finally, she leans across the table and tells him about the warning she got at Story Hotel, about how she'd been sure he'd ratted her out. She apologizes a hundred times. But she doesn't say anything about Fadi and the weapons. It's better to keep some cards close to your chest.

"But where did you get the gun from?" he says.

She shrugs.

"Long story."

Ignacio nods, licks pastry frosting from his fingers, and takes a final swig of coffee.

"But these pictures..." she begins.

He nods slowly and leans across the table, lowering his voice.

"I was hoping you'd just drop it, Yazz," he says. "I tried to warn you. People are scared. We started seeing that shit a few weeks ago. Those symbols? Around Pirate Square at first, then everywhere. One morning, it could be as many as twenty new ones. Just in Bergort. In one night."

"And the cats?"

He shrugs.

"I haven't seen that for myself. I think there was just that one you showed me. But that photo is all over online now. Fucking disgusting, *ey*? I mean, strangling cats? That's psycho."

Yasmine nods.

"Definitely. But what does it mean?"

"I don't know, Yazz. But did you see the news this morning?"

"The riots," she says. "Is that only happening in Bergort?"

"I think it started with us. But it's spreading now. I've heard people have seen that symbol sprayed all the way up in Fittja. But Bergort seems to be the epicenter. There are cars burning almost every night now. Even before what happened last night."

He lowers his voice again and looks around to make sure no one is listening.

"Something is going down, *bre*. And this shit is something more than just the usual kids, not the usual discontent."

"How do you know that?"

Ignacio leans back, as if he's offended.

"Don't you think I would know?" he says. "Seriously, give me a little credit. Anyway, this is something else. It's organized. There's some kind of plan. It started with the symbols. People posting that cat on the Internet and shit. Then cars started burning. Some rocks were thrown at the cops. Then it was quiet for a few days. Then it started again this weekend. And now? Shit, I swear, now all of Bergort is covered in those symbols. The last few nights ten cars have burned."

He lowers his voice again and looks around.

"I have to head home," he says. "Come with me, and I'll tell you what I know, OK?"

They stand up and walk out the door, which makes a

friendly ring as it closes. Outside the rain has ceased, and the night sky has started to clear.

"When you asked about those pictures on Monday, I didn't say anything. I was afraid for you, *querida*. You're an outsider now. Do you even remember how it works here? People see you as a traitor. You just took off, and nobody ever heard from you. There were a bunch of rumors about you. We knew they weren't true, but people who didn't know said you pinched a bunch of dough from Red and took off. You know, everything always gets blown out of proportion."

She nods. She knew that when she left. That it would be hard to go home.

"So I didn't want you to get drawn into it. But I understand it's serious now. You think it has something to do with Fadi? You think he's spraying the fist in the star in that picture you have?"

"I know it has something to do with Fadi," she says.

They walk quietly in the same direction they came from.

"So," he begins. "This is organized, Yazz."

He turns and looks at her.

"The kids are doing what they always do, you know? Spraying and burning and throwing stones and shit. But this time someone is behind it. Someone who tells them what to do and how and when. They have stencils? Shit, *bre*! Does that sound like the usual bunch of misfits to you? They barely know how to fucking set cars on fire."

"So you think someone's handing out stencils, or what?"

"Someone is, yes. And somebody's busing in people for those riots who aren't from Bergort. Really experienced *shunos* with helmets and slingshots and shit. "

"But who then?" Yasmine says. "Who's organizing it? And why, what do they want?"

Ignacio seems to think for a moment before he answers.

"*Ey*, Yazz, you know how it is? Always so much talk. I swear, one day people will talk themselves to death out there. Some say it's a conspiracy. Some corporation is behind it. Somebody's doing it to hold us down, ya know? Some say they saw some sweet Audi hanging out by the parking lot outside of school and one of those masked types took orders from there."

Ignacio laughs and shakes his head.

"Same stoner talk as usual. It's Jews and the Illuminati paying for everything as usual."

"But why break into my hotel room and spray that fucking symbol on my wall? What do I have to do with any of this?"

They're almost at the subway now.

"Someone ratted you out to them," he says. "Somebody told them you were asking questions, but it wasn't me. Somebody else must know. You must have talked to somebody about this."

They look at each other quietly.

"But one thing I'll tell you," he continues. "Or I don't know if I should tell you, because I'd rather you just forget this, Yazz."

"Say what you know, Ignacio. I'll find out anyway."

"I know," he says, looking worried. "OK, so. There were some crazy riots last night, right?"

Yasmine nods.

"I was out before it started," he says. "You know, after our talk. I wanted to know more. So I grabbed some kids I know. Ali Five's little brother and his friends. They're always out late, always got their hands full of rocks and bottles. And they told me they were getting their orders from some masked guy. Or not a guy, a man. They didn't know who he was, but there were several of them sort of directing the kids. And they usually meet at the Camp Nou, you know, the football field? So if you wanna find out that's where you should start. But I wish you wouldn't, Yazz."

She nods.

"Thanks. I'll be careful."

"Be careful with that snitch, and don't wave that gun around too much. Next time they might not settle for a warning, right? And it could be anyone."

Yasmine bends up and hugs him.

"I already know who it is," she whispers.

Chapter 30

Syria—May–June 2015

The days pass by. Our positions are locked at the frontline, neither we nor al-Assad are strong enough to destroy the other, and the battle is slow and increasingly mechanical. Among the sandbags, homemade grenades, and glossy eyes, we make fast, halfhearted attacks and even faster retreats. It reminds me of when I was younger, when we used to run toward the police on burning summer nights with our hands full of rocks and our heads full of poverty and overcrowding and testosterone. But now, our goals are grander, our motivation and perseverance something else. Now we're better armed and the enemy responds with barrel bombs and snipers instead of batons.

Brother Shahid takes me up to the front sometimes when he feels like I'm ready to give up. When he sees that I can't take any more boot polishing or shopping with the wives in the market.

"You shoot better now," he says, opening the door to the passenger side. "Maybe we can get some use from you today?"

And when he says that, I am filled with pride and anticipation, my shoulders rise, my chest expands, I jump in next to him, and we drive in silence up to the battle.

But when we get there I'm given no task, or I don't know how to find a task. The brothers are coordinated, like actors or dancers. They have their safe spots and holes in the wall where they shoot and duck, shoot and duck. They have places where they drop their homemade grenades, their patterns and rituals. And I have nothing. Just awkwardness and a lack of ability and balance. Instead, I boil tea and help them build the wall, filling sandbags and lining up our homemade mortars.

This is what my jihad is. Not like a sword, more like a brush to polish my brothers' shoes. Not like a spinning bullet, headed for the head of the enemy, but like an empty case, left on the ground, meaningless. But I say my prayers and I read my Qur'an. I take satisfaction from what we talk about in the evenings in the glow of the camp stove: we are in this together, we are fighting for our brothers and sisters, we are building a society that would please Muhammad, peace be upon him.

And some nights when I lie on my cool mattress I am filled with it. Some nights it's as if I could touch the very essence of it, as if I could hold it in my hands and my heart. Other nights it's not enough at all, and I sit in the window and look out over the dark and count the stars until the distance and emptiness threaten to destroy me.

I tell none of this to brother al-Amin during our short and irregular talks over the crackly satellite phone. Instead, I tell about the heroism at the front, replacing myself as the protagonist in my brothers' stories. And brother al-Amin listens and praises me and tells me how well I've integrated and how proud Allah, may he be glorified and exalted, must be of me. He often mentions the traitor and always tells me to be careful not to reveal that we're talking. He's not even certain brother Shahid can be trusted. But together we can solve this, he says. Meanwhile, it's important that he gets a good overview of how we live here. He's interested in the details, asks me to send pictures of my room and the area, which I do gladly. Then I don't even have to lie but can for once just document and tell.

"Our chance will come," he says often. "Be on your guard. I have a plan. Sometimes someone important comes to the front to check on the troops. You know, they sleep in different beds every night so that the dogs and lackeys who spy for the West, may they burn forever in hellfire, won't be able to execute them with their bombs and drones. When that happens, we'll put our plan into action."

"What's the plan?" I say and feel excitement growing within me. "What can I do?"

"Just make sure you tell me when that happens," brother al-Amin says. "Then I'll make sure we have the chance to save our leaders and reveal the *murtaden* who is behind this."

It's sometime in June, a little after lunch, when I see brother Tariq's car racing along the dusty red street outside our house. It's already as warm as a summer day in Bergort, and, after trying to fix a water pipe in one of the bathrooms, I'm leaning against the sun-warmed wall with a cup of mint tea in my hand. It's rare that someone comes back from the battle in the middle of the day, and I think something must have happened. Maybe somebody's been wounded or killed by those dogs in a cowardly attack, and when I see him slow down I rise up and jog toward him as he exits the car, weapon in hand.

"Brother Tariq," I say. "What has happened?"

As usual, he looks at me with a mixture of disdain and suspicion, and I regret that I ran toward him like an idiot, like a servant or a slave.

"I have a mission for you, Fadi," he says.

Always Fadi. Never brother. As if he doesn't think I'm worthy of even that.

"OK," I say. "I do what I can to serve Allah, may he be glorified and exalted."

"You know the guesthouse?"

I nod. The guesthouse is a deserted apartment building that stands near the village's small square, the only part of town where a few civilians still live. We've also slept in the guesthouse, it's important that we keep moving around so that the dogs and lackeys don't find out where we are and bomb us in the night.

"Sure," I say. "Why?"

"We're having guests tonight," he says. "I want you and the women to prepare three apartments with mattresses and sheets. For twelve."

"Twelve?" I say.

It's rare that we have any guests at all. Occasionally a group travels through on their way to another frontline, another eternal struggle, and stops for a night, but not more than once or twice since I came. And never so many at once.

"Yes," says Tariq. "Twelve. Do you think you can arrange that?"

Again, that superior expression in his eyes, that smug smile on his face. I swallow, and the thought occurs to me that perhaps this is what brother al-Amin has been talking about? Perhaps this is precisely what the traitor is waiting for? Important guests that the traitor can report to the government troops.

"Absolutely," I say. "Of course. Who's coming?"

"That's nothing you need to worry about today, Fadi," he says. "Just make sure there are mattresses and water. And ask sister Mona and the others to get a lamb at the market."

"A whole lamb?"

"That's what I said, wasn't it?"

Tariq turns around and goes back to his jeep, throws the Kalashnikov on the seat next to him, and drives back in the direction he came from.

I wait until the dust settles on the gravel, and the only thing I hear is the irregular, never-ending hack of gunfire from the front, before I pull up the satellite phone from my pocket. With my heart pounding, I call brother al-Amin.

Chapter 31

London—Thursday, August 20, 2015

Klara feels temporarily paralyzed by the sight of Patrick Shapiro wrestling with the seemingly jammed door. Not until he finally gets it open and disappears inside does she spring to action, knocking back the last of her wine.

Without looking away from the building, she crosses the pub and exits out onto the street to get a good view of all the floors. She lights a cigarette and stands close to the entrance of the pub, so as to be less obvious if Patrick looks out the window.

It takes about a minute, but then a light goes on in a third-floor window. It's too high for her to be able to see into the room, but she can make out shadows moving along the walls.

Patrick. Was he really the one who took her computer? Was he in the alley on Sunday night? Sure, he's an oddball, but she still finds it hard to believe that he would be involved in stealing her computer.

Maybe it's the wine, but for once she feels strong and focused, almost angry. What the hell is wrong with that fucking nerd? Stealing her computer, installing fucking spyware on it? Is he a stalker?

Or could it be as banal as jealousy that she's the one who's helping Charlotte with the report? Why else would he have *The Stockholm Conference* written on the whiteboard in his office? She's heard about how it works in universities, people stealing each other's work, backstabbing each other. But this? To steal and hack into a colleague's computer?

What did he hope to find? Or was it simply that he was out to destroy her: erase what she's done and make her look completely incompetent in Charlotte's eyes?

Here she'd been afraid all this had something to do with Christmas two years ago, the international scandal, the intelligence services. And it's something as petty as this. Something as petty as academic jealousy. Something as petty as Patrick Shapiro.

Before she has any more time to think, the light goes off in the apartment, and she recedes into the shadows. Soon a soft light flows through the door of 3 Formosa Street, and she sees Patrick's silhouette framed there. He shuts the door carefully and starts walking quickly toward the Tube station at Warwick Avenue.

She hesitates a second, lets him get a bit of a head start while trying to calm herself.

Before she's gone no more than thirty feet, she stops and retreats into the protection of the building again. From the shadows on the other side of the street, two figures have emerged to follow Patrick. And there's something about the stonewashed jeans they have on. Something about their shiny leather jackets and broad shoulders. Something about how they move, how they blend in and stand out at the same time. Something that tells her this might actually be more complicated than she thought. Something that's not just about Patrick and academic jealousy.

At the same time, she can't stay away. The wine and her newfound focus pull her along Warwick Avenue, surfing on a small, barely noticeable wave of recklessness and negligence, making her feel, for a moment, totally alive in the moment, without past.

She can't see Patrick anymore, focuses instead on leather jackets and keeps herself at such a distance that she almost loses them. And when she gets to the subway, she's sure she has. But at the last moment she spots a crew cut disappearing down the stairs. She doesn't see Patrick anywhere. He must already be down by the tracks.

She tiptoes carefully down the stairs to the platform. But she doesn't even get halfway before an incredible squeaking noise, steel screeching on steel, reaches her from the platform. It sounds like an incoming train is about to derail, like a disaster is under way.

Instinctively she stands up, feels her head spinning even faster, the world turning around her. What's going on? She can't stay here, she has to know, so she speeds up, taking two steps at a time until she's finally down on the platform.

The smell of moisture and metal hits her. The noise from the train subsides and is replaced by hysterical, screaming voices. She registers as if in a dream that the train has stopped now, halfway into the station, like a weary manga dragon, smooth and white and exhausted.

There are maybe thirty people in the station, some standing still, hands to their mouths or still on their ears, even though the station is oddly silent now.

Suddenly someone screams. A man and a woman run toward the front of the train. The whole scene is surreal, as if a window has opened between the normal world, where you wait calmly for the Tube, to a world of chaos, where people scream at the top of their lungs and trains look like dragons and stop halfway into the station.

She looks around but can see neither Patrick nor the leather jackets. She makes her way to the nearest person, a black guy in a suit around her own age. He looks calm, doesn't scream, stands silently just staring at the stationary train, as if it were an installation, a huge still life of isolated chaos.

"What happened?" she says.

The man is still in some kind of shock, she realizes, his mouth is half open, and he can't stop staring at the front of the train. Slowly he turns to Klara, his eyes not quite complying, as if they look past her, or through her. He points toward the train in a hesitant gesture of surprise and confusion.

"Somebody fell on the tracks," he says. "A guy. Just now."

Chapter 32

Bergort—Thursday, August 20, 2015

If not Ignacio, then there's only one other possibility, a betrayal that's even bigger, and even more surprising.

Parisa, Yasmine thinks as she winds her way through the commuters at the Slussen subway station. But why her?

Why would Parisa betray her? Bergort's loyalties are hard to grasp, even when you're part of Bergort. But now after being gone so long, she knows nothing. Still she'd believed their friendship was stronger than this.

But who knows? Maybe Parisa simply mentioned to Mehdi that she met Yasmine. Perhaps he'd drawn his own conclusions? The question remains why would Mehdi threaten her? All she wants to do is find Fadi. Find out if he's alive. If he's back.

She can't think straight in the subway among the dirt and tiles, and she pushes her way through the turnstile and out into the drizzle on Södermalmstorg. Gamla Stan is laid out like a pastel cake in front of her. When you say you're from Stockholm, is this what people think of? A Stockholm of water and yellow plaster. A Stockholm of green islands and outdoor cafés. She's never even thought of this as Stockholm. Her Stockholm is Bergort.

She crosses the street and leans against the fence, looks down toward the water and the city. What's going on exactly? Fadi is alive. It fills her with a strange tenderness. Happiness almost, or a hope for happiness. But also emptiness. And the guns under the bed? What is he mixed up in?

Suddenly she misses David. Not the David she left a week ago in New York, not the David whose fist is still pounding in her temple. She misses the David she moved to New York with. The David who helped her understand she couldn't stay in the concrete anymore, or not in that concrete, not Bergort. The David who made her realize that Bergort pulled her down and held her captive in its patterns and unequal, dysfunctional loyalties. She misses the David who worked all day and painted at night so they could escape together. That David had so much energy and love that if you squinted you couldn't see the hole and the emptiness inside him. That David allowed her to ignore the consequences and warnings, and he gave her the courage to let go. And how has she repaid the debt? How did she reciprocate what he did for her when she needed it most? By leaving him when he needed her most.

She sinks down next to the fence and exhales slowly. For almost a week, she's been able to avoid these thoughts. But she knew she'd end up here eventually. That what she provoked in Brooklyn was only a transient spell and couldn't protect her forever. But she couldn't afford to give in to these thoughts now.

She has to steel herself.

Slowly she stands up. David and Fadi. Her own mother. Everything she's run from. Everything she needs to keep running from. How can you live when you're constantly pulled in opposite directions?

But she's made her choice. She's known since Fadi disappeared, since the news of his death. Since the news of his return to Bergort.

She's been given just one more chance to never betray him again. Slowly she turns around and goes back to the subway.

There's something in the air in Bergort. She senses it as soon as she steps off the train. Something prickling and crackling just outside what the senses can catch. A lingering air of tear gas and acetone, batons and burning rubber. She sees broken glass on the platform, sees stencils sprayed onto every column, sees it in the eyes of the commuters. Bergort is filling up. Someone has left the gas on, and all it takes is one little match.

Yasmine recognizes it from other summers, other idle, unemployed summers. When frustration grew out of sandpits and empty refrigerators, closed recreation centers and lost football games. From the anxiety of the summer being all too short, from boredom because summer had been too long, the repetition and the lack of money, lack of will, lack of power. Summers when riots were sparked by almost nothing at all.

She sees that now as she walks down the ramp toward the shopping center. Sees a pair of burned-out cars in the parking lot. See the eyes of the kids outside the Syrian's shop, sees it in how they hold their cigarettes in the afternoon light, spitting and blowing smoke up toward the elusive clouds. Sees it in their eyes and their hyperactive focus. Hears it in their brief chuckles. It has begun now. The fuse is lit.

Parisa isn't at the salon, and Yasmine doesn't want Parisa's mother to see her, so she speeds up as she passes by on her way to Pirate Square. She sees the symbol sprayed everywhere. There's something unpleasant about it, something that reminds her of totalitarian propaganda.

The square is empty, and the checkerboard tiles remain smooth and slippery from morning rain. She walks past a stupid frozen chicken sign, and its complete lack of imagination suddenly enrages her, and she slams it as hard as she can. But it barely moves, just squeaks and wobbles in its rusty frame. She raises her eyes to the concrete and the satellite dishes.

"Fadi," she whispers. "Where are you, little brother?"

Parisa's building looks just like it always has, like all the other buildings always have. Ten floors of cracked plaster, balconies in peeling pastel, the lame attempt to lighten up the gray is irritating. The door is unlocked, just open it and trudge the seven floors up, because as usual the elevator is out of order.

Climbing up the stairs is like traveling back in time: the echo of her feet on the steps, the cool air, the smell of garlic and hamburger frying somewhere, the muffled sound of a baby screaming. She thinks of winter nights when they had nowhere to go, when the bus shelters got too cold and the recreation center had long since closed. How they pushed open the door to a building where none of them lived and drank low-alcohol beer they bought from the Syrian and the smoke from their cigarettes was blue and stiff as it poured out into the cold through the half-open door, out into the glare of the streetlights. She can't decide if that feels like a long time ago or yesterday.

She's out of breath by the time she reaches the seventh floor, behind her the echo of her own footsteps linger. The big gun chafes inside the waistband of her jeans. She approaches Parisa's door and rings the bell while placing her finger over the small peephole.

Someone's moving around inside, feet shuffling across the floor, a voice speaks soothingly, as if to a small child. The feet stop on the other side of the door, a moment while the person probably tries to look through the peephole, then the sound of the lock turning. The door opens a small gap, the door chain is still on. Yasmine can see a small child in Parisa's arms.

"*Sho*, Parisa," she says.

She turns her head, looks through the gap, smiles with her mouth, but not her eyes.

"Yasmine?" Parisa says and even in the dim light Yasmine can see her stress level rise.

"We need to talk, *sister*," she says.

Her voice is cold, obviously ironic. Parisa strokes the baby nervously across the cheek and shifts her eyes. She throws a glance over her shoulder, then leans closer to the gap and lowers her voice.

"Not here," she says. "Not now."

Yasmine feels anxious and frustrated, anger building inside her. She just wants to grab Parisa and pull her out onto the landing, throw her down onto the stone floor, and scream at her: Who the fuck are you, bitch? What are you doing to me?

But the baby on her arm makes all that impossible, and Yasmine allows her fury to slide away.

"So when?" she hisses.

"Tomorrow," Parisa says and lowers her voice even further.

Something gleams in her eyes, and she nods her head almost imperceptibly backward toward the apartment.

"I know something about Fadi," she whispers. "Just wait until tomorrow."

Again, a glance over her shoulder.

"The playground. At three o'clock."

Chapter 33

Syria—June 2015

I hear the engines in the distance, cutting through the silence where I sit in the open window facing the street. The moon is almost full, the village silver under the dim light, and the shadows are long and black. The brothers are down at the guesthouse, and I can smell grilled lamb from up here in the apartment where Tariq and I often sleep.

I should be down at the guesthouse too, but during my feverish call to brother al-Amin earlier today, he asked me to wait here and take pictures of the cars and let him know as soon as they're on their way.

It takes a minute before I see the bright headlights of the first car appear at the end of the street. They're approaching fast, and I soon count four vehicles, not like the dusty, shitty cars we drive, but two black SUVs with tinted windows and two pickups with large machine guns mounted to their beds. I pick up the phone and take a few pictures and text them directly to brother al-Amin before going down to the guesthouse.

I'm halfway there when I feel the phone vibrating in my pocket, and I pick it up. There's a photo of an Arab man with heavy, tired eyes and a huge grizzled beard, maybe he's in his fifties, maybe younger. It's hard to know with brothers who've been here a long time, battle ages you, as if one year equals five.

"If that's the leader of your guests, then we'll put the plan into action," al-Amin writes. "He's wise and strong. Confirm when you've seen him. *Inshallah*, soon we'll have the traitor, brother!"

I can feel the blood pumping through me, and I hold my Kalashnikov closer, and study the picture carefully. I don't understand exactly how brother al-Amin is going to solve this, but I'm sure the dog will soon be punished, and it fills me with joy as I speed up my steps.

The guests have stepped out of their cars and are standing with the brothers around the grill I built earlier. Just a couple of blocks of cement with an iron grate over them, but the smell of the lamb Mona marinated for hours is spicy and garlicky. We don't usually eat badly, just modestly and purely so as not to detract from our prayers and Allah. I haven't eaten large chunks of tender, grilled lamb since I got here, and I notice how hungry I am.

The guests are dressed like us, the same worn camouflage and scarves, the Kalashnikovs thrown over their shoulders. But there's something about them, something in their attitude, the way they stand, which makes it obvious they belong to another division. I think of Red and Blackeye and you. I think how we all looked the same, even if you were older. But we weren't the same. It was clear from the beginning who would die on the frontlines and who would leave in their SUVs with tinted windows.

Brother Shahid sees me and waves me closer.

"This is brother Fadi Ajam," he says in Arabic to the group. "Our newest member. Like me he's from Sweden, and he's repatriated, Allah be praised, to help us free our Arab brothers and sisters. "

"*As-salamu alaykum*," the guests say.

"*Wa alykum salam*," I reply.

That's when I see him. The man from brother al-Amin's picture. I see his grizzled beard in the glow of the fire, I see his tired eyes. He looks like he's at least fifty, maybe older. Suddenly brother Umar is standing next to me.

"You know who he is?" he whispers in Swedish.

I shake my head.

"He's from Yemen. Responsible for training camps and foreign soldiers."

He lowers his voice even further.

"Rumor has it he's totally ruthless."

I turn to look at brother Umar, but he looks away. We never criticize anything when we sit drinking tea and talking in the evenings. But you can read between the lines that many of the brothers have a difficult time living with some decisions. The attacks in Europe. Mass executions. I know that Umar and Shahid think as I do, that it's the wrong approach, barbaric, and pointless. The battle is here. Liberation is here. We can live as Muslims here. The rest can wait. But we say nothing. We leave it to Allah, may he be glorified and exalted.

Now I turn my gaze back to the man with the gray beard again. Brother al-Amin wrote that he was wise, he'll help us uncover the traitor. That's the most important thing now. I'm so hungry, but this is important, and when brother Umar moves on, I slowly make my way away from the fire until I'm sure no one is looking at me. Why should they care? I'm basically a servant, a gofer.

I sneak around the corner and out the back of one of the buildings. From the front you hear the occasional shot. Evenings are quiet, the brothers who are there now only hold our position. Cautiously, I take the phone out of my pocket and dial brother al-Amin. He answers on the first ring.

"Brother Fadi," he says. "Is that our man?"

“Yes,” I say. “It’s the man in the picture. The leader. What do I do?”

“Go back to the fire,” brother al-Amin says. “Eat and behave like usual. I’ll be in touch soon.”

And with that he’s gone. No *as-salamu alaykum*. No Allah, may he be exalted. I stand there, quietly, with the phone in my hand.

How did he know we have a fire?

But I don’t have time to think further before I hear steps behind me on the gravel. And before turning around, I hear the metallic sound of a rifle’s safety being disengaged.

Chapter 34

London—Thursday, August 20, 2015

Klara turns toward the rails again. It's as though the platform and the big white dragon are trembling under the yellow overhead lights, as if the people around her are moving jerkily, clumsily, and she struggles to get her bearings. She sees several people, two or three—she can't seem to count anymore—move to the front of the train, the driver opens the door, he's on his way out of the train. But it seems like he's moving in slow motion, eyes scrunched up, his fists knotted.

She hesitates, but her feet move as if by themselves toward the small group of people gathered at the edge. A woman has jumped down on the track, another leans over the edge of the platform. They talk loudly, yelling at each other, but their voices are strangely subdued, Klara can barely hear them. The driver is in front of the group now. He's angry.

"What a fucking idiot!" he roars. "In front of my train!"

His voice isn't muted, it's shrill and horrible, and he beats his fists on the train so hard that the plastic or metal, or whatever it's made of, thunders. Then he turns and collapses, empty and wrinkled like an empty balloon, with his back to the train. It seems like he's crying, like he's shaking with sobs, and someone squats down next to him and gets him to sit down on the platform with his legs straight out like a child.

And her legs move her closer and closer to the edge of the platform, apparently unaware that she wants to stay where she is, that she wants to turn around and disappear. But suddenly she's right in front of the track, and even though she wants to close her eyes and turn away, neither her eyes nor neck seem to obey her, and she bends over the tracks.

And then she sees him. And doesn't even notice that she's screaming until someone puts an arm around her and leads her away from the edge, toward the middle of the platform and sits her down on a green, scratched wooden bench.

When the shaky film ends and her vision goes back to normal, the platform is full of firefighters and paramedics, stretchers, bags that look like they contain important lifesaving instruments. But it's far too late to save any lives.

Next to her someone is talking to a police officer, not a bobby in one of those helmets, but a regular police officer in a hat and a belt full of pockets, but no gun.

"Then he just stepped right out in front of the train," the voice says. "It was as if he stumbled, as if he lost his balance and kind of jumped by mistake."

"You saw the whole thing?" the officer asks.

"I think so," the voice continues. "From the corner of my eye."

The voice is so pleased with itself, so pleased to be such a splendid fucking witness. Klara turns toward it and sees that it belongs to a man in his fifties, wearing a suit, short sideburns. Affluent, accustomed to being listened to. But he didn't see this. What he's saying isn't true.

"Someone pushed him," she says, quietly at first.

Sideburns loses his train of thought and turns toward her.

The officer turns too, his eyebrows rise above his friendly, brown eyes.

"Excuse me?" the officer says.

"Someone pushed him," Klara says, notices how difficult it is to speak, the words almost have to be squeezed out of her mouth. "Two guys. Two guys in leather jackets. Crew cuts."

Sideburns looks confused at first. Then he smiles uncertainly, catches the policeman's eyes. But the officer turns toward Klara.

"Did you see this?" he says.

There's interest in his voice now. Klara wraps her arms around herself, she's freezing suddenly. It was so hot before, how could it be so cold now? She shakes her head.

"I came down just as it happened," she says.

"So you didn't see the man fall in front of the train?" the officer says.

"Like I said, he didn't fall. He was pushed by fucking gangsters."

"But you didn't see it?"

She stands up. What is it he doesn't understand?

"No," she says. "I didn't see it happen, but I know how it happened. I know he was being followed."

There's a different light in the officer's eyes now. Another kind of smile on Sideburns' face. He puts his hand on her, protective, condescending, coddling.

"I understand," the officer says. "We'll talk later, OK?"

"Did you hear what I said?" Klara says. "They pushed him!"

She bends forward toward the officer, so close that she almost touches the brim of his silly hat. He pulls back slightly, pushes her away gently with his hands still resting on her shoulders. She knocks them away.

"Miss," the officer says. "Have you been drinking tonight?"

"Drinking?" Klara says. "What does that have to do with anything?"

The officer glances at Sideburns. They exchange a knowing glance, and the officer shakes his head. Klara takes a step toward him again, into his sphere, catches a whiff of soap and sweat. Inside her something red and dangerous is growing.

"No one else has reported anything similar to what you're saying now," the officer says. "I'll listen to you as well, but you need to calm down, OK?"

"Listen to me now, goddammit," Klara says. "I saw two gangsters follow him down to the platform. Men in their forties with crew cuts. Eastern Europeans."

She doesn't mean to raise her voice, but their condescending expressions provoke her.

"You can think I'm hysterical all you want," she says. "But I saw what I fucking saw. I know the guy lying there on the tracks. His name is Patrick."

She's shouting now, and she notices a strange silence has settled over the platform, the concrete seems to be sucking up every other sound except her voice. The officer turns to her again. His warm gaze has hardened now.

"Miss! Please, Miss. There's no reason to scream. I'll take your statement, I promise. As soon as I'm done with this gentleman."

He gestures toward Sideburns, who gives Klara a look that's so fucking condescending it drives her crazy. And that little smile.

"Just sit down here and someone will help you soon," the policeman says and takes her gently by the elbow, leads her back to the bench. "Wait here for a bit."

Then he turns to Sideburns again.

"We'll continue over here," he says, pointing toward the protection of a thick concrete column.

She tastes the wine and adrenaline in her mouth. They're going to ignore her. No one else saw those two men. She is hysterical, the woman who's seeing things. They've already made up their minds.

She puts her head in her hands and stares down into the concrete, sitting like that for a few minutes. No one comes to check on her. Suddenly she feels it again. Her rage is growing. They pamper and coddle. Fix and talk. But when it really matters, you're alone. Always completely alone. She looks down toward the pillar where the officer and Sideburns are still standing. She can see Sideburns gesturing and pointing as he gives his incomplete, inaccurate statement. It doesn't matter, his type are always believed.

She casts a last glance toward the pillar, then rises quietly, and walks away toward unmoving escalators. She's alone in this. No one but she knows what happened.

Halfway up the stairs her legs start to tremble, she can barely stay upright, and when she holds her hand in front of her she sees it shaking uncontrollably.

Patrick was pushed in front of the train. They pushed him in front of the train.

She feels sick. He took her computer, then he was murdered.

Chapter 35

Syria—June 2015

"Who were you talking to, dog?"

Tariq's voice is calm and cool. Almost the same as always. I spin around, and it feels like all the oxygen leaves my head, as if no matter how hard I try I can't get any air into my lungs. I just stare at him with the phone in my hand. Just stare at the muzzle of the Kalashnikov, large and round and black and aimed at me. He stands ready with the gun against his shoulder, safety off, looking at my chest through the sight. It's completely silent. No hacking from the front, no voices from our brothers. It's just me and Tariq here.

Everything rushes through me now. Brother al-Amin's voice. How did he know we had a fire? And the muzzle perfectly round and dark in front of me now.

Then the phone rings again. I feel it vibrate and see it light up in my hand, like a flashlight in the dark. Tariq waves the barrel impatiently.

"Who is it?" he says. "Who the hell are you talking to, dog?"

"No one," I say. "My imam at home."

"Answer," he says. "Speakerphone, or I swear to God I will shoot you here and now."

I hesitate. Whatever I do, I'm going to die. Is this a martyr's death? Shot in the chest because of a misunderstanding in a dusty yard behind an abandoned house?

Phone vibrates in my hand. I don't want to die. Martyr or not. I just don't want to die. Not now. Not for this.

"Take it easy," I say. "Take it easy."

I hold the phone in front of me, theatrically. Press "answer," press "speaker," hear brother al-Amin's voice, breathless and excited now.

"Are you back inside by the fire, Fadi?" he says without greeting me. "You have to go back to your leader now, you understand? Otherwise, we won't be able to expose the traitor."

I look at the phone and turn my eyes to Tariq. He lowered the gun slightly now, listening with a confused expression on his face.

"I..." I begin. "I'll go to him now."

"Hurry up!" brother al-Amin commands. "We have only a brief window to reveal who this is! Go now!"

"Just one thing," I say, and swallow. "How did you know we had a fire?"

There's silence for a moment, just al-Amin's breath. Then: "You said so, brother Fadi. You said you were going to grill. Don't you remember?"

"No," I say. "I didn't say that."

"Forget this, brother," al-Amin says. "Just go to the leader now so we can get this over with."

I look at Tariq who nods meaningfully. He's lowered his gun now and appears to think for a second. Then he stretches out lightning fast and grabs the phone. Screams straight into the receiver: "Who are you? Who the hell are you working for?"

I hear several voices in the background, hear a click as brother al-Amin hangs up. Tariq seems temporarily paralyzed. He just stands there with the phone in his hand.

"He said we had a traitor among us," I whisper. "That we had to expose him."

Tariq looks up at me with sudden insight in his eyes.

"He's right," he says. "The traitor is you, Fadi."

Then everything happens too fast. Tariq throws his gun on his back. He takes a few steps out of the house and studies the dark sky, which shimmers in the moonlight, seems to be listening. And then we hear it, both of us at the same time, and we look at each other, and I know that my life has changed now. That everything is falling apart around me. That nothing is what it appears to be. No one is who they appear to be.

It's as if we're paralyzed at first. Only that almost imperceptible sound. A gentle humming from high above getting closer and closer. A big insect on its way down. There is only one thing it can be. What we hide from and fear every day.

A drone.

And everything crashes over me as we stand there without moving. Brother al-Amin is the traitor.

All of them are traitors. Brother Dakhil and brother Taimur and brother Tasheem. They are all traitors. The realization hits me like a bomb, that's what this was about the whole time. That was why they took care of me, why they helped me and supported me. Why they let me go to Syria. They had this in mind the whole time. That one day I would give them the opportunity to complete their treachery.

The thought is dizzying. All the prayers and meetings in Bergort. For a whole year. They tricked me. Used me. For what?

Who are they? Whose side are they on?

Hatred and resignation wash over me like an ocean, a tsunami, obliterating everything in its path, all my piety and my desire to do right. Everything.

I sink to my knees. Above us the noise of the drone becomes even more urgent. What should we do? The gravel is cool against my palms where I kneel on all fours. What should we do?

But Tariq pulls me up by the shoulders.

"Come!" he roars. "We have to get out of here! Don't you get it? They're gonna wipe us out!"

The first explosion makes my eardrums shake, makes my head ring and howl. I feel the gravel under my chest and my stomach, my legs, and I open my eyes as the second missile hits the place behind the building where the other brothers sit and eat. The whole world is white and deafening. Phosphor and annihilation.

I lie on my stomach. I lie on my back. I sit up. I feel someone pulling me up, and I turn my head to the left and see Tariq. His face is dirty and bloody. I see his lips move, and I get to my feet, I follow him as he runs across the yard, through the door of one of the houses. We stumble and fall over each other down the stairs into the basement. Behind us the world explodes as a missile hits the place where we just were. Mortar and flakes of paint fall on us as we lie on our bellies on the cool concrete floor.

Then silence. Complete and absolute silence.

Chapter 36

Stockholm—Thursday, August 20, 2015

The subway back to the city. Yasmine hardly registers it. She climbs the stairs out of the central station and exits into the balmy evening. She can't stop thinking about the only thing that matters.

Slowly she walks along the water toward the Lydmar. It's almost automatic, she doesn't decide to go back to the hotel, it just happens.

Parisa knows something about Fadi.

She pushes aside thoughts of her friend's betrayal and the baby and Parisa's anxious gaze. It's impossible to understand all of Bergort's connections and motives. Not if you've been away as long as she has.

Yasmine feels the lingering effects of jet lag in her body. She needs to sleep a few hours before heading out to Bergort again to follow up on what Ignacio told her, whatever's happening in the artificial grass at Camp Nou.

Her thoughts start to spin. Parisa was the only one besides Ignacio who knew where she lived. Parisa must have mentioned it to someone with connections to the riots, or whatever this is. Maybe she did it on purpose? Maybe not. But who's trying so hard to keep her away from Bergort? Why is it so sensitive when she asks questions about Fadi and those symbols?

And now Parisa knows something about Fadi. Something she didn't want to say through the crack in the door.

Yasmine stops at Strömbron and looks up at the beige, dirty walls of the Royal Palace, then father out across the silvery water, she sees the boats near the dock, the green of Skeppsholmen behind that. It's beautiful, she thinks. There is a version of Stockholm that is breathtakingly beautiful.

But something makes her feel uneasy, and she turns away from the palace and the water and back toward the Opera House and the Royal Garden. Traffic stands still at the traffic lights, but between two cars she can see across to the other side. A man in a shiny blue tracksuit and a hoodie is standing there. White sneakers, shaved head, and a flat boxer's nose, green tribal tattoos wind their way up his neck from his shirt. He stares straight at her, and when he sees that she's looking at him, smiles calmly and arrogantly without moving.

The traffic light turns green, and the cars slowly start moving again. She stands as frozen as the asphalt, while her view is obscured by a gray van slowly rolling past. She feels the gun chafe against her back.

When the van finally rolls by, the man has disappeared. As if he'd never been there. As if he'd never seen her. She shudders in the heat. Oh my God, is she becoming paranoid?

She speeds up her steps toward the Lydmar. Every ten steps she throws a glance over her shoulder, but sees only the usual mix of tourists enjoying a late-summer stroll by the water and affluent locals pushing their strollers as neat as insects toward the Svenskt Tenn store. On her way through the reception she nods to the doorman and goes straight for the elevators.

But in the corridor outside her room she stops. Something is hanging from a thin string on the handle. Slowly she moves toward the door. At least it's not a strangled cat, she thinks. Instead, it's a small envelope.

She loosens the cord from the handle, opens the door, and goes into her room. With a pounding heart, she sits down on the unmade bed with the envelope in her hands. She closes her eyes and opens it, takes hold of its contents—a simple, folded letter-size page—and removes it.

She slowly unfolds the paper. It's a picture again, a printed photograph. This time it's a masked man pointing a large, black gun straight at the camera, at her. He's broad-shouldered and between the collar of the T-shirt and his mask you can see a green tribal tattoo. She turns the paper over. Four words: Go to the window.

She places the piece of paper on the bed and feels her head constricting. Without really wanting to, without being able to stop herself, she gets up quietly and walks the few steps to the window.

She gently pulls away the thick, opaque curtains, and the palace and the water towers emerge in front of her. She allows her eyes to sweep over the view before dropping them down to the street between the hotel and the water.

And there he is. No more than a hundred feet away, on the street, with his back to the water and his gaze on her. Shiny tracksuit and hoodie, white shoes and a green unmistakable tattoo scaling his neck.

When he sees her in the window, he raises his arm. The smile is now replaced by an indifferent, seemingly blank stare. He continues to slowly raise his arm until it is pointing straight at her. He shapes his hand into a gun and makes a motion, as if he's pulling the trigger. Then he lowers his arm and stands still for a second, before calmly turning around and disappearing along the quay.

Chapter 37

Syria—June 2015

I don't know how long we stay on the floor without moving or speaking. Dead still.

It's quiet outside. All we hear is the monotonous buzzing of one or two drones, which seem to be lingering to assess and evaluate the extent of what they've just wiped out. But eventually they disappear and all is completely silent.

"Tariq?" I say.

He moves beneath the layer of mortar and plaster, flaking paint and cracked glass, and turns to me. I see his face is covered in blood and ash and dirt. He says nothing, just looks at me.

"You're hurt," I say. "Blood on your face."

He looks at me with those cold eyes, eyes which despised me before and hate me now. Then he gets up and brushes off the worst of the dirt, roots around until he finds his Kalashnikov. He stands up on unsteady legs.

"We have to get out," he says. "You, too *khain*—fucking traitor. Especially you."

He goes ahead of me up the stairs and opens the door onto the gravel. A ray of moonlight falls through the gap in the door. I stand up, too. Grab the gun and phone, and follow him.

Just outside the door there's a deep crater, apparently the missile the drone sent after us when we fled. They really wanted to wipe us all out.

*

Brother al-Amin. The one who was my brother. Who I *thought* was my brother. In the end, he didn't hesitate to send me straight to my death. He urged me toward my death.

And why? Who are the brothers working for? Al-Assad? One of our other enemies? Jabhat al-Nusra? But only the Americans have drones, right? Somehow, they sold us out to the Americans. Sold *me* out to the Americans.

Deceit and my gullibility. Thinking about it, I'm overcome by sudden nausea, and I vomit crouching against the wall. By the time I'm finished Tariq has already rounded the crater and is halfway across the yard, halfway to the house on the other side of the square where the brothers were.

I don't want to see where the missiles hit. I don't know if I can take being confronted with the massacre I brought down on us. My head hurts so bad, it feels like I haven't slept for days, weeks, and I stagger forward, barely able to keep myself upright.

But I know there are no excuses now. This is something I have to face. There is no way to avoid this, and I hurry until I catch up with Tariq.

He doesn't look at me—pretends I'm not even there—as he walks with calm, firm steps across the courtyard.

"I swear, with Allah as my witness, I swear I didn't know anything about this," I say. "They tricked me. I thought we were going to uncover a traitor in the group."

Tears flow down my cheeks now, and I need to hear something from Tariq, need him to recognize that I'm here, with him. It's as if it would be a kind of blessing if only he turned and looked at me. But he doesn't. He just keeps walking, as if he's alone, as if I were air, less than air, nothing.

We both stop at the corner of the courtyard because we

hear voices and a car engine. After a second, Tariq squats down and peeks around the corner. It seems it's our people out there, and he stands up immediately and goes forward. Voices are raised inside the courtyard, feet run toward him, implore him to lie down, but he refuses.

I stay on the other side of the corner, barely breathing, not sure what it will do to me to be confronted by the consequences of what I've done. I lean against the rough concrete of the wall, close my eyes, and breathe as deeply as I can. But I can't hide any longer and force myself to look around the corner.

The entire courtyard has been transformed into a gravel pit. What was packed sand, stone, and yellow grass is now dirt and dust, eight-foot-deep pits where the missiles struck. Two rusty ambulances stand just inside the entrance to the courtyard, their snorting engines running. Medics and soldiers are scattered all over the yard. I see an older man with a stained white coat and a mustache holding a shoe in his hand. It takes a moment for me to realize that someone's shin is protruding from the shoe.

The ambulances are here, but there's no one to rescue. And the paramedics must have been here a while, even before the drones left, because they've lined up the bodies they've found. I try to avoid seeing the details. But I can't. I see torsos without legs. Bodies without heads, without arms. Bodies with holes blown out of their chests. And some bodies are completely intact, which is the most confusing thing of all.

I'm drawn to those bodies. Suddenly I have to see them. I need to know how many are there. So I go toward them, as if in a dream, and count them. I don't notice that someone's wrapped a blanket around me, until I'm right in front of the bodies, until I start to walk along them, pointing to them one by one.

"One. Two. Three," I count out loud in Swedish. "Four. Five. Six."

Sometimes I'm not sure if pieces of bodies belong together. Which bloody legs belong to which shattered trunk. If that one-eyed head belongs to that chest. It's like a puzzle.

"Seven. Eight. Nine."

Someone has put his arm around me, but I try to shrug it off. Twist my shoulders out of his grasp.

"Ten. Eleven. Twelve. Thirteen. Fourteen. Fifteen. Sixteen."

The arm tugs at me, and I stop and turn toward the person next to me.

"It's no use," Tariq says. "It was God's will. They're being rewarded now. We should rejoice for them."

He keeps his arm around me, and I find it incomprehensible that he's standing there, Tariq who thought I was a traitor, who knows it was me who caused this. Not Allah. Me. Yet he holds his arm around me and leads me away from the bodies, toward the ambulances.

"There were only sixteen bodies," I say to the man in the white coat, who was holding the shoe and the shin. "We must have been at least twenty-five."

He makes me sit down, gives me a bottle of water, and forces me to take a sip.

"You never find all the bodies," he says. "Some are just smoke and rubble."

And I feel it then, when he says that. I know that this is how it must be. That it's our only option.

Later I sit with Tariq at the rim of the crater. The stench is overwhelming now. Gunpowder and fire and death.

"I have to go back to Sweden," I say into the devastation. "I have to destroy those who did this."

Tariq says nothing. He just nods with his eyes down on the gravel.

"They can't get away with this," I say. "*Wallah*. I swear. They have to pay for this."

Tariq turns to me.

"How are you going to do that, brother?" he says.

"I'll become smoke," I say. "I'll become smoke and rubble."

Chapter 38

Stockholm/Bergort—Thursday, August 20, 2015

When she wakes up the sound in the room seems different, even though she pulled the curtains as close as she could, as if that would shut out whoever is watching and threatening her. She rolls over on her side and checks her telephone. 7:34 p.m. There's an email in her in-box. She sits up. She's been sleeping for over an hour. How is it even possible for her to sleep?

She drowsily clicks on the email.

> Hey Yasmine, It is in English. I just wanted to check how things are going for you in Stockholm. We have a project that the symbol you showed us is just perfect for. Please contact me as soon as you can. We've already started to think about campaigns, and we'd like to have the background work complete.

She blinks, trying to get some focus. It's signed Mark and comes from an address with *shrewdanddaughter.com* at the end. Damn, she's hardly given her assignment a thought. They're expecting something from her. After all, they're paying well over 400 dollars a night for this room.

She can't even think about that. Not now. She doesn't want them to freeze the card, so she sends a quick email saying things are happening, and promises to return after the weekend.

She gets up and goes over to the window again. She pushes the curtain aside with one hand and holds the gun behind her back with the other. She peeks out carefully toward the quay. But the man in the tracksuit is nowhere in sight, and she pulls the curtains again.

Whatever his reasons are for trying to keep her away, it's time to go back to Bergort.

"Do you have any other exits?" she asks the clerk at the front desk. "I mean for someone who doesn't want to exit straight out onto the quay, or whatever you call it?"

It's the same guy she ordered breakfast from the other day, the same mustache.

"I mean, you have celebrities who stay here safely. Do you have a back door for them?"

He doesn't hesitate, doesn't even ask. Just steps out from behind the counter and holds out his hand.

"Absolutely. The staff entrance is over here."

With all the stress and tension wound up inside her, the uncomplicated kindness he shows her almost makes her want to hug him.

It's almost half past eight by the time she gets back to Bergort. If the mood was palpable this morning, now it's magnetic, thick, and as oppressive as an approaching storm. There are clumps of kids in jeans and tank tops standing on the platform, smoking and spitting onto the tracks. But there's none of the usual pushing and laughing tonight, no catcalls or wolf whistles. The small groups are overfilled balloons tonight, with their own force fields, crackling and hissing, waiting to burst.

TV trucks are parked near the bottom of the ramp and excited reporters and cameramen are untangling their wires and microphones. And on the other side of the square the police stand with their police vans and helmets, their short, blond hair and neat uniforms. It's like a football match, Yasmine thinks. But it's unclear what the teams are. Unclear what the goal is.

Near the edge of the artificial grass everything is quiet—just a couple of small boys kicking a ball against the high fence. The rattle of it echoes among the buildings. Yasmine remembers what Fadi looked like when he was younger and came home from doing this—red in the face, with his T-shirt sweaty and dirty, his knees scraped bloody by the plastic grass. He'd eat bowl after bowl of cornflakes, standing in the kitchen, half of him still outside, still with his friends. He never looked more like a little brother than then.

She sinks down on a slanted bench a little ways away and leans back. That was a long time ago, but when she closes her eyes, the kids' voices on the field sound like Fadi's.

Finally, it starts to get dark, and somebody calls out for the boys on the field, it's time to go in, and there's something in their mothers' voices that makes the boys obey immediately. This is not a night to stay out, no night to disobey your parents, unless you're already part of the shadows, already a hoodlum, already hopeless.

Yasmine knows that if she and Fadi were still children, no one would have called for them. She sees the image of her mother before her, her tired eyes and scrubs. Thinks how she never shouted for them, never asked them to come back in. She just kept working. Just made sure there was food on the table, clothes in the closet. And the duality cuts through Yasmine. Her mother was never there for them. Her mother was always there for them.

The field is deserted, and Yasmine goes down to the kiosk to buy a coffee, mostly just to move a little. Cup in hand, she crosses between the buildings and the bushes, while light disappears along the rooftops and then away over the fields, and the pines, until darkness, or at least the shadows, settle over the balconies and the tunnels beneath the tracks. Finally, she goes back to the football field, uses her purse as a pillow, throws her legs up onto the bench, and gets ready for a long wait.

At midnight she sits up again, her body feeling stiff and heavy. The darkness has settled over Bergort, deep and heavy as velvet. The air is still warm, but summer is close to over. She turns her eyes toward the plastic grass, where she can now make out dark silhouettes through the mesh of the fence. She tries to count them. Maybe twenty or so.

Suddenly a voice is raised, louder than all the others.

"*Ey*, shut up! Listen to me now! Tonight we go like hell! We'll show them what Bergort is made of, won't we?"

Young guys shout and whistle. Pull on the fence to make it rattle. Yasmine carefully sneaks over to some bushes closer to the field. She recognizes that voice. She knows who it is. All these threads converge and part here. All these connections and interruptions. She peeks through the sparse branches and leaves. He's older now. Not fat anymore. More large and muscular. But with the same high-pitched voice.

Mehdi.

From Fadi's old gang. Parisa's man now.

She should have known, that was why Parisa looked so uncomfortable. That was why the cat ended up on her hotel wall. Mehdi is mixed up in this of course. But why all the drama? Why the threats and the craziness? Why the dead cats and tattooed gangsters? And what she truly doesn't understand is: What does Fadi have to do with all of this?

"Wait! Wait, brothers!" Mehdi's voice comes from the football field. "We have a friend here who's going to help us tonight, just like he helped us yesterday! *Wallah!* I swear! Tonight, the pigs are gonna get it!"

Another man steps out of the shadows on the other side of the field and goes over to Mehdi. Yasmine can't see his face—he's wearing a ski mask—but he's wearing glossy blue track pants identical to the ones the man outside the Lydmar had on.

On his upper body he's got a loose-fitting tank top and she catches glimpses of green tattoos from his back up to his neck. Everyone has those kinds of tattoos now, they're not rare, but it's the same man. She's absolutely sure.

But who is he? What is this?

"Listen carefully now!" says the man in the tracksuit pants. "Tonight we're gonna burn this shit down!"

He throws a bundle of ski masks down in front of him.

"Put these on. You've seen the square, it's full of TV cameras. You don't want your face to end up on the news."

The kids laugh and bend down and each one grabs a mask and pulls it over their heads. And in that moment, they are transformed. That simple gesture of pulling those hoods over their heads changes everything. They don't laugh or shove anymore. They're no longer bored or idle. They're no longer just boys.

With the ski masks on they become men, faceless soldiers. They're no longer individuals, they're a mass. They can no longer be understood or protected, they're something that must be fought.

They fall silent and the tension crackles around them, sending out shockwaves, which seem to flicker and jump, blue and red, along the chain-link fence.

"This is no game tonight, brothers," Tracksuit continues. "Tonight it's not just us. Tonight we'll spread chaos not just in Bergort, but everywhere. All brothers are united across every area!"

The mass, who were just boys before, stomp and bang on the fence, shouting and jumping.

All brothers united, thinks Yasmine. There are twenty of them. Maybe thirty. How many people live in Bergort? Three thousand? Four thousand? Hardly all the brothers have united here on the field. Just a bunch of guys who don't want to go home.

Tracksuit pulls out two large, apparently heavy bags, and opens them. He holds a glass bottle in one hand and a can of liquid in the other.

"Molotovs," he says. "Here are funnels and bottles and fabric."

He shakes the can.

"And fuel. All you have to do is make them."

The brothers divide and fill the bottles. When they seem ready, Tracksuit hands out what look like metal slingshots with thick rubber bands to some of the kids.

"We'll do like yesterday," he says then. "You start at the parking lot."

He points to a group of maybe five guys.

"At least five cars, *bre*," he says. "Ideally more. When the pigs come you run up onto the footbridge. Then wait under the bridge."

He selects maybe ten kids.

"Use the Molotovs. Rain fire down on those fucking pigs.

Make them pay for all the shit they've done to you. Let the fuckers burn!"

The guys are agitated now, can hardly stand still. The excitement rises like vapor off of them.

"And then," Tracksuit says, "you torch the grocery store."

He points to what looks like two big hammers on the ground.

"Smash the windows in with these," he says. "Take what you want and destroy the rest! Then we'll see where things lead, OK? Brother Mehdi will stay in contact with each group. Make sure you have his number and do what he says, okay?"

The soldiers, who were just boys before, stomp and jump. They're ready for this, ready for the streets, ready to set fire and flee, ready for chaos.

Mehdi says something, and then they set off in their groups, some with their ski masks on, others leaving them off so as not to attract attention. Finally, only Mehdi and Tracksuit remain.

"You'll take care of this, *len*?" Tracksuit says.

"You know it," Mehdi says. "It's cool, brother."

They shake hands and Tracksuit turns around and disappears toward the other end of the dark field.

Yasmine's thoughts are racing and she feels one of her legs beginning to shake nervously. Should she confront Mehdi now? But she can't risk not getting to hear what Parisa has to say about Fadi tomorrow.

But Tracksuit? Who is he? Without really making a decision, she moves farther back into the bushes and crouches down with her eyes fixed on the slowly disappearing figure of Tracksuit.

She thinks about the stencil on the wall, about the warning

he gave her earlier today outside the Lydmar. They, whoever they are, don't want her here, nothing could be clearer than that. But she's come this far, risked this much. Seen he's the leader of the riots. She's not about to stop now.

Slowly, carefully, she makes her way through the bushes until she's out of Mehdi's field of vision. Then she straightens out and follows Tracksuit between the buildings as carefully as she can.

He pulls off his ski mask as he walks from the high-rises toward the low-rises. She stays as far back as she can, so he won't catch sight of her if he turns around. The image of his hand shaped into a gun flashes before her eyes, but she forces it away with Fadi, by thinking this could lead her to Fadi.

The man is almost to the school now. The barracks are still there, just older, grittier, made more permanent by snow and ice and sun. The man slants through the snowball trees where Fadi used to wait for her, into a parking lot that's deserted except for a gleaming, midnight-blue BWM parked under a streetlamp. It's different from the few luxury cars you see around here, the ones that belong to footballers home to visit their family or to Serbs or Swedes who've scored an armored vehicle. Those cars are always black, always have chrome wheels and tinted windows, always scream gangster or superstar. This is streamlined and quiet, toned down and anonymous, not starved for attention.

Tracksuit leans down toward the driver's side and says something to someone in the car. From the other side of Bergort comes the muffled sound of explosions, a car being set on fire, and Tracksuit turns toward the sound. For a moment he looks straight in Yasmine's direction, where she's standing on the slope down toward the school, barely hidden behind the corner of one of the buildings, probably less than a hundred feet from him. For a moment she thinks he sees her.

But he quickly turns back to the car again and says something, then stretches out his hand. When he pulls it out again, he's holding an envelope in his hand, from which he removes what appears to be a small stack of bills. He counts them quickly and raises a hand in a farewell before leaving the parking lot and heading toward the subway.

Yasmine waits, unsure of what to do now. Should she follow him? There's a big risk that he'll see her on the platform—he knows what she looks like.

As he disappears behind the buildings, Yasmine hears the car in the parking lot start, the lights turn on, and she turns back toward it. Maybe this is the way forward? ERG 525. She types the license plate number into her phone without looking away from the car. As it slowly rolls out of the parking lot, it passes by her at a distance of no more than thirty feet, and she bends forward to look into the car. In the soft glow of the streetlight she gets a glimpse of the driver.

He's probably about ten years older than her. Blond, a Swede with a backslick and a blazer, a straight nose and high cheekbones. He's so far out of his context here that it seems surreal, like science fiction. He turns his head and their eyes meet for a moment in the yellow light. He looks tired.

Tired and empty and scared.

Chapter 39

Bergort—Saturday, August 8, 2015

Bergort. Everything is the same. The concrete and grass. The scent of pine and lukewarm kebabs from the food cart. Every step is a step I've taken before. Nothing has changed, nothing is new here. Nothing except me. I'm smoke and rubble now. Shaved head, dirty clothes, sleepless nights, and twenty pounds lighter. I have no wings, just shaky hands, and jumpy images of bodies without heads, bodies without feet, calves, thighs, legs, chests, shoulders, arms, hands. Everything is the same here. But I'm nothing more than memories of death, memories of betrayal. I'm nothing. Just the promise of revenge.

I wait in the grove behind the school until dusk. Rumors spread quickly, and I have to keep to the shadows, have to bide my time. And when the shadows are long enough, I throw my bag over my shoulder and head toward the shopping center. Only the kids are out now. Like seagulls flapping and croaking in the playground, spitting sand and gravel at each other, jumping around and squawking. It makes me sad to see them. I want to go to them, line them up, and tell them. I want to sit down on the slanting bench in front of them and point to my thin arms, my shaved skull. Want to say to them: "Look at me! Leave this place while you still can."

When I get there, I let my gaze wander up the cracked walls of the high-rise apartment building. I don't even know which apartment is his, but I know it's here.

I take out my cell phone and send a message without thinking about it anymore. Just two words. *Come out.*

Then I wait a little farther down the bike path, where I'm hidden from any windows. And it doesn't take long for him to come out the door, stretch, and look down along the asphalt. I stand up and stay perfectly still. He squints, maybe he's doesn't recognize me at first. Then he walks toward me slowly, his face pale.

"Seriously," he says. "This is can't be happening."

He stops and hesitates, runs his hands over his face. Closes his eyes and looks again, as if he thinks I might disappear, as if I'm just a film in front of his eyes that he can wipe away.

We stand like that for a moment. I don't look away. I know what he sees. A shadow from the past. A hologram, shaky and so thin it's almost completely transparent.

"Fadi?" he says at last. "*Brush*, is that you?"

I don't say anything. It's been so long since Mehdi and I even talked. He's come closer now and looks scared, hesitates, stops, squints at me, seemingly ready to bolt at the slightest provocation.

I just nod, try to smile, hold open my arms. It's been a long time since I had any right to expect something from him. He takes a hesitant step closer.

"This is crazy," he says. "Brother… You were dead? We heard you were dead. Everyone thought you were dead. "

He falls silent, still hesitant, as if I were a ghost. I try to smile again.

"But I'm not, *len*," I say. "Many of my brothers are, but not me."

He looks at me, curious and surprised. Then he takes another step toward me and opens his arms and puts them around me.

"Fadi," he says. "I swear, we thought you died in Syria. They said it was a drone strike, *bre*? Like a fucking movie, you know? They talked about it on the Internet. All the *shunos* from the projects wiped out along with some ISIS leader?"

I nod, shift my eyes away.

"Do you have a smoke?" I ask.

Mehdi stands completely still, just looking at me, as if I still might be a ghost.

"Yeah, yeah sure..." he says at last and hauls a pack of Marlboro Reds out of his jeans pocket.

I light one and cough on the first drag, gasping for breath. It's been over half a year since I smoked.

"There was a strike," I say. "A lot of people died, brother."

I gesture down the street.

"Come," I say. "Let's go, I don't like standing still here."

So we go across the asphalt, away through the smell of pine, away from our childhood and adolescence and who we are now. The playground is dark and empty, and as crappy as usual. We sit in the sand, like when we were kids. Let it flow through our fingers.

"Why did you come home?" Mehdi says. "You were so fucking *haddi*, brother, had the beard and everything. Fluffy beard!"

He laughs. It's been a long time since I heard someone laughing, so I laugh too, and I'm amazed by how it sounds, high and straggly and not at all like me, so I fall silent again.

He looks at me, bends forward to study my face, and it feels so intrusive that I back away.

"Damn, you're skinny, *len*. And your eyes? Shit, you look dead. Maybe you really are a ghost."

"I only came home for one thing," I say quietly. "Just one thing."

I turn my eyes to his again, hold his gaze with mine.

"I came home to kill the fuckers who betrayed us," I say.

It's not cold, but I shake in my light clothes as I tell Mehdi everything. About my false brothers, about my trip down. About my true brothers in the red sand, about brother Tariq. About their heads and exploded chests and feet. About the shoe with a shin in it. Everything.

"Daaamn," Mehdi says. "What the fuck! It's like a fucking movie, *ey*? Except you lived it."

A horror movie, I think. A nightmare.

"Where are you gonna live now? With your parents?"

I shake my head.

"I have to keep a low profile. Everyone thinks I'm dead. Them too. That's how it has to be. I have to be a ghost, *len*. You have to promise me, OK? Promise I can remain a ghost. You know, we grew up together. Then came all that shit. I know I ratted you out. I know I never apologized for it. But I'm begging you, brother, help me with this."

Mehdi puts his hand on my shoulder and leans toward me.

"For sure," he says. "I'm here for you, brother."

He falls silent and seems to be thinking.

"Maybe you can help me with something too."

Chapter 40

Stockholm—Friday, August 21, 2015

Tegnérgatan is hot and dusty now, just before eight in the morning. The traffic is constant and low-key, strollers exiting beautiful *fin-de-siècle* buildings. It took her only a minute to find number 10, and she's been standing for a half hour in the sunshine on the other side of the street, slowly drinking hot coffee from a paper mug she bought on her way here.

It had been easier than she thought to find the owner of the car she'd seen in Bergort yesterday. Or both easier and more difficult. She'd Googled how to find out who a car is registered to. Found the site, put in the number of the car the upper-class guy was driving. The only problem was that it was registered to a company. Merchant & Taylor. Some kind of public relations firm—it wasn't clear from their website what they did. "We create a climate for change," it said in the Swedish version; they seemed to be all over the world.

But one thing they were proud of was the appearance of their staff, all of their pictures and names were posted on the website, and the Stockholm office only had three guys who looked similar to the one in the car. All upper-class, bleached teeth, and smooth fucking skin. Golfers, sailors, whatever. But she knew immediately which one it was. Saw it in his fearful eyes, which he couldn't hide even in a picture in which he was supposed to appear confident.

George Lööw. A lawyer apparently. A specialist in "Government Relations" and "Interest mobilization." Whatever that meant. Fuck it. She was only interested in his address, which took a second to find by Googling his name.

She closes her eyes and runs her hand through her hair.

How the hell did you get yourself into this, Fadi?

When she opens her eyes again, she sees George Lööw coming out of the front door of the building. He's a real yuppie—dark suit, glossy blond hair. His white shirt is unbuttoned two buttons, which gives you a hint of a muscular chest beneath. In his breast pocket, he's carelessly stuffed a red-dotted handkerchief.

"Wolf of Wall Street," she says under her breath.

She detaches herself from the wall and follows him quietly in the direction of Döbelnsgatan.

George Lööw walks rapidly toward the inner city, and sometimes she almost has to run to keep from losing him. But he's tall, and it's easy to follow his bobbing lion's mane along the green of Johannes Cemetery.

At Malmskillnadsgatan, Lööw pauses and slips into a small kiosk. Yasmine stops and waits a bit farther up the sidewalk, unsure of what to do, but it only takes a minute before he's out on the street again with a bundle of what seems to be Sweden's four largest newspapers in his hands. She has never seen someone buy so many papers at once before. His eyes dash over the front page of a tabloid, then he folds it and checks one after another.

"Damn," she thinks she hears him say.

All the front pages are covered with pictures of burning cars, masked boys, and faceless policemen. Bergort is everywhere, riots so sudden and intense that the middle class can't look away. Lööw speeds down the street, and Yasmine follows calmly after. Suddenly he takes advantage of a temporary break in the traffic and crosses the street just before the Malmskillnadsgatan bridge over Kungsgatan. She hesitates a moment, then follows him, maybe thirty feet behind.

There's a yellow Dumpster on the street, which he disappears behind, and she loses sight of him. It's as if he's been swallowed. Did he enter a building? All she can see is an office building. But no upper-class guy. Fuck! Where is he?

But then she understands: The staircase down from the bridge toward Kungsgatan. She runs over to it and sees him halfway down the stairs. She heads down after him.

At the bottom of the stairs, he turns left. The street is somewhat crowded, and she has to take the last of the stairs two at a time to keep from losing him. He's walking under the bridge, Yasmine is only fifteen feet behind him now. When he comes out on the other side, he turns left again and disappears into a door that seems to be in the base of the bridge. She bends back and studies the building. The door doesn't lead into the bridge itself but into one of the two old towers that stand on either side of the street. They look like mini versions of Gotham, like the old skyscrapers on Wall Street, she thinks, but about a third as high. The King's Towers, she suddenly remembers. Is that what they're called? No skyscrapers, but at least ten floors high.

She hesitates a moment. If she followed him this far, she might as well go all the way. She hurries over to the door before it has time to shut behind Lööw.

The foyer is dark, and it takes a moment for her eyes to adjust and make out Lööw standing inside an old-fashioned elevator made of wood and mirrors. He's just about to close the door, but when he sees Yasmine step into the foyer, he holds the elevator for her.

"Are you going up?" he says.

He sounds annoyed at first, as if he didn't really want to offer her a spot in the elevator, but some innate civility compels him. She immediately feels a wave of stress. What should you do now, when the person you're following suddenly addresses you?

"Yes..." she says hesitantly and takes a few uncertain steps toward him.

"Don't you know where you're going?" he says.

His irritation seesm to have dissipated now that he's had a good look at her. He smiles a flirty, confident smile. She recognizes that smile.That smile is the same everywhere, in Bergort or in Östermalm. In New York or Tokyo. She thinks of Joey's clumsy, obvious pickup line in *Friends*, from the endless reruns she watched on those afternoons with Fadi: *How YOU doin'?*

For once it might be to her advantage.

"Yes," she lies and smiles back. "But where are *you* going?"

She can almost hear Lööw smack his lips with satisfaction that she's playing along.

"Fifteenth floor," he says. "Higher or lower?"

He runs his fingers over the buttons, and she reads the company names on the small sign in the elevator as quickly as she can. Higher, she thinks. Then maybe she'll see where he goes when he gets off. On the sixteenth floor there's something called Stocktown Pictures. It could be anything.

"Sixteen," she says.

George presses the button, and the elevator rattles upward. Yasmine checks the brass plate for the fifteenth floor. Two company names. The name of a law firm is etched into the plate, and beside it another name is printed on a narrow piece of paper, taped to the plate.

Stirling Security, she reads. There's something familiar about it, but she can't put her finger on what.

"Are you a lawyer?" she says and does her best to sound impressed and subservient.

Lööw stretches and clears his throat.

"Not exactly," he says. "I have a law degree. But I work in PR, I guess you'd call it."

"Oh, I thought you were on your way to that law firm?" she says, pointing to the brass plate.

"No," Lööw says. "Coulda been, but I'm going to the other company. One of my clients."

He winks at her. His eyes glitter, but she sees something else there too, something strained and stressed. There's something under that polished surface, that's for sure. He has unexpectedly deep furrows on his forehead, and his eyes are slightly bloodshot. At the same time, he can't help but let his hand touch her arm slightly as the old elevator makes its rocky way up in the building. Dudes are the same everywhere.

The elevator stops with a short rattle, and the papers under Lööw's arm rustle as he fiddles with the complex dial to unlock the grille gate.

"Bye," he says and beams one last smile at her.

It's the wrong time, she knows it before she even opens her mouth, but there's something about that smile, that uncertainty, that anxious face, something about the papers under his arm, which makes it impossible to stay silent.

"Why are you paying guys in Bergort to create chaos?"

Lööw is already out of the elevator when she says it, and her words make him stop as suddenly as a skinny, hungry lion hit by a tranquilizer dart.

He turns around, drops a couple of papers on the floor in front of him, and has to stoop to pick them up. She holds the door to the elevator open with her foot. Lööw rises slowly and approaches her. The smile is gone, he's a different person now than he was three seconds ago, but he's not intimidating, just scared.

"Who are you?" he whispers, standing much too close to her.

"Are these the people paying for those riots?" she says, pointing to the inconspicuous door with the tight, red logo of Stirling Security posted on it.

"Listen to me now," Lööw hisses. "I have no idea what you're talking about."

He throws a nervous glance over his shoulder. Far below in the building she hears a door opening, steps across the marble floor. Then someone presses the elevator button, but nothing happens because she keeps it firmly on the fifteenth floor.

"I have a meeting now," he continues. "And it's probably the people I'm meeting who have just entered down there."

She grabs her phone out of her pocket and pulls up the pictures she took last night. Without hurrying, she holds up the picture of Lööw handing over the money to the guy with the tattoos.

"This was last night, asshole," she says. "Your car, *len.*"

Down below someone continues to push the button with increasing vehemence. Lööw swallows and pales.

"This is not happening," he hisses. "Fuck fuck fuck."

He looks at her, something desperate in his eyes now.

"Are you a journalist?"

She shakes her head.

"I'm just looking for someone," she says. "Someone who's mixed up in this. I don't give a shit about you, George Lööw."

He jerks when he hears his own name. Uncomfortable

that he doesn't know anything about her, but she seems to know a lot about him.

"But if you don't talk to me, you'll have enough journalist vultures after you, *bre*. Do you understand? I'll send the pictures to their tip line, and then it's game over for you, buddy."

She nods toward the papers George has pressed against his chest like a shield.

"Seriously," he whispers. "We can't do this. Not here. Not now. This is not what it looks like, okay? "

The corner of one eye jerks, a tick from stress or something else, something deeper. Fear.

"So when?"

"Give me until tomorrow, OK? Give me your number."

Yasmine just looks at him.

"Are you kidding?" she says. "A time and a place. Early."

"OK, OK," he says. "The stairs in front of the City Library at nine then."

"Don't be late," she says and finally lets go of the door. "Don't forget I found you today. I can find you again. "

And with that, the elevator heads down toward the dark foyer again.

When she gets there, a short man in a tight, dark suit is waiting for the elevator. He's probably in his sixties, with a bald head encircled by a garland of short hair. He's somewhat slender, almost supple, like a gymnast, or martial artist. His eyes are cold and green, equally intense and indifferent, like a dragon.

"Why you block elevator?" he says in English with a strong Slavic accent.

"Sorry," said Yasmine says, and looks away as she sweeps past him.

Is that who Lööw is meeting? If so, she understands why Lööw's eye was twitching.

She's relieved to step out into the summer morning outside. A black Mercedes is parked halfway up on the sidewalk. It looks as evil and indifferent as the man by the elevator. She notes that it has unusual license plates. Blue and with a different combination of letters and numbers than regular ones. DL012B. She pulls out her phone and writes them down. How the hell could this have something to do with Fadi? She feels her desperation growing.

But maybe this is just a dead end.

Chapter 41

London—Friday, August 21, 2015

It's almost ten-thirty by the time Klara climbs up the stairs to the entrance of the institute on Surrey Street. Her legs feel as heavy as her head. Images from yesterday flash through her mind: glass after glass in the pub while she waited outside what turned out to be Patrick's house. Then the two men. Why had she been so sure they were following Patrick? They had appeared at a convenient time, definitely. But there wasn't really anything to suggest they were following him. Nothing except paranoia and too many glasses of wine. Nothing except a shard of intuition that sits deep inside and doesn't want to let go.

Then flashes of Patrick's pale face on the tracks. His lifeless, open, empty eyes. Flashes of the officer hinting she was drunk. She closes her eyes, filled with remorse and guilt. She had been drunk. Really drunk. Was that why Patrick was dead? Would she have done something else if she hadn't drunk those last glasses of white wine?

"No, no, no..." she whispers and pushes open the heavy door. "No, no, no!"

On the landing outside Charlotte's door, someone has set up a table with a small bouquet of lilies and a burning candle; the flame trembles slightly in the draft from the poorly insulated window. A card lies opened in front of the candle, and Klara can see that many of her colleagues have already written their condolences to Patrick's family. She hesitates a moment, then goes over to the table and picks up the ordinary, blue ballpoint pen, but something ripples through her, and she feels unsteady. The image of Patrick on the tracks. She has to grab onto the table to keep from losing her balance.

"Klara!" Charlotte says from behind her. "I suppose you heard the terrible news?"

She turns around and sees Charlotte standing in the door of her office. She looks tired, hollow-eyed, with her big, curly hair not pinned up, but left down, floating around her like an aura.

Klara just nods and remains completely silent. She wants to tell her about yesterday. About the computer and the men in leather jackets and Patrick on the tracks. But she remembers Charlotte's voice at lunch when she mentioned Stirling Security and suddenly feels too afraid. She takes a step toward the wall for support, closing her eyes.

"How are you doing, Klara?" Charlotte says.

Her voice is close to her ear, and she feels a hand on her shoulder, Charlotte's hair against her cheek. She turns her face away so Charlotte won't smell the remnants of alcohol on her breath.

"It's OK," she says quietly. "It's fine."

She slowly opens her eyes.

"It's just so awful."

Charlotte nods, catches her eye.

"Who would have believed it?" she says. "Maybe it's always like that, but even though he was odd, he didn't seem depressed."

"Why would he have been depressed?" she says and meets Charlotte's eyes.

They have the appearance of compassion. But underneath, Klara senses an icy abyss.

"Klara," Charlotte says and takes quiet hold of her arm. "The police told me that they found a suicide note printed out in his home."

"What do you mean 'printed out'?"

Charlotte shrugs.

"What do I know? That was what they said. "

"Printed out from a printer, or something?"

"Yes, that's what they said, but that's not what's important."

A cold wind suddenly blows through her, and she stiffens again.

If Patrick didn't use computers, why would he write his suicide note on one?

"How awful it all sounds," Charlotte continues. "We can't let this distract us now. We fly to Stockholm tomorrow. The report is ready. That's where our focus needs to be now. Everything else can be taken care of when we get back. Are we clear on that?"

No! Klara wants to scream. *We sure as hell are not clear! This is completely crazy!*

But she doesn't. Instead she nods.

"I'll do my best."

She waits on the creaking landing in front of Patrick's office until she hears Charlotte shut the door to her office on the floor below. She has to know what he was doing in there. Why he took her computer. What Stirling Security is and why Charlotte is acting so strange. And above all, why he died.

She takes a deep breath and presses down on the handle of the door to his office.

To her great surprise, the door is unlocked and opens on creaking hinges. Slowly she opens the door. The blinds are down and the room is dim as usual. She takes a half step over the threshold and listens to make sure that no one is on their way up the stairs.

When she's satisfied she turns on the lights and turns to the whiteboard where Patrick drew his mind map. But the board is an empty, gleaming white under the lights.

She stands directly in front of it. The whiteboard looks brand-new, not even a stain on it. She lets her eyes sweep across the desk, and notes that it too is completely empty. Not a notepad or paper. Not even a Post-it. On Tuesday, it had sagged under Patrick's square, and obviously well-organized, piles of paper.

When she turns toward the bookshelf, she sees it's still filled with Patrick's books on human rights. But the binders, which covered at least two shelves, are gone.

She remembers reading that people who are about to commit suicide often arrange their affairs before they put their plan into action. That would be Charlotte's explanation.

But she's sure this is not Patrick's work.

Chapter 42

Bergort—Sunday, August 9–Sunday, August 16, 2015

I wait for the stores to open then go into the city to shoplift some jeans, T-shirts, new sneakers, and a Lakers cap. At the mall I grab a black cap with *NY* written on it, but I drop it, because thoughts of you suddenly flow through me. I think about how you, just like everyone else, must think I'm dead, and it makes me feel so sad and so guilty, but at the same time angry. And I don't know what to do about it. In a way, I *am* dead, my body just a shell, uninhabited and hollow. As if my consciousness were weak, barely functioning, and only focused on one thing: my mission, all I have to live for now.

And I stand in my new clothes every night, with my new, thin body, my shaved head and chin, around the corner from brother Dakhil's apartment, where we brothers met almost every day, an eternity ago, in another life, another world, another body.

I see them come and go. I see Dakhil and his bushy, red beard, brother Tasheem, brother Taimur. But not al-Amin.

I don't really know what I'm doing. Maybe I'm surveilling them, maybe I'm trying to find the right time to strike. Maybe I'm just building up my courage or trying to find my way to the bottom of my hatred. And when I do reach the bottom? When I'm done mapping out the movements of the traitors?

What do I do then?

All their talk. How we prayed and cried when Kobane was lost. How we cursed American bombs and Kurdish ruthlessness. How we rejoiced at the progress in al-Hasakah and in the strength of the warriors getting closer and closer to Aleppo.

How proud they were when I finally got to go.

"The worst is over now after Kobane," they said. "The Kurds are strong, but in Hasakah it's al-Assad men. And they're tired. *Inshallah*, you will taste victory, brother."

All lies. All theater. All of it to destroy their own brothers.

So when I'm done watching them? When I've found my courage again? What do I do then?

Destroy them.

At night I sleep in a closet next to the garbage room in the basement of Mehdi's house. It's one of those spaces that someone always has a key to. The kind of place we used to drink in when we were kids or sleep in when we got kicked out or too fucked-up to go home. But Mehdi is a big deal around here now, he keeps an eye on the kids, and he's the only one who has a key, so nobody bothers me when I'm lying on my mattress in the dark, wrapped in a plastic sleeping bag I shoplifted along with some white basketball shoes from a sports shop. Mehdi brings me leftovers, and sometimes we go to McDonald's together, but not in Bergort, not in our neighborhood, somewhere else, where nobody recognizes me or the person I used to be.

A few days pass by like that. Mehdi is free, and we drive down to a lake in a little, shitty Mazda he borrowed. It's a warm day, and we've left the jetties and the small beach, left the kids and the noise, and gone up into a woodsy area barefoot, so pine needles cut into the soles of our feet. We're sitting on a small ledge, on a stone next to a pit where we used to grill.

"Damn, do you remember?" Mehdi says. "This was where you made out with Soledad!"

He laughs and slaps his thighs.

"Damn, I swear brother, she was not much to look at! But you were so fucking horny! Like an animal! A fucking rabbit, *len*!"

I can't help but smile too. It's been such a long time. How old were we then? Thirteen?

"*Khalas!*" I say. "Stop it, she was hot, brother."

Mehdi just shakes his head. The laughter dies out, and we sit silently in the heat for a while. Then he turns to me.

"Do you remember I said we could help each other out?" he says.

I look up at him, squinting against the sun, nodding.

"Sure," I say. "Anything, *brush*. I wouldn't be here without you."

Mehdi moves a little closer. Squats down next to me, so he can whisper.

"You know there's something going down in Bergort, *ey*? You've seen it, right? The symbol sprayed all over the place? You can feel it in the air, right?"

The sun feels warm and easy on my face, and I sink deeper into the pit, half lying against the stones and pine needles. Of course, now when he says it, I have seen those things sprayed all over the concrete, and I've seen something in the eyes of the kids, heard them whispering and crackling when I've been on my way to the basement in the evenings. At the same time, I'm so focused on my own world that I haven't cared, just noticed it, nothing more.

"Sure," I say. "I can see something's on its way, no doubt."

Mehdi nods eagerly.

"Good, good," he says. "You know, it happens sometimes. Something happens. The police beat up some dude, or somebody dies. And all of Bergort goes crazy, right? We've been a part of it, right, brother?"

I nod and remember a time, maybe five years ago, when it was a hot summer and Bergort exploded for a couple of nights. The police came with their fucking shields and batons and shit, but they didn't have a chance, we were like mercury and water, just found other channels to flow through all the time. But I don't remember now why, don't remember how it started or ended.

"But this time it's different," Mehdi continues. "This time it's planned. Do you understand? We're getting help from some people who know about this shit, who can help us start a fucking war. We're starting with this, with the symbols. It's psychological, brother, we're creating an atmosphere of fear, right? "

I shrug.

"If you say so, *len*."

"And then it's gonna happen. One hundred percent, brother! Not just us, other suburbs, other neighborhoods, too. A fucking war! And you can help us, *ghost*! You only go out at night. So you can tag the symbol when you do, right?"

I remember how it felt to go off like that. Remember how intoxicating it was. The thought of fighting back with my brothers. Paying them back for every fucking baton blow or stranglehold, for every night in jail, every meaningless evening spent in the backseat of a police van. To finally make the pigs run, make them confused and defensive. The fucking power in that! Showing them the power in Bergort.

But I don't feel any of that now. Just emptiness. Just a meaninglessness that vibrates and bends the pines over me, forcing away the sunlight and threatening with darkness. What's a few stones thrown at the cops, when our brothers are dying by the thousands? A few cars burned when brothers are being blown to pieces by drones? It's nothing—less than nothing. But I owe Mehdi this. After everything, he was still there for me, so I force myself to smile.

"OK, brother," I say. "I can spray those for you, no problem."

It's getting dark by the time we head back to Bergort, and Mehdi keeps harping on about the fucking riot, how huge it's going to be. He talks about how they're gonna cover all of Bergort with a symbol he shows me: a fist inside a star. How everyone will be terrified by what's going down, all of it done with stealth, only a few *shunos* will know. And he gives me some stencils with the symbol on them and a few cans of spray paint.

When we get back to Bergort, it's dark and the streetlamps shine pale and yellow in all that gray. I ask Mehdi to drop me off at my old house, and he looks surprised when I jump out with my heavy nylon bag.

"What the hell you gonna do here, brother? I thought you were in hiding?"

"They're sleeping," I say, and glance up toward the dark windows.

"What's in the bag? You drag it around like a fucking donkey. Must be important?"

I hesitate a moment, but I can't resist it. Can't resist the urge to show it to Mehdi. To show him how fucking serious this is. So I put the bag on the passenger seat and gently pull the zipper. He bends over and his eyes widen until I think they'll fall out of his face.

"What the fuck, brother?" he says. "What the fuck?"

"I'm not playing around," I say, lifting up the gun, which is cold and heavy in my hand. "It's an eye for an eye, brother. The people who deceived me are gonna pay."

He nods seriously as I push one gun down into my pants and zip up the bag.

"I'm gonna hide them here," I say. "There's no safer place. If you want, I can teach you to shoot a gun?"

The apartment is dark and quiet—they go to bed early if they're not working. The light blue nylon bag is heavy and rubs against my shoulder as I creep through the hall. The stale air fills my lungs. It's been several months since the last time I was here. That was another life.

I could have hidden the weapons in the woods, like we used to hide all our shit back in the day. Could have dug a hole and covered it with pine needles and leaves. They would have been safe there, maybe even safer.

What is it that draws me here? Is there some security in the past? Or is it the vague hope that a door will crack open? That a light will turn on and muted steps will come from the bedroom? Whispering voices that will ask me what I'm doing here, what I have in the bag? A confrontation that would force me to see myself through their eyes.

I stand still in the hall and listen. Maybe that would have been enough. Maybe it would have been enough with a ray of light, muffled footsteps, a questioning voice. Maybe that would have been enough to stop me from doing what I have to do.

Our old room looks exactly like it did when I left it, only cleaner. Silently I pull out my old mattress and flatten the bag's contents, insert it into the spot under the bed where I hid so much in the old days. But this will be the last time.

On the way out I stop. I stand frozen, the hair on my neck standing up. I could swear I heard a sound from the other side of the living room. Could swear something creaked.

Slowly I turn around. The living room is dark, almost black inside the constantly drawn curtains. The door to their bedroom closed. I stretch and listen again. Wasn't the door open a crack before? I stand completely still, unsure of what to do, my heart pounding. But I don't hear anything else. Just the hum of a fan somewhere below, deep in some basement. I stand like that until I get a cramp and gently turn around, creeping toward the door and back out into the warm gray evening.

On the bicycle path outside, I stop, filled with equal parts relief and disappointment. No one saw me. The plan is intact. This is what my life is now, what I live for, what I live with.

Chapter 43

Bergort—Friday, August 21, 2015

The afternoon sun is high. The sky is blue and empty above the ten burned-out cars dotting the parking lot. Shards of glass cover the asphalt, and the windows of the Syrian's store are smashed in. He's standing out there with a broom in hand, his eyes black and angry, his lips mumbling: "Goddamn kids. Stupid fucking kids."

Yasmine sees those same empty, tired eyes in everyone she meets. It's their cars that have been destroyed in the parking lot. Their grocery store that's been set on fire, their children who can't go out in the evenings anymore, and hardly during the day. And everywhere that red fist and star are sprayed. Everywhere that feeling of a threat, a siege, a countdown to chaos.

Yasmine continues down toward the shopping center. The gun chafes her lower back a little, but she's surprised how used to it she is by now. Ever since she saw that gangster outside Lydmar she's kept it loaded, too.

She was here just twelve hours ago, but even after last night's destruction, she's still amazed by how different things feel now, how normal. Broken windows at the grocery, milk cartons smashed against the dirty, checkerboard concrete. Still it's nothing like the turmoil she saw last night. No screams, no fire, and no running, faceless boys chasing after running, faceless police.

Two police cars are parked outside the grocery store, one police van and one squad car and four cops are leaning against them with paper cups of coffee in their hands and their hats pushed back on their heads. They're doing their best to look harmless now, as if they're something other than the dark shadows that ran through Bergort last night. But no matter how hard they try, they look like foot soldiers on leave. Like farmers' sons who've become an occupying army without understanding how. They don't look intimidating now, just naïve, almost innocent, as if they're unaware of the hatred around them.

She could almost feel sorry for them, but she knows that when evening comes, they'll be masked again. When evening comes, they hide behind their shields and grids and their batons and punches.

And the cops know that everyone knows that. So there's something strained in their posture, something tense and unnatural. They see the symbols sprayed all over Bergort. They see the cars burning. They tell themselves they can protect this powder keg from its burning fuse. But deep down, they think it's too late.

She sits on a bench in a sunbeam that streams down between two buildings. The rain has moved on, and the afternoon sun is hot again, but the sand under the forgotten spades and cracked, loose wheels of toy cars in the sandbox is still moist. It's nearly three by the time she hears Parisa's voice behind her.

"Yazz?" she says. "Sorry I'm late."

When she turns around, she sees Parisa standing by the warped gate to the playground and starts walking toward her across the damp sand.

"It's OK," she says.

When she reaches Parisa, she looks into her eyes and gestures in the direction of the center of Bergort.

"Quite the chaos," she says. "Last night, I mean."

Parisa nods cautiously, as if she hadn't really thought about it.

"*Ey*," she says at last. "That's the way it goes, *len*. You know how it is. The cops start bashing us, and it's payback."

Yasmine hesitates. Doesn't Parisa know her guy is involved in this? That he's some sort of leader?

"Whose baby was that?" she says instead. "Your sister's?"

Parisa flinches, and her gaze glides out over the playground and the square, and the battered stores behind it, bathed in light. She shakes her head.

"Did your mom have another baby?"

Yasmine laughs, doing her best to dispel the tension that's descended on them. But Parisa just shakes her head and looks at her again, something hard and rebellious in her eyes now.

"She's mine, Yazz. Nour is mine."

Yasmine takes a step back in surprise.

"What? You're kidding? You—"

She breaks off, unsure of how to proceed.

"Is that so strange, Yazz?" Parisa says. "Is that so fucking *wack* to you? That I might have a kid?"

"No, no. Or, I don't know, Parisa."

"Not everyone can run away! Not everyone can just say fuck it and move to New York."

"That's not what I mean, sister," she says. "I just mean... Why didn't you say anything?"

"Why didn't I say anything?" Parisa says, a small mischievous smile at the corner of her mouth now. "Why didn't I say anything? You weren't here, *sister*. It wasn't like you called me every day, right? Not like you were Facebooking me all the time, *sister*?"

The way she's saying sister is the same way Yasmine said it yesterday outside Parisa's apartment. Yasmine shrugs her shoulders now, feels Bergort creeping over her again, pressing down on her, pushing her closer. Feels its tentacles pulling her back. It doesn't matter how far you travel.

"Whatever," she tells Parisa. "She's sweet, *len*."

Yasmine's got her eyes on the ground now. She was the one who came here full of righteous anger. But that's how it always turns out. Nothing is permanent here except chaos.

"Is it Mehdi's? I mean, is he the father? "

Parisa doesn't say anything, just nods with the back of her head.

"Come on, Yazz," she says. "I wanna show you something."

Yasmine just looks at her.

"What?"

"You wanna know about Fadi? That's what you said. You don't give a shit about the rest, you're just looking for him?"

"I don't give a shit about the rest, whatever the hell it is. But if he's alive I have to get a hold of him. You understand that, right?"

She feels her fury growing again. Parisa and all of fucking Bergort. All this shit and stagnation and mysterious connections and guilt, guilt, guilt.

"Come on then," Parisa says, turns around, and starts walking.

Chapter 44

Bergort—Monday, August 17–Thursday, August 20, 2015

The following days are simple. On Monday, we load ourselves into that worthless fucking Mazda and drive out to the middle of nowhere. Just Mehdi and me. We listen to old Pirate Tapes classics and Mehdi raps along to the chorus with his worthless, stressed-out asthma-flow, always half a beat off, always saying the wrong words. It makes me laugh, and for a brief moment, I almost forget who I am, forget who I've become.

We park the car and take tiny walking paths out into the middle of a forest, just like mushroom pickers, I swear, just like fucking Swedes. It's quiet out there, just the clanking of the plastic bag filled with empty bottles and cans Mehdi's carrying. When we get far enough away from the small gravel road to feel secure, we line up the cans on some old logs and back up about sixty feet. I open the bag I took with me from Syria and lift out the well-worn Russian gun.

Of course Mehdi's seen guns before. I remember Räven's face many years ago when he showed us a rusty old revolver. So fucking proud. But you already knew by then he was on his way out, you could see the heroin in those dead fucking eyes, you could see how close it was, so we didn't even get that excited, just kind of depressed, and just a few months later he was dead, poor bastard.

But this is different. This comes from a war, and Mehdi's hands tremble as he holds it for the first time, his eyes glistening.

"Shit, *brush*," he says. "Where'd you get 'em?"

"Took them with me when I came," I say. "No one keeps an eye on all the weapons down there. It took a week to get home on trucks and buses. Couldn't exactly check them in at the airport, right?"

He holds up a gun and aims it toward the pine trees.

"Have you been in a battle with this?"

He looks at me with an admiration I haven't seen from him before, a willingness to believe whatever I tell him. So I tell him about the front, about the barrels al-Assad's pigs rain down on us, about our homemade grenades, about how the brothers hold their rifles above their heads and shoot through the gaps in the concrete out of the ruins, how it smells like sulfur and the desert, I tell him how many pigs the brothers have killed. And when he asks if I killed someone, I nod hesitantly and look away.

Because the only ones I've killed are my brothers.

We sit down on a couple of stumps and Mehdi starts gobbling down a Twix, without offering me one, just like usual, and it irritates me, even though I know he's done so much for me. But when I see him cramming chocolate into his mouth and smacking his lips it makes me angry. Why the hell are we out in the woods? Why does he need to learn to shoot? I hear his hissing fucking breath coming from the stump. I lean back against a tree trunk and look at him.

"Are you ever gonna tell me what the hell this thing you got going on is?" I say. "Why the hell are we out here in the woods like a couple of Swedes?"

He looks up at me and slurps in such a way that chewy toffee flows out of the corner of his mouth.

"What the hell's wrong with you?" he says. "You mad or something?"

I shake my head.

"Whatever. But surely you know what kind of shit is going down in Bergort, brother. The riots? What the hell is this about?"

He nods quietly.

"It's starting to grow now. This weekend it's gonna explode, brother. We have our *shuno* who's fucking coordinating, you know?"

I shrug.

"And what happens when it does, brother?" I say. "What the hell's the deal? Don't shoot anybody, asshole."

It's not that I care about the cops, but it just feels so fucking useless. Shooting some cop in Bergort. I think of the kids I saw on that first evening I got back, cawing and flapping around Camp Nou and the playground. What happens to them if they see guys like Mehdi trying to shoot cops?

"No, *relax*," Mehdi says. "I'm not stupid. And I don't give a shit about any of that? I'm getting paid by the Serbs, you know? A thousand a night, brother. To create some chaos? Back in the day, we did it for free!"

He laughs, and I spit in the moss before I look up at him. And I get it. It's natural. This is how we grew up. It's drilled into us. There's always a hustle somewhere. Always one more layer, always some ass-backward, phantom possibility under layers of bullshit and chaos. Always one more thing that can go to hell. Never further than our own noses. Never further than the next pay check.

That afternoon Mehdi comes to the door of my hiding place,

my cave. He looks stressed-out, his eyes jumping around the room like little rabbits.

"*Shoo,* brother," he says, giving me a hand and a half hug.

"What's going on?" I say. "You look stressed."

He pulls the metal door closed behind him, enters the room, and looks at me seriously.

"There's someone keeping an eye on you," he says. "Someone knows you're back. You know how this works, it's just a matter of time before everyone knows."

I sit down on the mattress. It was only a matter of time, even though I was careful. Things move fast out here.

"How did you find out?"

"I have my contacts. And this person is asking questions about the symbols, and it makes me worry. You know, this is big shit we have going on out here. The people involved... You know? The ones who are paying? They'll go batshit if somebody unravels all this before it's ready, brother. You don't want to mess with them, believe me. And if anyone sees you, you'll lose your chance for revenge. We have to be careful now."

"Who's seen me?"

Mehdi's eyes flutter away before he looks at me, annoyed.

"Somebody you don't know. You better fucking stay inside now if you don't want it to come out that you're back. Damn, you're *haddi*, brother. It may be *fucking* Säpo. We don't want Säpo snooping around here now, just a few days before this starts."

I'm confused.

"But what the hell, brother," I say. "Who is it? Is one of the traitors asking around? One of the men who sent me to Syria?"

I feel my mouth go dry. I've been hiding, sneaking around, barely out in days. How could they have discovered me?

"It doesn't matter," Mehdi says. "You need to keep a low profile for a while, then you can have your revenge, like you want."

So we move an old PlayStation and a TV down to the basement. Plug it into a socket out in the hallway. Mehdi's too stingy to lend me his new one, so I sit around with his old PlayStation 3, playing old, fucked-up FIFA and Halo games. On Tuesday, Mehdi picks me up, and we drive into the woods, where I teach him how to shoot with a pistol while he babbles on about riots and chaos.

I look at Mehdi, all hesitancy and wheezing breath, see how he flinches when he fires the gun, closes his eyes when he pulls the trigger and misses so badly that I almost start to laugh. A thousand a night to burn down Bergort. Masks and baseball bats and throwing rocks at the cops. We're not kids anymore, and it makes me feel sad and empty. Nothing ever happened for us; we never got a break.

On Thursday evening I stand across the street from the traitors' meeting place. I see them arrive one by one at Dakhil's apartment. From the other side of the shopping center, from the other side of Bergort, I hear the uproar of the kids getting worked up for the riots tonight. It's still too early. There will be some quiet before the explosion. Just like the last two nights. But every day it's more and more intense.

I don't know why I'm here tonight, sitting on the bench outside the apartment. Usually I go home as soon as I see that they've left, as soon as I see that al-Amin is not with them. But tonight I just can't leave, despite Mehdi's warnings.

The evening is warm, and I'm tired and lonely. I guess I have nowhere else to go. Maybe I feel that inside me. But I decide to wait here.

I have almost dozed off when I finally see him on the cracked asphalt of the parking lot. He locks the door to a small car, a Golf maybe, with a click and a beep and starts walking toward the apartment building at a rapid pace.

Brother al-Amin. Same clothes, same leather jacket, and small *kufi*. He has a phone pressed to his ear, and he's talking quietly. I freeze to the bench, stuck there, unable to move. All I can think about is that phone, if it's the same phone he used to call me a few weeks ago. If it's the same phone that wiped out my brothers?

He's inside the door before I'm able to collect myself, collect my thoughts.

Al-Amin hasn't disappeared. Maybe he always comes late now? Maybe it's the first time this week he's been here? Maybe it's the last time? Maybe he's been on one of his fucking missions. The adrenaline starts pumping inside me. Is this my chance? My only chance? All the brothers are gathered here. My whole body vibrates. I have never thought beyond this. But I've dreamed of it. And now it's real.

I stand up on the bench, try to see up into the window, but the curtains are drawn.

I don't know how long I stand there, paralyzed, unable to think one simple thought. But before it passes, I see the door open again and the brothers stream out. One by one they disappear over the asphalt until only imam Dakhil and al-Amin are left. They are too far away for me to hear what they say, but they seem to be done now, and shake hands, hugging one another briefly. Then imam Dakhil turns to go back to his apartment again, and al-Amin heads for the parking lot. Before they separate, I hear it.

"See you tomorrow, after Friday prayers."

I sink back into myself, and my focus returns, sharper and harder than ever.

See you tomorrow.

Yes, I think and close my eyes, we will.

Chapter 45

Bergort—Friday, August 21, 2015

They walk away from the shopping center in the sun, down toward the low-rise apartment buildings where she and Fadi grew up, past them, then out toward the mangy little field with its thistles and dandelions. Behind that there's a little grove where she and Fadi used to play when they were young, where she used to tell him about Ronia, and he got so afraid of trolls and robbers that he'd start to shake. Where they used to pretend they were grilling hot dogs at dusk and would sneak home numb and giggling to the darkness and silence of home.

"Where are we going, Parisa?" Yasmine says now.

"You'll see," Parisa answers quietly. "Almost there."

The grass is high, and Yasmine, suppressing the thought that there are snakes hiding and crawling there, hurries to keep up with Parisa.

When they arrive at the grove she stops.

"Up there," Parisa says with something forceful and impetuous in her voice now. "You go first."

"What the hell," Yasmine says. "You brought me here. You're the one who had something to show me."

Parisa sighs.

"Whatever you want," she says and climbs easily up to the sun-warmed rocks.

Yasmine waits a second and then follows.

*

She realizes she's been deceived as soon as she steps into the grove. Two men in wide jeans and long-sleeved, dark T-shirts stand in front of her. They don't say anything, and all Yasmine can see are their little eyes peeping out through the holes in the ski masks they're wearing. Ski masks identical to the ones the kids wore yesterday.

She feels adrenaline streaming through her, the world flashes around her, and she turns her head to look at Parisa, who has already turned around and started running down the slope without looking back.

Now the men approach her, and she backs up. They don't say anything, just walk quietly toward her with their arms out, black leather gloves ready to grab her. Finally, she turns to run, to escape, to leave all of this, whatever this is, behind. But then she sees a third man in a black ski mask coming toward her from the bottom of the slope, and she realizes there's no way out.

She sees that the man headed up the slope has on a shiny tracksuit and a green tattoo winds up from his back to his neck and in under his mask. In her fear she's watching all this from the outside, standing in a pale grove under a pale sun, with three masked men around her. She's alone here. Completely alone with these men.

She screams after Parisa: "What the fuck, *sharmuta*? What have you done?"

But Parisa doesn't answer her. Her back has already disappeared between the trees.

Chapter 46

London—Friday, August 21, 2015

Though it's still afternoon, the Friday-night rush has already started at the Library bar, and when she opens the door excitable French electronica washes over her. Klara forces her way up to the bar between thin bodies in thin dresses, between Breton-striped T-shirts and sweaty beards.

The press around the bar is extreme, but she's used to this place, and it doesn't take her long to catch Pete's eye.

"You look tired," he says over the music while filling a glass of Chardonnay to the brim and pushing it across the sticky counter.

"Thanks," she murmurs and takes a deep swig.

This makes everything feel a little better. Warmth spreads through her, and she closes her eyes. She's looking forward to going back to Stockholm tomorrow morning, although she feels guilty about not getting in touch with Gabriella yet. She's thought about it constantly for weeks. That she'll get to see her again in Stockholm. But then everything happened with Patrick, and her life was turned upside down.

I'll call later this evening, she thinks while taking a deep sip. Half of the glass. When she opens her eyes she sees Pete giving her a concerned look. She can see he thinks she's drinking too quickly. He's probably thinking about how things ended up last Sunday. Without looking away from him she downs the rest of the glass. *Fuck him and his bloody worry. Fuck all of them.*

She leans over the bar, signaling Pete to come closer so he can hear her: "Have you seen the guy who left my computer in again?"

Pete shakes his head.

"I told you he wasn't a regular? Never seen him before. Are you OK, Klara? I mean you look like—"

"No," she interrupts. "I'm not OK. Not at all."

Then she turns around and pushes her way out of the bar.

She stops at Tesco, as usual, on autopilot. Buys the same chilled bottle of Australian Chardonnay for £7.99 and a curry to warm up in the microwave. She pays and goes out onto the street again; suddenly everything feels a little too fast, speedy, as if she can't grab hold of her thoughts, as if they just shimmer and disappear as she tries to focus.

As soon as she's alone, it's as if she can't control her brain, as if it jumps back to the past then rushes forward, no matter what she does. There's Patrick on the rails, strangely intact and bloodless, but obviously lifeless. She's glad she got only a glimpse of that image. Then the leather jackets, glasses of white wine, Stockholm, the clothes she has to wash, Gabriella, her grandfather, Patrick again. Oh my God, in only two days they're going to present the report. Why is this happening? And then Patrick on the tracks again. The leather jackets again and the office.

Her thoughts drain her, and she feels too exhausted to take another step, even though she's almost home. In the end she sinks down onto the curb. But she forgets what she's holding in her hand, and the bottle in the thin plastic bag hits the asphalt hard and shatters, and wine flows out of the bag onto the street.

"Fuck fuck fuck!" she hisses and jumps aside to avoid getting soaked by wine.

She feels powerless. She thinks she might start crying, and she hides her face in her hands and leans forward. But the tears won't come, and through her fingers she sees the cracked asphalt, cigarette butts, candy wrappers, gravel.

When she finally opens her eyes panic washes over her, as heavy and stifling as a wave. And across the street, less than thirty feet away, a man stands staring straight at her. There's something familiar about him, something that makes the hairs stand up on the back of her neck. It takes a second for her to realize who he is. But then everything falls into place: the night in the alley, losing consciousness, the computer. She is completely sure. Patrick didn't take her computer.

The man across the street did.

Chapter 47

Bergort—Friday, August 21, 2015

The men are close now. They stop, maybe four or five yards from her, with their arms at their sides, black leather gloves, black masks. In the background, there's the sound of a train speeding out of the tunnel, glaring lights. She backs up, turning so that she always has all of them in sight.

"Please," she says, holding up her hands, she hears how empty it sounds, how helpless and pathetic. "Whoever you are… I'm just looking for my brother."

They stand still, just staring at her, completely neutral in their masks. She moves her gaze between them, tries to really see them or find some surface, make eye contact. The one with the tattoos and the tracksuit pants studies her calmly; his eyes are like small stones, dark gray and smooth in the holes of the mask. The one in the middle has brown eyes that seem completely calm and indifferent as well. But there's something in the eyes of the man at the very edge. It's as if he can't concentrate, his eyes wander back and forth from the others to her. There's something in them, something familiar.

She tries to swallow, but her mouth is dry and sticky. She turns to the familiar eyes, trying to catch them, begging them.

"I'm just looking for my brother," she repeats.

Tracksuit takes a step forward, holds out his hands with palms up, as if to show her he doesn't intend to hurt her. But she knows that gesture, she's seen it a thousand times.

Its meaning is inverted, not passive, but aggressive, and she takes a step backward. She sees the legs of the man with nervous eyes trembling, and she turns to him.

"Damnit, I'm from here," she says. "*Wallah*, I'm one of you."

"We warned you," Tracksuit says suddenly. His voice is deep and muffled like sound inside a prison cell. "We've made it clear that you needed to stop poking around. But you have shown us no respect, *len*. So you've left us no choice."

She doesn't know how it happened, but he's holding a knife now. The blade glitters, throwing reflections on the trees, and it blinds her.

"Please," she says again, "I'm just looking for my brother…"

"Seriously," says the one with the nervous, familiar eyes. "We said…"

"Enough!" Tracksuit hisses sideways and turns toward the person who questioned him. "Shut your mouth, you little cunt."

He turns to Yasmine again, leaning back a bit, self-assured, as if this is commonplace for him. The knife gleams in his hand. Yasmine takes a step back, she feels pine needles and gravel beneath her, feels the beginning of the slope, feels the trees around her.

"You don't seem to understand," he says, as if he were explaining something to a child. "You need to forget about that. There's nothing here for you. Nothing to figure out. Your brother, the *haddi*, is dead. We're nothing, you understand? We're ghosts."

The nervous eyes are fastened to the knife now.

"He's not dead," she whispers.

"What did you say, whore?" Tracksuit says.

He's almost next to her now, maybe an arm's length—a stab—away. And there's something in it that wakes Yasmine up, something in the way he says Fadi is dead, how he calls her a whore.

Something about the way he stands there with his shitty tattoos, his fucking knife, and his shiny, douchey Adidas pants. It's as if she falls headlong into a well from a mountain, headlong into where she came from. How many times has she seen them with their knives and knuckles and shaved heads, their broken noses, and their wasted fucking lives? Just like David, just like everyone here. Your own rules and expectations, your own violence and threats. And she thinks about Fadi and the weapons and David's fist against her temple. And she thinks: It's enough now, she can't take another second. It ends here.

And before she knows it the gun is in her hand. Before she's even caught up with her own reaction, she's cocked it, just like she remembers from the shooting range. Before the adrenaline even has time to flow through her body, she's holding it in two hands and pointing it straight at the forehead of the man in those tracksuit pants.

She took the blows in the living room and in the kitchen and in the bedroom all through her childhood. Took the bruises and the shame. But it was for Fadi's sake. She took the abuse and the blows from David. She let him do it, asked him to, forced him to. But it was for her own sake. No more. All the hatred she carried, for that, for Fadi and David and her mother and father and Parisa and this whole sad place, Bergort, is suddenly in her hands. It's as if she's embracing hatred, as if it's made of steel and death.

She sees how the eyes behind the mask change, something flashes in them. She sees how the other two draw back, how the one with the nervous eyes holds up his hands and backs away.

"Do not call me whore," she says. "My brother is not dead."

The glint of fear or confusion has passed.

"What are you gonna do with that?" Tracksuit says. "Are you gonna shoot me, whore?"

He says the last word quietly and slowly, and the last syllable is drowned out by the deafening sound that erupts when she pulls the trigger.

Chapter 48

Bergort—Friday, August 21, 2015

I get up before six. I read the digits on my cell phone, relieved that it's finally tomorrow, even if time is more complicated down here in the dark. I couldn't sleep last night. How can you sleep when your whole life is twisting around inside of you? How can you sleep when you see your sister's face every time you close your eyes, hear her voice, see the rows of your dead brothers, rows of bad decisions—a short, wasted life?

Sometime in the middle of the night I pushed open the heavy door to the hallway, found my way to the stairs in the dark, and was relieved to discover that the door opened without a key. I remembered one time about a hundred years ago when we climbed up onto the roof of one of these buildings, and I felt like that was the only thing that mattered. To get to the top, all the way up, as close to the sky as I could. And I crept up the stairs, all the way up to the top floor, all the way up to the attic, right up to the last staircase to the roof.

The air in the attic was so heavy and damp, so filled with concrete and abandoned junk that it felt like breathing in all of Bergort, and it made me so miserable that I hurried up the last stairway. Two steps at a time, then out the door, out onto the roof, ten floors above the ground, the wind so warm and mild, the stars faded in the gray summer night sky. I crawled on all fours right up to the edge.

It looked like the school was right at my feet, so small I could have put it in my pocket. There were high-rises all around me, like the towers of a castle, a fortress, or a prison. I saw Camp Nou, which looked like a postage stamp, and the playground and the low-rises. I turned my head and saw cars burning in the big parking lot, which looked like birthday candles, of no importance at all. I could hear voices even up here, could see the kids and the cops engaged in their meaningless dance.

When I crawled to the other side, I could see our building, so small and identical to all the others, and I thought, That's where it began, sister. That's where we started. It could have ended up differently, sister, but this is what is.

This is how it turned out.

And I turned my gaze just a few degrees, past the grove where we used to play and where I met the brothers, just a bit more, and there was imam Dakhil's apartment. This is where it ends, sister, I thought. Just an inch from where it started. And I crawled to the middle of the roof and rolled over on my back. Looked up at the sky, the stars, and everything else. And I made one last attempt. Maybe the only sincere attempt I ever made. For a moment I thought that now it was going to happen, that it happens when we are in need.

I stood up, turned in the right direction, made the right movements, mumbled the right words, and fell to my knees. Slowly, I let myself fall forward, my head on the rough, dry roof. All around me was dawn light and burning cars, timber and concrete, and my whole life. If God exists somewhere, I thought, he is here. And I recited the verses with a sincerity I'd never before been capable of. Right there, in that moment, I sought mercy and forgiveness and humility more intensely than I ever did before.

I don't know how long I lay there, how long I waited and prayed. Long enough to finally become so exhausted that I fell down on my side, in the gray, grainy light. Long enough to know that I got no answer. Long enough to know that I was completely alone.

Maybe being alone is somewhat of a relief, I think now, as I stand up on the warm concrete floor in my basement. All I want is to be reconciled to the past. I should have understood a long time ago that there was never any context outside of us. There was never anything that could fill the void you left behind.

But it's not true, that's not all I want. More than anything, I wish I'd never let you disappear. That I'd never given you any reason, that I never forced you to go. But these are thoughts I don't have the strength to think. Instead, I force myself to focus on the only task I have left. The traitors are going to have to answer for their betrayal. Beyond that, everything is dark.

I reach my hand into the sleeping bag, down to the foot, and haul out the old Russian gun, check the magazine. This was all I took with me from Syria. Two handguns, a rifle. The instruments to exact my vengeance. I double-check the safety and wedge the gun into the waistband of my jeans. I inhale and sit down on the mattress.

There is only one thing left to do. I tear a page out of my notebook, grab a blue ballpoint pen. And I start to write.

I write to Mehdi first. I thank him for everything. Then I ask him to save the rest of the letter. To hide it and wait for you. In case you ever come back.

And then I start from the beginning and write everything

down. I write about waiting for you next to the bushes outside the school, about how we slept on the floor in that cold apartment. About my brothers and the Syrian's car and the fires and all this fucking shit. About how I flapped and cawed and chased your shadow through Bergort. But most of all I write about how it wasn't your fault, nothing that happened was your fault. It was only me, just concrete and my brothers and the ones who call themselves our parents and the school and the darkness that pushes and pries... But mostly it was just me.

I write about Dakhil and al-Amin, I write about his betrayal and the bombs, about legs blown off and the line of bodies. I fill the paper and tear out one and then another. I write until the ink in the pen is gone, until the text becomes paler and thinner, ultimately just an imprint on the paper.

When there's nothing left, I collapse on the mattress, emptied out by the past, emptied by what led me here. Empty of everything except what I have left to do.

Chapter 49

Bergort—Friday, August 21, 2015

Everything happens fast now. Everything stands still. The sound stops and for a moment there is complete silence. One of the men in the hood has turned around and is running like a hare through the bushes and brush, down the slope toward the weedy field below. Yasmine lets him go, barely glances at him, confused by what she's done, confused by the silence and stillness.

The man in the tracksuit pants and tattoos lies in front of her in the long grass, rolled up in a little ball, whimpering like a kitten, with his hands pressed against his thigh where she's just shot him.

The other man, the one with the nervous, jumpy eyes is down on his knees now, holding his hands up in front of him.

"Yazz!" he says. "Please Yazz, don't hurt me! I didn't know, I didn't mean to..."

She just looks at them. It's surreal. The sunlight. The man whimpering. The other man begging for mercy. She realizes that she still has the gun in her hand. She's still pointing at the other man, aiming for his head. And she realizes she knows who he is. She's known it the whole time.

"Take off your mask, Mehdi, you little fucking *sharmuta*," she says.

He obeys, and when he lifts it, she sees tears flowing down his broad face.

"Yazz," he says. "I'm a father now, Yazz! Let me live."

She lowers the gun slowly.

"You're such a fucking ass, Mehdi," she says. "I'm not gonna shoot you. I wouldn't have shot him either if he hadn't pulled a fucking knife on me."

Mehdi nods quickly, pathetically.

"I swear, Yazz, I didn't know anything about this."

But she's not listening. She bends over the man she shot and pulls off his ski mask.

"We better put something on that wound," she says. But he just stares at her with cold hatred in his eyes and lifts one hand from the wound to try to hit her. She jumps away.

"Fuck it then," she says. "You've just been shot, *bre*. No matter how much I hate you, I don't want you to die."

She turns to Mehdi.

"Take off your shirt and tie it around the wound. Do you have a phone?"

Mehdi nods and takes off his jacket, pulls his shirt over his head.

"Call an ambulance, then, *len*. Your friend needs help."

"But what should I say? I mean, he's been shot?"

"No fucking ambulances!" the shot man says and tries his best to get up on his side.

But he collapses on his back, his hands pressed against the wound.

"Tell them he's shot. Seriously, I don't care. But don't pull me into this bullshit any more, I want to make that absolutely fucking clear to you."

Mehdi bends over the other man and wraps his T-shirt hard around his thigh. The man refuses to look away from Yasmine.

"You'll die for this, whore," he hisses. "You don't know who you're fucking with."

He tries to laugh, but it comes out as a hiss.

"This isn't just about Bergort, you little *sharmuta*. This is fucking real."

Yasmine bends over him again.

"So what is it then?" she says. "What's this about? And what does my brother have to do with it?"

"All I know is that you're gonna fucking die, whore," he hisses between clenched teeth.

Mehdi shrugs.

"We have to get out of here," he says. "Before the cops get here."

"I'm not going anywhere," Yasmine says.

She suddenly feels the weight of the gun again and aims it at the man on the grass, at his other leg.

"I'm not going anywhere until this fucker tells me where Fadi is and how he's connected to all this. Time to talk, *bre*, otherwise I'll fuck your other leg up, too."

There's something intoxicating about all this. Something almost arousing. After all she's had to take, all the blows and shit. She has the power now. The violence is in her hands. She almost hopes he'll keep his mouth shut. She wants nothing more than to put a bullet in his right leg, too. But Mehdi pulls on her shoulder, sobbing.

"No, Yazz," he says. "I swear, he doesn't know anything about Fadi. I swear! Nobody knows. No one besides me."

They're all the way to the high-rise where Mehdi and Parisa live with her mother when they hear the sirens singing over the expressway, then slow down and turn off on the other side of Bergort.

"Damn, they were fast," Mehdi mumbles.

Yasmine doesn't answer, just snatches open the door to the staircase. She doesn't have time to care about what just happened. All she can think about is—Fadi is here, Mehdi's been with him the whole time.

She stops inside the damp, echoing stairway and turns to Mehdi.

"And now?" she says. "Where are we going?"

He walks past her, unlocks the door to the stairs to the basement, and heads down in front of her. Their footsteps echo dully behind them. He leads them farther down into the dampness, past rusty, dripping pipes and a humming laundry room. Finally, he stops in front of a white steel door that's identical to all the other white steel doors down here.

Yasmine's head is pounding, and she's having a hard time breathing. Mehdi goes to the door and leans forward to insert the key.

"Wait," she says.

She sinks down on her haunches, and her throat feels thick and rough from suppressed tears. It's been four years since she left him. Four years of betrayal and emptiness, and life without him and Bergort. Just weeks ago she learned that he was dead. She closes her eyes and sees the cat hanging from a lamppost, the symbols on the walls, the burning cars. Sees Fadi when he was small, asleep on her arm. Sees his eyes that last night, when she left him to his fate. She sees blood on the grass in the grove just minutes ago. What happens now? she thinks. Where do we go now?

She swallows and looks at Mehdi, gestures for him to open the door. He knocks gently.

"It's just me, brother," he says.

Then he pushes open the door to the basement storage room, and Yasmine closes her eyes, unsure if she's able to do this. When she opens them, Mehdi has turned on the light in a bare and empty room.

"He's gone," he says.

But he's holding something in his hand, a small bundle of handwritten papers.

"But I think he left something for you."

Chapter 50

London—Friday, August 21, 2015

The sight of the man on the other side of the street paralyzes Klara. All she can see is his black T-shirt, his black jeans, and his long, messy hair. She suddenly remembers his sinewy hands as they tore away her backpack. Remembers what he whispered to her.

When she gains control of her body again and manages to stand up, she backs up toward the building behind her, without looking away from him. She sees he's holding his hands up, as if to show he's unarmed.

A car drives slowly down the street, creating a moment of distance between them. But as soon as it's gone, it's as if she's hypnotized again, she can't look away from him, can't run, can only back up slowly toward the wall.

Remember, remember, the fifth of November.

That's what he whispered to her, that's what he has tattooed on his wrist, and now he's slowly crossing the street, with his hands still held up, palms outward, trying to show he's not a threat. But he's already proven he's a threat, already proven what he's capable of.

Remember, remember, the fifth of November.

She backs up until she's against the window of a vintage boutique. He walks slowly toward her, steps up on the sidewalk now, just a few yards away. A group of young Spanish people laugh outside the shop behind her and disappear down the street.

He waits until they're farther away.

"Klara," he says calmly.

His English sounds American, and his voice is surprisingly friendly and strangely high, almost childlike and alarmingly harmless.

"Klara, please forgive me, we need to talk."

He's close now, could almost touch her if he held out his hand. His face is pale and smooth as a winter moon, his fingers long and thin. He doesn't seem like he spends much time outdoors.

She holds up her hands, signaling that she doesn't want him any closer—he's already too close.

"I don't know what you know," he says. "I was the one who took your computer."

She nods, steels herself, tightens her fists. A single fucking motion and she could hit him between the legs, just like she kicked Calle in sixth grade when he tried to touch her breasts. None of the boys tried to pinch her after that. And she's close now, ready to explode.

"I'm so sorry," he says. "It was a mistake, OK? So fucking stupid."

She doesn't relax, even if there's something about him that seems genuine, sincere. She says nothing. Just waits for him to continue.

"Patrick is dead," he says. "They pushed him in front of the train."

She swallows.

"How do you know Patrick?" she whispers at last. "Who the hell are you?"

"You can call me Cross," he says, throwing nervous glances up and down the street. "I don't have much time, but do you mind if we take a walk?"

*

"It was my idea," Cross says as they walk slowly along Virginia Road toward the long shadows of the trees in Ravenscroft Park. "A fucking stupid idea. Patrick was pissed off of course. But I'd been up for a really long time, if you know what I mean? Coding and doing speed for a couple of nights. And Patrick was so close to figuring out what this all was about. I knew he needed access to one of your computers, that he'd tried before. Me too."

Klara shakes her head, stops.

"What are you trying to say?" she says. "What the hell are you talking about?"

But Cross doesn't seem to care. He just waves at her to continue walking. She keeps her eyes on him, glancing at him sideways, ready to fight or flee if it were to become necessary. Should she even be walking with him?

"Patrick said you were in Sweden last weekend, so I checked the flights and waited for you at the airport, I thought you might leave your bag unattended for a second. But you never did. Not until you went to that hipster bar. I had some roofies with me, for personal use, I was really speedy. But I had another idea when I got to the bar. So I waited a while and then crumbled a couple of pills into your drink. You drank them up fast, so it didn't take long for it to have an effect."

She just stares at him. What the fuck is he talking about?

"Wait," she says, shaking her head. "What the hell are you saying? You put something in my drink? That is fucking deranged."

Cross nods, avoiding her eyes.

"Not my best moment, I have to agree. Would have been better if I just let Patrick do it in his own way. Maybe he wouldn't have..."

They've arrived at the park now and head down one of the gravel paths toward a park bench. She takes out a cigarette and lights it without offering him one.

"Are you going to tell me what the hell this is all about?" she says. Cross's eyes continue to jump back and forth across the park. Finally, he calms down again and turns to her.

"It's about your job," he says. "Something to do with whoever is paying for your research."

She tries to catch his eyes, but they're hopping across the park again, and Cross has stood up now, rigid and anxious like a hyperactive child.

"Stirling Security?" she says.

"He got a hold of some stuff," Cross continues, as if he hadn't heard her.

He shrugs off his backpack and takes out a thick, red cardboard folder.

"Here," he says and lays it on Klara's lap. "I don't know what it is. Patrick hid it in the courtyard behind the institution where you work. As soon as I realized he was gone, I went and got it. When I came home, someone had ransacked the apartment."

Klara feels the weight of the folder on her knees. She puts her hands on it, pulls it closer, and looks up at Cross. He has tears in his eyes now.

"It was our culture, you know?" he says. "Anonymous. Digital rebellion. But that it would end up like this? That he'd die?"

"Were you two a couple?" she says quietly. "Was he your boyfriend?"

Cross nods hesitantly.

"He was the reason I came to London. You know, he got this job after Harvard? So idealistic. Human rights and all that. But soon he realized something was off about your boss. Something off about the entire institute."

Klara gets up too. Gently, she takes his hand.

"What's off?" she says. "And why did you take my computer?"

He seems to calm down for a moment when she holds his hand.

"Something's not right about that report you're writing," he says. "And the conference in Stockholm. Patrick was sure your boss had been bought, you know? She's writing the report on behalf of someone, a business or a lobbyist. He thought the report was going to end up having a lot of influence. But we couldn't get a hold of what she wrote, or what her conclusions were. So Patrick said you were also working on the report, and then I thought maybe we could find it on your computer? But of course you didn't have it either."

Klara shakes her head.

"Our boss wouldn't let me see her recommendations," she says. "But why do you trust me? Maybe they bought me too?"

Cross looks into her eyes, shrugs.

"Who else do I have?" he says. "I don't even know what this is about. Just that I have to leave now. It's not safe for me here anymore. And if they find out what you have you won't be safe either."

He points to the cardboard folder Klara laid on the park bench.

"I have to go," he says. "Get out of London. Do what you want with that. Everything's over for me anyway. But I'm sorry about that thing with your computer."

And with that he turns his back to Klara and disappears deeper into the shadows of the trees.

*

Afterward, she's sitting rigid and perfectly straight in the back of a taxi. On her knees sits the red folder, which she hasn't even dared to open yet.

What should she do with it? What does she dare to do? Patrick is dead, probably murdered. The trip to Stockholm is tomorrow. She hasn't packed. The whole world is upside down again. She needs a drink.

The taxi stops outside the Library, but when she sees the warm light and the people laughing and having a good time inside, she feels sick again. She leans forward and tells the driver to continue, and with a sigh he drives on. She has to go somewhere. Anywhere at all. As long as nobody knows her there.

Chapter 51

Bergort—Friday, August 21, 2015

It's late afternoon by the time I'm back in front of the building I grew up in. It's as if time has stopped. One second is an hour now. One minute a whole morning. Four or five hours left now until it's time. I try not to think about it, push it away, push it down, but the adrenaline still makes my head spin. It's not that I'm afraid of it. On the contrary. I look forward to it. The thought of al-Amin's eyes when he kneels before me. Will he beg for his life? The man who was ready to destroy me, how will he look when I destroy him?

Our parents aren't home, the apartment is dark and quiet and clean. I stop in the living room. Squat down. This is where we used to lie, sister. On the floor in the afternoons. This is where you read the subtitles and quizzed me on the dictionary. This was where we struggled to stay warm, where I lay my head in your lap and felt a sense of security I've never felt since.

For a moment, I think I'm going to cry, but I know it doesn't matter, there's no going back. It's all over now, has been for a long time.

But when I open the door to our room, it's as if the world trembles, as if the whole universe hesitates and restarts. I stop at the threshold with my temples pulsing—overcome by a feeling I can't quite put my finger on. A sense that something has shifted in the foundation, and now nothing is the same. The light streams in through the blinds and across the floor like it always does. Your bed is made and stretched tight like it has been since you left. Nothing is different, yet everything is different. I turn to my own bed and its light blue bedspread. And I see it's wrinkled now, not smooth like last week.

Slowly I go over to the mattress. Slowly I lift it up, pull it off, close my eyes. Time is uneven again. It feels like two seconds are an hour, but at last I feel the mattress become heavy in my hands, feel it fall off the bed and onto the floor.

When I open my eyes I already know the bag is gone. My heart is pounding as I go to the bed and bend over it. A paper is lying there. A folded letter-size page. I pick it up and see your blocky handwriting. Just one line. "I will always protect you." And your number. Nothing more.

Chapter 52

Bergort—Friday, August 21, 2015

It's as if she can't move and she falls slowly down onto the thin mattress with the letter pressed to her chest.

Fadi's jerky handwriting. The desperation of the letter, the confusion that increases throughout the text until it finally ebbs away completely. The last page where the ink has run out, and he's carved the words into the paper with the dry tip of his pen.

Somewhere far away, she can hear Mehdi lifting things up and moving them around, as if he's looking for something.

She thought Fadi was dead, only to discover he was alive, and now he's on his way to die, on his way to choose death. If only she had taken him by the hand four years ago. If only she had put her arms around him and pulled him close. If only she had taken him with her. If only he'd done what he's asking Mehdi to do in his letter, stay and wait for her.

Perhaps that's what he was trying to do? But Bergort wouldn't let him go. The ties were elastic and pulled him back. In the same way they dragged her back now. She feels Mehdi put his hand on her shoulder, and she opens her eyes.

"Yazz," he says. "He's taken his gun. And he has another gun and a Kalashnikov hidden at your parents'."

She shakes her head.

"Not anymore. I found them and took them away."

She pulls the gun out of her waistband.

"How do you think I got a hold of this?"

Mehdi nods and squats down with his face in his hands.

"OK, OK," he says.

She looks at him with his head hanging down, his eyes jumping around, his baggy jeans, his sneakers. He looks like he did when he was little. Like when Fadi was little. Like when she was little. All that attitude is gone now, revealed for what it is: bluster and bravado. A façade that hides the usual bad decisions and chaos. Her whole life. Fadi's whole life. Just bad decisions. Just chaos.

She shuffles off of the mattress and grabs Mehdi's arms, takes his hands from his face. He opens his eyes and looks at her in surprise.

"*Ey*," she says. "Mehdi, brother, we need to fix this. You understand? Right?"

He continues looking at her silently, nods slightly.

"How?" he says.

"You have to tell me everything you know. Everything about what just happened up there in the grove. Everything about those fucking symbols. Everything about Fadi and what he's up to. You understand, *len*? Time to come clean, OK?"

Mehdi tells her what Fadi told him. About Dakhil and the men who recruited him. Everything he knows about the mysterious brother al-Amin and the satellite phone. Everything he's been told and has pieced together. It all sounds like a movie. The drones, the dead brothers in the sands of Syria. Fadi's eyes and his weapons.

"I swear," he says. "If I hadn't seen his eyes, *len*. If I hadn't seen the guns and how he can shoot. If I hadn't seen his eyes, Yazz. I promise, I would have thought he was crazy, I would have thought he was crazy."

And he tells her about Bergort. About the gangster, Rado, who she shot in the leg. About how he showed up out of nowhere a few weeks ago, with a few other dudes just like him. Mehdi tells her about their tattoos and their dead eyes. They're Serbs, and dangerous as hell.

"I promise, Yazz, they were like *Straight Outta Kumla*. Totally psycho. He brought a dead cat with him, *len*. He hung it on a lamppost! Crazy shit."

"But why, Mehdi?" she says. "And why did you stay around? What's the matter with you? You have a baby now, brother!"

He shrugs and shifts his eyes, rubs his hands over his face.

"Fuck, I can't take it. Neither can Parisa. We weren't ready, you know? Not me. We live with her mother. In one room. With the baby. Like fucking beggars. This *shuno*, Rado, who you shot, he put me in command, ya know. The kids looked up to me like a king! And he paid. Fuck, Yazz, Parisa and I don't have shit. A thousand kronors a day for two weeks is a lot of cash for me."

He falls silent and clears his throat, looking embarrassed. But Yasmine doesn't give a shit about his fucking anxiety.

"You're a fucking jackass, Mehdi. I swear, if it weren't for all this chaos I'd laugh, brother. Do you think people hand out cash for free? So fucking stupid, I swear."

"Sorry," he mumbles. "Of course it was wrong, Yazz. I shouldn't have snitched about you looking for Fadi. But we were getting ready for the riots, and I thought if you could just calm down for one week that this would go smoothly. I get my cash, and Fadi has time to get his revenge. Everybody would win if you just stayed away. But I didn't think they'd hurt you. I just told them that somebody was asking questions about the symbols and the riots and that we had to make it stop. And what happened today... that was Parisa's fault."

Yasmine is startled by that and leans toward him.

"Parisa's fault?" she says slowly. "What do you mean?"

"I wanted to tell Fadi, I swear. I mean, he deserved to know you were looking for him, right? But Parisa thought that was too dangerous. Nobody should know, not even you. We needed the cash, Yazz. And I don't know..."

"Don't know what?"

"You just took off," Mehdi says and looks her in the eye. "Never answered her emails, lived your cool life. Maybe it was payback for her?"

He looks ashamed.

"So I did what she wanted, didn't say anything to Fadi. Asked them to scare you. But they promised they wouldn't hurt you, Yazz."

"Fuck, Mehdi, what did you expect? You said yourself they are completely *loco*, brother?"

They sit in silence for a while. Mehdi can't look her in the eyes. Time is precious, but it's too much to take in. Too much Bergort to take in at once.

"So what's the deal with Rado and the riots and all that shit, then?" she says. "Who is he? What's the fucking point, brother? Just to create chaos for its own sake? That's so fucking useless."

Mehdi shrugs, looks at her furtively.

"There are rumors," he says.

"And?"

"People say someone is behind it. Somebody who wants Bergort to be in chaos."

She nods.

"But who? And why?"

He shrugs.

"There are rumors that some Swede has been handing out cash in the parking lot outside the school. They say some huge corporation is behind it. I don't know, Yazz. I didn't ask much, I needed the cash, OK?"

"I know something about that," she says. "But this Rado? Who is he?"

Mehdi shrugs.

"He's probably like me. Just a *shuno* who wants to make a little coin. He doesn't give a shit about riots. It's all about cash. But they're gonna be really fucking angry now."

He shudders, and it sounds like he's sobbing, helpless.

"I doubt Rado is a *shuno* that forgets," he continues. "He's a real *g*, Yazz. Not a wannabe like me. They'll kill us after today."

She knows he's right. You can't just go around shooting gangsters. You don't threaten their game. She knows what the price for that is.

"It doesn't matter," she says.

She leans forward and puts her hands on his arms.

"The only thing that matters right now is Fadi," she says. "Everything else we'll take care of later."

"Jesus, I'm so fucking stupid," he says. "All of this? What the hell was it good for?"

"Fuck all that right now. We have to find out where Fadi is, and where he's headed. And where those jihadists are. That's all we worry about now."

Mehdi raises his head finally and looks into her eyes.

"I know where he's going," he says.

Chapter 53

London—Friday, August 21, 2015

She doesn't know why she asks the taxi driver to take her to One Aldwych Hotel. She's read about it somewhere, that it's luxurious and in some way anonymous, and far from the places she usually goes. After she's paid and stepped out onto the street, she sees through the high windows of the bar men in tailored suits ordering sophisticated cocktails for women in severe makeup with their hair up. It's perfect. She sees a reflection of herself in the glass and is surprised she doesn't look grittier after a week like this.

It takes half a glass of wine for her to muster the energy, or courage, or whatever it is, to remove the plastic folder and put it on the low mahogany table. She takes another sip of wine. And then another. Feels how it relaxes her, how the stress slowly flows out of her. She takes the plastic folder in her hand and goes to the bar and orders another glass. Sits down. Takes a deep breath and lifts out the first page.

The folder is thicker than she thought at first. It seems to contain around thirty pages. She reaches for the wine-glass—small sips, now that she feels calmer, not as greedy—and leans over the stack of paper. The first pages seem to be printouts from Stirling Security's website. The same pages she was browsing the other day. The same vague descriptions of what they do. The same empty boasts.

She feels her pulse quicken. Stirling Security again, but nothing she didn't already know.

The next document is a transcript from the Liechtenstein Bank's website. Ribbenstahl & Partners. *"Market-leading confidential private banking."* OK. But she's also already made this connection as well.

She quickly thumbs forward to what looks like an article published in a large British business magazine a few months ago. CORPORATE KREMLIN ENTERS EU LOBBYING ARENA is the headline.

She pulls the sheets out of the stack and leans back in the chair with wineglass in hand. The article is a review of how companies with ties to the Russian government have started to position themselves in Brussels in a variety of ways. The clearest examples according to the author are how Gazprom and the other Russian energy companies who have hired major U.S. lobbying firms and law firms to push through EU legislation.

Klara sighs and takes another sip of wine. None of this is news to her either. She remembers this discussion in Brussels a few years back. With half an eye she turns the page and skims the reader comments on this article. Halfway through the thirty or so comments her eye is caught by some familiar words: Stirling Security. She stops and looks back through the comments until she finds that name again, in the middle of a comment by someone with the pseudonym RedThreat99.

She glances quickly through the comment in which RedThreat99 warns that it's not just energy companies with murky ownership structures that are active in Brussels and elsewhere. The commenter points specifically to businesses in the growing security industry, which RedThreat99 says he himself works in.

> During a period of increasing acceptance for the outsourcing of some police tasks to contractors, it's particularly important that policymakers are aware of who is behind companies such as MRM, Vienna Continental, and the aggressive and resourceful Stirling Security, which in recent months has established itself in several European countries. I myself have been in meetings where the latter's representatives were accompanied by Russian diplomats. It's important that we don't give away the keys to the city in our desire to save money!

Klara turns the page, but no one had commented on RedThreat99's short text. She lays the paper down in front of her on the table. Russian-owned security companies want to enter the European market? But there's nothing concrete here. Everything she's read so far, she could have found online.

Her wineglass is almost empty, and she stands up to order another. But there are several pages left in the folder, so she changes her mind, sits down again, and pulls out the last seven or eight pages, which seem to be copies of receipts for payments.

She moves the paper directly under the table lamp. Her eyes are drawn to the sum of the first page. It's for five hundred thousand kronor, and it's dated two months ago. She flips forward and sees a similar payment dated on the same day this month, just two weeks ago. She flips back and sees that the money was sent to an account at the Ribbenstahl & Partners bank, with an address in Vaduz, Liechtenstein. It was paid by Stirling Security.

She feels her pulse quicken and tackles the last pages in the folder. They look like printouts of an email correspondence. The sender of the first email has the initials GL and the address *@stirlingsecurity.com*. But it's when she sees the recipient that she freezes, and it's as if the murmur in the room suddenly subsides: Charlotte Anderfeldt.

As she reads through the messages between GL and Charlotte, it all seems more and more surreal. They're written in Swedish, and there's something about how GL formulates things that feel familiar to her, but she can't quite put her finger on what. She can't seem to concentrate on it either. The first email is sent from GL nearly two months ago:

> Thanks for yet another constructive meeting in London! It pleases me and everyone at Stirling Security that we'll be working together on this, and we look forward to supporting your important research. I'm attaching proof of payment so you can see the first installment has been deposited in the account we arranged at Ribbenstahl. Obviously, as previously mentioned, I can't stress enough how important it is that our cooperation remains private. Please erase our email correspondence, as agreed. Looking forward to a productive collaboration!

Then come a couple of emails about a meeting in Stockholm a month ago. She vaguely remembers that Charlotte was in Stockholm, but she travels so much that it's hard to remember exactly. And then comes the last email from GL, dated just a few weeks ago:

> Charlotte!
> Here comes the second proof of payment, which you've surely already seen in the account? As we said on the phone, a meeting the day before the conference at our office on Kungsgatan

30 would be perfect. I suggest 11:00 A.M. I've shown your rough draft to Orlov, and he's going to clear it with international management, but he's very positive for the most part. Just some details to adjust, as I'm sure you can appreciate. Good work!

Best, GL

There's a ringing sound in her ears. She lifts her eyes and suddenly it feels like all the well-dressed guests are looking furtively at her. She quickly rakes up the papers and heads out to the street.

The early evening is warm and sticky. She leans against the glass windows of the bar, takes out a cigarette, and feels a sort of calm spread through her when she lights it.

A Russian-owned security company. A bank in Liechtenstein, where Charlotte has had a million kronor deposited. The conference in Stockholm, where Charlotte will present her expert recommendation to the EU justice ministers about the possibility of privatizing certain policing functions. A recommendation that Klara has not yet read.

And Patrick's body on the tracks in Little Venice. The contents of the folder she's holding in her hand are probably what got him killed. The men in black leather jackets were following him. She wasn't crazy.

"Charlotte," she whispers quietly to herself. "What have you got yourself mixed up in?"

Chapter 54

Bergort—Friday, August 21, 2015

They're sitting on the slope that leads up to the subway tracks, on the other side of the sidewalk, and the afternoon sun flashes off the dusty windows of the low-rise apartment building Mehdi pointed out. To the right of the building Yasmine sees the neglected field she walked across earlier today. It's incomprehensible that was just a few hours ago. You can still make out the tracks of the ambulance and police cars that drove over the field.

She looks up at Mehdi and shades her eyes from the sun.

"Damn, Mehdi," she says. "Are you sure about this?"

They have been here for almost an hour, and the longer nothing happens the more desperate she feels. Fadi is about to do something terrible, something unforgivable. Something that will make him have to disappear for good—before he's even come back. At the same time she can't help but understand. They betrayed him and turned him into a murderer. Everyone has betrayed Fadi. Eventually you strike back, no matter the consequences. She understands that too well; in the end nothing else matters.

Mehdi nods, but not very convincingly.

"This is the where the beards meet anyway," he says. "Somewhere near the top."

"Fadi told you that?"

Mehdi shrugs.

"Everyone knows that. If he's gonna attack some beards in Bergort, then it would be them."

Yasmine leans back. What she wants most is to just curl up and sink into a deep darkness until this whole thing is over. But she barely has time to close her eyes before Mehdi shakes her leg.

"What did I say?" he says, pointing down toward the sidewalk.

Yasmine sits up halfway and follows his finger with her eyes. Two men are approaching across the asphalt. One is North African and the other has a long shirt, wide trousers, a *kufi* on his head, and a long straggly beard. The other guy is younger and wearing more Western-style clothes. But still has the beard. Their voices are low, only a hum, and disappear completely when they open the door and enter the stairwell.

"They seem to be meeting up there," Yasmine says quietly.

She bends down toward the bag they picked up from within the thicket behind the school and gently pulls out the well-worn Kalashnikov.

She sees Mehdi turn. His eyes are frightened and shaky when he sees the gun.

"What the hell are we gonna do, Yazz?" he says. "I don't understand."

"I don't care what you do, loser," she says. "I'm gonna do whatever needs to be done, *len*. That's all."

She keeps her eyes on the sidewalk, but all she sees is a large man jogging toward the building. He has no beard, but he's wearing a *kufi* on his head.

"There's another one," she says, nodding in that direction.

The man disappears through the front door, which slams behind him.

She crawls out of the bush to get a better overview.

She can't see him. Yet it's as if she can feel Fadi's presence, like a radio frequency, a vibration in the air that only she can pick up. She turns back and gets down on her knees to pick up the gun and get it ready.

She's scarcely grabbed hold of it, when she hears a crash from somewhere above, followed by screaming voices through an open window or a balcony door. The sound of something falling to the floor and smashing. More voices screaming and begging. She stands up, her legs trembling, rifle in hand.

"Fuck," she says. "He's already in there. He's inside!"

Chapter 55

Bergort—Friday, August 21, 2015

Your note in one hand. At the top of the stairs, outside the attic. My gun in the other. Suddenly I'm so close to you. A phone call away. At the same time, I'm so close to what I came home for, the only thing I've been living for during the past month. Just minutes from it, the light is already falling at an angle through the dirty windows half a floor below me.

The brothers will be here at any moment. I let go of your note and unfold it again. Your handwriting, your words. Why did you come back? Why now? Four years, sister. Why only now?

Sometimes brother Shahid told us about martyrs in the evenings, and we listened half terrified, half impressed. How they prepared for their suicide missions. How they kept to themselves, without any outside influences. How someone else took care of food and everything else for the week before, so they could spend their time praying and thinking about their mission, and the paradise that awaited them. And how, finally, when the bomb was wrapped around their chests, they were led nearly the entire way to their target. So they only had to focus on going straight forward, without any distractions, no thoughts except of paradise, so their task would remain simple and clean.

This is how I've thought of myself since I came back. This is how I thought of my days in the basement. Like preparation, sharpening the blade. Even if I don't pray anymore. Even though I'm no longer hoping for paradise. One final act of courage. One last act of chaos and justice. Then nothing.

But here you are. Here's your note.

And with it come thoughts I shouldn't have. Thoughts of my life, myself. Thoughts I've been pushing away, that I no longer have the right to think. Not since my brothers were wiped out. Not since I destroyed them. Since then I have no life beyond this. I press the gun harder into my hand. Look at the magazine for the thousandth time. Since then I can't allow myself any thoughts other than revenge.

I take out your note again. Read your words one more time before I tear it into a hundred pieces and let it go. The pieces fall down the stairs like confetti, like snow, like forgetting.

They land soundlessly on the worn stone steps just as I hear the front door opening far down in the building. I hear the brothers' voices echoing in the concrete. The gun is heavy and cold in my hand.

I close my eyes and listen. First, I hear brother Taimur's voice, almost a whisper in the concrete.

"I don't mean hands aren't *awrah*, brother, but when they're so strict, they risk losing people, you know?"

The usual talk about life in the Caliphate. The other brother just hums, and I guess that it's brother Tasheem. He's always silent, lets the others do all the chatting and complaining. It flashes before my eyes. In my head, I have executed them all every waking hour for a month. One by one. Had them kneeling in front of me with their hands on their heads. Then just let the bullets sweep over them. But now, when I'm so close? I force myself to remember the body parts in the red sand. Force myself to remember the rows of dead. They have earned this. They have brought this on themselves.

My heart is pounding, and I take the second magazine out of my pocket. Turn it over. Look at it. Fourteen bullets in total. This wasn't my plan. I was supposed to have the rifle. But I can't wait any longer. Especially not now, not after I found the note. I don't know how long my determination will last. I can already feel it tottering.

The men who were my brothers are at the door now. The same door I went through many times. The doorbell is still broken, and I hear them knocking, hear the door open. Then Dakhil's voice.

"*As-salamu alaykum*, brothers. Come in."

And the door closes behind them. Three of them. Only one left. The biggest traitor of them all. I feel the sweat running down my neck, even though it's cool here inside these concrete walls. I feel the blood rush through me, way too fast, and I wish I could will it to flow more slowly, wish I could force the calm.

Then I hear the door open downstairs. Hear rapid footsteps coming up the stairs. Hear someone taking the steps two at a time. And I creep down two steps, peek out through the black metal railing. I hear his increasingly heavy breathing coming closer. I swear I can smell him.

Suddenly he's standing in front of me, his back to me, with his fist against Dakhil's door. He looks the same as always. Broad-shouldered and wearing a little hat. Jeans and boots. He barely has time to knock before the door opens.

"You're late, brother," Dakhil says.

He doesn't make it any farther, because I hurl myself down the stairs—two steps, three steps at a time—holding the gun with both hands in front of me. He doesn't make it any farther, before I'm pushing my gun into the back of al-Amin's head and pressing him toward Dakhil. He doesn't make it any farther, before the world starts spinning around me, and he screams fearfully and starts to back down the hallway, and I push al-Amin in front of me, and I scream something too.

I wave my gun, and a shot goes off, and the sound is deafening. I hear them screaming and crying as well, something crashes to the floor. And I scream again, more loudly now: "Do as I say! Do as I say!"

Again and again. It's as if I hear my own voice from outside, and it sounds high and shrill. Al-Amin tries to turn his head backward, but I beat his head with the barrel of the gun until one of his eyebrows splits and bright red blood streams down his face and neck and onto his T-shirt and jacket. But I don't care, I just yell and push and pull them into the living room. I force them in front of me in the room where we, where *I*, used to sit. And I'm yelling and screaming and waving the gun. It's chaos, like being in the middle of a wave, I can't see clearly, don't know the difference between space and time. I just force them onto the thick rug, force them down onto their knees. Force their hands behind their heads, and they do what I say. They see the madness in me, and they do as I say. And I look at them. I hear Dakhil's voice somewhere below my own.

"Brother Fadi, this is my home, our home, please, brother…"

And I hit him too with the barrel of the gun so that his head bounces to the side. He collapses on the floor.

"Shut up!" I scream. "Just keep your mouth shut!"

And then silence, everything falls silent for a moment.

I look at them, and in their eyes I see such complete surprise, such fear, that for a moment it fills me with doubt. But I can't stop now, can't let this feeling disappear. And I raise the gun at them again. But at the same time, something doesn't make sense.

There are more people than I expected. I count more than four. At the edge, there's a little boy on his knees. Or he looks like a little boy, younger than me. He stares straight ahead and a tear runs down his cheek. I lose focus again, I struggle with it, move toward him.

"Who are you?" I scream. "What the hell are you doing here?"

I'm waving the gun, and I see his lips moving. He's praying.

"I am brother Firas," he says. "The brothers have shown me the path to Allah, may he be glorified and exalted."

And he closes his eyes and prays again, with trembling lips, quivering nostrils. And I feel my emptiness and anxiety increasing. Brother Firas is me. One more just like me. One more they found to turn into a traitor.

But anger and hopelessness have blinded me. I realize it's too late when I turn around and find myself staring straight into the muzzle of a gun far larger, far more modern than my own. I feel my own gun twisted out of my hands. And there is nothing I can do.

"Give me that," al-Amin says and looks at me with his empty eyes. "This ends now."

Chapter 56

Bergort—Friday, August 21, 2015

Down the slope. It's as if she's flying, as if she's floating over the sidewalk and through the heavy door and into the chilly, damp stairwell. The sounds above, maybe coming from a half-open door. The rifle heavy and cold in her hands. The stairs taken two at a time, and she hears Mehdi behind her somewhere, his damn wheezing. Second floor. Third floor. It's quiet up there now. No more banging, no raised voices. And it scares her almost as much.

Fourth floor. Just one floor left, and she stops to listen, catch her breath, still hears Mehdi's footsteps and his whistling lungs somewhere far down behind her.

She collects herself and takes hold of her gun with two hands, moves the safety to the side like they showed her at the shooting range, in what now seems like another life. The gun is set to fire one bullet at a time, not automatic. She glances up. What awaits her up there? What will she do when she's there? Slowly, stealthily, she takes a first step toward the fifth floor. Then another one. And another.

When she comes around the corner, she sees that the door is ajar. No neighbors have come out. They probably know better than to get involved. Or they're at work or in the mosque down in the shopping center. As she gets closer to the door, she hears voices from inside. And suddenly they get louder. Suddenly someone is talking loudly, not Fadi, someone else.

"This ends now!" she hears.

And it's followed by a crash, as if someone has fallen to the floor. And then cofused, agitated voices.

She's arrived at the door now. Stands with her back against cold concrete, the rifle leaning against her upper arm, barrel pointing downward. In the corner of her eye, she sees Mehdi coming up to the same floor. She glances at him, gestures for him to stay back, doesn't want to worry about him fucking this up too.

Now the voices from inside the apartment again.

"What are you doing here?" the deep voice says. "You were dead, dog. What are you doing here?"

Then something that sounds like a kick, followed by a muffled groan.

Fadi, she thinks. Fadi, Fadi, Fadi.

"He's a fucking dog," says the deep voice. "That's the only explanation. He's a *takfir*—worse than that—worse than an apostate. A murderer!"

Another voice now. Tense and stifled and strained: "Brother Fadi? What's going on? What are you doing here?"

She hears sobbing, shallow breaths, moaning. Then other voices. Disbelieving at first, then furious and accusing. She keeps the gun pressed against her shoulder. Feels her heart pounding inside of her. She's halfway across the threshold, halfway inside the room, but she can't yet bring herself to make herself known. Fear and confusion. What's happening in there?

Then the air is filled with chaos again. Sound cuts through the voices. Like someone rolling on the floor, tearing something down, bodies against bodies, and then voices again. Agitated and confused.

"What's he doing?"

"Hold him!"

And then she hears Fadi's voice. Thin and lonely and almost impossible to discern through the cacophony of other voices. But it's him, and she feels her grip on the rifle loosen.

"Quiet!" someone shouts inside. "Let him speak!"

They fall silent, and she hears it in his voice, recognizes it from times when he's been cornered and accused. When everything was stacked against him, when no one was on his side. Hears how he spits out the words and accusations.

"It was you!" he sobs. "You did this. You killed them."

"What are you talking about?" says the calmest of the voices.

But it's interrupted by the deep voice.

"We've heard enough, *takfir*. You come in here with a weapon and threaten us? Who do you think you are? You know the punishment for leaving the faith."

"Punishment?" Fadi spits out the word. "Punishment? It was you who murdered our brothers! It was your phone! It was you who sent the drones. I got the phone from *you*!"

The higher voice again, slow and doubtful now.

"What phone? What is he talking about?"

"Brother al-Amin's satellite phone," Fadi says.

And when he doesn't get an immediate response, he continues: "What? Don't you know anything about it? The telephone al-Amin gave me?"

A dull thud interrupts him, and Yasmine flinches behind the door.

"Shut up!" the deep voice says. "He's lying! He's a murderer and a spy, I swear!"

"What is this telephone he's talking about, brother al-Amin?" says the calm voice.

Behind him now she hears the voices of the others, puzzled and confused.

"There's no phone, he's made it up. He's afraid to die. Afraid that God will punish him as he deserves, that's all, brother Dakhil."

But the voice is different now, stressed. There is desperation in it. A tone of fear that frightens her. Slowly, with shaking legs, she pushes open the door to the apartment. Slowly she twists her head around the door and looks into the dark hall. Her temples are damp with sweat, her knuckles white around the rifle. The door on the other side of the hall is half open, and she can see backs and shoulders moving in what seems to be the living room. The widest back is bending over someone lying on the floor. She can't make it out really, just a leg, which might belong to Fadi. With lungs pumping, heart thundering, she presses herself into the narrow, dark hallway.

"Stop lying!" roars the deep voice from inside. "Everyone knows you're lying!"

The other seems to gasp for breath. Voices screaming and upset. She hears only what the high voice says: "Put down your weapon, brother al-Amin, let's sort this out."

But the broad back doesn't seem to be listening. It looks as if he's standing, legs apart, leaning forward, with his arms in front of him. As if he were preparing to shoot.

It's quiet for a moment. Then she hears Fadi's voice, low and half smothered.

"It was you," he mumbles. "You killed them."

"Shut up!" screams the deep voice. "Your lies stop now."

And then the shot.

*

The sound is deafening, shocking, compressed inside a small apartment. The world shrinks inside her, and she thinks she's going to vomit in the silence that follows, but instead she puts the gun to her shoulder, feels her temples pounding, her chest thump and cramp. She takes three short, quick steps through the hall, inhales, and kicks open the thin door to the living room. The room sways and turns, a moving mosaic of faces and bodies, a kaleidoscope of blood and confusion. She shuts out everything. Just aims for the man holding the gun. Shuts out everyone else. Shuts out everything except the gun.

Until she sees Fadi. He's lying on the rug on the floor, with his head down. When she finally takes in this image, it's as if everything ends. As if the whole world is made of bricks that are falling around her. There is nothing left. The world is nothing. She feels her hands around the barrel. Feels her finger on the trigger. She opens her mouth and screams.

Chapter 57

Bergort—Friday, August 21, 2015

It's when I hear you that I realize I'm not dead. It's when I hear your voice, hear you screaming, like that Syrian woman did when the brothers arrived carrying her dead son from the front. Completely raw and endless, like an animal or a monster. Terrible, sudden sadness, nothing else.

But I'm not dead, and I try to move, try to say something.

"Yasmine," I hiss with my mouth still pressed halfway on the rug, filled with the taste of blood and anxiety.

I look up and see Dakhil standing there. He holds the gun I had in his hand. But he bends down now and lays it on the floor slowly, his eyes on the door where I heard your voice. I think he must be the one who shot, shot into the air, maybe he just wanted to scare al-Amin? Al-Amin, who has now given up.

When I realize al-Amin is no longer pointing his gun at me, I turn to you, pushing myself up on my elbow. I see you for the first time. I see your eyes and they are unlike I've ever seen them, void of emotion, inhuman, eyes that are ready to kill, eyes without any thought of consequence. I see how skinny you are, how you have a swelling on your temple, how your mouth is half open, and how your lips are moving, soundlessly. And I see that you're holding the gun I took home with me, and it's huge in your arms, grotesque, and you're aiming it at the man that I have almost forgotten about for a moment.

I see that you are close to doing it. Close to firing and stepping over the threshold to something else, into a world you, my sister, should never enter. Into a world no one should enter. I scream: "Yasmine! I'm alive, Yasmine! I'm here!"

You look away from the man and at me for a moment, surprised, almost frightened. As if I'm a ghost, and maybe I am. You blink and your eyes change, going from empty and indifferent to something else, something I remember. Something I lost and couldn't live without. You lower the gun, take a confused, uncertain step aside.

That's all they need, all al-Amin needs. He's empty-handed—he must have dropped the gun on the floor when you came in—but now he bends down quickly with his eyes glued to you. You are so shocked or confused that you barely react, your mouth is half open, the rifle vibrates in your hands.

I spin around, groping for the gun Dakhil dropped, the gun I brought with me. It's slippery, but I grab hold of it, my hands clinging to it, the blood sticking to my face. I don't think, just turn around, both hands outstretched, just a few yards from al-Amin. I close my eyes and press the trigger.

Chapter 58

Bergort—Friday, August 21, 2015

She collapses to her knees with the gun to her shoulder again. She turns toward Fadi, sees him holding the gun with one hand while trying to get up with the other, his face covered in blood.

"Stand still!" she roars and moves the barrel of the gun toward the men. "Get into the corner! All of you! Now!"

They obey instantly and silently, moving into the corner of the apartment with their hands up and their eyes wide and frightened.

"Mehdi!" she shouts out toward the staircase. "Go get the fucking car!"

He doesn't say anything, but she hears his heavy footsteps disappearing down the stairs, echoing through the suddenly palpable silence. Fadi has stood up now, and he turns toward her.

"Yasmine."

His eyes are full of something, maybe love, but also something else.

"You came back," he says.

But he doesn't go to her. He goes over to the burly man lying on the floor, his face striped by the sun shining in through the blinds. He breathes and groans slightly, hugging himself. Fadi bends over him.

"Who are you?" he says. "Who do you work for?"

The man turns his gaze up toward Fadi, and Yasmine sees that he's holding his shoulder.

"I don't know what you're talking about," he hisses.

Fadi looks at the man with something like a smile at the corner of the mouth. Slowly he raises the gun and points it at the man's forehead.

"I don't give a shit really," Fadi says. "I don't care. You murdered my brothers, that's all that matters now. And there's only one punishment for that, brother."

He spits, which sprays a thin coat of blood over the man's face. Yasmine shifts her gaze between Fadi and the men still standing in the corner. It can't end like this.

"Fadi!" she says. "It's over, brother! Let him be!"

"Who?" he repeats. "*Wallah*, there is nothing I would rather do than to execute you, dog."

"Fadi!" she screams. "Damnit, Fadi, it's over!"

The man looks away, toward the floor, mumbling something, quietly, almost inaudibly.

"What did you say?" Fadi says and bends over him.

The man closes his eyes and clears his throat, coughs.

"I work for the police," he mumbles.

"What? The *fucking* police?" Fadi screams.

"Swedish intelligence, Säpo. Brother, I swear it's true," he says.

Fadi looks confused, suddenly uncertain.

"Säpo? You've been working for them this whole damn time?"

The man turns his eyes up toward him and looks him straight in the eyes.

"Fadi," Yasmine says as calmly as she can. "We have to leave now. We can't stay here. Especially if he's a cop."

She nods toward the door, taking a half-step toward it.

Fadi doesn't seem to hear her, remains with a gun pointed at the man on the floor.

"But who sent the drones?" he says.

"Don't be so fucking naïve. Don't you realize the West is working together?"

"So I was just a mark for you? An idiot you could murder in order to get to someone else?"

Fadi presses the barrel harder against the man's head and breathes heavily. Yasmine sees it expanding in his eyes now, a darkness that is so big and black that the whole room suddenly seems dim.

"Fadi," she says. "It didn't happen. You survived."

She takes a step toward him and stretches out a hand.

"You got another chance. Don't throw it away, please."

His face twitches as he bends forward again and pushes the cop down onto the floor with the gun.

"I trusted you," he whispers, and Yasmine sees tears flowing down his cheek.

She quietly lays her hand on Fadi's and twists the gun slowly away from the man's forehead, and down onto the floor.

"*Jalla*, Fadi," she whispers. "Come with me now."

Chapter 59

Stockholm—Friday, August 21, 2015

We're out of Bergort now. I heard the police on the way out, saw the blue lights and police vans, but Mehdi took it easy for once. He kept driving under the speed limit, like somebody's dad.

We're out on the highway and calm now. The car is full of guns, but it's fine, the brothers were confused and furious, but they will certainly make sure al-Amin doesn't get the chance to rat us out before we get away.

I saw the shame in Dakhil's eyes as we left the apartment. Despite all their precautions, they had an infiltrator in their midst. And if they had any balls they'd kill him. But they're all talk and airline tickets. In the end, they're just like everyone else. They don't know anything about war.

The sun shines over the concrete and industrial buildings, and I try to wipe the blood off my face with some wet wipes Mehdi found in a diaper bag in the backseat.

I know you're looking at me. I feel your eyes on my cheek, on my shaved head, my eyes squinting against the sun. But I can't turn to you, can't look at you. There's too much between us, too much time, too much of me.

"Is it really you, Fadi?" you say.

I nod and keep my eyes on the chimneys and warehouses, brown brick covered by billboards and newly built, paper-thin office buildings made of thin steel and reflective glass. And then we're up on the bridge. Then everything is sparkling water and gleaming façades. It takes ten minutes for the world to change, and now we're flying again, and I can't help glancing at you.

The sun falls over your hair where you sit with your face turned toward the dirty windows, toward the city, toward the view that's impossible to ignore. It's impossible to understand that you came back. And I whisper it quietly, so you might not hear.

"How'd you find me?" I say, and my voice isn't even a croak anymore, just high and thin.

You turn to me, and I meet your gaze for the first time without averting my eyes. Your eyes are tired and full of something I don't recognize, something I don't know what to do with, not yet. Something that looks like love.

"Fadi," you say. "You *wanted* to be found, *habibi*."

Mehdi drives along the waterfront, past the Opera House, and those white boats out among the islands, past Kungsträdgården, the Royal Garden, and then along the water past fancy buildings and museums. Finally, he slows down and stops outside a large building, which also looks like a museum. On the other side of the water, behind the boats and quays, sits the gloomy, gray palace. He bends forward and checks on another building a little farther up the street with large trees in front of it.

"You live there? At the Lydmar?" he says over his shoulder. "Pretty fucking luxurious, sister!"

"Seriously?" I say. "How the hell did that happen, Yazz?"

"Long story," she says.

"Look," Mehdi says from the front seat.

He points at two guys sitting farther down the street. Two *shunos* in jeans and hoodies, with their caps pulled low on their foreheads.

"Who are they?" Yasmine says.

Mehdi shrugs. "No idea, but they sure don't look like guests at the hotel do they?"

His phone rings again, it has been ringing constantly on the way into town, but he's ignored it. Now he lifts it up and looks at it nervously.

"Fuck," he says. "Parisa."

He presses the phone to his ear, and his whole appearance changes. He's no longer the guy from the streets, but the sweet boyfriend, willing to serve.

"Hey, baby," he says, and Yasmine and I smile at each other in surprise.

But then he says nothing more, and from the rear-view it looks like he turns pale.

"I don't know where they are," he says resolutely.

It takes a few seconds before he hangs up without saying anything more. He just sits there completely silent with the phone in hand.

"Mehdi?" Yasmine says. "What's the deal? What's happening?"

"*Ey*, brother!" I say.

"Talk. What's happening?"

"They want Yazz," he says calmly.

"What?

I don't understand anything at all. We're out now. You came back and rescued me. Surely there's nothing keeping us here any longer. We're free now? They can't catch us.

"What's happening?" I say. "What is this? Yazz?"

You turn to me again, your eyes are tired and heavy now.

"Mehdi's gangsters," you say. "All that bullshit in Bergort, the riots and all that, you know? It's a long story, but Mehdi tried to get them to scare me so I wouldn't find you. He is loyal. An idiot, but loyal. Anyway I ended up shooting one of them in the leg."

You shrug, as if it's not such a big deal.

"And now they want to get us so we'll shut up or for revenge, or who the fuck knows why," you continue.

I lean back and close my eyes.

"You shot somebody in the leg?" I say.

You don't answer, just bend over to check on the two guys standing guard outside the entrance. I shake my head, hoping it will clear.

"What's the matter with Parisa?" I say.

Mehdi inhales deeply and slowly lets the air out.

"They were with her now," he says. "I heard it in her voice. They made her call. Their way of sending a message, right?"

I nod. We all know all about that. About messages and alliances and threats and the endless fucking futility of it all.

"I have until tomorrow to find you," Mehdi says.

"What the hell are we gonna do?"

We sit in silence for a moment.

"I might know where to start," you say at last.

Chapter 60

Stockholm—Friday, August 21–Saturday, August 22, 2015

It's evening by the time they end up at Tegnérgatan 10. They're all so tired, they're close to collapsing. She looks at Fadi, who can hardly sit up in the backseat, and he looks transparent, even more of a ghost than before.

They drive slowly past the address and turn up on Döbelnsgatan. It's almost seven. Where did the afternoon go?

"Stop there," she says and points to a gap between two cars in the other direction.

Mehdi does a U-turn at the next intersection, drives back, and parks his Mazda in the spot. Then he leans back in his seat with his eyes closed. The stress is eating away at him, of course. He hadn't expected this, hadn't anticipated that those *shunos* would threaten him and his family.

Mehdi was never the brightest guy, and he's brought most of this shit on himself through his own stupidity, but she still feels sorry for him. She feels sorry for Parisa too, despite her betrayal. She remembers how it is, or how it was, all those interlocking alliances, all the trouble it caused. And now they're in deep water, and Yasmine is the only one who might be able to save them.

She leans forward between the seats and looks out through the window, down Tegnérgatan. She can easily see the door at number 10.

"There's a hostel on Observatorielunden," she says now, turning around toward Fadi.

"You have to sleep, *habibi*. I'll stay here."

"What do you mean you'll stay here?" Mehdi says and rubs his eyes.

"This is where he lives," she says. "Lööw, the guy who pays those *shunos* at night. He's sort of your boss, Mehdi. I'm meeting him tomorrow, but I want to keep an eye on him. You stay with Fadi and keep your phones on, OK? I'll see you tomorrow."

When she opens her eyes again, the street is still deserted, light gray with splashes of gold and green farther up the street near the park, and she's shivering from cold in the morning light. Her neck and back are stiff as she straightens up in her seat, and her teeth chatter. How long has she been sleeping? Her cell phone display shows a few minutes to seven.

Lööw got back to the apartment late yesterday, after eleven, and she initially considered surprising him. But in the end she decided to wait and follow him to their meeting at the City Library.

She doesn't trust him. Who knows what he's up to?

She's freezing, and there's no way to get warm in the car. She's wearing nothing but a black tank top and a thin bomber jacket. Her head feels scratchy from a few days of lack of sleep, and she pushes open the car door and climbs out onto the street. It's quiet and almost impossible to imagine that a city could be this empty and deserted.

On the passenger side there's an old, red hat thrown on the floor. With a grimace, she tries to pull her long hair into a ponytail and pushes the cap onto her head. Not the world's most sophisticated disguise, but it's all she has right now.

She slowly starts to jog up toward Tegnérlunden, just to warm up and get her body going.

Nearly two hours later, she's managed to procure a cup of coffee and a stale cheese sandwich from a café that isn't supposed to open for another hour. Now she's back in the car again, and the morning has gone from raw cold to tepid late summer, and she feels the life slowly returning to her body and limbs.

She sends a text message to Fadi.

Everything okay? I'll contact you after I met Lööw, OK?

She checks the time on her phone. 08:35. He should be heading to their meeting soon, she thinks.

Still she almost has time to doze off again, leaning back in the driver's seat, when she sees with half an eye someone coming out of the door at number 10 and heading toward Sveavägen. It only takes a second for her to wake up and stand up. George Lööw is dressed in stiff, skinny chinos and brown shoes. A narrow, dark blazer. Hair like yesterday, slicked back.

While keeping her eyes glued to him, she jumps out onto the street, locks the car, and follows him down the street.

She's aware that she has to be more careful, even if he would hardly expect to be followed to their meeting, he knows now how she looks.

But when he takes out his phone and presses it against the ear, she hurries up and closes the distance between them to just a few yards. The streets are almost empty; if he turned around now he'd see her. Does it matter, she thinks? It feels more important to try to hear what he's talking about on the way to their meeting.

It takes a moment before someone answers. Then: "I'm on my way now," he says in English.

A few cars drive by on the street, obscuring what Lööw says next. The only thing she picks up is that he repeats the words *makes me uncomfortable* several times. At the same time, he runs his free hand nervously through his hair. As if he really felt physically uncomfortable.

When he finally takes the phone from his ear, and lets it drop into the pocket of his chinos, she ducks into a doorway and lets him get a good lead on her again.

At the Stockholm School of Economics, he crosses Sveavägen, but she continues on the right side of the street. They're almost walking side by side now, Lööw with his eyes straight ahead, and Yasmine never letting him out of sight. He looks stressed and seems to be searching for something or someone along the sidewalk while continuing to manically push his hand through his hair, as if no matter what he does, he's not satisfied with how his slickback lies against his head.

At McDonald's, he slows and takes out the phone again. It's 8:50, ten minutes to spare until their meeting. There's a white van parked across the street from the path that leads up to the library entrance, and she slips in behind it. Through the van's side windows, she can see him ascending the long steps to the library, alone and visible from all directions. He is all alone.

Time passes slowly. Twenty minutes seems like a whole morning. Apparently, George Lööw feels the same, because he's finding it hard to stand still on the other side of the street, and keeps alternating his gaze restlessly from his phone to the library entrance.

Ten minutes. And then only five. The time is approaching nine-thirty, and it seems like Lööw's restlessness has started to turn into apathy. How long will he wait before he gives up and realizes that she's not going to show up?

He lifts the phone to his ear again, glances toward the shadows on the side of the library. Is that where they're hiding, whoever they are? He lifts his arms in resignation, and turns his wrist to check the time on his huge, dull gray watch. Finally, he ends the call, shrugs, and goes down to Sveavägen again. Morning traffic has started now, and for a moment she loses sight of him. She feels stiff all over from her night in the car and nearly an hour spent standing behind the white van. When she catches sight of him again, he's halfway across Sveavägen, heading back to her side. He's calmer now, and turns to the right, back in the direction they came from.

She waits a moment and continues to look up at the library. And sure enough, down the stairs they come. Two of them, one after the other, not side by side, but it's obvious that they belong together. She squints to see better. These are no typical gangsters, but they've got straight backs and a wide stance. Indifferent eyes peer out over the street. One of them has a hat on and looks almost Swedish. Whatever. It's clear they were George's backup. A Volvo stops at the curb, and the two guys jump into the backseat.

She exhales; Lööw is alone now. She feels the reassuring weight of the gun against her back. Quietly, she jogs after his back and his bobbing lion's mane. Now she's ready for a meeting.

Chapter 61

Stockholm—Saturday, August 22, 2015

She waits in a doorway just thirty feet farther down Sveavägen while Lööw goes into the espresso bar Sosta. It takes only a few minutes before he's back out on the street again with a small cup in hand. He finds a skinny ray of sunshine to stand in and leans back against a wall. A cup in one hand, scrolling on his phone with the other, a tight expression on his face.

She scouts up and down the street for a glimpse of the dudes from the library or the Volvo they disappeared into. Nothing. Fuck it. It's make-or-break time.

Quietly, she goes toward the café, and soon she's beside Lööw without him even looking up from his phone.

"I have a gun under this jacket," she says calmly, staring straight at him while she discreetly lifts her bomber jacket to prove what she says is true.

He jumps and spills the little tiny coffee cup onto the sleeve of his blue blazer.

"What? What the hell!" he says, and takes a step away from her.

"Don't move," she hisses. "Put the fucking cup on the table and follow me."

He looks tense but obeys and they walk side by side away from the small terrace.

"You don't need to do this," he tries. "We had a meeting planned an hour ago. You never showed up."

When she turns around and looks at him, his gaze is roving around the traffic, toward the Stockholm School of Economics and up into the sky. He's blinking so frequently she thinks he might be going into an epileptic seizure.

"I saw your gorillas, asshole," she says. "So we're doing it like this."

She leads him across the street back toward the City Library.

At the foot of Observatory Hill is a small deserted playground where she signals to Lööw to sit on a bench. Then she stands in front of him, forcing him to meet her eyes.

"Do you think I'm so fucking stupid that I'd walk straight into your dumbass trap?" she says. "Give me a little credit, dork."

He leans back on the bench and shifts his eyes.

"It wasn't my idea," he mumbles. "What did you want, anyway? Who are you?"

He meets her gaze for a moment before glancing out over the swings and jungle gyms again.

"I don't give a shit about you," she says quietly. "I don't care about whatever you're up to in Bergort, don't give a damn about whatever Stirling Security is. Do you understand? But somehow, my brother and I have become involved in this. And you're gonna make sure we get uninvolved. I don't know what you're doing, but the gorillas need to leave us alone. Do you understand?"

He slowly shakes his head.

"I..." he begins but breaks off and runs his hand nervously through his hair again.

"I have no control over this," he says. "There are very powerful forces in play. More powerful than you can imagine."

"The Russian you met with at Stirling Security yesterday?" she says. "What's Stirling Security? Who are they?"

Lööw turns toward her and looks her in the eye again, his gaze calmer now.

"I can't talk about it. It's in their interest to make sure the riots in Bergort continue. That's all I can say. They're behind some of it. For example, that symbol? The star and fist? Have you seen it?"

Yasmine nods.

"Everyone has seen it."

"They created it. Stirling Security. They made it, and I gave it to the guys who are coordinating the riots. But believe me when I say that I can't tell you more than that right now."

"The Russian then? Why is he driving around in a fucking diplomatic car?"

Lööw shakes his head.

"He's basically the head of Stirling Security," he says. "But I'm begging you not to poke around any more right now. There is a lot at stake."

"What's *your* role in all this?"

"I do whatever they ask me to. Stirling Security is my client."

He looks pleadingly at her.

"But not everything is what it seems," he says. "I agree, this is all crazy. But you have to understand I've already said too much. This is very fucking complicated."

He stops and collects himself.

"I have a meeting in about a half hour," he pleads. "A meeting that has to do with Stirling Security. If I don't show up..."

"Then what?" Yasmine says.

He just shakes his head.

"You have to let me go," he says. "You don't understand, I can't miss this meeting. It's just not possible."

"I don't give a shit about your fucking meeting. Your only chance is if you get us out of this mess. We don't have a fucking thing to do with this."

"I understand. I really do. Believe me, I'll do what I can, OK?"

It takes less than ten minutes to walk down Sveavägen to the Stirling Security office.

"But you realize that you can't follow me up, right?" he says nervously, stopping outside a café.

"I'll wait here," she says. "And if you try to trick me or ambush me or play me..."

She lets the words hang in the air and sees how Lööw cautiously holds up his hands, before turning around and disappearing toward a woman in her fifties who's waiting at the front door. They've just gone inside when Yasmine feels her phone buzzing in her pocket. She moves into the shadow of the building and takes it out. It's a message containing a video. She takes out an earpiece and puts it into her ear, and when she clicks on the video she feels herself falling, her world splitting apart and collapsing around her.

Chapter 62

Stockholm—Saturday, August 22, 2015

I wake up to Mehdi standing in the doorway. He looks worn-out, as if he hasn't slept at all. His breathing whistles and hisses as he leans his two hundred pounds against the doorframe of our little room at the hostel. The sun is shining in through a gap in the blinds.

"*Shoo*, Mehdi," I say and sit up. "Where the hell you been, brother?"

He closes his eyes and breathes rapidly—the two flights up have apparently knocked him out completely.

"Couldn't sleep," he mumbles. "Took a walk."

He looks stressed and fiddles with his phone.

"I get it," I say and pull my T-shirt over my head, stand up, and grab my jeans.

"This is tough shit."

I get hold of my phone next to the bed and see a message from Yasmine. She'll call after her meeting with Lööw. I text quickly: All good. Talk later, and stand up.

"Yazz is smart, brother," I say. "You know she'll fix this? She fixes everything."

Mehdi shrugs and goes to the window, raises the blinds, and looks out onto the street. His hands tremble as he turns backs with wandering eyes, his lungs wheezing—the stress seems to be eating him from the inside.

"Come on," he says. "I can't stay here any longer. Let's go get something to eat."

Vasastan is warm and sun drenched despite the fact it's not even half past nine, summer is apparently making its last stand, and despite all our problems, which I don't fully understand, I feel calmer now than I have since I can't remember when.

Yazz is back.

It was not my fault that the brothers were murdered. Or not only my fault.

The guilt is not mine, not wholly mine. For a moment I feel almost free. I can't even remember dreaming about blown-off legs and white lights in the night.

"Have you talked to Parisa?" I say after we've each bought a coffee and are headed to where we left the car parked yesterday.

Mehdi has his eyes on his cell phone and seems distracted and shaky. It pisses me off that he's so absent, and I stop and throw my arms open.

"*Ey*, brother!" I say. "We're gonna fix this, OK? Are you texting with Parisa now? How is she?"

He looks up at me and throws his half-drunk coffee in a trash can.

"Yeah, yeah," he says. "Sorry, it's fine. She's worried, that's all."

"What did you tell them?"

"About what? About this?"

His eyes look everywhere except at me.

"Um, yes? What else?"

I've never seen him like this before. Not even when we were

little. It feels like last week—when he was all macho with his talk about riots and chaos—was a thousand years ago.

"They seem to have managed without you tonight anyway," I say, pointing to a headline in large black letters:

BERGORT BURNS

Mehdi just nods.

"Come on," he says. "Let's drive around while we're waiting for Yazz."

The old, red Mazda sits where we left it. It looks like a cheap toy among all the SUVs and BMWs on this block.

"Where are you going?" I say. "Yazz said we need to stay far away from Bergort until she's fixed this."

Mehdi doesn't seem to hear me, just heads straight for the car with the key in hand, fully concentrated. I speed up and catch up to him at the car. He already has the key in the lock.

"Brother," I say. "Talk to me. What the hell is going on?"

He opens the door and folds the seat forward so I can climb into the backseat. I'm still wondering why I'm supposed to get in the backseat, when he turns around with an expression on his face that's so sad it confuses me.

"I'm sorry, brother," he hisses, his lungs whistling. "I'm sorry, Fadi."

It's the last thing I hear before someone pushes me up against the side of the car and pulls my hands behind my back. The last thing I hear, before someone ties my hands behind my back and throws me headfirst into the backseat of the car. I try to scream and turn around, but someone hits me in the back of the head with what feels like a hammer or a gun. From the corner of my eye I see a shadow, a shaky silhouette. The shadow has a hood in his hands, and there's nothing I can do when he pulls it down over my head, and the whole car disappears into darkness, the whole city disappears, the whole summer.

They push me onto the floor and keep an arm on my head while we drive calmly through the city. The darkness around me is confusing, and I struggle to breathe and to keep my breathing calm. I hear frantic voices, but not what they're saying. Mehdi is talking to me, in his shitty, stupid, badly pronounced Arabic so the other person in the car won't understand: "Sorry, Fadi. Very sorry. They want Yazz. They promise they will let you go."

I don't give a shit about why, just lie still in the backseat. Feel the hood grow wet from my tears.

Chapter 63

Stockholm—Saturday, August 22, 2015

After the last few days, she should feel much worse than she does when she sinks down into her seat on the airport's express train to Stockholm. Her headache isn't bad, barely noticeable. She ate a couple of dry samosas from a corner shop and drank almost a quart of water as a preventive measure when she finally got home from One Aldwych last night. But she couldn't sleep, even though her head felt heavy and pleasantly buzzed from wine and fatigue. Instead she lay awake, tossing and turning until at least three, then finally fell asleep. The room had been too hot, the sounds from the street too loud, her mind filled with stressful thoughts, images of Patrick on the tracks, Stirling Security, Charlotte's mysterious emails. She must have gotten up a dozen times to check that the door was locked, the stove turned off, her passport packed in her bag...

She was supposed to fly in the afternoon because she didn't need to be there until the presentation on Sunday morning, but for a fee of fifty pounds, she managed to rebook in time to make it to Stirling Security's office on Kungsgatan for Charlotte's meeting. If nothing else, she wanted to find out who was behind GL.

She turns her eyes up toward the express train's small flat screen, which plays ads aimed at business travelers and news clips on a loop. The screen shows burning cars and masked young men throwing stones at retreating policemen. The riots that started in Bergort earlier this week have apparently spread to other suburbs in Stockholm during the night. Same as in London, where riots and demonstrations took place throughout the summer. It's a summer of unrest.

But before she has time to take in what exactly is happening in the suburbs of Stockholm, the news clip is replaced by a serious-looking advertisement for a company that provides "comprehensive and holistic security at the macro level." As the screen goes black a familiar company name slowly appears in red: Stirling Security.

It's not even ten when she arrives at Kungsgatan 30, which ends up being the address of one of the Kung's Towers. Not a bad place to establish yourself.

There's a café just forty feet from the entrance, and she finds a table by the window, from which she can keep an eye on whoever goes in or out of the door.

She listlessly orders a croissant, a cappuccino, and a mineral water at the counter. When she sits down at her table, she realizes even though she's been eating poorly the last few days, she's still not hungry, and she thinks again of the terrible week she's had.

The only thing she really wants now is a glass of cold white wine. The thought should make her feel worried, she thinks. A person shouldn't drink every day. Not so you end up with blackouts and can't sleep until you've had at least half a bottle. And she definitely shouldn't be craving a glass of wine at ten in the morning, even if she's been up since five.

She takes out her phone and checks the time. Ten-fifteen. Forty-five minutes until the meeting begins.

*

At ten-forty, she sees a taxi roll up and stop outside the door. She leans back quickly when she realizes it's Charlotte jumping out of the backseat and walking toward the entrance. Charlotte takes out her phone and seems to make a short call. When she's finished, she stands, waiting on the sidewalk.

A few minutes pass, then Klara sits up in her chair. At first she thinks she must be mistaken, and she leans toward the window to get a better angle. There's no doubt. Outside the entrance to the café, she sees George Lööw, in fresh-looking, perfectly fitting chinos and a dark blue blazer with a small handkerchief sticking out of his breast pocket. Brown, shiny shoes. His hair is a little longer than she remembers it, combed back, and sun-bleached, she's sure, from dinners in Sandhamn and sailing trips outside Marstrand. But his jumpy gaze is just as tormented and haunted as she remembers it.

George, she thinks. What a coincidence that he'd show up here right now.

Seeing him brings back everything that happened last Christmas in Sankt Anna. George Lööw, the Brussels lobbyist who, without knowing it, nearly got her killed in the archipelago at her grandparents'. George Lööw, who at the very last second developed some sort of moral compass and saved both her life and Gabriella's.

She closes her eyes for a moment and shakes her head. It feels like a dream now. The snow and storm. Her father, who she never actually met, dying in her arms. And George was the one who finally rescued her.

They'd only been in contact sporadically since then. He'd emailed her a few times and asked how things were going in London, but lately she hadn't felt up to answering.

George stops right outside the café, and she sees that he's

with someone else. A young Arabic woman dressed in jeans and a bomber jacket, her long, curly hair in a ponytail, sticking out from under a red cap. She looks cool, exudes a kind of self-confidence that makes it impossible to look away from her. Her youth and attitude feel like the opposite of George's conservative, polished surface—they are undoubtedly a rather odd couple.

They stand outside the door of the café, and George appears to be trying to convince the girl of something. Klara see his hands flying around, sees him run them nervously through his hair. Finally, he leaves the girl and continues up the street. When he does, he passes right outside the window where she's sitting; if not for the glass she could reach out and touch him.

She's about to get up and run after him until she remembers Charlotte is standing just a little ways up the street. And that's when she finally realizes where he's going.

Without hesitation, George heads straight toward Charlotte and shakes her hand, then they head up the stairs, open the door, and disappear inside.

She flashes back to the email address in Patrick's folder: gl@stirlingsecurity.com. GL. George Lööw. Even after all the bizarre fucking shit she's been through, she did not expect this. She hadn't expected that George Lööw would be representing Stirling Security. At the same time, she's not the least bit surprised. What she knew of him indicated that he moved in the darkest corners of the already shady world of lobbying.

She turns her gaze back down the street to where the young woman is standing outside the café with her cell phone in one hand, apparently looking at something on the screen with one earbud in her ear.

Then the young woman takes a step back toward the façade and collapses, as if she's received a blow to the stomach.

Chapter 64

Stockholm—Saturday, August 22, 2015

The video is only fifteen seconds long and not particularly violent. Someone wearing a black hood, white ties around his hands and feet shackled, is lying on a made bed. Two hands pull the hood off to reveal that it's Fadi. His cracked lips and gaunt cheeks. He's squinting at the glare after the darkness of the hood. He spits and throws himself around on the bed and screams: "Fuck them! Don't do what they say!"

Someone gives him a hard slap with an open hand across the cheek. Then the camera turns toward another masked face. The same masks she saw in Bergort the other night. Same as what Mehdi and the gangsters wore yesterday.

"You have until five, bitch," the man says. "Six hours. Maybe we'll find you before that. But if you don't show up in front of the school by then, that's it for your little brother. Do you understand?"

She closes the phone and backs up against the wall. Her eyes no longer focus, and she sinks down on her haunches, afraid she might vomit. It's too much. Too many threads and knots. Too much pulling her and Fadi back. Too much to ever escape Bergort.

How did they find Fadi?

Mehdi?

The betrayals are piling up. Nobody but Mehdi could have ratted them out. Again. It's the only explanation.

*

Tears flow down her cheeks, and there's nothing she can do to stop them. It's just her and nobody else. Like always, just her.

And she doesn't notice that she's no longer alone until she hears a quiet voice somewhere to the right of her. Slowly, she turns toward it. A slender woman with big brown eyes and a dark pageboy cut is squatting beside her. She's holding up a napkin. Yasmine takes it reflexively, but then just sits there with it in her hand, as if she doesn't know what to use it for. Then she feels the dark-haired woman put a hand on her shoulder: "Can I help you?" she says. "What's your name?"

Chapter 65

Stockholm—Saturday, August 22, 2105

She looks at the weeping girl sitting on the sidewalk with a napkin in her hand. The girl looks confused, as if she barely knows where she is, as if a steel rope that kept her upright had suddenly broken under the burden of a tremendous weight and dropped her straight onto the cement.

There's no feeling in the world she's more familiar with right now, and Klara gently puts her hand on the girl's thin shoulder.

"I can help you."

The girl doesn't respond, but Klara gets her to her feet, leans her against the wall.

"I can't stay here," she mumbles. "I can't..."

The girl twists out of Klara's vague embrace. At the same time a kind of spark illuminates in her eyes, and she looks at Klara as if she hadn't really noticed her until now.

"I'm OK," she says. "You can let go now."

There's an automatic, suppressed aggressiveness in the way she says it. As if she's not the kind to take anyone's help. Not someone who relies on good intentions. As if she's accustomed to being disappointed. She turns around and heads rapidly down the street toward Stureplan.

"Wait..." Klara says. She stands there for a second considering her options. She can find George Lööw again. But there's something about this girl. Something that makes her need to know more.

"Hey," she shouts. "Wait!"

The girl glances over her shoulder but doesn't slow down.

With a few quick steps, Klara catches up and puts a hand on her shoulder. But the girl brushes her hand away.

"I told you not to touch me, bitch," she says. "Sorry. Thanks for the napkin, but I'm fine now, OK?"

"I know George Lööw too," Klara begins. "I saw you with him."

The girl just looks at her, but then shakes her head slightly.

"I have no time for drama," she says. "Believe me, he's all yours, lady. He's probably screwing around, but not with me."

Klara can't help but smile.

"Probably," she says. "But how do you know him?"

"Seriously," the girl says. "I don't care. Bye."

She turns and starts walking down the street again.

"Do you know anything about Stirling Security?" Klara calls out in a last desperate attempt.

Then the girl stops and turns around. She looks at Klara for a moment. Then she walks slowly toward her.

"What did you say?"

"Stirling Security? Do you know anything about them? I promise, it's important."

"What do you mean important?" the girl says. "What the hell do you know about important?"

Klara swallows and doesn't look away, there's something about the girl's reaction that makes her continue, something in her eyes that convinces Klara she's on the right track.

"I know that people have died," she says quietly. "And it has to do with them. And somehow it has to do with George too."

Something happens, something changes in the girl's eyes. Desperation pushes through that tough surface.

"What do you know?" she says. "I have very little time."

"My name is Klara. I guess you could say I know George from past experience, and I know he works with shady stuff. I know that Stirling Security is up to something awful. Something connected to Russia, or at least a Russian company."

She can hear how fuzzy all this sounds, and she digs into her pocket to pull out a cigarette and a lighter. Her mouth is dry from the tension, and the smoke tastes bitter on the first drag.

"I think it has to do with the meeting of EU justice ministers that begins here tomorrow," she continues. "It has something to do with a report my boss has written."

She takes another drag. The cars roll past them on the street. A sparse stream of Saturday shoppers and tourists stroll by them on the sidewalk. The world is moving on like usual, but they're in a separate, surreal bubble.

"A colleague of mine was murdered," she continues. "Because he started investigating this."

She's lowered her voice to a whisper now, and the girl comes closer. She looks at Klara with intense, searching eyes while she fiddles with the phone she's holding in her hand. She looks as if she's trying to make some kind of decision. Then she opens her mouth: "My little brother has been kidnapped," she says in a completely hollow voice.

"Oh my God," Klara whispers. "And you think it has to do with George?"

The girl nods slowly.

"Somehow," she says. "In some fucking way."

"Have you called the police? I mean, can you call the police?"

The girl just looks at her.

"Are you kidding?"

Klara nods calmly. "But what happened?" she says. "Why was he kidnapped?"

"Long story," the girl replies. "Fadi, my brother, disappeared. To Syria. We thought he was dead, but then he came back and got involved in the riots somehow."

"The riots in the suburbs?"

"In Bergort. His friend was involved, and Fadi got involved too. And now he's been abducted."

"By whom?"

"The people involved in this. The people behind it. Or by their hired thugs."

She points up along the street.

"Stirling Security, or whatever the hell their name is," she continues. "That Lööw works for, he's the one who pays the kids to create chaos night after night. And there's also some fucking Russian behind Stirling Security. He drives around in a car with blue diplomat plates and a chauffeur."

Klara sees the whiteboard in Patrick's office in front of her. The Russian Embassy. She sees the payments to Charlotte in front of her. The bank in Vaduz. And amid all this: George Lööw.

"But what do they want in return?" Klara says. "I mean, what do the kidnappers want?"

"Me," the girl says quietly. "They want me. I only have a few hours."

As she stands there on the street with somebody who needs help even more than she does, Klara realizes it won't work. She can't do this on her own.

"We need help," she says. "You need help. And if you let me, I think I know someone who might be able to help us. I can't promise anything, but it's better than nothing. "

The girl's façade has collapsed now, and tears flow down her cheeks. She nods slowly.

"I don't know what I'm going to do," she says. "I haven't got a clue."

"Come," Klara says and pulls her down toward Stureplan. She's going to call someone she should have called a long time ago.

Chapter 66

Stockholm—Saturday, August 22, 2015

The bay is so shiny and gray it looks like polished stone, as if she could walk across it from Skeppsbron to her room at the Lydmar on the other side. But that room is in the past now, and she will never set foot in it again.

She left an old version of herself behind there. It started when David's fist hit her temple a week ago, a memory that's already cracked and yellowed, and feels like it happened to someone else. For the last week she's been reduced, layer by layer, until only the core remains. The prototype. That which survives. That which protects.

She glances at the woman walking beside her, Klara, who still has a phone to her ear. Who is she? Why does she trust her? Maybe it's those brown eyes with small sad wrinkles at their corners? Perhaps it's how she speaks with that peculiar, rural accent, and her gentle touch? Maybe it's because she cares? Or maybe she just can't do this by herself anymore.

The time is half past eleven. They have five hours to come up with something. Five hours until she has to take the subway out to Bergort for the last time.

Klara finally gets off the phone. She talked with someone nonstop from Kungsgatan down through the Royal Garden, and all the way here to the far end of Gamla Stan.

Yasmine tried not to listen, but it was clear that the call started tentatively and anxiously. Klara sounded like she had something to apologize for. But then her voice changed and became livelier and happier, even though she was talking about someone being pushed in front of a train, mysterious banks, research institutes, and finally Yasmine herself.

Now Klara turns to her.

"My best friend Gabriella is a lawyer," she says. "Not only that, she's smart. And has contacts everywhere."

Yasmine nods cautiously. *Fuck*, she wants to scream. How the hell is a lawyer going to help me with this?

"Also," Klara continues, "she can fix stuff. If anyone can help you now it's her."

Yasmine stops and turns toward the water. Out toward those fucking white ships with their tall masts, moored along Skeppsholmen on the other side of the bay. She can feel herself leaking, feel the energy streaming out of her. Slowly she sinks down on her haunches.

"Damn," she mumbles. "It's not gonna work, you don't get… How could this work?"

Klara squats beside her and puts an arm around her.

"Maybe not," she says quietly. "Maybe it will all go to hell."

Yasmine gently turns her head and looks at Klara's serious cheekbones, her slanted eyes searching the Södermalm cliffs, before turning her gaze inward again.

"I can't promise anything," Klara says. "How could I? But sometimes you just have to let go, close your eyes, and hope. Sometimes that's all you have."

Chapter 67

Stockholm—Saturday, August 22, 2015

They're sitting on the steps to the entrance of Skeppsbron 28, where the law firm Lindblad and Wiman has its office, when a taxi slows down on the street in front of them. Yasmine's legs are trembling, and Klara has seen her checking the time on her phone every fifteen seconds since they arrived.

By the time Gabriella jumps out of the backseat, Yasmine is already up, still with phone in hand.

"Is this her?" she says over her shoulder.

Klara nods, rises more slowly, and walks out into the sun and toward the car. Gabriella is dressed in tight, dark jeans and a long, blue-striped linen shirt that almost reaches her knees. Her curly red hair is pinned up carelessly in two loose braids. She looks more like a well-scrubbed hippie than a criminal lawyer and a partner in one of Sweden's most prestigious law firms.

When Klara glances at Yasmine, she can't avoid smiling at her skeptical expression.

Gabriella is in front of them now. She takes Klara in her arms, and when she presses her close, Klara is surrounded by the familiar scent of her perfume. Sandalwood and magnolia, she thinks. The smell of friendship.

"I'm so sorry," she mumbles in Gabriella's ear. "I thought so many times…"

"Shh, shh," Gabriella whispers. "Me too, Klara. Me too."

She pushes Klara tenderly aside and holds her hand out to Yasmine.

"You must be Yasmine?" she says. "My name is Gabriella. I know it may not look like it right now, but I'm actually a lawyer."

She takes a bunch of keys and an advanced-looking key card out of her pocket.

"Look," she says. "They gave me the keys to the place."

Gabriella unlocks the door, disables the alarm with the card, and leads them up the dark, impressive staircase to the third floor, where her office is located. She looks into a small camera, and there's a tiny satisfying popping sound when her retina scan is approved. She unlocks the door with a key and leads them through a beautiful but unexpectedly heavy mirrored door, which opens silently. When Gabriella knocks on it, it barely makes a sound.

"Steel plates inside oak panels," she says contently. "It's like a hypermodern retrofit inside an ancient Gamla Stan palace. I love it!"

"Wow," Klara exclaims. "It wasn't like this last time."

Gabriella laughs and looks at her.

"The last time you were here I was doing a summer internship in the broom closet on the second floor. A lot has happened since then."

The corridor they go down is dully lit by some invisible light source that comes on automatically when Gabriella opens the door. On the walls hang a series of black-and-white artsy photographs of serious, tattooed men from some sort of institution. The warm, thoughtful light makes the office seem more like a hip record label than a law firm. Gabriella stops at the tall, white door at the end of the corridor and unlocks it. The room isn't huge, but it's roomy. Big enough for a light and modern sofa set beside the door and a massive antique desk in dark wood. And behind the desk: a window with uninterrupted views of the bay.

"Wow," Klara says again and goes over to the window. "I can't believe you're a partner now."

Klara turns around and meets her gaze. Gabriella suddenly looks a little sad.

"They didn't have much choice after what happened in the archipelago," she says. "Plus all the work I put in before that. It was my turn."

Klara just nods. Gabriella was the one who'd figured out how to solve everything. She'd negotiated with the big shots at the CIA. She'd managed to make everything calm down, made sure no one had to lose face. She'd convinced the CIA that she and Klara wouldn't leak the information they'd come across but would instead guard it. She'd negotiated a balance of terror.

Klara couldn't imagine anyone who'd earned this view more than Gabriella. Still she knows that Gabriella also thinks of Mahmoud every day, that she can't fully avoid the idea that his death paid for her career.

When she turns away from the window Gabriella is already sitting on the sofa next to Yasmine with a computer in her lap.

"So," she says in a quiet, neutral tone, "your brother has been kidnapped? Tell me how you found that out, and we'll go from there."

Chapter 68

Stockholm—
Saturday August 22, 2015

The office is fucking crazy, like something from a movie, better, even better than the Lydmar. Because this is for real, not a backdrop you buy with a credit card.

It reminds Yasmine of the *Ally McBeal* reruns she and Fadi used to watch on the living-room floor in Bergort. Who knew that the whole time it was happening for real just a subway ride away?

It's hard to stand still, hard not to constantly check the time, so she sits down on the gray couch.

She can't stop her legs from bouncing. Time flies by. She wants to scream at them that it's time to fucking do something, anything, but before she knows it that Gabriella woman sits down beside her, still looking like some kind of inner-city hippie, like she should be into pottery or painting or something. But her eyes are open and cool, and also experienced, and that makes Yasmine relax for a moment.

"So your brother has been kidnapped," Gabriella says. "Tell me about it."

And so she begins to tell her, fast and shaky, stumbling over words because time just rushes by, and they've already wasted too much. She tells them about the film they sent to her phone and then about the pictures her mother sent. About the symbols on the walls of Bergort and the weapons in the bag. About the riots and George Lööw and his stacks of money in the school parking lot.

When she mentions him, she sees Klara and Gabriella exchange a quick glance, as if they actually know much more about this, about him, than she does. But she continues to tell her about the betrayal and the grove beyond the dandelion field where she shot the gangster, whose name is apparently Rado, in the leg.

And then she tells them all about Fadi, about his trip to Syria, and how he came back for revenge. How Fadi managed to shoot a brother in the shoulder, who claimed to be working for Säpo, Swedish intelligence. How they fled to the city, how Fadi must have been betrayed by Mehdi. And then she tells what she knows about George. What he said about the box of stencils and money and Stirling Security.

And then she talks about the video they sent her again; she's forgotten where she began.

Meanwhile, Gabriella says nothing, she just keeps her eyes on the screen and types so fast and irregularly that it sounds like someone popping popcorn.

But when Yasmine brings up the film again, Gabriella gently puts a hand on her arm.

"We can stop there," she says.

Then she's silent for a moment as she scrolls through what she's written, and Yasmine looks at Klara, who's leaning over to follow the text as well.

"Tell me about the man who claimed to work for Säpo again," Gabriella says. "Everything you know."

Yasmine shakes her head and feels her leg start jumping again. They're wasting time. They're focusing on the wrong things. How will this help anyone at all?

It was a mistake to agree to this. She stands up, presses her hands against her temples.

"Seriously?" she says. "I promise you, Swedish intelligence didn't take him. Not jihadists either. This is about making sure I'll shut up. And revenge for shooting Rado. These are the gangsters that Stirling Security hired to whip up the riots. They took Fadi. Whether Stirling Security knows something about this is another thing. You don't get it, in Bergort if you shoot somebody you don't get away with it."

She falls silent and her eyes are black with stress and frustration.

"Can we concentrate on saving my little brother now instead of talking about this secret agent shit?"

Gabriella leans forward and takes Yasmine's hand in hers, pulling her back down on the couch.

"Believe me," she says. "That's what I'm doing."

And there is something in those eyes, something in this room, that stops any further protest. So Yasmine tells her again. But all she has is what Mehdi told her, and what Fadi wrote in the letter to her, the ink getting fainter and fainter and then turning to nothing more than a fingerprint in the paper. She hasn't even had time to talk to him about it.

"And then?" Gabriella says. "When you were in the apartment yesterday with the jihadists, as you call them, you realized it was only this al-Amin who was behind the betrayal?"

"Yes," she says. "He admitted that he worked for Säpo. The others seemed completely shocked."

"So your impression is that al-Amin infiltrated the group, and that he steered Fadi to these soldiers in Syria who he then annihilated? And that he also wanted to get Fadi killed?"

Yasmine nods impatiently.

"Would you be willing to talk to the press about this?" Gabriella says.

Yasmine shakes her head. "Seriously," she says. "I know you're trying to help, but I just want to save Fadi, OK?"

"But if it would help Fadi, would you be willing to talk to newspapers on the record? I don't think it will be necessary, but I have to know."

"If it would help Fadi. Absolutely. Of course. I would do anything."

Gabriella smiles at her and strokes her hand.

"Good," she says. "Then we really have something to work with. Let me make a few phone calls, before we continue, OK?"

Chapter 69

Stockholm—Saturday, August 22, 2015

Gabriella is gone for a quarter of an hour, and with each minute that passes, Klara sees Yasmine disappear more and more into herself. She barely even checks her phone anymore, just stares straight ahead and answers Klara's attempts at conversation with monosyllabic answers.

It's difficult to take in everything Yasmine told them—even when Klara grabs hold of Gabriella's computer and scrolls through her notes. The brother who was radicalized and then brutally exploited. She feels her stomach knot up when she looks over at Yasmine. If she'd read in the newspaper that Swedish intelligence, working with the Americans, had infiltrated a jihadist group and it led to the death of an ISIS leader, how would she have reacted? Maybe she would have raised an eyebrow, but she might also have thought it sounded like a successful operation. Now, when Yasmine told her the sad story of her brother, she feels only disgust for what Säpo did. Is it possible that they would be so ruthless as to recruit and sacrifice a Swedish citizen?

And then George Lööw and Stirling Security on top of that.

She leans back in her chair. Trying to understand what this is all about. Is it possible that a company would go that far? Buying a researcher is nothing new in and of itself, even if this seems particularly egregious, what with the huge sums in the Liechtenstein bank account. But to assassinate someone for trying to piece together the puzzle? Are the stakes that high?

She thinks about Yasmine's story again. How the riots in the suburbs seem to be orchestrated by Stirling Security. How even the symbols sprayed on the walls were created by the company. Even the ski masks that the kids wear at night come from them.

Slowly it dawns on her what Patrick was on to.

Stirling Security's intentions must be to create a new market for private security companies—a market that they of course hope to dominate. If they can get political support for the privatization of some of the duties of the police force, they could earn a lot of money selling their services. And that's why Charlotte's report by an "independent academic" is so important.

And if it also appears that the police force isn't up to the task, if the people are fed images of burning cars and hordes of faceless protesters... They're hoping people will get fed up and start to believe there's no other option but to privatize parts of the police force.

Could that be how this all hangs together?

She sees the screen from Arlanda Express in front of her. How news reports from the chaos in the suburb were interrupted by advertising that offered a solution: Stirling Security. And as if that weren't enough, Stirling Security seems to have some connection to the Kremlin?

She has to get a hold of Charlotte. She has to tell her that she knows how this all fits together, to prevent her from presenting that report tomorrow.

Still, that Patrick would be murdered for this. And Yasmine

would find herself in danger. And what does this mean for her personally? What kind of danger is she in?

There is no alternative but to talk to Charlotte. And with George Lööw.

She's just taken out her phone, but doesn't have time to call, before she sees Gabriella standing in the door again.

"Yasmine," she says quietly and sits down next to her. "Things are going to happen very fast now and be very messy. But we're going to save your brother, OK?"

Chapter 70

Stockholm—Saturday, August 22, 2015

Gabriella barely has time to explain what the plan is before Klara says from the window: "I think they're here."

Then Gabriella pats Yasmine's cheek, stands up, and goes downstairs to open the front door and let in the people who are here to pick up Yasmine.

But Yasmine aches with uneasiness. This is so fucking wrong. They've taken control of this now, Gabriella and Klara, and they mean so fucking well. They believe in order when Yasmine knows that all of this is chaos, and she wants to protest: *Listen to me! You don't get how this works!*

But the words stick in her throat. Because she knows the only thing that will work is if she turns herself over to the kidnappers and Bergort. This is eye for an eye, tooth for a tooth. There are no shortcuts. Bergort will not be content with anything less than blood. She knows that she hates herself for having allowed these middle-class ladies to take over. They know nothing about this. And she hates Klara and Gabriella for lighting that little light on the horizon, the light of another solution. She hates them because they raised her hopes, and made her stumble from her own crooked, pitch-black path, which is the one that leads home.

But now it's too late, the cops are standing in the *Ally McBeal* office with their ironed jeans and leather jackets, their close-cropped, gray hair and holsters on their belts for cell phones. Now they open their mouths and introduce themselves with their hillbilly accents as Bronzelius and Landeskog from Säpo, and they speak calmly and sit down next to her on the couch, pretending they're all friends, like they don't hate her kind.

"So from what I understand," the one named Bronzelius says, "there's just a few hours left until this deadline?"

She says nothing, just stares straight ahead. Gabriella takes a seat next to her.

"Yasmine," she says. "I understand that you don't trust me or these two. But I promise you that they won't do anything to you. I have explained to Bronzelius what Fadi has been through, and it will be a huge scandal if it's true. I've told him that if anything happens to you or him, anything at all, we'll go to the press immediately. And I can promise you that's the last thing they want. So you don't need to trust them because they're nice, but you can trust they don't want their mistakes to be made public. We have more on them than they have on you. Do you understand? What happened to Fadi would be a scandal for them."

"But it won't help, you don't understand," Yasmine mumbles.

She turns her head and looks at Gabriella. She wants to trust her. But she'd also like to tell her to go to hell, tell all of them. But that light is dancing on the horizon. That tiny hope that for the first time ever, they can win without anyone having to lose. Win-win. She knows how false that hope is, but what's the alternative? Going out there and handing herself over to a bunch of hardened gangsters? Risking getting both herself and Fadi killed.

"Fuck it," she says quietly. "What do we do?"

"First, we need your phone," Bronzelius says. "Then we'll take you in and go through everything you know in detail."

She sighs when she hears "take you in," but she still takes out her cell phone and hands it to him.

"Can you unlock it?" he says. "And show me the video Gabriella told us about?"

She does what he tells her to, and he enters the number the video was sent from into a text message on his own phone and sends it.

"Hopefully, our technicians can track the number," he says.

Then he leans forward and takes out a pair of handcuffs from his back pocket. He lays them on the table in front of her. She recoils.

"Are you armed?" he says.

She hesitates a moment before she lays Fadi's gun next to the handcuffs. She sees Klara's eyes from across the room widen in surprise.

"For this to work," Bronzelius says, "I have to put these handcuffs on you. It's just theater. If someone is watching you, it's better if it looks like you were arrested rather than going in willingly. Do you understand?"

She turns her head and meets Gabriella's eyes.

"What the hell is this?" she says. "Fucking shackles were not part of what we discussed!"

Gabriella looks at her confidently.

"It's for your own safety," she says. "If someone followed you here, they'll think you're being arrested. It will explain why you didn't go to the school in Bergort at five o'clock. Do you understand?"

No! Yasmine wants to scream. *I don't understand any of this! I don't trust any of you! And it can't fail! It can't!*

But she doesn't scream. Instead, she bends her head and holds out her hands so Bronzelius can chain her like an animal, and lead her out into the muffled hallway, down the echoing staircase and put her into the backseat of the dark Volvo parked on the sidewalk outside.

Fadi, she thinks. *Habibi, what's going on?*

Chapter 71

Stockholm—Saturday, August 22, 2015

Klara and Gabriella stand in the afternoon sun outside the front door on Skeppsbron, and Klara lights a cigarette. The smoke hangs nearly motionless in the air around them.

"What just happened?" she says. "Are they really going to fix this?"

It's only been minutes since the dark Volvo rolled off toward Slussen.

Gabriella shrugs. "I think so," she says.

"And if they fix it? If they manage to get a hold of her little brother? What happens to them then? He's basically a jihadist and both have committed several crimes in the past few days. I mean, they certainly would have reason to stay away from the police, right?"

"Yes," Gabriella says. "But that's the whole point. Those kids have so much shit on Swedish intelligence that it's better for Säpo to just ignore them when this is over. When I mentioned 'newspaper' and 'eyewitnesses,' that seemed like enough for them to want to keep this away from the police."

"But do you really believe that kid's story? It sounds totally nuts," Klara says.

"There's a lot of shit that happens behind closed doors," she mutters. "A hell of a lot of shit."

She extends her hand to Klara, asking for a cigarette.

"It's my last," Klara says and hands it to Gabriella, who takes a few drags before handing it back.

For a moment, it feels like old times. Like when they used to smoke on the steps of the library when they were at Uppsala University together, always dead broke, always sharing the few cigarettes they had. That was a long time ago. A lot has happened since then.

"I think it's true," Gabriella continues. "Since Bronzelius was so quick to respond. But I agree with you, it's hard to believe. Collaborating with the Americans to infiltrate a jihadist cell and eliminate a terrorist leader. I mean, they've basically disregarded every rule and regulation on human rights that they're supposed to adhere to."

"Is this even part of their mission?" Klara says. "Aren't they supposed to protect Sweden, not get involved in the Middle East? Do you think the minister of justice even knows about this?"

Gabriella exhales the smoke slowly. "Maybe, maybe not. But they reacted a little too quickly when I contacted Bronzelius. That suggests, unfortunately, that these activities aren't exactly unknown to the rest of the organization. What if this is part of a larger project? I mean, maybe there are more Fadis?"

Gabriella takes another drag from Klara's cigarette and leans back against the wall.

"Can you imagine the headlines?"

Klara nods. It's too crazy. She thinks of the Bronzelius they met in the aftermath of what happened in Sankt Anna archipelago. A completely unremarkable man in a leather jacket and jeans and gray, short hair. Like a dad. But he'd proven to be some kind of spider in the Swedish intelligence net, full of secrets and resources. He was the one who had connected them to the U.S. security apparatus back then, which helped them extract themselves from the terrible situation that led to both Mahmoud's and her father's death.

It was a stroke of genius by Gabriella to contact Bronzelius now, and Klara couldn't understand why she hadn't thought of it. But that was why Gabriella is a partner in a law firm even though she was only a few years past thirty, and why she, Klara, was just a perpetual fuckup, ruining shit for everyone all the time.

"Sorry," Klara says and stomps out her cigarette on the sidewalk, looking away from Gabriella.

She can't look her in the eye. Can't quite take her quick thinking and helpfulness. At the same time, she can't manage without her either, apparently.

"For what?" Gabriella wonders.

"For everything," she says, leaning against the wall. "For not answering your emails and not calling you. And I never really thanked you for what you did last Christmas. And I'm sorry for going into hiding basically. God, I wouldn't be upright if it weren't for you. And then here I come stirring everything up again."

Gabriella leans back against the wall beside her, their shoulders touching, and both squinting up at the sun.

"It's not over yet," she says. "Hopefully Bronzelius will solve this situation with Yasmine and Fadi. But in terms of the report and George, that's up to you."

Klara nods. Despite her mild headache, she still feels some kind of security. Here with Gabriella. Despite everything that's happened. Despite everything that remains.

She leans her head against Gabriella's shoulder, her cheek against her hair. "I'm not doing well, Gabi," she says.

Gabriella strokes her cheek, her hair. "I know, Klara," she says quietly. "But we can do this. I promise."

Chapter 72

Bergort—Saturday, August 22, 2015

They won't let me take off the hood, but I know where we are anyway. It doesn't matter if I can see, they can poke out my eyes, and I'll still find my way around Bergort. I know every single echo, every aroma of cumin or *harissa* or sausage. I know the stairwells and front doors, recognize the tone of voices between the buildings, feel the cracks in the asphalt, and I know how many steps there are between the parking lots and front doors. I know everything about Bergort. Everything.

And now we're in a high-rise, in an apartment on the top floor that smells like weed and burned popcorn. They've locked me in the bedroom, and they're sitting out there playing FIFA, and speaking in Serbian. Sometimes they peek in to check I'm still here, as if I had anywhere to go.

After they videoed me, they left me alone here, and in the beginning I counted the seconds. *1001, 1002, 1003*. I don't know why, just to keep track of something, I guess. Just to keep the darkness outside my eyelids, keep it from getting in.

But then I remembered what brother Shahid told me in Syria one evening as we sat around the camp stove in the cold apartment. We were talking about imprisonment and martyrdom—and everything else that feels so far away now, like a dream, like another life—and he said that if you're taken prisoner by al-Assad's dogs you'll be a martyr by sunset. But if one of the rebel forces takes you, you might sit there for weeks, months, years. And the faster you let go of the world and go to Allah, the more likely it is you won't lose your mind.

Now I no longer have Allah, not even the dream of justice and jihad. Now I have nothing, but a sudden desire to live.

I've burned the ground behind me, and I want nothing more than to return. But those ideas are too big for the darkness of the hood. I need light. If I can't reconcile myself to death, then I intend to reconcile myself with life.

So I think of you. I think about how you knew exactly that for such a long time, and you tried to teach me. I think, that's what those dictionaries were for you, graffiti and music too. That's what those clubs in the city were. Maybe even that loser David.

Life!

I thought you were running away. From Bergort. From me. But everything you did was in order to live. Everything you did was to make your life better. Everything was in order to create something bigger and better than the conditions we'd been handed. And all I did was adapt. All I did was live up to minimum expectations.

The afternoon is long, and I do everything I can to keep my mind focused on something simple, rather than thinking about what you're doing now, what you're planning. So I force myself to believe that we will get free. It can't end like this, there has to be something else, something bigger and more beautiful. A bluer sky we can fly through until we're just dots that disappear forever. Somewhere there has to be a sea with a boat that can carry us both.

*

I hear something first near the window, maybe on the balcony outside. It's a scraping sound, and I turn my head toward it, not that I can see anything, just a reflex. I think it might be a bird, a pigeon, or a seagull, landing on the railing. Then I hear it again. One time. Two times. I don't know why, but it makes me nervous. Maybe because I'm so vulnerable with this hood over my head and my arms tied. The sound makes me uncomfortable, and I feel my heart start to beat faster. Then come a few seconds of silence, maybe minutes.

And then it happens. The whole room explodes, the whole apartment, with a frenzy and a volume that makes my head shake, and I scream. There are several explosions, quick, one after another, so deafening that I actually lose my hearing. A flash so intense I even sense the light through the hood, it's like I'm inside the explosion, inside the bomb. I don't know what I'm doing, I have no sense of myself, but I think I curl up on the bed like a child.

All I hear is ringing in my ears, but I imagine the room filled with people. And I feel someone grab my shoulders and pull me down onto the floor. I sense someone yelling at me. Then the ringing sound stops, or subsides a little, and I hear screams, things being crushed. I hear someone shout close to my ear: "Police! Hold still! Don't move! Police!"

Again and again he roars that, and I don't understand why, because I'm not moving. I lie perfectly still.

And then someone pulls the hood off my head and the darkness disappears. I gasp for breath and squint against the sudden brightness.

It's quiet now, only the sound of boots and the occasional orders coming from the other room.

"Keep still!"

"Look at me!"

When I open my eyes, I see a man in a ski mask and a helmet, dressed entirely in dark blue Kevlar, squatting down beside me. I see his weapon and gas mask on the floor beside him. A dark blue label is attached to the left breast: POLICE in gold.

Gently he unsnaps his helmet, rolls off the ski mask, and smiles at me. He's dark, almost black, and it doesn't make sense. He's not blond like a cop. He looks like us. Sweat runs down his cheeks.

"Take it easy, brother," he says, smiling. "It's over now. We have you."

Behind him, through the open door to the living room, I see other men with identical masks on their faces and helmets on their heads, dragging what I assume are my captors over the wooden floor and out toward the hall. I close my eyes. When I open them again, they're gone, but there's one body left on the living-room floor—stiff and still.

The world slows down now, and it feels like it takes seconds for me to get up on my knees, seconds to creep one step toward the door, seconds for the officer in front of me to stand up, put his hands on my shoulders, gently push me back into the room, and shut the door behind him with his boot.

"It's okay," he says. "A shot went off. But you're safe now."

But I've already seen what he's trying to protect me from. I've already seen Mehdi's pale face. Already seen his dead, unseeing eyes.

Chapter 73

Stockholm—Saturday, August 22, 2015

So they lied, of course, and now she's lying on the bed in a cell, staring straight up at the gray ceiling. They lied, like they always lie, and now her head burns with hopelessness and anxiety and the thought that it's all over.

She closes her eyes, presses her fists to them, presses as hard as she can, and screams.

She trusted them. How could she? How many times has she seen that same naïvéty in a teacher or some fucking academic doing fieldwork? Swedes, who mean well, but who brought nothing but destruction with their hollow promises and false hopes. She spent her entire childhood avoiding their bullshit and their empty phrases, their *belief in the individual* and their fucking pity. As if their sad lives are any better, full of day care drop-offs and box wine. They come to Bergort with their theories and methods, and think there's some method, some way to get ahead. When all we have is chaos.

But she wanted so much to believe this time. She forced herself to believe, even though the plan was full of holes and required her to put her life and Fadi's into the hands of their enemies. And now she's lying here, trying to force herself not to think about what's going to happen to them.

All she knows is that they interrogated her about Mehdi and his gangster friends, and she told them everything she knew without mentioning George Lööw. She'd told Gabriella she wouldn't. That was something they would take care of later, so the cops wouldn't get confused and would focus on saving Fadi first. After she'd told the abbreviated story to Bronzelius, he vanished and left her alone in an interrogation room, until a regular cop with a regular cop attitude picked her up and brought her here, without listening to any of her questions or protests. He's just pushed her down on the bed, despite her screams and blows. Locked the door and left her alone.

She doesn't know how long she's been in the cell when she hears the sound of the lock being turned in the door. When it opens, she's already sitting up on the bed with her feet on the floor. It's the same fat cop as before, crumbs still on his uniform.

"It's time for questioning," he says. "Stand up."

"Hold out your hands," he says.

"What?"

Yasmine has risen up from the bunk, and she sees he's got a pair of handcuffs in one hand.

"Did you hear me?" he says. "Questioning. Hold out your hands."

Humiliation courses through her, mixed with worry for Fadi. But she has no other choice, and anything is better than this cell, so she extends her hands, and he chains her again like an animal or a slave, and they walk slowly through the sterile, greenish-gray corridor to the interrogation room she was in earlier in the day.

"What time is it?" she says.

But the fat cop pretends not to hear her, unlocks the door to the room, and pushes her gently inside.

"Sit," he says. "They'll be here soon."

But it takes awhile, and the handcuffs chafe her wrists. This room is so close to hopelessness that it takes all her energy to even sit upright, to keep her mind from wandering too far. Finally, she hears the door being unlocked and straightens in her chair, steels herself, preparing for whatever, for the worst. But she refuses to turn around, refuses to give them that, so she sits there stiff and straight with her back to the door.

"Where is my brother?" she says quietly, straight into the wall.

She hears a man enter the room and go around the table. From the corner of her eye, she sees Bronzelius is back.

"Who the hell handcuffed you?" he says.

But she doesn't hear him. The panic is growing within her, a jet engine accelerating beyond her control.

"Where is my brother? Where's Fadi?" she screams.

She beats the table with her handcuffs and stands up.

Bronzelius takes a step toward her, holding up his hands to calm her.

"Fadi is doing well," he says. "We took him to the hospital just to make sure. It's routine, nothing to worry about."

It sounds like he's speaking inside a jar or a tunnel, his voice is muffled and echoing and what he says is impossible to believe.

She collapses, suddenly too weak to stand, and she feels the plastic cool and slippery under her as she sits down. Bronzelius squats down beside her.

"Breathe," he says. "Your brother is safe."

He gets up again and opens the door to the hallway.

"Somebody better get their ass in here and unlock these fucking handcuffs," he shouts.

A half hour later, she's sitting at the table again, this time without handcuffs and with Gabriella at her side. Gabriella's eyes, which were so warm when they hatched this plan a couple of hours ago, are now so hard they seem to bore straight through Bronzelius.

"I find this completely fucking incomprehensible," Gabriella says with such calm and focus that the air vibrates. "Is there no end to how fucking incompetent you are? Locking her up? Refusing to let me see her? Handcuffs? After what my client has been through. How is that even possible?"

Every word she says goes straight into Yasmine's body. Every word makes her struggle harder to keep her tears from flowing. Has anyone ever been so unreservedly on her side? Has anyone ever taken her side at all?

"Calm down now," Bronzelius murmurs while staring across the table. "A thank-you might be in order. We have solved your problem, so to speak."

"It's cool," Yasmine whispers cautiously to Gabriella. "Seriously, Fadi is safe, that's all that matters."

"Fadi wouldn't have needed saving if it weren't for the interference of these imbeciles," Gabriella mutters.

Bronzelius just looks at them with ice-cold eyes.

"Fadi Ajam is a terrorist," he says dryly. "I'd take it easy with the accusations if I were you."

"A terrorist that you created, yes," Gabriella says and nails him with her eyes.

Bronzelius doesn't avoid them, and they sit like that a few seconds until he turns toward Yasmine.

"After some reconnaissance work, we found them in an apartment in Bergort," he says. "At that point, we brought in a SWAT team, because our assessment was that the perps would not be open to negotiation, and the apartment was then stormed with minimal risk."

He stops, and Yasmine leans back in her chair. Slowly,

slowly it's starting to sink in that Fadi is alive. Whatever happens now, he's not dead. That knowledge spreads out like a net over her, a net that stops the free fall she's been in for such a long time. A new, profound fatigue sweeps through her. They're both alive. Everything else can wait.

"Unfortunately, it turned out the assault was not quite as straightforward as our friends in Kevlar had hoped it would be," Bronzelius continues.

"What?" Yasmine says and looks up at him.

She turns toward Gabriella.

"What does he mean?"

But Gabriella just nods for him to continue and gently takes Yasmine's hand.

"Mehdi Fahim," Bronzelius says. "As I understand it, he was a friend of your brother's?"

Yasmine swallows and closes her eyes. All she can see is the image of Parisa with the baby on her arm.

"He was in the apartment, and right now we're looking into how this could have happened. There were only two shots fired apparently. But for some reason they hit Mehdi Fahim. It was probably a mistake. He was unarmed and, as I understand it, more or less a hostage himself. It's a little unclear how this all fits together."

Now Yasmine can't hold back the tears any longer. Slowly they fall down her cheek. It's both relief and sadness. Hope and constant hopelessness. Mehdi betrayed them. But he protected Fadi too. Parisa betrayed them, but how many times in the past had she protected Yasmine? Eye for an eye, tooth for a tooth. Someone always pays the price.

Behind her, she hears someone knock on the door and push it open.

"Yasmine Ajam?" says a voice behind her.

She turns around and sees a female police officer looking through a gap in the door.

"If you're finished, I can take you to your brother now."

All she can do is nod and look questioningly at Gabriella, tears still running down her cheeks. Gabriella finds a handkerchief in her purse and gives it to her.

"You go," she says. "I have a few things to discuss with Bronzelius."

Chapter 74

Stockholm—Sunday, August 23, 2015

It's drizzling as the taxi turns off the E4 freeway toward Brunnsviken and the SAS Radisson Blu, where the conference is being held. Klara's heart is making small, short, insufficient beats in her chest. The stress of the report and what she should say to Charlotte kept her up all night. At the same time, she's relieved to not be hungover, for once. She's almost forgotten how it feels not to have a headache.

Yesterday she and Gabriella stayed up late in Gabriella's new apartment on Mariahöjden trying to figure out what the next step should be. Apparently, another perk of a partnership in a law firm was an apartment with a great view of Stockholm, and they'd sat on Gabriella's small balcony late into the night. She'd rarely seen anything so beautiful. The August sky turned a deeper and deeper blue above the thousands of lights of Kungsholmen and Gamla Stan. And the water below was completely still. They'd wrapped themselves in thick blankets and huddled around their teacups. No wine—for the first time in several weeks it didn't feel necessary.

But the conversation itself had been less enjoyable. Together they went through everything that had happened that afternoon and what Klara went through in London in detail. Gabriella had also told her about her frustrating meeting with Bronzelius at the police station. He'd listened with what seemed like half an ear to what she knew about

Stirling Security, George Lööw, Bergort, and the EU meeting, and had finally dismissed it all as speculation and irritably asked her what she thought he was supposed to do with it.

"I guess he might be right," Gabriella had said. "There's nothing truly concrete there. Sure, we have those bank statements. But they've been made from a Swiss bank account to an account in Liechtenstein, and nothing was said in the emails about what they're for? Sure, it seems like your colleague was pushed in front of the train, but nobody saw it. Your boss's institute is also in London, outside of Bronzelius's jurisdiction. And as for George..."

Gabriella shook her head in resignation.

"There's not even anything to go on there yet. One eyewitness statement that he gave money to someone who's rumored to be leading the riots? There's nothing here for Bronzelius and his buddies to really hold on to."

"Well damnit," Klara had said. "Isn't the whole idea that Säpo should be one step ahead, acting quickly before it's too late—"

"I pushed him on it, and he's reluctantly agreed to check on Stirling Security and get back to me tomorrow. But the fact is that the most interesting part of this is going to happen tomorrow when your boss presents that report to all those EU diplomats. When she recommends that certain police functions could be privatized, then of course that will put all of this in a different light, right? The email and the payments and all the rest. What a scandal! I think all we have to do is wait until tomorrow, then we present the whole thing."

Now Klara glances out over the green of Haga Park as the taxi slowly approaches the hotel. Gray, heavy clouds and almost ten degrees cooler than yesterday. The summer ended overnight.

The scent of autumn in the air is a relief. The taxi finally stops outside the entrance to the conference hall where today's preliminary meeting will be held.

"Do you think there are enough police officers?" the taxi driver says, nodding toward the roped-off area around the conference hall.

Klara smiles wryly and pays.

"Well, we'll have to hope," she says.

She realizes he's right when she steps out onto the gravel. She counts at least ten police cars and buses scattered around the parking lot, and there are barricades set up by the entrance. A couple of policemen are unloading shields and helmets behind one of the buses. Of course, a meeting of EU justice ministers on the theme "The Impact of Liberalization" is an obvious target for the antiglobalization movement. Tomorrow Haga Park will be full of left-wing activists.

Today is just the preliminary meeting. The ministers don't come until tomorrow. But if there's one thing Klara learned from her years in EU politics, it's that the preliminary meetings are what's important. It's here, among the more important civil servants and politicians' advisers, that agendas are set and guidelines drawn up. It's here that decisions are born, and foundations laid. That's why Charlotte's report is so important.

It's half past seven, and Klara is standing in line with suit-clad representatives of the collective, dubious European democracy. The security check is rigorous, like at an airport or the European Parliament, bags are x-rayed, and everyone has to go through metal detectors before entering the old armory, which has been renovated into a five-thousand-square-feet, Nordic-style conference hall of white and blond wood.

Klara registers and receives her name tag.

"Has Charlotte Anderfeldt registered yet?" she asks the young, blond intern in a tight dress, working behind the counter.

The woman taps on her tablet.

"No. Professor Anderfeldt doesn't seem to have signed in yet. But according to the program, her presentation will be at eight-thirty, just after the introduction, so she can't be far away."

Klara nods and heads for the table where they're serving coffee and a continental breakfast. She looks at her phone. No missed calls. No messages. The time is a quarter to eight. Fifteen minutes until this all kicks off. Then another half hour until Charlotte's presentation. Klara is staring to sweat. It's not like Charlotte to show up at the last minute. Not at all.

Then someone gently grasps her elbow, and she turns around so quickly that the black coffee spills onto the saucer.

"Klara," George Lööw says. "I need to talk to you."

He looks like he always does—freshly showered and immaculately groomed. The suit looks new. The white shirt and red tie as well. Another attendee —a round man in his forties—shakes hands with him in passing: "George! They set the fox loose among the chickens, I see!" the man says in a thick German accent and laughs heartily.

George forces a laugh as well and pats him affectionately on the shoulder.

"Otto! Good to see you!" He makes a gesture to indicate he's busy but happy to talk later. He pulls Klara through the crowd, toward the security checkpoint while waving, smiling, and making "call me!" gestures with his free hand. This is obviously his milieu.

Finally, they exit into the foyer, which is less crowded.

"George!" she says, making an effort to smile. "It's been a really long time!"

"Yes it has," George says, his smile as strained as hers. "We can catch up later. The thing is that we have a little problem on our hands right now."

"OK," she says. "But what a surprise to see you here!"

"Is it?" he says, looking at her in surprise. "Didn't Charlotte tell you I would be here?"

She frowns and tries to meet his eyes, but he's scanning the crowd behind her.

"No," she says cautiously. "She's never mentioned you."

"She hasn't?"

He sounds genuinely surprised and looks straight at her.

"I was the one who recommended you to her in the first place. How did you think you got the job?"

She takes a step back.

"Excuse me?" she says. "What did you say?"

"Klara," he says and focuses his eyes on her again. "Where is Charlotte?"

"Wait," she says. "What do you mean you got the job for me?"

"Forget that right now," he says impatiently. "She needed somebody who could speak Swedish, and I sent over your name. That's all. But where is she, Klara? This is really fucking important! You can't imagine how much is at stake."

Klara is very close to saying that she knows all too well what's at stake, and how important it is to him, but stops herself at the last second.

"I really don't know," she says. "She should be here any second. How do you know her, George?"

But before she can finish her sentence, he's turned his back on her and disappeared into a sea of identical suits.

Chapter 75

Stockholm—Sunday, August 23, 2015

A half hour later, the meeting's rules of conduct have been covered and the keynote speaker—a world-famous venture capitalist with a newly awaked interest in democracy—is obviously approaching the end of his presentation. It's probably ten minutes tops until Charlotte's presentation.

What do they do if she doesn't come? The report has already been written, and it will be published at lunch whether she's here or not. A woman in her fifties with short, blond hair squats down beside Klara.

"You work with Charlotte Anderfeldt?" she says in English with a slight French accent. "I'm one of the organizers of this conference. And this is a catastrophe!"

Even though she's whispering, her French desperation is all too clear.

"Where is Professor Anderfeldt? Has she been in contact with you?"

Klara shakes her head.

"I've been trying to reach her with no luck," Klara says.

"I can see no other alternative," the woman says. "You will have to present the report. I mean you and Charlotte wrote it together, right?"

Klara's chest tightens. She shakes her head emphatically.

"I've only written a small part!" she says, struggling not to raise her voice. "Just the chapter on legal limitations. I haven't even seen the finished version. Besides, I believe Professor Anderfeldt and I came to completely different conclusions."

The woman just looks at her.

"Catastrophe," she hisses back. "Complete catastrophe."

At the podium the moderator is finishing his brief summary of the speaker's introduction and looks out in confusion into the audience.

"Now we were supposed to begin with the first item on our agenda," he says and looks around worriedly. "The presentation of a report on the outlook for the privatization of police functions from a European perspective. The report has been compiled by Professor Charlotte Anderfeldt at the King's Centre for Human Rights in London. But I've just learned that it appears that Professor Anderfeldt has been delayed. I therefore suggest we postpone this item and instead begin with..."

He's interrupted by a door opening in the back of the conference hall. The whole room turns around. Charlotte enters through the door.

"I take back that last," the moderator says over the subdued murmur in the hall. "It seems Professor Anderfeldt has finally found her way here!"

"I beg your pardon for this unnecessary drama," Charlotte says as she takes her seat between the moderator and the other panelists.

Klara can hardly believe her eyes. Charlotte looks fairly calm, but her eyes jump back and forth between computer and the audience in a way that Klara doesn't recognize.

Charlotte sighs deeply, as if preparing, while her presentation opens on the screens around the hall.

"I'm here to present the first case study at this conference that will take a position," she begins. "And it concerns a question that has been raised recently in several EU countries: what would be required in order to privatize certain police duties. This is particularly relevant in the context of the large popular protests we've seen lately."

She looks up and lets her eyes play across the hall.

"Stockholm itself is a perfect example; in just the last week we've seen recurring riots in the suburbs. Riots for which the police have been severely underequipped, lacking the flexibility necessary to effectively deal with the problems that have arisen."

She pauses and looks out over the audience.

"This conference is no exception. The large police presence here today is a testament to the expectation of civil unrest."

All around the room attendees nod and lean forward to listen more intently. Klara feels the hairs rise on the nape of her neck. George and his customers have succeeded in creating an atmosphere that fits Charlotte's presentation with incredible skill. How could you possibly protect yourself from this kind of lobbying? What are you to do with a company that can create its own reality by fomenting and exploiting grievances in the suburbs, while simultaneously purchasing an "independent expert" to present a solution that best suits their case?

The cynicism of it is staggering and utterly ruthless. Klara turns around and meets George's gaze for a moment. He looks calmer now, she thinks. Onstage, Charlotte continues to speak.

"It is obvious that our communities face major challenges in terms of resource allocation and efficiency within the policing sphere, and it is therefore natural that questions regarding alternative solutions have been raised."

She makes it sound so reasonable, so technocratic.

"In several member countries, there have been claims that private actors would be more flexible and cost-effective. Parallels have been drawn to the positive economic outcomes of privatization in health care enacted in recent years, including here in Sweden."

Charlotte turns her head and looks directly at Klara. For a moment she falls silent. Then she slowly turns her eyes back toward the audience.

"But what our research has shown is that the problems of privatizating policing are almost insurmountable from a purely democratic point of view."

Klara gasps for breath. Could she have heard correctly? What is Charlotte saying? It must be precisely the opposite of what Stirling Security has paid her to say. Has she changed sides?

"What we've chosen to focus our work on are the legal issues and the risks to democracy that arise when considering the privatization of central government functions, such as policing. For this part of our work, I have to thank my colleague Klara Walldéen for her careful research that highlights these legal problems and for her summary of case studies in this field."

It's as if she's inside a kaleidoscope where the pieces have rotated to form a completely different pattern than what she expected. Klara sits perfectly still, while on the stage Charlotte carefully goes through the part of the report Klara wrote.

She turns to see how George is reacting. But his seat is empty, and she catches a glimpse of him exiting toward the lobby with his phone pressed to his ear.

On the screens around the room, she sees her own conclusions being presented one by one. Without a doubt, the focus is only on the problems of constitutionality and on democratic constraints.

For a moment she wonders if she imagined everything that happened over the past week: The emails between Charlotte and George. The money paid to the Liechtenstein account and to the people in Bergort. The symbol Yasmine told her about. All of that for nothing?

"The entire report will be posted on the conference website this afternoon," Charlotte says at last.

And then she's finished. Klara hardly notices that the monitors have been turned off, that the moderator has announced a coffee break, and that the attendees are moving around her, buzzing on their way toward the refreshments table at the back. Charlotte's final words ring in her ears: "The privatization of policing, beyond purely administrative tasks, appears very difficult to defend from a democratic or legal perspective."

Charlotte's report is exactly in accordance with what Klara wrote. If Stirling Security, whoever they are, were aiming to create a positive image for the privatization of the police force, they've failed spectacularly.

What exactly is going on? She's seen the payments made to Charlotte, seen her meeting with George, who works for Stirling Security. Everything indicated that they were about to get what they wanted, that Charlotte was in their pocket. What is it that she doesn't know?

Klara heads toward the exit through the mass of conference attendees. Where did Charlotte go? Klara completely lost sight of her boss after the presentation. But out there in the foyer she spots Charlotte's back on the way out through the metal detectors. She seems to be in a hurry, and Klara speeds up her steps.

Where is she going? Typically, a presenter stays after a presentation to answer questions.

She exits into the sunny, cool morning, only a few dozen feet behind Charlotte and is about to shout her name, when she sees her hop into a waiting taxi. As the car slowly rolls past the entrance, Charlotte looks up and meets her eyes for a moment, but then looks down without acknowledging her. There's nothing in those eyes of her former, obvious self-confidence. Just defeat, and something that resembles fear. Klara's thoughts are spinning in her head. What exactly is happening here?

When she turns around George is standing right behind her, and she's so surprised to see him that she takes a step back. He looks different now. His eyes aren't stressed or haunted anymore, instead they look older, almost sad.

"Come with me," he says, pointing to an Audi parked in the driveway. "We really need to talk."

Chapter 76

Stockholm/Bergort—Sunday, August 23, 2015

It's my brothers who wake me. I am surrounded by a great darkness, but suddenly I hear them whispering and moving around me, and when I open my eyes, I'm standing on Pirate Square. The cracked concrete slabs are covered by red sand that swirls and colors the whole world. In front of me lie long rows of shattered bodies and behind me Mehdi's lungs whistle after an afternoon at Camp Nou. When I turn around he smiles and waves, then slowly backs up and vanishes into the red wind. Then they come, one by one. Bounty, Räven, and Dakhil. Al-Amin and Umar. I stand there in front of the rows of my dead brothers, like a guard or a representative. No one says anything. The wind blows harder, the red sand covering everything until I can no longer see them. Finally nothing is left but sand, and I squeeze my eyes shut and sink down with my hands pressed against my face.

And then I hear you, your voice in my ear.

"*Habibi*," you whisper. "Wake up, *habibi*, you're dreaming."

When I open my eyes the red sand has disappeared. The square has disappeared. The concrete and the brothers have disappeared. I'm lying in a bed in a white room filled with wires, tubes, drapes, full of cool morning light, breathing, and whispering voices. I turn toward you, and it's like seeing you for the first time. Your long hair is down now, thick and wild, and the swelling around your eyes is no more than a shadow.

You lean over me and put your cool hand on my forehead, press like you did when I was little, when you thought I had a fever.

I gently grab hold of your wrist and press it firmly against my forehead. Your hand is as cool as I remember from when we were little. You used to play hooky when I was sick and sit beside me all day. How could I forget? How could I forget how you told me the stories your teacher read to you at school again and again, until it felt like you'd made them up yourself? I remember them now. I remember everything now, and I feel like I can't keep it inside me anymore, can't be alone another minute of my life.

"Remember what Birk told Ronia in *Ronia the Robber's Daughter*?" I mumble and squeeze my eyes so you won't see me crying like a child.

You move your hand away from my forehead and lean down until your cheek is against mine. And you nod quietly.

"How many times are you going save my life, sister of mine?" I whisper.

And you press your cheek even harder against mine, so close that I can feel your heartbeat through your skin. But you don't answer as Ronia answered Birk. You don't answer that you'll save my life as many times as I save yours. And I can't hold back my tears any longer. I let them run slowly down my cheeks and onto my pillow. I'm not crying for the brothers or for the past. I'm crying with relief. I'm crying because you're my sister, and you don't ask anything in return. I'm weeping because only in stories does love balance out, only in fairy tales is sacrifice symmetrical.

They release me from the ward early in the morning. I could have left last night, but you wouldn't let them wake me and convinced the doctors to let us stay the night. Maybe because we don't have anywhere else to go.

A police officer is waiting outside the door, and I feel myself being sucked into darkness again, but you take me by the hand as he comes toward us.

"Everything's fine," he says. "Do you have someone who can take care of you now? We can drive you if you want?"

But you shake your head.

"No more police," you say. "Thanks for your help."

"What are the cops doing here?" I say in the elevator on the way down.

"They wanted to check that we were OK. If you remember you were kidnapped? But we have a lawyer now, Fadi."

You smile when you see my questioning look.

"I'll tell you later," you continue. "But she fixed all this. All that old stuff is over now."

On the street outside Söder Hospital your friend Igge is waiting next to a dusty, old BMW. I didn't even know which hospital we were in, hadn't even thought about it. He hugs you and opens the door for me to the backseat.

"*Wallah*, you're both as skinny as reeds," he says as he starts the car. "Where are we headed?"

You sink down in the front seat beside him.

"Arlanda," you say. "But first we need to go home."

We stand outside while Igge goes up to Parisa's apartment. He's back in five minutes with the bag of stuff Mehdi was taking care of for me in one hand and my passport in the other. His eyes are dark and sad as he hands them to me, and he turns to you.

"You were right," he says quietly. "She doesn't want to meet you. The funeral is tomorrow. You know, they wanna do it quickly, according to the Qur'an. You're not welcome, it seems."

You nod silently, and I can barely breathe as you both head slowly down the footpath back toward the parking lot. I turn my head upward, looking along the cracked facade for their windows.

"*Jalla*, Fadi!" you shout. "Come on!"

Finally, I find it. And just before I turn around I see Parisa's face behind the curtains, see the little bundle she's holding in her arms. Our eyes meet for a second. Then she disappears into the darkness of the apartment again. There is no forgiveness, there's nothing, but it's enough for my feet to come unglued from the ground. Slowly I turn around and leave it behind me.

"Just one more thing, Ignacio," you say. "Then we go."

He nods and understands without you having to tell him. His crappy BMW swings out onto the street again, down past the school and the woods and Camp Nou, between the low-rises, up onto the little bike path and all the way to our front door, all the way back to where it began.

But when we get there, we can't bring ourselves to leave the car, just lean out to try to see through the windows. But it's impossible. Everything is dark inside, and the windows just reflect the sun and pine trees outside.

"Those fucking blinds," you say quietly.

"She's working," I say. "And he probably hasn't woken up yet?"

You nod, lean back in your seat, and look at me.

"Is this how it ends?" I say.

You shake your head. Then bend back and stroke my cheek.

"No, *habibi*," you say. "This is how it begins."

Chapter 77

Stockholm—Sunday, August 23, 2015

They say nothing to each other while George maneuvers the car between the barricades and drives onto the E4 ramp. The news is playing on the radio. The riots have subsided in the suburbs. Last night was quieter. George turns it off.

"Jesus Christ," he says. "What a fucking trip."

Klara turns toward him. He looks tired and much older than she remembers.

"What's going on, George?" she says. "Are you going to tell me or not? What happened in there, for example? With Charlotte and the report?"

He glances at her but quickly returns his gaze to the road.

"It's a pretty complicated story," he says.

She looks at him doubtfully. It's strange to be sitting here in his car. Suddenly it feels like it was only yesterday they rode her grandfather's boat through a blizzard in the Sankt Anna archipelago.

"You owe me an explanation, George," she says quietly.

"Yes, I surely do. How much do you know?"

"Stirling Security paid Charlotte for the report, and they paid kids in the suburbs to riot. And you're mixed up in all this. But can we start with what happened just now at the conference?"

"Something convinced Charlotte not to present the report she wrote for Stirling Security," George says quietly. "When she realized she'd been exposed, she was quick to do what was in her best interest. Charlotte's good that way. She has what you might call an intuitive understanding of what's most advantageous for her."

He smiles crookedly. She shakes her head.

"What do you mean 'convinced'?" she says. "You work for Stirling Security. But you don't seem particularly upset?"

He takes a deep breath and sighs.

"Stirling Security is basically the Russian government. There are a number of such companies. More now than ever. They contacted us, my firm Merchant & Taylor, almost a year ago, when there started to be talk of doing this report and holding this meeting. They wanted a fancy lobbying firm that didn't ask too many questions. My bosses were very interested, of course. Russians pay full price, if you know what I mean. For no questions asked. And I started working with them almost immediately after what happened over Christmas, one and a half years ago. It was one of my first meetings after getting back from… You know, what happened in the archipelago."

"You certainly do attract a particular clientele," she says.

He shrugs.

"That's part of the job… But after what happened, I got a little—how to put this?—more scrupulous about my clients."

He smiles and glances at Klara again. He doesn't need to say more than that. It was one of George's clients that had come close to murdering all of them that Christmas.

"And we were already in contact with Säpo, if you remember?"

"Bronzelius," Klara says quietly.

"Exactly. I couldn't take getting embroiled in this kind of shit again, so I decided to tell Säpo about Stirling Security—I told him that they didn't exist officially in Sweden yet, just rented an office under another name, and their CEO seemed to be some kind of attaché at the Russian Embassy. Bronzelius thought it sounded interesting."

She nods, but she can hardly believe her ears. Just yesterday Gabriella told all of this to Bronzelius, who dismissed it entirely. What an ice-cold bastard.

"I'd hoped they'd arrest somebody and get me out of my vile assignment," George continues.

"But?"

"Instead, they asked me to go forward as if nothing had happened. So I continued working with Charlotte. It wasn't so difficult. I knew what she was made of. Ambitious and money-hungry. Not much for scruples. And the Russians pay well, like I said. They didn't want the report to be too obvious, just enough doubt to give them an opening."

She nods and closes her eyes. Despite everything that happened, it's still too much to take in. Too much to be sitting here with George on the E4 freeway headed toward… well what?

"But the last few weeks really got out of hand," he continues. "Stirling Security started to subsidize the unrest in Bergort—the riots were already under way, but they were quick to see an opportunity to exploit them. They sent me out into the suburbs with stencils to paint onto the walls, you might have seen the fist? Totally sick stuff by the way. And the other day, some ghetto chick popped up who'd seen me in the suburbs. Bronzelius got really nervous, of course, and when the girl and I decided to meet at the City Library, he sent out some thugs to pick her up. And she ended up holding me at gunpoint! Can you believe it! Fucking crazy shit!"

Klara nods, doesn't want to interrupt his monologue to tell him she actually knows about that. Not yet.

"But what did Säpo say about it?" she says instead.

"They were ice-cold: *just keep going, do what they ask you to.*"

"What the hell?" Klara says and turns toward him quickly. "They allowed Bergort to burn when they could have stepped in and prevented it? It's so cynical it makes you nauseated."

George just nods.

"It was important to gather evidence, they said. They weren't interested in rowdy teenagers, they wanted to get higher up in the hierarchy. But it seems like the only one we got is Orlov, and he's officially just some minor diplomat at the embassy. They're good at lying low."

Klara feels her anger growing. Anger at the ruthlessness and indifference of it all. How the hell could Swedish Intelligence just let all this continue? First Fadi and now this?

"But what do the Russians want exactly?" Klara says. "Is it economic? Is it really just about money or do they have some other aim?"

George shrugs.

"I think it's both. Those Russian companies... They are always connected to politics in some way. The company would earn big money if EU countries started to privatize their police powers. At the same time, Russia would be in a pretty strategic position if businesses with Russian owners suddenly controlled parts of European police forces. You follow?"

"It sounds totally fucking bizarre."

"Yes, but Bronzelius say it's more like a submarine violation. Not exactly a direct invasion, more like a warning shot: *Look at us, we've got the muscle to create some real political chaos.*"

"I can't believe Charlotte actually allowed herself to be bought," Klara says.

"Oh, bought reports aren't exactly anything new. But she probably wasn't feeling so cocky last night when Bronzelius picked her up and laid his cards on the table. She denied it of course. Swore that the money she received in Liechtenstein was completely irrelevant to her academic independence."

He laughs dryly.

"But then Bronzelius showed her the draft she'd given to me during our meeting yesterday. A version in which the conclusions were the opposite of what she claimed today. She apparently turned white as a sheet and went straight home and stayed up all night rewriting the report. Like I said, she knows what's best for her."

"Was that the plan all along? I mean, to expose her right now, just before the presentation? Or was he planning to push things even further until he had a real emergency on his hands?"

"As I understand it, the plan was to stop now, before the Russians got any real influence. Säpo probably wanted to take it as far as possible without risking any real impact, in order to see how much information they could obtain."

Klara nods thoughtfully.

"And what's going to happen to Charlotte now?"

George shrugs. "I suppose she'll go back to London and lick her wounds until it's time again." He laughs. "Unlike a weakling like me, it will probably take a bit more for the likes of Charlotte to see the light."

"What the hell, people have died because of this," Klara says quietly.

The images from the London Underground flash by. Patrick's rigid, pale body on the tracks.

George nods gently.

"I didn't know about that until yesterday. Stirling Security hadn't anticipated Anonymous would sniff out what Charlotte was up to. Or that you'd start poking around either. The Russians are pretty damn nervous now."

"Why did you send me into the middle of this?" Klara says. "If you knew what the hell this was about?"

George glances at her cautiously.

"I guess I wanted to help you. I knew you wanted to finish Mahmoud's dissertation, and I could see that Charlotte would let you do that because I was paying her. I didn't realize you'd end up getting this involved. And I really didn't know everything would end up taking on such epic proportions. Bronzelius has made it sound like we were almost done since the beginning of the summer. But then he just wanted to push it further and further."

He falls silent. They've arrived at Sergels Square now, and he turns onto Sveavägen.

"Where are we going?" Klara says.

"You'll see. Somebody wants to meet you."

He stops at the sidewalk outside of King's Tower.

"Fifteenth floor," he says. "He's waiting for you there."

"You're not going up?"

George seems to shudder and shifts the gear of his car.

"No way. I've had enough of the view from that office."

She nods.

"Will I see you later?" she says.

George laughs. "Whenever you want. I think after this we'll both have quite a bit of free time."

"What do you mean? Do you think you'll get fired?"

He shrugs. "Who knows? It's not exactly company policy to actively work against your client's interests. Whether they're Russian or not. We'll see. I'm sure I'll be fine."

He hands over a business card.

"Call me whenever you feel like it," he says.

Chapter 78

Stockholm—Sunday, August 23, 2015

The first door on the fifteenth floor belongs to a law firm, and the other one is unmarked and ajar. She pushes on that one hesitantly.

"Hello?" she calls out and takes a step into the dark hall.

"In here," calls a voice from somewhere inside.

She walks through the hall cautiously and enters a large room with a magnificent view of Stockholm. The room is completely empty, except for a pale desk and two chairs in one corner. Bronzelius rises from the chair and walks toward her.

"Welcome to Stirling Security!" he says.

She looks around confused. Bronzelius is dressed in his usual uniform of dark blue jeans and a short-sleeved, plaid shirt. The shiny leather jacket is slung on one of the windowledges.

"It's... empty?" she says.

Bronzelius nods.

"Not that there was much here before either," he says. "But they seem to have been in a hurry to pack up what little they had last night."

"You let them get away?"

She feels her anger growing again. All this bullshit, everyone who had to suffer for it, and he just stands there and smiles and shrugs.

"The man who organized this left the country on a flight

to Moscow almost twenty-four hours ago," he says. "He has diplomatic immunity anyway. The rest of Stirling Security isn't in Sweden. They aren't even registered as a company here. Besides the sign on the door, they don't exist in Sweden at all. And now the sign is gone as well."

"But..." she says. "It can't end like this? My God, they were behind the riots in Bergort. They bribed a professor. And they got my colleague murdered."

"George Lööw paid those guys in the ghetto," Bronzelius says. "And he sent the money to your boss too. As for your colleague, we have been in contact with our British colleagues. They're fully aware of the situation, but unfortunately there's not much to go on at the moment."

"What the hell was the point then?" She's raised her voice now, can't hold back any longer. "If no one is going to be held accountable? What the hell is the point?"

Bronzelius waits until her voice stops echoing in the empty office.

"What's the point?" he repeats. "To send a signal. To show we know what they're up to. It's not just here, of course, there's been a more widespread attempt to disrupt the work of the EU, and we've been working together with our European colleagues. Just the fact that Russians liquidated this office, and sent the ambassador responsible for it home, is a victory in and of itself. They don't lose face, but they understand we see them. Just like the navy chasing submarines in the archipelago. The worst thing you could do is make one of them surface. That's when the problems really start. What we want to do is to stop them without attracting attention. That's the real victory."

She shakes her head. All this for nothing.

"And Yasmine then?" she says grimly. "And Fadi?"

Bronzelius goes over to the window and looks out over the rooftops glittering in the late summer sun.

"Not my operation," he says. "I knew nothing about it until Yasmine popped up yesterday with her story."

"But is it true?" Klara says. "Did Säpo really infiltrate extremist groups and help to radicalize people? Is it true that you worked with the U.S. or whoever the hell is flying those drones?"

Bronzelius doesn't say anything. He just stands there with his back to her. A few seconds pass. Then he turns to her and considers her indifferently with his blue eyes.

"Whatever was done was necessary. These groups are recruiting terrorists, you know that, right? Do you watch the news, Klara? This was a very successful operation."

"A successful operation? You radicalized Fadi and sent him down to Syria to his own death? That's a successful operation for you?"

"A senior leader of ISIS was taken out along with twenty of his fanatical followers. That's a successful operation no matter the context."

He doesn't look away.

"And as for Fadi Ajam, we didn't radicalize him. He found his own way to a radical group. We didn't want to kill him, he sought that out himself."

Bronzelius had helped them in the Sankt Anna archipelago. Säpo had been involved in the hunt for her and Gabriella at the time, but Bronzelius still found a way to help them. She thought he'd done it because he cared, because he had a good heart. Now she realizes that he did it because his interests in one way or another happened to coincide with hers. He's nothing more than a cynical and opportunistic intelligence official.

"I was silent once," says Klara quietly. "About everything that happened a year and a half ago. And I will continue to be. But I won't keep my mouth shut about this. What Fadi and Yasmine do is up to them. That's their choice. But I won't keep quiet about what I've been through. I owe that to Patrick. And myself."

Something twitches in Bronzelius's face, and he takes a small step toward her, looks into her eyes even more intensely.

"I strongly recommend you stay quiet on this matter," he says slowly. "You don't want me as an enemy, believe me."

She stands still, without moving, without a flicker in her eyes.

"Do what you must," she says. "And I'll do the same."

Chapter 79

Arkösund—Monday, August 24, 2015

They're sitting at the far end of the jetty, shivering in the biting wind. Above them the sky and the sea are the same dull gray color as the rocks. The trees and bushes will be green for a few more weeks, but summer is over now, there's no doubt. She snaps the rain jacket up to her chin and squints at Gabriella through the drizzle.

"Are you sure about this?" Gabriella says.

Klara turns her gaze toward all that gray again before answering. A pair of seagulls are hovering perfectly still in the wind above Hästö. This moment is the first time in two years that she's felt sure about anything at all. She turns back toward Gabriella and nods.

"Yes," she says. "Completely sure."

"And you don't want to be named or contacted? You're also sure about that?"

Klara nods calmly again.

"It's not about me," she says. "And I don't think it would be good for me to get too much attention right now. I'm not what you'd call super stable."

She smiles wryly and puts her arm around Gabriella.

"Besides you were always better at talking than me. Isn't that right, partner?"

She leans her head against Gabriella's shoulder.

"The most important thing is that it comes out," she says.

"That people know how cynically Säpo acted. They could have put a stop to the riots in the suburbs but instead watched as the rioters were encouraged and organized. And they were involved in bribing an independent expert before an EU meeting. But not a word about the rest, not a word about Yasmine and her brother."

Gabriella shakes his head.

"Damn," she says. "That's an even bigger scandal, a major overstep. It's so fucking brutal that they're going to get away with it."

Klara straightens up and nods.

"But they survived," she says. "It really wasn't clear that they would, especially not the brother. We have to take what we can get. And it's not our story. We have no right to share it."

"And Bronzelius?"

Klara shrugs.

"He threatened me," she says. "But what the hell can he do? I think he's mostly talk. Sometimes you just have to do what's right and not think too much, don't you think?"

She stands up and looks out across the islands. A familiar boat is rocking its way through the gray. She feels the rhythm of her heart change, calm spreads through her. Maybe it will work out this time too.

"Well then," Gabriella says as she also stands up. "I'll call George from the car and see how far he's willing to go with this. At least as an anonymous source, I hope. Then we'll talk to my contact at DN and see where this goes."

The boat is almost at the jetty now, and Klara sees the round head of her childhood friend Bosse through the window by the helm. She holds up her hand in greeting and prepares to jump on board. But first she turns and hugs Gabriella tight.

"Thank you," she says. "For everything. For taking care of me."

She feels Gabriella's cold lips against her wet cheek.

"Take care of yourself," Gabriella says. "I'll call you when I know more, so keep your phone on until it's time for publication. Then it might be best to turn it off."

Klara nods. With a practiced hop, she lands on the deck of Bosse's old boat. It smells strongly of tar and diesel and seaweed.

It smells like home.

Chapter 80

Brooklyn, New York—Wednesday, August 26, 2015

The breeze drifting in from the East River is still warm, but there's something else in it now, something that smells like dry leaves, something that makes the menus at The Ides outdoor terrace flutter, and Yasmine's bare arms tingle. She raises her eyes and looks out over the Manhattan skyline glittering with money and tension in the twilight. She was only gone a week, but now that she's back, everything seems new, except Shrewd & Daughter's credit card, with which she paid for both of their airline tickets and for their room at The Wythe in Williamsburg. But not even the card will last long when she tells them she doesn't have anything to report about the symbols in Bergort, that there was nothing behind them.

"*Wallah*, Yazz," Fadi says on the other side of the table. "We really have been living different lives."

He can't take his eyes off the silhouettes of skyscrapers against the navy blue sky, bewitched by the lights and life on the other side of the river.

She glances at him across the table, thinking that it's like looking at herself when she first came here. She wants to put her arms around him, wants to hold on to this crazy magic, these days of confusion when everything is still possible.

"I promise you that my life didn't look like this, Fadi," she says. "I lived in a glorified closet with David in Crown

Heights. Slept on a concrete floor, while he did drugs. Not exactly the high life."

He nods but barely seems to hear her. They've been here for two days now without thinking about the future. Two days of waking up jet-lagged before dawn and walking along the streets and bridges and carefully finding their way back to each other again. Sometimes they don't talk at all, but just walk beside each other in the dawn light while the city wakes up around them, as if it's enough to just be alive.

"Still," Fadi says. "It's a long ways from Bergort."

Darkness has fallen, and the lights of Manhattan are reflected in the river beyond the warehouses and galleries by the time Yasmine sees Brett coming out onto the terrace. She immediately feels anxiety press down like a sash across her chest.

"*Jalla*, Fadi," she says. "Here comes the guy I'm meeting with. Brett, the guy I work for. Jesus, this is gonna be rough."

Fadi straightens up in his chair and turns around to look at him. She's told Fadi everything. Everything about how their mother sent her pictures of the symbols, how she used them to get Shrewd & Daughter to pay for her trip to Stockholm. And how Brett was the one who made it happen. And now she's going to betray him.

Brett arrives at their table now with a bag in one hand and some kind of whiskey drink in the other. He bends down and kisses Yasmine on the cheek.

"Great to see you," he says with a smile, flashing his straight, white teeth.

"You too," she says with a little less enthusiasm in her voice. "This is my brother, Fadi."

They shake hands, and Brett sits down at the table and takes out his computer.

"First time in New York?" he says to Fadi, smiling.

Fadi nods. "How did you know?"

Brett leans back in his chair, takes a sip of his drink, and looks out over the Manhattan skyline. "Your eyes," he says. "They're still big as dinner plates."

"Brett," Yasmine says. "It's just as well that I confess immediately. A lot of strange stuff went down in Stockholm."

She takes a deep breath. What will be will be. She can't tell him that the symbol was created by a Russian company in order to foment unrest in the suburbs of Stockholm, and that she still doesn't quite understand the meaning of it. Better to say that she hadn't found anything at all. That it was a false alarm. What will be will be, she'll have to find a way to pay back Shrewd & Daughter for her expenses if that's what they want. Fadi is alive, nothing else matters. But Brett doesn't seem to be listening to her, he's busy searching for something on YouTube.

"Look here," he says, and turns the screen so she and Fadi can see.

The film seems to be shot in some kind of basement venue. A deep bass-line vibrates in the laptop's small tinny speaker, and on the screen a man stands with his back to the audience. He's dressed in worn jeans and a black T-shirt with a ski mask over his head. The monotonous bass turns into a dull, deep beat and the crowd pushes up against the stage, screaming and shaking their hands in the air. The beat stops, and for a moment you hear only the cheering and screaming of the crowd. There is an electrical intensity in that venue, an expectation that threatens to turn into a riot. But just before the audience explodes and attacks each other, the beat speeds up, and the man in the ski mask turns around and throws himself headlong into a rap that's fast and syncopated, but so clear every single word is discernible if you concentrate.

"What's this?" Yasmine says.

She listens to a few bars and glances at Fadi, who's swaying his head.

"That's a sick beat," he says.

The rapper is close to the audience, sometimes touching their hands, sometimes hitting them. He jumps and kicks, dances, curls up on the floor of the stage, and prostrates himself in front of the audience. It looks more like a punk concert than hip-hop. Then the beat slows down again, and the rapper stands still for a moment. Brett pauses the movie and turns to Yasmine.

"Check out the T-shirt," he says.

Yasmine leans closer to the screen. On the rapper's T-shirt there's a clenched fist inside a five-pointed star printed in red.

"What..." Yasmine says and looks up at Brett's smiling face.

"A pretty elegant symbol, right?" he says. "And a great fucking rapper. Sort of a younger, angrier Eminem. He calls himself Starfist."

"Starfist?" Yasmine says. "Like the symbol? I don't understand a damn thing."

Brett laughs and closes the computer.

"Shrewd & Daughter have been watching him a long time. He's from Baltimore. Very political. He's been performing anonymously for a few months. Geneviève has been leaking his songs on SoundCloud and YouTube without giving him a name. Basically that 'no brand' shit. Especially during the riots in Baltimore this spring, he became a kind of faceless symbol of the unrest in some circles. Everything was Geneviève's idea, a way to build up hype for the right people. And now that he's been established as a concept, they think this is the right time to launch him more conventionally. And if that's the case, he needs a name. And something more, something that clearly identifies him. When you showed up with the symbol... it was perfect, and now the symbol has become his trademark, or he's become the face of the symbol. However you want to look at it. He's scorching hot now, and he'll be huge soon. He's already done interviews on CNN, and Vice made a documentary about him. He's always wearing that T-shirt now and the ski mask, of course. Strong fucking look."

Brett holds up his glass to Yasmine for a toast.

"Nobody cares where the symbol came from anymore, Yasmine. In fact, our instructions are not to talk about it at all. It's from Baltimore now. People are already spraying it all over. Starfist. The record companies are crazy about him. This will end up being the biggest deal since the music industry died."

Brett laughs and takes a sip of whiskey.

"I don't understand anything," Yasmine says. "When did this happen? And what do Shrewd & Daughter get out of it?"

"Like I said, they've been working with him since early this spring, but everything moved quickly at the end," Brett says. "I emailed you right? The riots in Baltimore and other cities have been rolling back and forth for a while. But after our pitch Geneviève decided they finally had something to work with, so they named him Starfist, and she's officially his agent. She's promised to make him a star if he lets her run his PR. And she'll take twenty-five percent of his income, of course. Not bad money if you consider this will end up being a three-record deal worth ten million. And that's just the advance."

He stops and reaches into the bag.

"Which reminds me," he says. "This is your share. After I took my own twenty-five percent, of course. This time

I really think I've earned it. It's a lump sum, just so you know. A finder's fee. But I think you'll be pleased."

He finds what he's looking for in the bag and hands her a check. Then he swallows the last of his drink.

"Okay, kids," he says. "Time for me to leave. Stay here a few nights. Geneviève is beyond pleased, so she'll be happy to pay. We can talk later this week? I have some other stuff in the works for you."

He bends down and kisses Yasmine on the cheek, shakes Fadi's hand, then heads off between the tables and the bar until they can't see him anymore. Now they're alone again, just Yasmine and Fadi, and the indescribable sight of Manhattan. No plans. Nothing to return to. Just two new lives. Just two new lives and a check for $150,000, which flutters gently in the very first autumn wind.

Acknowledgments

Thanks to:

My publisher Helene Atterling, editor Jacob Swedberg, agents Astri von Arbin Ahlander and Christine Edhäll for all the discussions, read-throughs, and invaluable input;

My wonderful translator Liz Clarke Wessel, for a stunning translation;

My American editor, Jennifer Barth, for thoughtful comments and all the support;

Professor Leif Stenberg at the Centre for Middle Eastern Studies in Lund for the interesting conversations about radicalization and ISIS, and for all the help with terminology and Arabic;

The eighth-graders at Värner Rydénskolan in Rosengård, for allowing me to spend time with you in the spring of 2015;

To everyone at Södra Esplanaden in Lund;

To Tobias Almborg for friendship and for reading the first few chapters before I knew where I was;

Johan Jarnvik for friendship and laughter; Daniel Zander because you are my brother; Liisa, Milla, and Lukas. Without you, nothing.